THREE MONTHS

a novel by

Ben Hinson

Llumina
Press

Author pic: Timothy Greeson
Front cover image concept/design: Benjamin Hinson-Ekong
Please visit my website: www.benhinson.com

Requests for permission to make copies of any part of this work should be
mailed to Permissions Department, Llumina Press, PO Box 772246, Coral
Springs, FL 33077-2246

ISBN: 978-1-59526-893-8

Printed in the United States of America by Llumina Press

Library of Congress Control Number: 2007906785

Author's Note

HIV is very real and has not left a single part of this world untouched.

According to the 2007 UNAIDS AIDS epidemic update, globally there are 33.2 million people living with HIV. In that same year, 2.5 million people were newly infected. Regionally, Sub-Saharan Africa remains the most affected region in the global AIDS epidemic. 22.5 million people in this region live with HIV. The majority of the 1.7 million newly infected in 2007 were women.

Southern Africa accounts for 35% of people living with AIDS globally. In Eastern Europe and Central Asia there are 1.6 million people living with HIV, and in the Caribbean AIDS is one of the leading causes of death among people 25 to 44 years old. In Latin America, 58,000 people died from AIDS in 2007. In North America and Western Europe there are 2.1 million people living with HIV, and 78,000 people acquired HIV in the past year. The United States of America has one of the highest infection rates in the world, with men and adolescents accounting for 74% of HIV/AIDS diagnoses in 2005.

These figures are just reported numbers. The real number of people living with and dying from HIV and AIDS infections is probably staggering. These numbers are not going down, but are rather on the rise.

What would cause such a spike in infections? The lack of funds to provide life-saving education? Increased high-risk sexual activity? More drug abuse? Sexual crimes? Negligence? Ignorance? The possible reasons are many, but in this book I focus on two factors, which, in my opinion, top the list: negligence and ignorance.

Ignorance has been defined as "The state or fact of being ignorant; lacking in knowledge, and in many cases is seen as a pleasant alternative to a harsh reality" (www.dictionary.com). A high percentage of people, irrespective of race, creed, culture, or background choose this "pleasant alternative" to the realities of life, ignoring safe sex practices or resorting to unhygienic drug use.

HIV exists. It is not a myth. It really exists. On the street, in the bedroom, at the gym, in class, at the workplace, at the nightclub; it touches all classes of people, and crosses all boundaries. In most cases, you can't see it, because HIV does not wear a face; its face is all of ours, until a cure is found.

Despite the alarming statistics, there is still hope. Behaviors that put one at risk of acquiring HIV can be controlled. Injection-drug users should beware of the dangers regarding used needles, because such instruments, especially when used by multiple people, can carry HIV. Protected sex should be practiced when dealing with partners we are not committed to. Sex can still be a fun and pleasurable experience while keeping yourself and your partner protected.

In my opinion, the hardest part of dealing with the HIV epidemic is the negative stigma that victims get tagged with.

In our society, no one wants to touch, talk to, hold, kiss, sleep with, or in some situations even walk near a person they know is HIV positive. How ironic it is, then, that so many people with this ignorant attitude themselves have unprotected sex, and may carry the virus themselves.

In general, too many of us tend to pass judgment on and stereotype others, with regards to race, economic status and social class, when we ourselves are far from perfect.

A person with HIV cannot infect you by touching you, breathing on you, rubbing you, and so forth. I have been around many HIV infected people, and a friend of mine passed away from the progression of HIV to AIDS after many years. I am in perfect health, partly because I don't take unsafe sexual risks and also because maintaining my health is a big part of my lifestyle. So, if you do not believe anything I have just written you can use me as a testament: the only way HIV can be passed on is by the transfer of bodily fluids, which is why having safe sex is so important until you are sure of your partner's status.

Having HIV is not the end of the world. There are many people who have lived with the virus for years and are managing it well. With the right medication and proper exercise, HIV-positive people can live fruitful and healthy lives, longer than those who use drugs, are in gangs, live in warzones, and so many other things.

Many people write scholarly articles about the rate of HIV acquisition in certain areas, and the threat of a pandemic, but the core of the issue is education and prevention. You can find practical information in hospitals, clinics or workshops, sometimes in schools and perhaps the occasional television advertisement. But it is our responsibility, our duty, to educate ourselves. Knowledge is power, and power is only effective when used in the right manner. I hope this story I have created will help put things into perspective for many people and promote healthier living standards in our world as a whole.

HIV is very real. Protect yourself and the ones you love, and remember: "an ounce of prevention is worth far more than a pound of cure."

Acknowledgements

I thank You, God, for all the lessons you have taught me in this short but eventful life I have lived thus far; every obstacle that has come in my way, every trial and all the hurdles have been priceless life lessons that I have received directly from You. I do not have much to offer in return but a deep and sincere expression of gratitude. I thank-You for being my only Teacher, I thank- You for every experience that equals a lesson, and I thank-You for finding favor with me. I take no credit for this work, and I just thank-You in using me in such a manner, and for finding favor with my life.

Many thanks to my mother, mummy dearest, my brothers Nii-Boy and Koko, and to my father, Mr. John Ekong for being there for me; to all the experiences and wonderful mentors I have had on the various journeys I have made through life—from my life in Nigeria and in Ghana; to all my adventures here in the United States; to all the good people who have genuinely wanted me to succeed; Elom for priceless feedback; to LaDawn for being such a good friend, excellent publicist and for pushing me all the times I felt lazy and ran out of ideas; to Dr. Herbert Chien for all the lovely conversations about Playstation 3 games, movies, health theories and so forth – those conversations gave me ideas in ways you couldn't imagine; to Debbie Dawson, Debbie Greenspan, Robyn Benson, Cassandra, Rocky, Wynston and the staff at Llumina for being efficient, reliable and fun to work with; to Lana for all the words of encouragement; and finally to Therese—a great friend. Many thanks to you for reading and rereading and rereading my work at odd hours in the morning, and for putting up with my crazy questions, as well as critiquing my work in an objective manner, thus helping me make my book the full package that it is today.

And to you the reader—I thank you for granting me an audience☺

We know that the law is spiritual; but I am unspiritual, sold as a slave to sin. I do not understand what I do. For what I want to do I do not do, but what I hate I do. And if I do what I do not want to do, I agree that the law is good. As it is, it is no longer I myself who do it, but it is sin living in me. For I have the desire to do what is good, but I cannot carry it out. For what I do is not the good I want to do; no, the evil I do not want to do – this I keep on doing. Now if I do what I do not want to do, it is no longer I who do it, but sin living in me that does it.

-Romans 7:14

Chapter One

She screams my name as we both climax, and then we laugh. "Bad boy," she whispers in my ear.

"Look who's talking…it takes two to tango," I whisper back. I enjoy her breath on my cheek. It's cool, in sharp contrast to our sweaty environment.

She smiles and rests her head on my chest. "So, how about we do breakfast later?" she asks. I sense where she's going with this. To be quite frank, this was just a lay for me, nothing more.

"We'll see."

She climbs out of the bed and heads to the bathroom. I stare at her beautiful body as she walks away. The sweat from sex on her skin combined with the moonlight from the open window gives her curves a slight glow in our dark surroundings. She stops at the bathroom door, turns her head, and gives me a smile.

I don't smile back. I feel that after sex, her value has depreciated—or been lost altogether. After all, I met her just yesterday while I was driving my new car, a gift from my parents. She was willing to have sex with me, and considering that I had nothing better to do, I made good use of my time with her. For some reason, I think it was the car that got her attention. Pretty interesting, how willingly some women will open their legs at the sight of something that they will never have but only taste. Anyway, I got what I wanted. I might even put her in a cab to send her home but not until I have another taste of her body.

This is what I do with my free time now: hook up with different girls and eventually have sex with them. I'm living every young man's dream, I guess. As I am not in school; I only work night shifts at a diner right down my street; and during the day, I pretty much do nothing. In my quiet suburban town, I lead a simple life. I was away at college for four years, and my time away seemed to have enhanced my status here. Now, every girl in this town seems to want a piece of me, especially because I drive the best car and wear the best clothes. So, I have my whole day to do some major damage while I wait, biding my time till I get a job and become a success in the big city.

It's a shame that Carl, Luke, and Abel, my college buddies, are not here with me. I wonder if they're having as much fun as I am having. Well, I can't speak for Abel; of the three, he is my best friend, and he recently moved to

Brazil to further his "education," while Carl and Luke both got jobs in the big city. They have all left me behind and have graduated to sleeping with new levels of women. I am still here in my town with these same girls I have seen a million times over. I'm beginning to get bored.

Hey, at least I graduated from college. I have been out of college for about eight months now. It felt great to graduate and leave school. My name was spelled in big, bold print on my diploma: "Bachelor of science awarded to John Casey." It really felt good knowing that my hard work had actually paid off. I got the chance to make my family proud: my mother, my father, and my adopted brother, Alfred. And I think I am one of a select few from my hometown to have actually graduated from college in the city. So that definitely makes me feel proud.

The process of finding a job has not been an easy task. I send out about forty résumés per day on the various career Web sites, but no one calls me. Could it be my inexperience? Maybe I should lie a little on my résumé. Well, let's hope that soon I get some offers; I feel it is about time that I got out of this town and started making some serious cash. I would like to work in the big city nearby; there's just something about that place—the energy, the people. There always seems to be something going on, and everyone there seems focused. Even the bums seemed focused.

It's all about the money—the city and its concrete jungle—just what I need. Working in that environment must be a thrill, not to mention the variety of women…ah, man, the women, by far the most beautiful I've seen in all the places I have been. They come in all shapes and sizes, in all ethnicities and in every class imaginable…yummy. That is definitely one reason I hope I get a job in the city. That definitely would be a blast. I have been applying like crazy, so I hope something presents itself soon. Then I would be able to make up for all the time I spent in college, working and not having fun. Imagine the fun I will have when I get my own place, have my boys come by, have some ladies and—man, it's good to dream. But as of now, I am still a semi-fresh college grad, working part-time at a diner, being a manager and hoping my time to shine comes soon. It's not to say I have a bad life here. After all, my parents are wealthy, and I can pretty much get anything I want, including women. But I would like to start making real money and start living my life. I would also like to start fooling around with all the hot ladies I see walking around in the big city whenever I go there. Let me stop daydreaming; it's almost time for me to head to work.

I climb out of bed and join my female friend in the bathroom for one more round.

***

I got a call from a company in the big city about the position I applied for three weeks ago. They want to see me for an interview. Hurray! I really have to prepare myself so I can impress them. Have to do my research on them and their industry, get my lucky suit together, and maybe buy some new black shoes. Oh, yeah, and I need a tie. I am so excited—an actual interview in the big city! I can't believe it. I hope it's a good job that pays well.

***

I went for my interview today, and it went really well. It is basically a sales position, outside sales to be exact. But I wouldn't be working to meet my sales quotas selling printers or insurance; I would be promoting and offering services to various clients for an asset management company. Apparently, they like the fact that I studied finance in college, and I think they also liked my demeanor. I guess my charm got them. I was very confident during the interview; I knew the job was mine and I showed it. I think I will get the job. In fact, I know I will. I guess all I have to do now is to wait.

I'm getting calls from other companies I applied to, mostly crappy sales jobs, probably selling office equipment and stuff. But I really want the job with the firm I visited today. I feel it is meant for me. And man, the women I saw while I was there...wow! I will certainly go crazy working there—too much flavor! On a side note, I have been talking to this chick I met after work the other day. Her face is okay-looking, but her body is top-notch. Definitely Grade-A meat. She'll make a good lay, I'm guessing. And I think that's all she wants from me as well; I could tell by the way she looked at me. So we'll see. It's August and it's about to start getting cold. I sure could use someone to keep me warm.

***

I got a letter from that firm in the city. They offered me the position! Wow! An incredible salary plus bonuses and commission—not bad for an entry-level hire, eh? I am so excited and so happy! So, so, *so* happy! I could not wait to tell my mother, my family, and my friends the good news! This was by far one of the best days of my life! And to make my day even better, I bagged that girl I met after work! Talk about two good things happening in one day! I ran out of the diner, hopped in my car, and planned to drive home to show my folks my acceptance letter—but first, I had to share the news with another important person in my life.

***

His name is Jerry. I am not sure how old he is or where he is from, for that matter, but from his accent, I would assume he's from down South somewhere. My brother, Al, and I met him one day as kids, as we were riding our bicycles around the neighborhood. We had never seen him before, but on this day, he was sitting on the side of the road, looking like a wretch and singing a song.

We thought his accent sounded funny, so we stopped to check him out. He was very dirty, he walked with a very bad limp, and he was blind. He asked us for money, but we insisted he had to work for it, so he began making paper airplanes with paper we gave him. How he made paper airplanes with no sight, I could never understand, but the planes he made were nothing short of perfect. They flew in straight lines and stayed in flight for extended periods of time. Ever since that day, we have been good friends. He claimed he fought in Vietnam, but we never believed him, although now that he is an old blind man and I am older, I do not rule out that possibility. I never dared to ask him how he lost his sight or if he ever had it in the first place. Over the years, we have gone to him for advice on anything from girls, how to cheat on exams, or even for reasons to skip school, all in exchange for a little money and sometimes for food.

As we got older we brought food to him free of charge. Five years ago, he relocated from the streets to an abandoned shack by the railroad tracks. He greets passersby and assists them with directions, if needed. This is how he makes a little money each day.

I reach his door and find him sitting by the window, humming the same tune I heard him humming when I first met him.

"Hey, Jerry," I say.

His head turns in my direction. "Hey, Johnny, how's it goin'?"

"I'm good. I just got a letter offering me a job in the city, so I don't think I'll be around here often anymore."

He stops humming the song. "Hmm, that news certainly makes my heart sad, y'know? Certainly makes me sad, Johnny. I am certainly going to miss you coming around."

"Yes, Jerry, I know," I reply, "but Al is still here, and he will still come around to keep you company and bring you food. Besides, I will be here on some weekends, just not as often. And I will definitely stop by here whenever I am around."

He smiles. "All you young ones chasing money in that place, the big bad city. Be very careful in that place, boy; the glitz and glamour can sure seem appealing, but just remember that not everything that glitters is gold."

"I know this, Jerry."

"Yep, sure you do. There are lots of women out there, boy; lots of bad people as well; lots of people no good for you out there. But if you keep your head on straight and stay out of trouble, you should be fine. Two rules that can never steer you wrong, Johnny: stay focused on your mission, and don't let your penis, your little man downstairs, do the thinking for you. Oh, no, don't let him think, that little man. Once he gets control over your body, he will make you do the craziest things that are not always good for you, no sir."

I look at my watch and realize that it's time to leave. Besides, I feel Jerry is about to get into another one of his rants about his problems with his manhood. "I'll be back, Jerry, and next time I see you, I'll have great news to share with you!"

"Sure you will," he replies. "You just remember what I told you."

I head for his door and drop some money in his begging cup. "See you later, Jerry." As I leave, I hear him humming his tune again. Trust Jerry to always try to give me advice, even in a good situation. Anyhow, I look forward to being in the city. I can finally abandon this slow lifestyle I have here. Time to make some changes and begin living my life.

I can't stand my job. I'm a waitress at this Ethiopian restaurant situated downtown in this big city. My manager is always making me work overtime, and tonight is a particularly bad night for me to be working extra hours—it's Saturday night. I had made plans with my girlfriends, Anna and Jessica, to go out tonight to this new nightclub. But here I am, stuck here, pacing back and forth, taking orders for people, carrying plates of food, and smelling like onions. Granted, this is just a temporary job I do a few days a week, but I had no intention of working on a Saturday night! And to make things worse, there is this really weird-looking guy sitting at one table who keeps on trying to flirt with me every time I walk by, and at another table, there are these guys who keep on calling names at me. I just want to go home, take a nice long shower, do my hair, try those new heels I bought yesterday, and go out tonight. Yeah, go out tonight and hear all the stories from Anna about her new boyfriend. He probably won't last very long, knowing Anna. I hear he is really cute. Well, I only have a few more hours to go— two and a half, to be exact—so I'll just have to stick it out. During the day I work as a secretary in this law office. The money is actually not that bad, and in all honesty, I do not need to be doing this waitressing gig. This is one reason that I broke up with my ex-boyfriend, Cody—he kept on insisting that I made no time for him, but you know what? I think he was using that as a front. I know he was cheating on me and wanted to get out of our relationship. Men. They're all full of crap. And it sucks because you can't live without them. My ex really hurt me, you know? Yes, okay, maybe I do work a lot, but I know for a fact that he was cheating on me, and I know he is still seeing the girl to this day. Anyway, I am over him now; we were not going out for that long—eight months—so getting over him was not too hard. Or so I think. Anyway, I am single again, and I feel free! No more drama, no more arguments—total, complete freedom! So for now, men are the last thing on my mind. I want to begin saving some money because I want to move out of my current apartment, first of all, and I also want to have

5

enough money for this cruise my girlfriends and I are planning next year! That should be fun and a nice getaway from the hectic environment in this big city.

"Michelle! Order ready for table three!" I hear my name being called. Oh, well, I will just sweat this out 'til it's time to leave, and I will go back to my place and get ready for a night on the town. But before I go out, I have to stop by my older sister, Alexia's, place, because she wanted me to do her hair. And seeing as how her place is not too far from this restaurant, I might as well. If I had thought about it, I would have left my clothes at her place and just gotten ready at her place after work. Oh, well.

"Michelle!"

I hate this job....

***

I get to Alexia's place after work and let myself in: I had her spare keys. Alexia is not really my sister; she is a good friend—my best friend, in fact—and we have become so close that I call her my sister. I have one real sibling, my brother, who is younger than I am (I am twenty-six; he is twenty). I never knew my parents. I see Carl, my younger brother, once in a while when he is not in college. But in the big city, my only family is Alexia. She has been my best friend for the past six years, and I love her to death. I share everything and anything with her, from how I feel when I am on my period, to why I do not like corn flakes and she does, to what I want to do with my life, to how bad certain men are in bed, to certain bad things we do to men when they are in bed, to why men suck, to how beautiful Alexia's six-year-old daughter, Tara, is, to just about everything. We share everything with one another. I met her at this fashion show six years ago; I was on a date and she was on a date as well, and our dates happened to know each other. Strangely, we found our dates boring, so after the show, we left them and decided to get dinner together. And we have been the best of friends ever since.

"Hey, sweetie," Alexia says to me as I walk in. "You look tired."

"I am tired, Sis," I reply. "Do you have anything to drink?"

"Yeah, look in the fridge. I bought some stuff today." I head to her kitchen. "So how was the job? Any cute guys hit on you today?"

"No, I wish. Same old losers."

"Hmm."

"How about you? How was your day?"

"It was okay—went to work, came back, took Tara to the hairdresser after I picked her from school, same old."

"Where is Tara now? Where is my baby?" I ask.

"She is sleeping. I'm sure she'll be up asking for a drink soon. Of course, if she doesn't that'll be a good thing. So, let's get this hair done, okay?"

"Sure, let me just take off my jacket." I take off my jacket and soon I am standing behind Alexia, straightening her hair as we delve into current events.

"So, have you heard from Cody since you guys split?" Alexia asks.

"No. I guess he's still using the fact that I work too many hours to cover up for him cheating on me."

"But I keep on asking you, how do you know for sure that he was cheating on you?"

"C'mon, Alexia, with all his lame excuses for why he was never home or the few times I checked his phone and saw other girls' numbers? And to top it all, one of his lady friends called me, telling me that he was cheating on me."

"But, sweetie, what if that girl who told you that was lying? You know how some females can be."

"Stop trying to take sides, Alexia. I know you were fond of Cody and you approved of him, but that does not excuse what he did. He hurt me, you know."

"Hmm…well, all I want is for you to be happy, Michelle, that's all. And for you to make the right decisions. I mean, we both know men are not perfect, but who is? Cody was not such a bad guy. Yeah, he did typical guy stuff, but compared to a lot of guys out there, he was pretty decent. He had a good job, had his own place, made good conversation, had depth…"

"Yeah, I know, but it's over now. I know my Prince Charming is out there waiting for me; maybe Cody will be a good learning experience for me, you know? I mean, I do kinda miss him sometimes. Anyway enough about me. How are you holding up, missy? You never want to go on dates, even though I always tell you to come out with me and the girls."

"I know, Michelle, I should start dating again. I am just a little scared, you know? I was with Tara's father for eight years, and him leaving me hurt pretty bad. I don't know if I have it in me to start seeing guys just yet. But you're right; I should start dating again. I am only getting older, and I would like a father figure in Tara's life while she is still young."

"Great! So I take it that you'll come out with us tonight? C'mon, it'll be fun!"

"I don't know Michelle, you guys go to clubs and stuff. I am a grown woman; I don't know if the caliber of men that I would be interested in would be in such places, so I'll pass. But you guys should go and have fun" Alexia says as she picks up a magazine with a male model on the cover. "He's cute."

"Yes he is, but he is too pretty for me, and back to you coming out with us, you should, c'mon, Alexia, there are mature men who go out to night-clubs."

"Men, in general, only go to nightclubs for one of two things: to get girls to have sex with them, or to get girls to fantasize about having sex with them later."

"Alexia! You really think so? There are some decent guys who go to clubs. I met Cody in a club, and he, as you put it is, 'pretty decent.'"

"Yes, I also said 'men in general.' I know there are a few decent guys who make it into such places, but you have to be lucky to bump into them, and you were lucky to bump into Cody."

"You're not going to let me go with this Cody thing, eh?" I remark.

"Nope. I seriously think you made a mistake dumping him. He was a good guy" Alexia replies as she sits down in front of me.

"Anna and Jessica disagree. They could swear that he cheated on me" I say as I start to blow dry her hair.

"Anna and Jessica were not dating Cody; you were. Why don't you think for yourself instead of making decisions based on what your friends say to you? How do you know that Anna and Jess did not approve of Cody as I did or possibly were even jealous of what you had with him? Try to understand why people say things and don't just go off face value."

"You're right, Alexia, you always are. Damn, now I feel bad about Cody. See what you did? Ha-ha. But I can't run to him now; I dumped him, remember?"

"No one is suggesting that you call him, just learn from this experience, like you said. You never know—you might meet another Cody again."

"Well, that's why I am going out clubbing tonight!"

"Ha-ha, good one," Alexia replies. She gets up to go look at her hair in a mirror and sits back down. "Michelle can you please make sure the hair is as straight as possible?"

"Be patient I'm not done yet…you sure you don't want to come out, Alexia? It'll be a lot of fun."

"No, I'll pass, sweetie. I'm sure I'll have more fun here, snuggling with Tara in bed. But you go; you deserve to have a good time tonight, especially after doing my hair, which, by the way, looks great."

"Thanks, Sis," I reply, as I put the finishing touches on her hair. I walk off to wash my hands and grab my coat. Soon I am at the door, ready to leave.

"Be careful out there when you go out tonight, Michelle, and don't go home with any guys."

"C'mon, you know me better than that."

"Just checking. Well have fun, Sweetie. I'll kiss Tara good night for you."

"Please do. Bye, girlfriend."

"Bye."

I step outside, contemplating what perfume to wear tonight. I will have to get dressed quickly and then head to Anna's place for drinks before we head out. Should be a fun night.

Chapter Two

oday is my first day on the new job. On the train ride to my office, I spot this really cute girl. She has that exotic thing going for her, and she has lovely long hair. Not a bad figure, either. But what I like most about her is the way she dresses and carries herself. I know that looks can be deceiving, but she looks like she would be good girlfriend material. Well, you never know. I am happy that at least I have someone to flirt with on the train as I go to work. What a great way to travel.

When I get to work, things seem great. The people here are so nice and polite. The females in my office are hot! And they look ready to mingle. As soon as I stepped in, I felt like I was fresh meat. I got my own cubicle, and I was given a little orientation.

I will begin my training tomorrow with the sales team. My territory is in the downtown area of the city, as if things couldn't get any better. The girl who runs the orientation is called Lorraine. She is very sweet, and I can tell she is a tease; she is wearing this short skirt that goes well with her business attire and accentuates her derriere. Hmm. Okay, Lorraine, I'll have to keep my eye on you. Well, I am happy everything worked out. I plan on getting an apartment in the city so I am close to all the action. One of the sales guys I was introduced to said he could help me out with that, so that was cool.

I feel so good; I smile all the way home.

***

Today I met all the sales guys. There's Tom, our boss; Brad, a loud-mouth who seems to think he knows everything about everything; Craig, a really cool guy who seems shy; Sully, a former college basketball star whose eye twitches whenever he laughs; Anne-Marie, a very nice, decent girl—pretty, but she doesn't seem like the naughty type; and Sue, a blonde chick with big boobs, who I am guessing is the office whore. Cesar is the smooth playboy of the group. I see myself hanging out with him a lot in the future.

I will train with Craig on different sales techniques, and later, Anne-Marie will bring me up to date on the firm's numerous clients. Then Sue will show me how to work with some of the databases on her computer. Sounds like fun.

***

It's been about two weeks since I was hired. Training has been going well, and I am learning a lot from these guys. I see how Craig got the sales job; even though he seems shy, he is very charming, a quality most people will be drawn to. Plus, he knows his stuff.

I got an apartment right here in the city, in the downtown area, the same as my sales territory. I heard that's where a lot of the action is. So we'll see. The sales team is all supposed to go to some bar this Friday for drinks after work; I am guessing that event will serve as my induction into the sales group. This company must make a lot of money; it's amazing the things these guys talk about in the office. Their discussion topics range from some exotic vacation someone went on, to which new car someone else just bought, to what fancy new restaurant just opened somewhere in the city—my kind of talk. The chance to make some good money is what keeps me motivated in this company. After work, Cesar invites me to hang out with him around the downtown area, which also happens to be my neighborhood! Boy, it feels good to say that. Well, this Friday night will be a night to remember.

Winter is coming, and I need to begin lining up some women to keep me warm and comfortable.

***

It has been a blast since I started working here in the big city. The energy here is great, and there is so much variety. The women here are unbelievable. I sit next to beautiful women on the train every day as I go to work; I stand next to beautiful women on the subway; I see beautiful bodies in my office; and I walk by wave after wave of women as I head home after work. I am in heaven. I meet and see so many interesting people here as well. I love this place.

I have been working here for about a month now and have been meeting many new people, mostly through Cesar. This guy knows a lot of women! Damn! I guess I was right about my assumption of his being a playboy. He's cool, but his eyes are not honest, so I feel I have to be careful around him. I have been meeting and making a lot of friends outside of work as well. This city is crazy. Last week, for example, I went to this club and picked up this girl and brought her back to my place. She gave me a blow job, and then I slept with her! Wow! And she was hot. I couldn't believe that a girl that good-looking would deal with a bloke like me. And two days ago, I got this hot girl's number—she lives about four blocks away from me! I met her at the florist shop down my street. I think she is Persian or something. She looks like a supermodel. Man, this city is every bachelor's dream!

***

I hooked up with the Persian girl two nights ago. She is so sexy. She cooked for me the next morning and got my clothes ready for work! I love this life. I went to work with a big smile on my face.

At work, everything is going well; I took the sales qualifications exam and passed. Now I am beginning to deal with actual clients, under the guidance of Cesar for now. Cesar has a slick approach to sales. He is not as sharp as Craig with the actual information, but he is very good with words, and he has a talent for being able to make anyone believe a situation is great when it really isn't. I guess he fits his role perfectly and is ideal for this fast-paced rat race. I was raised with proper morals—at least with regard to dealing with other people—so sometimes I question the ethics of his approach to life, but who cares? We all lie once in a while, don't we?

I am at my daytime job, and today has been a slow day in the office. I have not answered many phone calls, and my bosses are not asking much of me. Took a few messages here and there, but nothing extravagant. So I have been surfing the Internet for most of the day, looking at movie reviews, sales for blouses, some Victoria's Secret catalogues and such. The last time I went out with Anna and Jess a few weeks ago was fun, as I thought it would be. Anna showed up with her new boyfriend, and they were kissing for most of the night. Jess was hit on by practically every guy in the nightclub; well, she is very attractive—a bit younger than the rest of us, has that naïve-college-student thing going on, and is very curvy—so that is to be expected. I had a good time as well. I got hit on by a lot of guys, and I took a few numbers, but then I met this really hot guy who walked up to me right before we left the place. He was tall with dark hair and had sensual eyes. I thought he was really cute, and the girls liked him as well. His name was Braxton, I think—I have it in my phone. I think he said he was an engineer or something. Well, we exchanged numbers, but he hasn't called me yet, so I am waiting. And last night I spoke to Alexia, and she says that she is sort of seeing someone! Wow, I definitely have to hear what she has to say. It's about time!

My cell phone rings. It's Anna. I have known Anna since college; she came as an exchange student from France and was my roommate. She has always been loud, outspoken, and a huge flirt. In school she slept with practically the entire male student body. But she was never branded as a slut in those days—at least, not to my knowledge.

"Hey, girl," she greets me.

"Hey. How are you?"

"Good. So I don't like my boyfriend anymore, and I am going to dump him."

"What? But you just started dating him not too long ago!"

"Yeah, but we went out to dinner, and it was me, him, Jess, and two of Jess's girlfriends, and he didn't even offer to pay for all of us!"

"C'mon, Anna, don't you think that is being a bit vain? I agree that a guy should offer to pay for meals, hold doors for us and stuff, but there were four of you, including him! C'mon!"

"No, that doesn't fly with me. How do you think the girls thought of me and the kind of guys I date? They probably won't respect me anymore."

"Yeah, Anna, but you can't just dump a guy because he did not pay for dinner for you and your friends."

"Well, it's too late; I dumped him already."

"Ouch. How did he take it?"

"Don't know; don't care. I am sure that there are better guys out there."

"What did Jess have to say?" I ask.

"You know Jess; she will always support any decision I make. So Anyway, has that hot guy called you yet? You know, the one from the club?"

"No, not yet."

"He was hot. So what will you say when he calls?"

"I don't know Anna. I'll just be myself."

"Yeah, he is probably a smooth talker. Hopefully, he will be better than Cody."

"Cody was not that bad, Anna."

"Yeah, okay. Well, I have to go girlfriend, but let's get together this weekend or something."

"Okay, I will call you. Bye."

"Bye."

We hang up, and I think about what Alexia said to me regarding making decisions for myself. I personally think Anna made a vain move to judge a man just because he did not pay for dinner for her and her friends. I pick up my phone and call Alexia.

"Hey, sweetie," she greets me.

"Hey. What are you doing?"

"Not much. Just getting ready to leave work and get Tara from school."

"I will be leaving shortly as well. I want to see you. Maybe I could join you as you go get Tara. Then we could all go get some dinner. Plus, I want to hear more about this guy you're seeing."

"Oh, boy, it's really not that big of a deal, and I am still not sure if it is going to go anywhere. He seems like a nice guy, but looks can be deceiving. But yes, you should join me when I get Tara from school. I am sure she will be happy to see her Aunty Michelle."

"Okay, so I will call you when I am outside your office. Then we can take the train together to get Tara."

"Okay, sounds good. See you soon."

"Okay, bye."

We hang up, and I resume surfing the Internet until it's time to leave.

***

I meet Alexia outside her office, and we start walking toward the train station to take the subway to Tara's school. There is a slight chill in the air, which reminds me that Christmas is around the corner. I've always had a boyfriend around Christmas.

"So-o-o…" I say with a smile as I nudge Alexia.

"So what?" she replies with a smile.

"So who is this hunk you tell me you're seeing? Fill me in!"

She gives a calm smile. "Just some guy I met at the florist the other day. I think he just moved in around here and was checking out the neighborhood and happened to bump into me."

"And?"

"Well, he was cute and a bit funny, so I gave him my number, and we had dinner once, and he seemed charming."

"You had dinner with a guy, and you didn't tell me? Alexia!"

"I'm sorry, sweetie, everything happened so fast. Anyway, we had dinner and the next night we hung out. We went to go see a movie, and then I— umm, yeah, that was it."

I give her a stern look. "Alexia, that was not it. What else happened?"

"Well, I, umm, somehow ended up at his place."

"Alexia! Oh, my gosh! Did you sleep with him?"

She looks at me with a sad puppy face. "Yes, yes, I did."

"Alexia! Wow, I never would have thought! You, sleeping with a guy, so early!

"I couldn't help it, Michelle. He was nice to me, and let's face it—I hadn't had sex in so long, and I was attracted to him, and we were at his place. It was bound to happen."

"Oh, my, well, I hope it was worth it. Was he good in bed, at least?"

"Yes, he was, actually," she replies. "And I did something the next morning that I regret now."

"What did you do?" I ask.

"Promise me you won't laugh."

"I promise I won't laugh."

"I made him breakfast."

"Ha-ha-ha-ha-ha-ha-ha-ha!"

"You promised that you wouldn't laugh!" she says as she slaps my arm.

"I'm sorry. What made you do such a thing?"

"Well, I had not cooked for a man in such a while, and I actually felt good doing it. Well, that, and also because he was a gentleman with me. He made me laugh, and the sex was not bad at all."

"I bet it wasn't. What is his name?"

"John."

"Will you see him again?"

"Dunno. I get a bad vibe from him, like he's only after sex with me, but we'll see. How about you? Who is this super-hunk you tell me you exchanged numbers with?"

"Well, his name is Braxton. He is tall, dark, and handsome. Said he was an architect, engineer, something to that effect. He will probably call me, so we'll see."

"Well, I want all the spicy details, every last drop."

We both laugh and hop onto the subway to go pick up a little girl called Tara.

Chapter Three

Christmas is around the corner, so I'm taking off this week and next to spend time with my family back home. I am sure they are curious about how I am faring with my new job and all. I make the train ride back home, wondering which new girl had come to our town, which one I could take advantage of.

As I walk from the train station to my parents' place, I bump into the last girl I had sex with before I left to go to work in the big city. Her name is Mary. She is in a car with another girl. I know she will probably ask me why I never called her after that day and if we can hang out while I am home. Then I think that would not be such a bad idea, having some sex before I head back to the city. But I also know I have to see my family first. She pulls up beside me as I walk and rolls her window down to chat. I stop walking and bend down to chat as well.

"Hey, sexy," she says.

"Hey," I respond, "how are you?"

"I'm good. Where are you headed?"

"Just going home. I got a job in the city, and I came home to see my family."

"I see. You never called me back. I was hoping we could do breakfast or something—you know, seeing as how we had a good time together."

"Yeah, sorry I didn't call. I just got a bit busy, that's all. Who's your friend?" I ask, as I nod in her friend's direction. Her friend smiles back at me. She is attractive, has a flirtatious smile, and is wearing a cut-off shirt that reveals her cleavage and large breasts.

"Oh, this is Eileen. Eileen, this is John."

"Hi, John" she says in a smooth, sultry voice.

"Hey. So, umm, I will be at my parents' this evening, but maybe later on tonight we can meet up or something, and maybe you can bring Eileen, here, with you."

I already know it was vain of me to make such a request, but I also assume that these girls are desperate and will sleep with any man for attention, especially a man just coming in from the big city.

"Okay, sounds good, but only if Eileen is up for it," Mary comments.

"Sounds good to me," Eileen responds.

"Cool. So I'll give you a call when I am free, okay?"

"Okay, John, whatever you say," Mary says. "I guess we'll see you later. Bye for now, John."

I wave good-bye as they speed off, and I feel good that I have made plans with the both of them. I have never been with two women; I am one arrogant man. Before long I am home and am greeted at the front door by my father.

***

I love my dad. My father is one of those types who gets straight to the point whenever he's engaged in conversation, and he's a man of few words. My dad is hardly ever involved in a group discussion, and your first impression might be that he is not a friendly person. But make no mistake; my father is a charming individual. I would say that of both my parents, although my mum is the more outgoing of the two. My mum is quick to give hugs and make everyone feel comfortable, whereas my dad prefers being in his study, alone, working on his various projects. But when my dad speaks, I find that he always has something remarkable to say. At least, I find what he says to be remarkable. Maybe he gets that from his experience with life; my dad came here as an immigrant with nothing. Through hard work and determination, he married my mother, set up three successful businesses in town, and is revered and respected around these parts, partly due to all the contributions he makes to the community. He is an ideal role model.

"Hey, son," he says.

"Hey, Pops. How are you? Feel like carrying some luggage?" I say, handing my bags to him with a smirk.

He looks at them and then at me. "No, I think you're strong enough to carry them yourself. I have to step out to the grocery store. Go inside; your mother is waiting for you."

"Okay, Dad." I step inside our home. One thing I love about both my parents, especially my mother, is that they have a great sense of style when it comes to designing a home. Our house is very comfortable, very clean and modern-looking. Perhaps it has that touch because my mother is an artist. The walls are covered with her paintings, and almost every room is filled with scented candles. There are at least four very comfortable couches in the living room, and there is never a shortage of good food whenever I am home.

I find my mother curled up on a couch in the living room, reading a book, looking as elegant as ever.

"Hi, Mum."

She looks up through her reading glasses. "Hi, baby," she says with a lovely smile. She gets up and gives me a warm hug. I can see why my father chose to marry a woman like my mother. She is a genuinely good person, and

I can't imagine any man not being satisfied, having such a nurturing lady taking care of him. When I look at my mother, with her gentle face, humble demeanor, dark eyes, natural elegance, petite frame, and strong character, I see a real woman. Plus, she's a good cook.

"So, how is my baby boy doing?"

"Your baby is doing okay, Ma. Say, where's Al? Is he home?"

"No, he went to do some boxing training with his friends. I think later on he will be leading a youth group at church, with some discussions on sex, diseases, and stuff like that. Maybe you should go, after you have a bite to eat."

"Umm, yeah, sure, okay. I don't see why not," I say, knowing full well I intend on seeing both Mary and her cute friend in a couple of hours for some possible action.

"Good. Well, I was cooking some food for you, so grab a drink and fill me in about work and then I will finish making up your plate."

I pour myself a chilled glass of lemonade in the kitchen and walk back to the living room to join my mother.

"Work is going well, Ma. I think they are all happy with my work so far. I have made a couple of friends, and the city is great" I say as I sit on a couch adjacent to hers.

"I see," she responds, "so you see yourself being there for a while?"

"Yeah, I think so. I like the energy there."

"Good. Just don't get caught up in a destructive lifestyle, and don't go chasing all the single girls in the city. And please remember all the teachings we have given you, so you don't lose track of who you really are."

"Okay, Mum," I reply, knowing that I lost track of their teachings a long time ago.

Just then my father walks in.

"So, how's it going, son?" he yells from the kitchen, as he puts his groceries away. My mother heads to the kitchen to fix me a plate.

"I'm doing good, Dad."

"And work?"

"Work is good, Dad."

"Good. Have you found a church to go to up there?"

Geez. I get uncomfortable when they start asking me religious questions. I mean, I love my parents and all, but I am not really a big church guy, and I am definitely not really into Christianity in general. I believe there is some supreme force, power, whatever you want to call it that created all that we see, but I have no contact with this thing. I make everything happen for me. Plus, I am not really big on this whole Jesus Christ talk.

"No, Dad."

Thank goodness that at that moment, my mum hands me my food, so I have something else to focus on.

"You should join a good church, John," says my dad as he joins us in the living room. "It will help keep you grounded in good values and, if you're serious about it, it will keep you from leading a reckless lifestyle. I really think you should join a church."

"I agree with your dad," my mother chimes in. "It is helpful when you have a church family that can hold you accountable for your actions. It will keep you focused on what is important and keep you out of trouble."

"I understand, Mum, and I promise that I will join a church when I get back to the city."

My mother does not look convinced. Neither does my dad.

"Well, John, we cannot force you to make such a decision," says Dad. "That, my son, is entirely up to you, but in my experience, I have learned that it is important to be a member of a healthy church family that can provide you with support and spiritual strength when you need it."

"Okay, Dad, I get your point," I say, taking my last bite. I feel that they are grinding me down with this sort of conversation, and to be frank, I am not in the mood to hear any more of such talk. I have to make an exit. "I think I will go see Al now at the church and join them for the youth group thing."

"Youth group?" my dad asks.

"Yes, honey, Al is running the youth group meeting at church today," my mother says.

"Oh. Well, then, that's good, John. If you leave now you might just make it in time and not miss much of their discussion."

"Okay, Dad. Mum, thanks for the meal. I'll see you guys in a bit, okay?"

"Okay, son, we'll be here," replies my mom.

I wash my plate, go upstairs to freshen up, and then step outside and hop into my car. My parents think I am heading to Al's discussion group at the church, but I have other plans that involve two girls called Mary and Eileen.

So Braxton finally called. It doesn't really matter that it was two days later; I was still excited to hear his voice. I like his style, so I agree to go out with him to dinner when he asks. He is an engineer, and he works for some firm in the big city. For one thing, he is very handsome; for another, he dresses really well. He has good taste when it comes to restaurants, so that's another good thing because I love food. He works out, so he doesn't have flab on his belly or anything, so that is another plus. But on the downside, he tends to talk about himself a lot. Well, then again, what man doesn't? He makes semi-decent conversation and has a commanding presence about him, so I guess, overall, he makes decent dating material.

The first time we go out he takes me to a very fancy Indian restaurant, and we actually have a good time. He tells me about his family, who he hardly ever sees, his love for travel, and what he looks for in a woman—general first-date conversation stuff. But it is good enough for me to want to see him again.

The next time, we go on a date to a movie, which I personally think is a bad idea for a date, because you don't get to talk for most of the time; you just watch the movie. And I know he wants to put his arm around me, but I don't let him, so I can tell he is a bit frustrated. But he does not take it personally; he asks if we can see each other again. We go to an art exhibit, which is nice because we get to talk a bit more, and it is then that I realize what lovely eyes he has. So that date goes okay, and he calls me again, asking if we can hang out again and I agree, because I like his company. So he suggests we do something a bit more intimate this time—dinner at his place. At first, I was going to say no, but after speaking with Anna and Jess, I accept his offer. Many thoughts run through my head. He has a really nice place; I wonder how many girls have been in this seat before me. I am sitting in his living room while he is in his kitchen. It is a nice apartment; he has very comfortable furniture; scented candles are everywhere; and the apartment itself has a very modern look to it. I am impressed.

"So, can I get you anything to drink? Red wine, white wine, water, juice, anything?" he asks as he emerges from the kitchen.

"White wine will be fine for now. So, are you going to tell me what you are making for dinner?"

"No, it is a surprise, but you will enjoy it, I am sure."

"How do you know that I will enjoy it?"

"You will. Everyone enjoys my cooking." What a cocky jerk. But I like his confidence. "Hold on—let me get that wine for you." He disappears into his kitchen and re-emerges with a glass of wine.

"Thank you."

"You're welcome. So how are you? Do you like my place?"

"I love it. I was expecting a messy apartment," I say teasingly.

"I'm sure you were. I like to keep the place clean because keeping the place clean makes me feel good. So since you like the place, maybe you'll come around more often."

"Maybe," I say sarcastically.

"You know, I have really enjoyed seeing you over the past few weeks," he says. "I like your company."

"Thank you. You're not so bad yourself," I reply.

He gets up and takes a seat really close to me on the sofa. "So, how do you feel? Anything I can do to relax you even more?" he asks.

"No, I am pretty relaxed, thank you. You are doing quite enough."

He smiles. "Okay, well, I had better go check on the food. It should just be about ready now."

He disappears into the kitchen, and I think to myself, *Why did he sit so close to me? What do I do if he tries to kiss me?* I mean, I am attracted to him physically, and we have seen each other a couple of times. I retrieve my cell phone and send Alexia a text: "He sat really close to me. I think he wants to kiss me. What should I do?" I wish she would respond, but just as I finish pressing send, he re-emerges from the kitchen.

"Food is ready. I hope you're hungry."

We sit down at his dining table and have good conversation over crab, lobster, and steamed vegetables, not typically what I am into but good food nonetheless. After dinner we resume sitting on his sofa, with red wine to keep us company.

"The food was great, thanks. Maybe you're not such a bad cook after all," I remark.

"You're welcome. Here's to a great relationship with each other," he says as he holds up his wine glass for a toast. I raise mine and smile. Then he moves even closer to me and stares at me directly in my eyes. I can smell his cologne now.

"You know, I am really happy you decided to come by," he says as he touches my hand. I hate to admit it, but his touch feels good. He is really close now, and I am looking directly at his lips. I know he wants to kiss me, and I think I want him to. At least, my body does.

"I am happy I came by, Braxton. I've had a good time tonight," I reply. He leans over, looks in my eyes one last time, and kisses me. I let out a slight moan as he does because it feels so good! And as we kiss, his hands start going places, touching me in certain places. I feel a bit guilty—I mean, I met this guy at a club. Granted, we've gone on a few dates, but do I really know him? But he is still touching me. I have to make myself stop.

"Wait, Braxton, wait!" I exclaim, out of breath.

"What? What's wrong, Michelle? Did I do something wrong?"

"No, no, no, you did everything right. It's me. Don't you think we are moving a bit too fast?"

"Michelle, we have been seeing each other for the past couple of weeks. How fast have we been moving?"

"I don't know. I just don't want to get carried away, that's all. I mean I have been hurt by guys in the past, and I just don't want to get carried away with you."

"Michelle, I will never do anything to hurt you. You can trust me," Braxton replies. "I really like you—you know that," he says as he draws me closer to him and kisses my cheek.

"Yeah, Braxton, but every guy says that, and I just don't want to be hurt again."

"I am not going to hurt you, Michelle. C'mon, let's enjoy the rest of the evening, shall we?"

He kisses me again, and strangely, I feel reassured by what he's just said to me. I kiss him, and soon I feel his hands taking off my shirt and reaching under my blouse.

Well, it looks like I will be staying over at Braxton's place tonight. I just hope that I have no regrets.

Chapter Four

It's been about a year since I started working for these guys in the big city, and what a year it has been! Work has been going well; I acquired three new clients in six months, which is ideal for a fresh hire. Well, I guess I'm not so fresh anymore. My superiors have been impressed with my work, so they have been dishing out more and more responsibility to me, as well as increasing my bonuses, which is a good thing, I figure. My mom is very proud of me, as is my dad, and I am happy that they're happy. I cannot afford to do anything that will disappoint them. My parents always tell me to stay close to God when I am in the city, but I must admit I was never a big religious or spiritual type of guy. I used to talk to God a lot when I was a kid, but as I grew older, I realized that I could do most things on my own. After all, why should I believe in something I cannot see? I live life by my rules; I work hard and I make money, and can get any woman I want. Who needs God? As long as I am semi-nice to people, mind my business, and look out for me, I will be fine.

As far as my social life goes, I am on full blast. I work during the week and party hard on weekends. I know almost all the hot spots now, and they know me. I have met so many women here and gotten so many numbers, it's unbelievable. Cesar, another guy, Shawn, who seems to be Cesar's prototype, and I have been hanging out a lot lately. Shawn is also in sales but for a different firm. He looks like he doesn't belong in the big city; he's got the long blonde hair and a real chill attitude, and I feel he would fit in better in some beach town or something. I can see him being a surfer out there. But the ladies love this guy; he's a chick magnet, I tell you. Well, we all are, if I may be so bold. Okay, I'm just kidding. And these guys party hard. They must have an endless supply of money, because they throw away money like it's nothing whenever we go to a bar or a club. Sometimes I feel ashamed that this new life of mine is in stark contrast to my parents' teachings, but hey, no one knows. My mom and dad cannot see me, and what they don't know won't kill them, so I am good. Or so I think.

I am still seeing the Persian girl, by the way; Alexia is her name. She's a good girl after all, just looking for attention. I think she really is beginning to like me and wants me to be her boyfriend, but I am too young for that. That's how these girls trap you, you know. That's how it starts. Nah, what am I saying—I am a playboy having a blast in the big bad city!

***

Alexia has been inviting me places and calling me like crazy, so I have been avoiding her. I know it's wrong, but hey, I need my space as well. Maybe she'll get the idea soon enough. Plus, she has a kid, a little girl. Granted, I get along with kids sometimes, but I am not at that stage in my life to start baby-sitting. Yes, I said it, but it's true: I'm not. I'll just stop calling her; maybe she'll get the picture.

***

I have not spoken to my mom or my dad in a while, which is wrong. I am getting too engulfed in this fast-paced lifestyle; maybe I had better slow down.

My job is going well, as usual. I am in charge of ten clients now, and have someone under me, a new hire by the name of Chris. I still hang out with Shawn and Cesar. As a matter of fact, Shawn wants me to be his wingman at a party he is going to next week, and so we'll see how that goes.

Life is good, but for some reason, I am not satisfied. I still feel I am missing something. I try to meditate and pray here and there, but my spirituality is definitely not the same as it was before I came here. But I will pick it up soon, I promise. Like I said before, I was never really a religious person, and I am not too keen on what any religion has to offer, including Christianity. Sometimes I feel I am losing track of what my real agenda is, but hey, I am young and handsome, I have a prestigious job, I live by myself in an apartment in the heart of the city, and I've got money, so I can't be doing that bad…can I?

***

I went out drinking after work last night with some friends. It's amazing how much vanity I have picked up since I have been here. People around here seem to find drinking alcohol fun, so much so that they actually go out with the sole purpose of getting drunk. Now, I do not mind having a drink, but I just cannot see the "fun" involved in going out just to get drunk. I would rather be with a woman or two. At times, I wish I could see my old friends on a more regular basis. I would love sometimes to just chill with good friends, have some good food with some wine, and just talk. I really miss that. But I am on my own now, so I have to act the part I guess. Friends come and friends go, at least until I see them again.

I went out drinking last night with two new friends who I met through Cesar. Steve and Job were their names. They are really funny. We went to a bar and then made a stop at a crowded club. The music inside was so loud, nothing else could be heard. I was having a pretty bad time and was about to leave when I saw this good-looking lady dancing all by herself. It was almost as if she had been reserving the next dance for me, because she looked at me and smiled. I decided to walk over to her and grabbed her from behind and started dancing. She had no objection to my doing so. She had rhythm. She felt good. She had long, beautiful, dark hair and smelled extremely fresh and clean. She had the smallest waist, which blossomed into curvy hips and what felt like a perfectly round behind. We danced together until the club shut down. And after it shut down, she took me to her place…

Well, it's been about a year since I met Braxton. After a couple of nights of sleeping with him, he suddenly lost interest in me. I would call and he wouldn't respond, and when I would ask if we could meet, he would make up some excuse, and it seemed he only wanted to see me when he wanted to have sex. So I stopped calling him. I guess he got what he wanted. I talked to Alexia about it, and she told me to just let it go. But I can't understand why some men act like that! I was interested in him, and he just slept with me and forgot about me! I don't get it. Alexia has been seeing that John guy she told me about, but I think she is having the same issues with him. It's funny, because I have met every guy she has ever dated, but this guy is the first that I have never seen. He doesn't come out when she invites him to dinner with me, and whenever we plan to go out together and we invite him, he never shows. So I know she is considering cutting him off as well. Can't hurt. From the way she described him, I figured he was a player anyway. It must be hard for her, because she has Tara, and I know she just wants someone to be there for her, a manly presence to lean on whenever she needs comforting. She deserves better. And so do I. I am still a little pissed about this Braxton guy. Who does he think he is? I can still recall how our last conversation went.…

"Hello?"

"Hey, Braxton, it's Michelle."

"Hey, you."

"What do you have planned this weekend?"

"Oh, nothing much. I don't have any major plans, just tidy my apartment, that sort of thing. You?"

"Well, I wanted us to go out to dinner this Saturday night, and since you have nothing planned, I was hoping we could go out—my treat."

"Oh, well, umm, I actually told a friend of mine that I would help him move some stuff out of his apartment this Saturday evening, so it all depends on if he calls me or not, and I just don't want to leave him hanging because I sort of promised him, but I will definitely keep you posted."

"I see. How about Sunday? Can we meet for lunch then?"

"Well, I will be washing my clothes, cleaning my place and stuff, but let's play it by ear and see how it goes. How about I call you as soon as I am done? Will that be okay?"

"That'll be fine."

"Okay, so, umm, listen, I have to run for a sec. Can I call you right back?"

"Sure."

"Okay, thanks, Michelle. You're a sweetheart. I'll call you right back."

"Okay."

And of course, I did not hear from him after that. Like I said, that was the last conversation we had, about three months ago.

So I've made up my mind that I will cut him off. I've made plans with Anna, Jess, and Alexia to meet at this lounge tonight to get some drinks and discuss our favorite subject: men. I will probably share with them my recent decision concerning Braxton and see what they think. I told Alexia I would go with her to drop off Tara at her sister's place; then we could make the trip down to the lounge together.

***

We got to the lounge around 8:30. The girls were all already there, and we walked over to their table and joined them.

"Hey, girls!" Anna bellowed. Jess was sitting next to her, quiet as usual. Jess is a lovely person. I met her through Anna a few years back at some house party here in the big city, and she has been a part of our group ever since. She is very smart and very shy, which is surprising, because she is a very pretty girl. And oh, yes, she is a virgin.

"Hi, guys, have you guys been waiting long?" I ask.

"No, not really; just here discussing my men issues with Jess, as usual" Anna replies.

"And what are your men issues, Anna?" Alexia asks.

"Hi, Alex. I was telling Jess how useless men are, at least the ones I date."

"Oh, boy, what happened this time, Anna?"

"Okay, so I met this guy at the grocery store last week, and he walked up to me and started trying to flirt with me."

"Wait, so what happened to the last guy you were dating?" I asked.

"Oh, he's history."

"Oh."

"So listen, I met this guy, and he walked up to me, and at first I did not want to give him my number, but he was really cute, and I could tell that he had a nice body, and he had a nice butt."

"Oh, this sounds spicy. Do tell, Anna, did he have broad shoulders? And did he have nice eyes?" Alexia asks.

"Yes, all the above. C'mon, girls, you know my taste in men. He didn't have the best pickup lines though. I think he was confused as to what to say to me when he walked up and tried to get my number, so he said something like, 'Oh, umm, me and my friends throw parties downtown every weekend in the big city. Maybe I could get your number and invite you if you're interested.' Some crap like that."

"So what did you say?" I ask.

"I said sure…only because I thought he was hot."

"And that's why you gave him your number? Because he had a nice body?" Alexia asks.

"Yeah. But I that's not the point of my story. So check this out—we spoke a few times over the phone, and I decided to go see him at his place a few days ago."

"Wow. Already? Did you guys at least go out to the movies or have dinner or something before that stage, Anna?" I ask.

"C'mon, Michelle, I am a grown woman. What difference does it make if I have dinner and all that stuff or I just go directly to his place? It all ends up with the same thing happening, right? Look at you; didn't you end up sleeping with the Braxton guy?"

She had a point.

"So like I was saying, I went over to his place, and we started talking, and he was wearing this tank top that was showing all his muscles and stuff."

"Man, this sounds like it's really going to be spicy!" Alexia exclaims. We all laugh.

"So we were hanging out, and I started getting really hot, so I moved closer to him on the couch."

"And?" we all chimed together.

"And I was doing my best to flirt with him, but he wasn't responding."

"What do you mean he wasn't responding?" Alexia asks.

"He wasn't. He kept on talking about how he wanted to wait until he was married before he had sex with a woman and all that crap. And then he said he wanted to hold me as it got really late and lie down with me. So there I was, lying in bed with one of the hottest guys I have ever talked to, and he just fell asleep."

"What?" Alexia asks. Jess giggles.

"That's right…he just fell asleep. That's *asleep*. Asleep. Like you know when you shut your eyes and do that thing your body does when your body shuts down."

"Wow. So what did you do? I would have poked him" I remark jokingly.

"Funny. Well, I waited for some minutes, and then I got up and just left. One of the most frustrating encounters I have ever had."

"Yeah, that sounds frustrating. Maybe he was gay," Alexia suggests.

"No, I don't think so. I did not get that vibe from him," Anna replies.

"Well, you're a very attractive girl. Maybe he was just being respectful. Maybe he was a little intimidated," Jess suggests.

"Wow, she speaks—listen, Jess, I know you are still a virgin and have yet to venture into the world of animalistic, carnivorous men, but no normal man will sit there past midnight with a girl whose skirt is hiked up her side to reveal her smooth legs, no normal man will sit and do nothing while the girl next to him is giving all the physical signs that she wants to sleep with him."

"Then maybe he was not normal," Jess replies.

"Oh, he was not, we've established that," I chime in. "Maybe he wasn't attracted to you, Anna."

"Rubbish. I caught him looking at my legs a bunch of times as I tried to seduce him. He wanted me, I know it."

"Then maybe he was gay. Maybe he is a gay guy who is considering sleeping with women, but he is not ready for it yet. Maybe he wanted an extra push from you," Alexia remarks.

"I gave him all the push he needed. I need a real man, not half a man. I need a man who can 'rise' to the occasion, if you know what I mean."

"Rise to the occasion, ha-ha. You're crazy, Anna" Alexia laughs.

"Yeah, I was really hot and ready that night. He tried calling me again, but I did not answer. I mean, he's a nice guy, I guess, but not what I am looking for."

"Seems to be a lot of that going around. The last guy I was seeing just stopped calling me, and I feel bad because I slept with him," Alexia remarks.

"Oh, well he's a guy. What do you expect? Let me tell you something, if you do not know it already. Many guys lose interest in a girl if they do not have much trouble getting her in bed. They will only want to see you for sex again if the sex was good. Which is why many guys call me all the time."

"Oh, gosh, Anna, you really are a maniac!" I remark.

"But it's true," replies Anna. "I have to go use the bathroom. guys. Give me a min." Anna gets up and walks off.

"Anna's crazy," Jess remarks. "Hey, Alexia, what is this guy's name, the guy who you slept with?"

"John. I think his last name is Casey. Why do you ask about his name?"

"Oh, just wanted to put an identity behind the story, that's all," Jess replies.

"Long line for the bathroom; I'll go later. So, Alexia, was the sex good at least?" Anna asks, having returned from the bathroom area.

I knew it was because Alexia had told me so, before Anna and Jess even knew about this John guy. "No the sex wasn't even that good; it was just okay," Alexia says without making eye contact with me.

"Oh, so give him the boot then! This is not even up for discussion. How about you, Michelle? I know you said you were thinking the same about Mr. Braxton. Any updates?"

"Yeah, I'm done with him. He only wanted sex with me and nothing more, and I can't believe I invested this much time in him."

"Jess has been really quiet over there. What's cooking with you, Jess? Any guys waiting in line? You never talk much about yourself," Alexia remarks.

"Yeah, Jess never says much. Miss Goodie Two Shoes over here. C'mon, Jess, let's hear it," Anna teases.

"Well, I don't know. Every time I hear you guys talking about sex and stuff, I get a little intimidated."

"You know what's interesting about Jess? In my opinion, she is the prettiest out of all of us, and she is a virgin. Go figure."

"I'll take that as a compliment. I do date guys. I am just a bit reserved about that kind of stuff, that's all."

"I can't believe you've never had sex, Jess. You do know this is the twenty-first century, right?" I exclaim.

"So what exactly have you done when it comes to sex and stuff?" Anna asks.

Jess turns bright red.

"Aw-w, she is shy. Okay, okay, so Jess, have you ever kissed?" Anna asks.

"Of course."

"Yeah, but kissed where is the real question," I remark. We all laugh.

"Okay, okay. Jess, have you ever, umm, had a guy touch you down there?" Anna asks.

"Yes. Twice, but I wasn't comfortable, so I made him stop."

"Okay, have you ever given a guy a blow job?" Alexia asks.

"No!" This time Jess turns a really bright red.

"Do you ever think about sex?" I ask.

"Yes, sometimes…but it is not something I dwell on."

"How can you not dwell on it when you hang around Anna all the time?" Alexia remarks.

"I'm not sure how that works, but I don't…at least for now. How about you, Alexia? How do you handle sex?"

"Well, I prefer to be in a steady relationship before I have sex with anyone. It makes me feel more secure with who I am dealing with."

"You had sex with the John guy, and you were not in a relationship with him," I say. Alexia just gives me a look.

"Well, that was a one-time exception, Michelle."

"And you, Anna…you're here questioning everyone. What's your stance on sex?" I ask.

"Well, I personally prefer that it be with someone I am attracted to. I would even sleep with two guys at the same time if I was able—I've done it before."

"Wow, really? How did that turn out?" I ask.

"Heaven."

"I don't know; I think I would be a bit intimidated. I would personally prefer to fall in love, get married, and then make love to the man of my dreams," says Jess.

"Keep on dreaming, girlfriend. Those stories don't happen in the real world. Maybe you should get together with the last guy I told you guys about. You guys would make a good match," Anna says.

"Okay, okay, let's stop all this sex talk. It's getting me worked up. How about family? It's going to be my daughter's birthday in two weeks!"

"Aw-w, little Tara!" the girls reply. We quickly switch the subject to Alexia's daughter, and soon the thought of men and their uses becomes a distant memory…or so we think.

Chapter Five

I see my folks for the weekend. They seem well, although some wear shows on their faces. I wonder if that is an effect of age, a hard life, or both. Of course, I tell them everything is fine with work and all, and naturally, they give me advice on handling myself in the city.

My father is planning a trip to South Korea, so he only speaks with me briefly and then goes to his study to work on his trip. He leaves in three days for two weeks. I will miss him.

My mother asks me about work, life, and if I have a girlfriend now. After telling her no, she suggests finding a good girl to settle down with, one with a good head on her shoulders and one who fears God. She says I should avoid the "loose" lifestyle that the big-city nightlife supports. If only she knew the ugly truth. My mother is especially concerned about my faith and spirituality. I tell her I am still close to God, but in my heart, I feel bad about telling a lie to the woman who gave birth to me. I have always been skeptical about religion and the unknown. I have always relied on my wits and my logic to make sense of all that happens around me. I mean, I believe in God; there has to be a divine source that began all things, but the truth is, I just do not focus my energies on understanding or developing a relationship with God.

I live day by day, and I work hard to make ends meet. I just did not feel like getting into a spiritual conversation with my mother. She thinks it is important that we, as human beings, develop our spiritual side, along with our physical and mental sides, as this is the only way to attain contentment with life. And my mother seems like a very content person. A staunch Christian and believer in Jesus, she never seems to need anything and always seems satisfied. She always seems secure. I wish I could attain that level of spirituality one day; for one thing, it will keep me from chasing women so much and spending so much damn money.

After talking with my mother, I head into Alfred's room. Alfred is in his early thirties. My parents adopted him when he was fourteen; both his parents were victims of a homicide in their own home. Luckily for him, he was at school at the time. He was a boxer at one point, but bodily injuries prevented him from progressing further in that sport. So he currently works in a docking yard, and at night he is a youth preacher at the neighborhood church. He has become an older brother to me over the years. My conversations with Alfred are composed mainly of debates on his beliefs and on the authenticity of Christianity.

He's flipping through a boxing magazine on his bed when I walk in.

"Hey, dude."

He looks up at me. "Hey, John," he says in his calm manner. "So how is the city life treating you?"

"Fine, I guess." I feel ashamed, in a way, to bring up my exploits with women to him, as I respect him and his beliefs. So we chat about old times, boxing, and work. As I get ready to leave, he asks me about my faith.

"Well, Al, you know I was never really a religious person, but I guess I am okay."

"It's not about being religious, John; it's about having a personal relationship with God, your creator. They are two separate concepts."

"Well, Al, I am nice to everyone. I believe I have a good heart, and I work hard. So I guess I am doing okay. I guess I am doing fine."

"Well, John, that's good, but remember, sometimes just doing good is not good enough. To excel at anything you need to put in extra effort to understand why things are the way they are, so you are better equipped to get by."

"I know this, Al, and I do put in extra work in all I do, and I am getting by."

"You're getting by in just a small part of a much bigger picture, John."

I open my mouth to fire a response back at Alfred, but then realize that doing so will just start another debate that probably will not end that day, so I resist the temptation. "Okay, Al, whatever you say."

He smiles. "Giving up so easily? That's very unlike you, John."

"Yeah, yeah, whatever you say, Al. You still didn't convince me" I say as I glance at a basketball magazine on his dresser.

"Maybe it's not my job to do so. All I can tell you is that I accepted Jesus Christ as my Lord and Savior four years ago, and it has been amazing what He has done for me. Anyway, enough on that topic. Have you found a girlfriend yet in the big, bad city?"

"Not exactly."

We end our conversation on that note, and the rest of my time at home is spent eating good food and having good conversation. Well, overall, it is splendid seeing my parents, as well as hanging out with Alfred. I really want to make them proud of me. I cannot do anything that would disappoint them, especially seeing how much they have done for me. Whenever I feel down and out, whenever I am drained, they are always supportive and seem to always have the right things to say. So going home for me serves as a sort of boost to my character, as well as to my spirit. Going back home relieves me from so much stress.

And it is a good way for me to get my dirty laundry done for free.

***

I just got back to my apartment. My bedroom seems to say that it misses me. I check my messages, and I have about five waiting for me on my landline, of which three are from women. I love my life. Alexia wants to see me, apparently. Damn, I wish she would just leave me alone. She's cute and all and seems like a "good" girl, but I am not ready to settle down just yet. I just got here. Well, it's been a little over a year now. Besides, how "good" can a girl be when she opens her legs to me within two days of meeting me? Lord knows who else has been in there. Or what else, for that matter. No, thank you. I've still got the girl who took me home from that club on my mind; I think Sophia was her name. She has near-perfect tits and that beautiful contoured butt that I love. Plus, she is very sensual. Sounds like my kind of girl. I have to give her a call; sex with her wasn't bad. It wasn't bad at all.

***

I messed up. I messed up big time. I messed up. I messed up. Oh, boy, did I mess up. Damn. Sophia called me and asked me to come over to her place last night, so I obliged. Like a trooper, I packed a bag and went to her place after work. We went right into sex; didn't even pause for greetings when I got there, like two wild animals. She gave me a blow job, which was incredible, by the way, then asked me to enter her. Crap. It was then I realized that I'd left my condoms at home. Of all the ammunition any dirty bachelor like me should be carrying, a good condom should be the first thing on the list. So there we are: two naked, sweaty bodies on top of each other and like an idiot, I forgot my condoms. I asked her if she had any, and she said no. And as we lay there, sweaty bodies and all, I didn't want to, but I just couldn't think right, just couldn't control myself, and…well, I guess you can figure out the rest.

Now it's the next day. I am at work. I am freaking out and feel so paranoid. I don't know this girl too well, and I was inside her, unprotected!

How could I be so stupid? I have to meet up with her and discuss her background and share mine as well. I am such a fool. Well, I have had the experience; let's hope I learn the lesson.

***

I call Sophia, and she agrees to meet for dinner and discuss our "event." We meet on Friday after work and have dinner at a Dominican restaurant. I tell her about my numerous sexual exploits, in college and beyond, always protected, of course (I think). Then she tells her story. Basically, she is fine, she says, and has been living on her own for the past nine or so years. So, naturally, she has been through all kinds of things.

Oh, boy, like that makes me feel any better. I won't go into the details of exactly what she told me.

I immediately tell her I am clean. I ask her to get tested and to let me see the results. She agrees. I know it is a bit selfish to ask her to get tested when I did not offer to get tested myself, but in my eyes, she is the bigger threat. I hope I'm not lying to myself.

We go back to her place. It is late and I do not feel like going home, and for the first time in my life, I watch a movie in bed without having sex. The movie plays, but our minds are in a different place.

***

I am at work and am so nervous. I cannot think straight. What if this girl has an STD? Worse yet, what if she has HIV? I am doomed if she does. That would finish me. I am so stressed out. I look at my computer screen, but my mind is far away, imagining all sorts of negative outcomes. Will I be sick? Will I die? I can't seem to think straight. The only way I will be able to clear my head is when I see her test results. So I call her again, and she tells me she will be getting her results back in about three days. So I have to wait. I will take my test after she lets me know her status.

***

I'm going to Sophia's today because she asked me to. She says she has something important to share with me. Uh-oh. My heart starts pounding as I hear her say those words. "She's got to be okay," I say to myself. "I will be okay." Her message does not sound too positive, though. She sounds very serious. I begin to imagine all sorts of possible scenarios. Then I begin to pray and ask God to help me. "I will never sleep with another woman again until I get married; I swear! Please help me, God!" What a hypocrite I am. It's funny how most of us only turn to God when we need stuff done for us.

I get to her place, and she offers me tea, which I accept. Then she receives a phone call and tells me to hold on. As she speaks on the phone, I start to play out all these possible scenarios in my head. "What if she's sick? What if she has HIV? And why does she choose now, of all times, to answer her damn phone?" I am very impatient, and I want her to show me her lab results so I can clear my conscience. But she looks so calm; in fact, she is wearing a smile on her face, so nothing can be wrong, or so I hope. As soon as she gets off the phone she walks over to me and calmly shows me the results of her lab test: HIV-negative.

"No STDs?" I ask?

"Nope." I feel this weight lift off my shoulders. I am so happy—so happy that I begin kissing this girl. And she loves it. I kneel down and thank God for this news. And then, of course, kissing this girl, with her bodacious body, leads to other things, but this time I am prepared. But having a condom this time does not stop me from being a hypocrite, and I know God is watching.

It's Saturday today, and I am accompanying Alexia to a school play which Tara is participating. I love that little girl; she's so cute. She's only six years old, and she is the most adorable little thing you'll ever see. She looks just like her mother, and she has strong Persian features. She has big, round, beautiful eyes, and she always has a smile on her face. I could spend the whole day with Tara. Sometimes when I am around her, I feel like having a kid myself. I told Alexia once that I was going to steal Tara from her and give her back when she became a teenager. Anyway, we are heading to the play now at Tara's school. As Tara is in the play herself, we have to get there ahead of the other parents so she can get ready. We approach the school steps, with Tara holding both our hands, skipping between us.

"Are you excited about the play, baby?" Alexia asks.

"Yes, Mommy, I'm very happy."

"And you know what? We are going to have a special little party for you after the play, just us three, to celebrate your being in the play! Won't that be cool?" I ask Tara.

"Yes! It will be. Hey, Lanna! Mommy, look, it's Lanna!" Tara exclaims excitedly as she points across the street at one of her playmates who is also heading to the school. We all wave at little Lanna and her parents, but something else catches my attention.

There is a man standing with Lanna's family. He is beautiful. He is tall, well built, and well dressed in a sports coat, slacks, and loafers. But what catches my attention are his eyes. His eyes are very sensual. As Lanna's family approaches, he looks directly at me and smiles. I melt. I look over at Alexia. "I know," she comments with a naughty smile. "Let's say hello."

Tara is the first to make a move. She runs and gives her buddy a big hug, and the little girls start giggling. We adults greet each other the adult way.

"Hi. I think we met once before. I am Tara's mom, Alexia."

"Oh, hello. Lanna talks about you all the time. I think you volunteered once to host tea time for the kids," Lanna's mom replies. "My name is Jane."

"Hi, Jane. This is my best friend, Michelle."

"Hi, Michelle. This is my husband, Stephen, and his best friend, Darius, who also happens to be Lanna's godfather."

Darius. So Darius is his name. I think Darius just became my favorite name for men, as of today.

34

We all head inside the building. Tara is so excited that I have to physi-cally hold her to stop her from running off and playing with her friends. We leave her in the care of the teachers who are organizing the play, and Jane finds some seats with the guys, while Alexia and I head to a bathroom.

"Oh, my gosh! Did you see that guy, Alexia?" I exclaim. "He was fine!"

"Mm-hmm," Alexia exclaims as she straightens her hair. "Well, it seems we both fancy him, but I did see him smiling at you."

"Oh, Alexia, are you interested? If you are, I will back off."

"No, it's okay. Let's see who he focuses on. He had beautiful eyes, I have to say."

"Okay, but no matter what happens, this is just a guy, and we are best friends. He is not that important."

"Michelle! C'mon! You are exaggerating the situation. It's fine—if he talks to you, flirt with him and see what happens. I already told you that I saw him smiling at you."

"Okay, okay, let's head out there."

Alexia takes a seat between Jane and Stephen. I sit right next to Darius. I am so shy that I cannot even look in his direction. I want him to talk to me. Soon, I feel a tap on my arm. Oh, boy.

"Hi, did you say your name was Michelle?" he says. I love the smell of his cologne.

"Yes, that is my name, and you are Darius, right?" I reply.

"Yes, nice to meet you again. So you guys are best friends. How long have you known each other?"

"Umm, a several years now. We met each other randomly, and we have been best friends ever since."

"Randomly? Care to explain?"

"Well, I went on a date with a guy whose friend was also on a date that same night with Alexia in the same place. We got bored with our dates, so we ditched them and decided to go out by ourselves, and we had such a great time that we decided to keep in touch. And now we are best friends."

"Ha-ha, you ditched your dates? Wow, don't you think that's a bit mean?"

"Well, they were boring."

"I see. Well, what makes for an interesting date then for you?" he asks.

"Well, for one thing. don't be one-dimensional and talk about average things, like what happened on what television show, or how much money you make, or what new shoes you bought—boring stuff like that should not be brought up."

"That's it? Is there more to what makes for an interesting date, Michelle?"

"Well, just be genuine, you know. I personally like guys who can carry a conversation—a meaningful conversation, for that matter. And don't talk too much about yourself; that is not attractive at all."

"A-ha, well, I hope I do a good job of carrying a conversation with you," he says.

"Well, you're doing a good job so far," I reply. He smiles at me and looks at the stage. Tara and Lanna step on stage and start singing something that sounds like a nursery rhyme. Alexia and Jane start screaming. I want to scream as well, but this guy's eyes have me in a different state of mind.

"Those little girls are adorable," he says.

"I know, aren't they? Do you have any kids?"

"No, no, kids for me."

"Why not?"

"Is that a trick question? Well, I haven't met anyone yet that I see myself having kids with."

"I see. How about a girlfriend. Do you have a girlfriend?"

"No, no, girlfriend. And yourself? Boyfriend?"

"No, I'm taking a break from men. You guys are too much work. But no, no boyfriend. I am taking applications though."

He giggles at my last comment. The play goes on for another thirty minutes, and after it finishes, the parents and kids file into a hallway for some refreshments. The girls and Alexia are standing with Jane and her husband, commenting on the play. Darius and I choose to stand behind them and chat.

"So, you never told me what you do Darius," I remark.

"I'm sorry. I'm a chef. And you?"

"I work two jobs. During the day I am a secretary in a law office, and at night I sometimes work as a waitress. So you're a chef, huh? Will you cook for me sometime?"

"Absolutely. I will need a number to arrange that, though, if that's okay with you."

"Sure," I say as I notice Alexia look over at me and smile. Darius and I exchange numbers.

"Well, I better get going. We planned on throwing a little party for Tara after the play. But it was nice meeting you, Darius."

"It was nice meeting you as well, Michelle. I will call you, and we can arrange something."

I take one final look into his eyes, and then I smile and force myself to walk away. Later, as Tara, Alexia, and I sit in Alexia's apartment and play Scrabble over hot chocolate, I can't help but daydream about this guy, Darius, and his deep, sensual eyes.

Chapter Six

It's been about a month since the Sophia incident. I met a Spanish girl two weeks ago at a lounge, and I have been talking to her on the phone. Her face is decent, but what a body she has. She is so "bodacious," as I like to say. I never got tested after my event with Sophia. I don't think I have to; she was clean, and I think I am clean. What I don't know won't kill me. You know, they say these days that you can't trust people. You never know what people have, what baggage they carry, myself included. But in my defense, not that this is an excuse, but taking a test for HIV and STDs and waiting in line for the results is one of the scariest, most distasteful activities one can engage in, especially if you are a dog like me. I know that is an ignorant response, but hey, for now I would rather not know—it makes my life easier and less stressful.

So for now, I will just focus on excelling at my job and being a good person. And I'll also deal with all the ladies who come in large supply in this city! But I have to admit—sometimes I wish I had an actual girlfriend, one female who would enhance me and contribute to making me a better person. Yes, that would be great. The problem is that good girls are hard to find these days. They often are very materialistic, too full of themselves, always complaining, not focused, not grounded, not spiritual, not smart, or just not decent. These are my opinions, of course. I find most girls in bars or clubs or both. And it's hard to find a good woman in such places, generally speaking. Lord knows who else they meet every time they step out. But who am I to talk? I am out there with them as well. It seems I set a double standard, and I am sure women say the same things, if not worse, about men. But it's true. I guess I should be asking two questions: Should I change my lifestyle? And where do all the good people go?

***

I have been talking to the Spanish girl. Her name is Gendrey. She's twenty-five years old, and she works in an accounting firm. She speaks fluent English, and it seems like she has a decent head on her shoulders; at least, you can tell she went to school, which is more than I can say for a lot of people I meet these days. Nice smile. Very nice smile, actually. Nice full lips. Long curly hair, tan skin, big butt. Small waist. Big breasts. My type. No potential for anything long term; I think we both know that, but we are still talking, delaying the other obvious outcome. Sometimes I wonder why people drag out the introductory, getting-to-know-you process. If there is no potential, both parties may as well see if they are willing to sleep with each other, and if not, go their separate ways. I guess that's the stereotypical man's way of looking at things. And I am a stereotypical man. But seriously, I just find it a big waste of time. I call it a courteous and nice way of asking another person to bed. Just as you would ask someone to dinner, but with a different menu. If you're both hungry, and don't really need each other's company, I say, just eat. Hopefully, the food won't taste that bad. Hopefully.

***

It's Saturday, and I have invited Gendrey over to my place for the "main meal." Figured I'd had it with all the small talk. Ate my appetizers; time for the main course. Do the math.

We agree to watch a movie, knowing full well that we plan on "making" a movie afterwards. So things are going normally, and then we get into it. Then we really get into it. We start messing around in my living room. Then I carry her to my bedroom. She's very aggressive, this girl. After some foreplay, I put my condom on—Magnum, of course—and begin the main course on top. I am inside her and going for a good fifteen minutes when all of a sudden I feel a different sensation. A very raw, juicy sensation. Almost too good to be true. And that's exactly what it is. My condom slipped off. I must not have put it on properly, and I was in this girl for about five minutes with that sensation.

Oh, boy, not again. I immediately stop and pull out, my manhood wet and all. She was so into it, I don't even think she realizes what has happened.

"Gendrey," I say.

"What?" she screams at me, panting and out of breath. "Why'd you stop, John?"

"The condom came off."

"What?"

"I said the condom came off, Gendrey."

There is a brief silence. She sits up in bed and looks at me with a serious expression. "What do you mean, the condom came off?"

I hold the used condom up to her. "I mean the condom came off, Gendrey."

A look of worry comes over her, and rightfully so. "Oh no, oh no!" She begins to cry, and I am still sitting up in bed, buck naked, looking at her like a fool.

"Why me? Why me? You are clean, right? Nothing is wrong with you, right? You did not cum in me, did you, John? You sure you did not cum in me? I cannot afford to be sick or have kids now. You sure you did not cum in me?" The questions keep coming.

I am in a brief state of shock, not really listening to her but wondering what I did wrong when I put on the condom. Squeeze the tip, maybe? Maybe she was too wet? Wrong-size condom? Expired condom?

"Hey!" she screams. I look up, and realize this girl has been crying for the past couple of minutes. I move over to her and hold her in my arms, and she sobs. I feel good comforting her.

"Don't worry. I am okay. I am healthy, and I did not cum in you. But if it makes you feel any better, I will go get tested and let you see the results."

She still sobs in my arms, and I stare at the wall, feeling bad for lying because I myself do not know if I am okay or not. But now I have no choice. I have to face the heat and get tested. It's amazing how one night of pleasure has turned into a longer period of stress. I hug her until she falls asleep in my arms, and I stay awake, staring at the wall like a buffoon.

***

I am at the testing center today, a rainy Wednesday. I choose a center that gives anonymous testing, located on the west side of the city. Anonymous, just in case there is something wrong with me. Then I and only I will know about it—you know, for my job safety and stuff. You never know; better safe than sorry.

So anyway, here I am. They gave me a ticket number; I am fifty-four. Feels like I am on death row. I don't even have a name, just fifty-four. What makes it even worse is all this anxiety I feel. All these memories of my past sexual exploits come flooding back. My heart is pounding. What if this girl gave me this? That girl gave me that? I met some girls for just one night; Lord knows who else they have been with. What if they gave me something? I realize I have not been making the most strategically beneficial decisions in my short life. What if, when the condom broke, I got something? What if, what if, *what if?*

I ask and I ask, but I know it is too late to ask questions now. I am about to cross a line and receive one of two answers: yes or no. No maybe, no probably, and no what if's. So there is no point in asking now. No medicine I can get will cure me instantaneously, if at all, in the event that I caught anything. I am in a no-fly zone now. No-man's-land. I face the unknown. I learned as a child to pray to God whenever a situation got beyond my control. Well, this situation was in my control, but I lost control, and now I am helpless, about to receive what is, in my eyes, either life-or-death sentence.

So I get on my knees, right here in the testing center, close my eyes, and say a silent prayer, the best way I know how, to the Master of the Universe: "Lord, I am sorry for what I have done. Please, I beg You with my soul, body, heart, mind, and spirit not to have the results come out positive for any STD or for HIV. I beg You, please spare me, and I promise I will not have sex again until I marry. I promise. Please, I beg You."

I open my eyes, and I feel a little better, but I am still nervous. Everyone in the room is staring at me, and one nurse is in the corner with a smirk on her face. She's probably thinking, *Look at this guy, only praying to God because he is in trouble.* But I put myself here so I have no right to be mad. If anything, I should be mad at myself.

Half an hour passes, and I entertain myself by watching a video of the different STDs, as well as one on HIV. It shows, in graphic detail, the after-effects of each. In one screen shot there is puss emerging from what looks like a penis. This is torture, I tell you, having to watch this and wait for my test, knowing that those images could be me. I think the staff here intentionally plays these movies to scare the patients. Good strategy.

"Number fifty-four!" That's me; it's show time. I walk into a private area where a man, who I assume is a doctor, is waiting. He tells me to relax, and then he takes a cotton swab device and swipes all around the exterior of my gums. Next, he draws my blood from my arm. I don't feel a thing, maybe because I am too preoccupied with worry. Then I am instructed to go back to the waiting area for the results. This is the part that sucks. A whole thirty minutes sitting there, watching horrific videos about STDs and waiting to see if I have the guilty sentence.

"Number fifty-four." I spring to my feet, nervous about what my result will be. I follow the nurse into a separate room, and she whips out my results. She hesitates, and I almost leap over the desk between us to yank it out of her hand. Finally, she hands me the result slip: HIV-negative. The STD results will come in four days. Phew. I can't believe it; I just can't. I feel this huge weight ease off my shoulders. I am so happy. And I feel I have to spread the good news, so I call a close friend by the name of Abel, who is almost like a brother to me. We grew up in the same neighborhood. but he chose to move to Brazil because of his obsession with the women there. For some reason. he gives good advice on women but never seems to live by his advice. He is the biggest womanizer I know, and this is the one person on this planet who knows all my dirty secrets. I had already shared the details of my accident with him. I call him up.

"Yo, I tested negative, man!"

"That's good news, man," he replies. "Let me say this to you though, John; you're gambling with your life and dodging too many bullets. Keep on playing like this and one day you're bound to get hit."

I agree, but let's hope for my sake that I remember his advice at the right time.

I spent the next two days after I met Darius chatting with him on the phone. He seems to be quite a nice guy. He comes from a good home and is a chef in one of the top restaurants right here in the big city. It helps that I work part-time as a waitress, so at least we have something in common. We talked for two hours straight the first time he called me, and then talked for three hours on the next night! So I have a good feeling about him. We agreed to meet today for our first dinner at his restaurant, and I was curious to see what he had planned, being that it was his restaurant and all.

I wanted Alexia to help me get ready and talk a bit before I went on the date, but Tara is not feeling well, so she has to stay at home with her. In addition, her mother, Miss Pryce, is coming into town to spend time with her, so she also has to get her place ready to accommodate her. So I decided to get together with Anna, who, surprisingly, had no one to do this Friday evening.

Anna comes over to my place, and before long we start chatting about our favorite topic: men. I sift through various jeans and shirts for Anna's approval.

"So what is this guy like anyway?" she asks.

"He seems to be pretty laid back. He is very soft spoken and all. I don't know; there is this mysterious thing going on about him."

"Well, you sound excited, so it seems like the date will be fun. You're so lucky; you have a chef making dinner for you tonight."

"Aw-w, thanks, Anna. I'll make sure to tell you all about it."

"Please do, and I want all the spicy details as usual. Wait, wait! I like that! You should wear that," Anna exclaims as I hold out some clothing from my dresser.

"Okay."

"Great, so my mission here is complete. Enough about you; let's talk about me, I have some crazy stuff to share with you," Anna remarks.

"Go ahead. What happened?"

"There is this guy I have been seeing, or should I say sleeping with, for the past few weeks."

"You're seeing someone and you didn't tell us?" I say.

"No, no, I was going to, but he is no one important. I just see him for sex, that's all."

"Oh, okay, so what happened?"

"I was walking through the city two days ago, and I saw him chatting with two other guys."

"Guys are allowed to talk to other guys, you know."

"No, no, no, I am not done. So I see them talking, and my guy—the one I'm seeing—waves his hands in a very—how do I say this?—'girlie' manner."

"Wow, so you think he's gay? Or bisexual, maybe?"

"I don't know, Michelle, but the friends he was standing with were all acting very feminine. I was shocked because he acts very manly around me. I had never seen him act like that."

"Maybe he was just joking around with his friends?"

"No, Michelle, this was definitely gay. Half my male friends are gay, so I know gay when I see it, and this was definitely gay. And that made me think about another thing. He doesn't really get turned on with actual sex, at least not all the time, but he enjoys my performing oral sex on him. I always found that a bit strange."

"That is a bit off. Well, you know they say these days that there are a lot of men seeing other men for sexual reasons. Shame; they should at least tell the person they are seeing so everyone is clear on what is going on."

"I agree, and I don't think I will see him anymore. I like manly men, and when I saw what I saw, I could not believe it. I wonder what his reaction would have been if he had seen me looking at him."

"I don't know. That is a good question. I would be curious to know as well. But yes, I don't think you should see him anymore. Who knows what other secrets he may be hiding if your assumptions are true? Well, Anna, that's what you get when you sleep with all kinds of men. You get exactly that: all kinds of men. Ha-ha!"

"That's not funny, Michelle. Okay, enough on that guy. He doesn't deserve conversation time. Are you ready for your date tonight with Mr. Sexy, as you described him?"

"I can't wait. He has the most beautiful eyes, and I can't wait to spend all night staring into them. Wish you could join me, Anna, but you have a gay man to attend to. Ha-ha."

"I told you; that's not funny. Okay, maybe it's a little funny," Anna giggles. "Just remember to look him directly in his eyes when you talk, and let him know that you're into him."

"I know, I know. I'm sure I will be a little nervous, maybe shy, but I will get over it as we talk."

Anna and I spend the next few hours chatting about how to act when on a date with a hot guy, a conversation we've had many times before, and then I am on my way to dinner with a handsome chef called Darius.

***

I get to Darius's restaurant, Odyssey, around 8:30. It is a really nice, chic place that is situated within a hotel. There is some smooth jazz playing but surprisingly, the restaurant itself is empty. Darius lets me in and seats me at a candlelit table in the center of the room. The dim lighting really brings out Darius's good looks, and if it wasn't for social norms, I would jump on him right now. Sometimes I wish I was more like Anna.

"So…" Darius says as he sits down in front of me. "How are you?"

"I am well. I am excited to see what you made for dinner."

"Well, normally I make Japanese, Italian, and Swedish dishes, but tonight I thought I would surprise you with something a little different, something that you don't get every day but is very tasty."

"M-m-m-m, are you going to tell me what it is?"

He grins and disappears into the kitchen, re-emerging with dishes that he sets around the table. The aroma coming from the food is irresistible.

"This smells delicious. What is this?"

"This is a dish from West Africa—Nigeria, to be exact—called pounded yam and egusi stew. The white stuff is fresh yams, which have been pounded to a thick paste, and we will eat it with egusi stew, a stew that I made with smoked shrimp, goat meat, stock fish, fresh spinach, basic veggies, like onions and peppers, the egusi powder, which I had shipped from Nigeria, and some rare spices. It is a really tasty meal and very filling."

It isn't a typical meal, and I like that. This Darius is proving to be a little different. We spend the next few hours digging into his tasty dish, which is, as promised, very filling and very, very tasty. After dinner he cleans up and we sip on wine as we talk.

"That was a heavenly dinner, Darius. I like a man who can cook."

"Thanks. I enjoyed your company. What else do you like in a man?"

"I like a man who has goals; I like a man who doesn't just sit around the house doing nothing; I like a man who has a job."

"Yeah, that's important."

"Yeah, I like a man who is respectful and can treat me well, someone who can make me laugh, and, umm, good looks don't hurt."

"Looks like you just described the perfect man."

"No, no one is perfect."

"Very true, so I remember you saying that you work part-time as a waitress?"

"Yeah, at an Ethiopian restaurant. It is a pretty nice place. The dishes also have that nice flavor like what you just served. But I am getting tired of working there."

"Well if you don't like working there, you could work at my restaurant. I could always use more help."

"Thanks, but I don't know if I will be able to work around you" I say with a smile.

"And why is that?"

"Because I find you very attractive, and I am beginning to like you. I might drop the plates and stuff as I try to serve customers."

He turns red in the face and smiles. "Thanks, Michelle. I'm starting to like you as well. You have a great personality."

We look at each other and then he leans over and kisses me, and I almost pass out. And then he looks at me and holds my hand and starts kissing me again. Then his hands start going places and for some strange reason, I think about Braxton.

"Wait, Darius, wait," I exclaim.

"What's wrong, sweetie?" he asks in his calm demeanor. I melt.

"I find it hard to resist you, and I just want to take it slow. I have been hurt by guys when I got physical too fast. and I want to take it slow with you."

He lets out a sigh, then looks at me and smiles.

"Okay, I understand, and I apologize if I moved too fast. You can trust me, and I will respect you."

I smile back, and he holds me in his arms as we gaze out one of the restaurant windows. Maybe this guy is different. He is respectful and he seems genuine, and he is in no rush to get physical with me. So I feel I can trust him.

Chapter Seven

I t's been five days since my test, and I just got the results—my STD blood test is negative. Phew. I must admit I was a little nervous, opening the envelope.

I meet up with Gendrey later at a café downtown and show her the results. As soon as she sees them, she gets up and gives me this huge hug. I can sense her relief. She is as happy as I am. We speak a bit about that night, and I tease her about how she cried. Then we part ways; no doubt I will see her again. I watch her butt jiggle as she walks away. I guess I am back to my old self. Well, I'm happy I got that off my chest; I don't want to go through this ordeal again. Now that Gendrey has left to go do whatever she has to do, I sit back in the café and do some thinking. I am a young, good-looking guy, if I may say so—a smart, semi-successful man in this city, making decent, if not good, money. I am a magnet for women. As long as I am careful and make sure to use condoms properly, I should be fine. I just have to be a little more careful, that's all. I have to set higher standards. My goal now, while I am still single, is to tag a celebrity. Imagine having a celebrity chick as a booty call? Now, wouldn't that be something? My boys back home would never believe it. I imagine all these self-centered, sexual conquests for myself; ironic and hypocritical, especially after I just prayed, telling God I would change and asking God to spare my life.

***

I decide to lay off women for a while. That whole experience with Gendrey shook me up a bit, so I am trying to involve myself in other activities besides making money, drinking, and sex. I joined the gym to keep myself in shape. I also signed up for yoga classes after work. I decide to make a list of all the things I want to accomplish as I try to redirect my energies. I even have given a name to my new project aimed at redirecting my sexual energies: Operation Change. I know it sounds corny, but hey, it's a start. It helps when I write down my goals on paper. I hope that my "operation" will help me focus on other issues besides women, because at the rate I am going, I am bound to crash soon. But even in the gym, when I try to focus, I can't help but notice some girl on the treadmill, running with her butt cheeks flapping around, or another girl on the mat, stretching, with her tits protruding in my direction, or another girl doing squats in the smallest of shorts, her butt doing what butts do when good-looking women do squats in the shortest shorts. Oh, boy, this is going to be hard. I try to concentrate, but I find that I can't. Am I the only one in this predicament? Are there other men out there who suffer from this sexual addiction like me? Everywhere I turn, I find sexually appealing women. and I can't help but undress them with my eyes. And this city has a lot of good-looking women. The ratio here has to be ten to one. Of course, this is the big bad city, so just because I see someone who looks like a woman does not necessarily mean she is female. Do the math.

But I realize my predicament as I leave the gym today: I am an addict, and my drug is women.

***

I am heading home from work when I get a call from Shawn, Cesar's buddy.

"Yo, what's up, man?"

"Hey, Shawn," I reply. We indulge in small talk for a bit, then get down to business and his reason for calling.

"Yo, tomorrow night I am heading to this bar-slash-club and meeting up with European models who moved into the city last month. They want to party. Should be about five girls, and as far as I know, I am the only dude. I told Cesar, and he's in; thought you might want to tag along and meet these girls. And you know how freaky and wild these model kinds of girls are."

I think about his proposition, and all my previous attempts at changing for the better go right out the window. "Sure thing, man. I'm down. Where should I meet you guys?"

"Well, first we'll be hitting a bar downtown, and then we'll head to their pad. They live about three blocks away," he replies.

"Sounds good to me. Text me the address, or I can head there with Cesar after work tomorrow. Either way works for me."

"Cool, dude. I'll call you around seven."

"Cool."

He hangs up. I have a big smile on my face, imagining how lucky I am to have friends who know European models who live in the city. And I imagine that if we three guys and five girls go back to their place with liquor in our systems, something interesting will go down. I am definitely going to get laid, and it helps that I live in that area. I can't wait. Operation Change has been in effect for only one day, six hours and forty-two minutes. So much for that.

I am at my daytime job, surfing the Internet as usual. I get a call from Anna.

"Hey. So how did the date go with Mr. Darius?" she asks.

"It went okay. I am seeing him again tonight."

"Oh-h, so have you slept with him yet?"

"No, Anna, I'm taking my time with him, and he has been respectful. I actually spent last night at his place."

"And you did not sleep with him?"

"Nope. But I think I might the next time I do see him. I don't think I can resist much longer."

"Hmm…do you think he will be good in bed?"

"I think so. We have a strong sexual attraction, so I think it will be a really passionate experience. Well, I'm hoping it will be."

"Hmm, okay. Well, drink lots of water, because it will be a long, sweaty night!"

"Anna! You and your foul mouth. So, what's up with you, anyway?"

"Well, not much. I cut off gay guy."

"Really?"

"Yeah, I intentionally pissed him off to see his reaction, and he reacted a bit too feminine for me, but I don't want to talk about that."

"Oh, so anyone new?"

"Nah. Some friends of mine from Europe are in town, and we are meeting up with some guys in the city. So it should be fun with them. You should come out with us. I know for sure we are going out tomorrow."

"I'll pass. I told you I will be with Darius, remember?"

"Oh, yeah, I forgot. Well, that is more important, but I will definitely keep you posted about how the night goes."

"Okay. Well, have fun, and try to get a nice guy."

"You know me. I'll talk to you later, girlfriend."

"Bye, Anna."

"Bye."

I hang up and feel good that I am going to see Darius rather than hanging out with Anna. I am beginning to like his company, and I know I will definitely be sleeping with him tomorrow night.

Chapter Eight

After work today, Cesar and I take a cab downtown and meet up with Shawn at a new bar that just opened. He flashes his usual big smile—his big smile with bad intentions.

"What's up, fellas!" he greets us.

"What's up, man," I reply.

"Yeah, what's up, Shawn?" chimes in Cesar.

"Okay," says Shawn, "so four of the girls are here. They're inside; they're really nice, so be cool. The fifth is on her way. Let's go in, and I'll introduce you guys."

We follow Shawn inside. The club is dimly lit and seems to have an Arabic theme. It is really crowded, and everyone inside seems really happy or maybe really drunk. Most people are standing and talking, but in random corners I see people kissing, fondling, or dancing really close. The crowd itself seems to be very mixed, with a representative from every race here. There are blacks, whites, Chinese, Spanish, Filipino, and I am sure lots more—different colors, different shapes, and different sizes, but all in the same place. I guess birds of a feather do flock together. Interesting place.

Shawn introduces us to the girls: Olga, Anastasiya, Arisha, and Darya. Their names seem very Russian to me, but I mention nothing of my observation. Then again, what do I know? They are very friendly and look great. Great skin, beautiful smiles, and they are all very flirtatious. This promises to be a great night. Shawn cunningly orders more and more drinks for the girls, who can't seem to get enough. I am sitting by Arisha, and her hand is resting in my lap, and she doesn't even seem to notice. Olga keeps glancing at me. Wow. This is going to be a great night. I wonder what the fifth girl is like. And then she walks in.

***

She is built like a Greek goddess, very curvaceous and in prime shape. She has very long hair. Even in the dim lighting I can tell she has great skin. She has clear blue eyes, and her full lips just seem to be made for kissing—or something else that my perverted mind suggests. She has nice, perky breasts and the roundest ass I have ever seen. She is made for sex, in my eyes. I stare at her like the dog I am for some time, until she makes eye contact with me. I notice Cesar has noticed her as well, and I think he also notices my interest. Let the games begin. Cesar makes the first move. As I sit with Arisha's hand still resting on my lap, he walks over to the new girl and starts talking in her ear. She smiles and stares at him, but she also looks at me from the corner of her eye. I keep my cool. I shift my attention to Arisha, remembering that the night is still young, and there is still time. After some time, the new girl walks over to be with her friends. She introduces herself to me.

"Hi, I'm Anna," she says.

"Hello, I'm John." I can't seem to stop staring at her cleavage and her round butt. "Are you from around here?" I ask.

"Yeah, I live in the city but am originally from France. And you?"

"I just moved into the city myself," I reply.

A conversation between us grows from that initial icebreaker. Turns out she's a buyer for some fashion house in the city. And she lives alone. That information is music to my ears. She looks me dead in the eye as she speaks and occasionally glances up and down my body, as if she is sizing me up. When I crack a joke, she laughs and holds my arm and leaves her grip there longer than usual. She has that look in her eye; that seductive look that I am sure has wooed many men, that seductive look that is wooing me now, and I love it. I spot Cesar from the corner of my eye. He is talking to another of the European models, but he glances every so often at Anna and me. I know he wants her as well, so I make a power move.

"Hey, I would love to hang out with you sometime. Why don't we get a drink or a bite when we are both free?"

"Sure," she replies.

"You have a number I could call you on then?"

She smiles, puts her hand in my pocket, and grabs my cell phone, making sure to feel my thigh in the process. My hormones immediately start going crazy, and all I want to do now is have sex with this girl. This girl called Anna from France. She hands me back my cell and gives me a kiss on the cheek, while whispering in my ear, "Call me."

Wow. She leaves to use the bathroom, but I know the real reason she leaves is to keep her options open. There are a lot more people in the club, and I am sure I am just one of many guys who will hit on her tonight. I move around the room and talk to different people, but my mind is on this new girl with her curvy body, thick lips, round derriere, and full breasts—Anna.

***

The night ends on a sour note. Shawn gets into a fight with some guy at the bar, so we all have to leave. Cesar vanishes from the scene without even saying good-bye to any of us. The girls suggest we get something to eat, so we go to a diner, and I get some one-on-one time with Anna. She seems very laid back, and there is something mysterious about her, but I can't quite put my finger on it yet. She is very energetic when she speaks, which to me is very attractive. She has a red dot on her lip, though, and I can't get my eyes off it; it could be an STD or just a cold sore. It's probably just a cold sore and is so small, it's hardly even noticeable.

We talk for about an hour, and then I try to go back with her to her place, but she doesn't want me to, so I take my lonely self back to my apartment. We agree to meet up sometime in the coming week, so I am definitely looking forward to that.

***

It's Thursday evening, and Anna and I are here for dinner at this Japanese restaurant. I order fried rice, and she orders a dish whose name I cannot pronounce. We start chatting; apparently she used to work in London and decided to move to the city because of all the excitement that supposedly can be found here.

I tell her my story. Then we talk about the night we first met. Apparently, Cesar got her number as well and has been calling her, but she is not interested. At least, that is what she says to me. But you can't trust people, and who knows what she is really doing behind the scenes? She starts talking badly of Cesar, saying his approach with her was not working. She adds that he was acting childish over the phone. She then asks me to swear not to tell Cesar. I nod, while I think of what she just said. As she talks about others like that to me, I wonder what she says about me to others. Then I think: why should I care? After all, I am going after what I want. I can't stop looking at her cleavage. When she gets up to use the bathroom, her butt moves in a way I cannot describe appropriately. We part ways after dinner, but agree to meet up for a movie over the weekend.

***

It's Saturday, around 5:30, and I am getting dressed to go meet Anna. My phone rings. It's Cesar—weird coincidence.

"What's up, man?"

"Hello, Cesar, how are you?"

"Cool, dude, doing just fine."

As usual, we make small talk, then get down to his reason for calling.

"Say, umm, have you heard from that girl from the club that night?" he asks.

"Which one? There were five girls there that night, buddy."

"I mean the one with the big boobs and nice butt. You know, what's her name again?" he says, acting as if he's forgotten her name when we both know he has not.

"Anna," I reply.

"Yes, her. Did you ever see her or speak to her again?"

"Umm, yeah, I spoke to her once and that was that," I respond.

"And you never spoke to her again?"

"Nah, not really," I reply, feeling guilty that I am getting dressed to go see her as we speak. But hey, may the best man win.

"Oh, okay, yeah, just wondering how it went, that's all. Cool, well, we'll have to link up soon. I think there are some more parties coming up this weekend."

"Okay man, let me know."

"Okay dude, I'll talk to you later. Peace."

"Peace, Cesar." I hang up and wonder what the point of that conversation was. Maybe Cesar wants to sleep with Anna as well. I catch my words, thinking what a shame it is that most men like us see women as nothing more than pieces of meat. I step out the door of my apartment and hop on the subway to go meet Anna for dinner—and a movie I plan on making.

***

Dinner with Anna is a similar experience to the last meal we shared. Same conversation, the only difference being the cuisine; we eat at an Ethiopian restaurant this time, per her recommendation. She says she had a friend who works in the place, although not tonight. We arrive on time for the movie after dinner, but did little watching. Our hands were on each other the whole time. Our faces were on the screen, but I know our minds weren't. After the movie, she invites me to her place for tea. Yeah, okay. I obliged. I spend the first fifteen minutes sitting on her sofa as she changes into silk pajamas, and then she slides down right next to me on the couch. My hormones start going wild at this point. We start to kiss, touching each other all over, and then I carry her to her bedroom, put on a condom, and do very little sleeping the rest of the night.

I haven't spoken to Anna in a few days. She called me to tell me that she brought some guy she met to the restaurant where I work, but I was on a date with Darius that night. She said he's cute, though—probably just another guy she'll sleep with for some time and forget about. Or maybe he'll have some impact on her life and make her stop sleeping around so much. Who knows?

I have been seeing Darius on a regular basis for the past couple of weeks. I guess you could say that he is my boyfriend now, as I am not seeing anyone else and neither is he. I really like this guy. I don't want to mess this up, so I think I will learn from my mistakes with Cody and approach my relationship with this guy with a little more sense. He is so sweet; he cooks for me all the time, he takes me out to different opera shows, he surprises me at his apartment with candlelit dinners—I am in heaven. He seems perfect. And sex with him is not bad, either. Jess asked me last week to straighten her hair for her, so we agreed to meet at Alexia's place to hang out. Besides, Miss Pryce, Alexia's mom, wants to see us.

We all meet at Alexia's. Little Tara has some of her friends over but they are in her room, so Alexia has some breathing space. I begin straightening Jess's hair, and Miss Pryce sits with Alexia across from us.

I have known Alexia's mother for as long as I have known Alexia. She is a beautiful woman—she is an older version of Alexia. She has become sort of a mother figure to us all, and whenever she comes around, I feel like she shares some truths with us, some of which we do not want to hear. But that's the thing with some truths, isn't it? Sometimes they hurt.

"So how are you girls doing?" Miss Pryce asks.

"Okay" we all answer.

"Good. So, Michelle, Alexia tells me that you are working in a law firm now. What do you do for them?"

"Oh, nothing special, Miss Pryce. I just answer the phone."

"And surf the Internet," adds Alexia.

We all giggle.

"Are you planning on finishing college? What happened with that?" asks Miss Pryce.

"Well, that's on hold for now, Miss Pryce. I'm trying to get myself together first," I reply.

"You're a young woman now, Michelle. This is the time you should be finishing school and making plans to get a steady job. You can't work two jobs forever. A degree is very important; it separates you from the pack and gives you some credibility. You have to be realistic with life, you know. If you want to get a steady job that pays decent money and offers some form of stability, it starts with your getting a degree. It is a very important investment to make in life; trust me. I had to force my daughter here to go back to school after she dropped out, and now she is reaping the benefits."

"I know Miss Pryce, I know. I guess I've just been lazy about it. I will start looking into it. I've just been out of school for so long, and I don't know how I will get my old study habits back," I reply.

"That will come with time, I'm sure, but you have to make the effort, Michelle. Nothing worth having in life is ever easy, so you have to try."

"Okay, Miss Pryce, I shall," I reply, feeling guilty as I say so, because I do not mean it.

"Good. And how are you doing, Jess? I know you are in school. How is that going?"

"It's going okay. Same old. We just had our midterms, so I have a little break now from studying."

"That's good. Next time you go to class, be sure to take Michelle with you," Miss Pryce jokes. "And what about boyfriends? Which men are you guys dealing with now? I know Alexia was seeing someone briefly that turned out to be nothing promising. How about the rest of you guys? Jess?"

"Oh, nothing is going on with me. I never have luck with guys."

"And why not? You're so beautiful!"

"I think that's the problem, Miss Pryce. I meet many men who always want to get sexual with me, and I want to save myself for my future husband."

"You're still a virgin, Jess?" Miss Pryce asks.

"Yes."

"Wow, even I wasn't a virgin at your age. That's commendable."

"Anna says she is not normal," Alexia comments.

"Anna—that's your other friend, the French girl, right? She was a wild one, if I remember correctly. Where is she, and how is she doing?"

"She has not spoken to us in a while. Last time I spoke to her personally, she was going out with some friends, and she said she was seeing some guy she met, and that was the last I heard," I say.

"Knowing Anna, she's probably asleep in his arms, whoever this guy is," Jess says.

"You girls should be careful with whom you sleep with you know. Especially in a big city like this," Miss Pryce remarks.

"You're right, Miss Pryce. It's too risky to be sleeping around, and I don't think any of us wants to get pregnant by a man we are not in love with," I reply.

"Michelle, getting pregnant should be the least of your concerns. What about diseases? Don't you realize how many infections, viruses, and so forth are floating around these days? What about HIV? Pregnancy should be the least of your worries, Michelle."

Everyone becomes really quiet. I am sure at that moment we all begin to think of our past exploits with men. Well, maybe all of us, except for Jess, the only virgin in the group.

"Listen, I don't want to scare you guys. Remember that I am an old woman, and I have had a lot more experience with men than you have. All I am saying is be more careful and know who you're dealing with, that's all. I love you all and don't want any of you to get hurt in any way, shape, or form."

"You're right, Mama. It's just that sex is such a favorite activity for so many people, so that makes it hard to think about such things," Alexia remarks.

"That is what makes talking about it so hard, because no one wants to have the bad things associated with something they love thrown in their faces, especially if it is something they do so casually. But that's the world we live in these days, girls, and you have to know what's going on, or else you might hurt yourselves and others you love. So you should take such things seriously," Miss Pryce replies.

"At least Jess has nothing to worry about. She doesn't have sex," I say.

"Well, I have performed oral sex," Jess replies.

"I can't believe what I am hearing. You gave a guy a blow job, Jess?" I ask. "Wow, when did this happen?"

"Some time ago, Michelle."

"Wow, the world is definitely coming to an end. Jess is giving blow jobs now," Alexia comments.

"You should be careful with oral sex as well, Jess," Miss Pryce replies. "Do not be naïve about the subject."

"Damn, Mama, you're making sex become such an un-pleasurable experience now," Alexia remarks. We all giggle.

"No, it can be, if we approach it the right way," Miss Pryce replies. "Don't sleep around, and talk to the person you're dealing with so you know more about him. The hard part is talking."

I think about all my past relationships and all the men I had called boyfriends, being that I had never slept with anyone outside of a relationship—well, I did have two flings and a one-night-stand in my past, but I trusted my boyfriends, and I know they would have told me if there was anything I needed to know. I reasoned that I was good to go. I was lucky to have dealt with good guys, for the most part. And the one-night-stand? Well, that was many years ago, and I would have noticed something different on my body by now. So I decide not to worry.

"Well, girls, let me go spend some time with my granddaughter. I'll see you ladies later."

"Good-bye, Miss Pryce," we all reply. Alexia walks off with her mother to go check on Tara while I finish up with Jess's hair.

"Well, I am kinda sorta seeing someone, like, we kiss and stuff, and I have been seeing him for a while."

"Is this someone from your campus?"

"Yeah, some kid I see frequently in the library. He seems like a nice guy, but I know he wants to sleep with me."

"And how do you know?"

"Well, he is always very touchy whenever we get together, but I really like his personality."

"So why don't you date each other? How long have you been seeing each other?"

"A few months, but I think he is scared to commit. You know how guys are."

"I definitely do. Well, just don't perform oral sex on a guy who doesn't want to be with you."

"Well, maybe he will change. We are starting to do more things together. And he has not shown any sign that he is not interested in me."

"He is interested in you because you give him free blow jobs, Jess. C'mon, you really can't see that? I think you've been hanging around Anna too much. You need to spend more time with me and Alexia before your lips fall off."

"Michelle! How could you say that?"

"I'm just kidding, Jess. But seriously, chill with the blow jobs or at least have sex if you do."

"I think what Miss Pryce said made sense. I have to be more careful with this guy and with guys in general."

"Yeah, she is right," I say, not adding anything more, because I have work to do in that area myself.

I finish Jess's hair, and for the rest of the night Alexia, Jess, and I stay up talking about all the other issues in our lives, and as we talk, for some strange reason I think about Anna.

Chapter Nine

It's been two weeks since I last saw Anna, and I am still having the afteref-fects from my night with her. By far the best sex I have had in a very long time. What a body she has. And she is very sensual.

I am sitting at my desk, daydreaming about that night, when Cesar walks up. I have been seeing him a lot more often now. I wonder why.

"Yo," he greets me.

"Yo," I reply.

"So, have you spoken to that girl from the club? Anna or whatever?"

"Nah, not since the last time I told you I did," I lie.

"Oh, okay, cool. I actually spoke to her last week. She agreed to meet me at this club soon, so if she is bringing her friends and you're free, you should definitely come hang out with us. I am sure she and her friends would like to see you again."

If he only knew. "Yeah, sure, let me know, man."

"Okay, cool, talk to you later." He leaves, and I resume the task of day-dreaming about Anna and her great body. She wants to see me again this upcoming Friday.

***

It's Friday, and I am about to get off work. I have a knapsack packed for my "sleepover" at Anna's. As I shut down my computer and get ready to leave, Craig, my one-time mentor at work, approaches my desk with a buddy of his from another department—Sully, the guy whose eye twitches whenever he laughs.

"Hey, Craig. Hey, Sully," I say.

"Hey, John," Craig answers, "We are going to party at a club downtown, should be fun. You are more than welcome to come join us."

"Yeah, you should. You never come out to hang with us; you're always with Cesar," Sully jokingly chimes in, his eye doing the twitching thing as he says so.

"I know, I know, okay, send me a text message with the address of the club and I will see if I can come by."

"Okay," Craig says, "hope to see you there."

"Okay, Craig, see you soon. Talk to you later, Sully."

"See you later, John," they reply.

I step out of the office into a cool evening breeze. As I trudge to the subway, I debate whether I should head to Craig's event or spend the night at Anna's. It would be nice to hang out for once, but those guys like to drink and yell. Not typically my scene. And besides, Anna is fun in bed. Maybe I can go see Anna for a movie and leave immediately afterwards to Craig's event. But Anna will be disappointed, and I will feel I missed out on some good sex. But then again, she is not going anywhere, and this party is just happening once. I continue debating as I hop on the subway heading in Anna's direction.

***

Anna meets me at a café down the street from her apartment. She is wearing really tight black pants that accentuate all her curves. The more I look at her curves, the more going to Craig's party seems like a bad idea. She is looking especially sexy tonight. That red spot which was on her lip when I first met her is gone as well. Probably was just a cold sore. I give her a hug and notice how her body feels so good next to mine.

We sit down at the café and have random conversation for about an hour. Then we decide to go to her place. As we walk out of the café I receive the text from Craig with the address to the party. I debate for one last time whether or not I should go, then decide I would rather hang out with Anna. My mind and my conscience are officially switched off at this point, and my body is officially turned on. I've fallen for the bait; ironically, I'd set the trap. We jump right into sex as soon as we get to her place. She performs oral sex on me, and then we move to her bedroom. I literally rip her clothes off and put a condom on. I go inside her. She is extremely turned on for some reason. I start working it, when I hear the worst noise in the world. A pop.

"Damn!" I exclaim. Not again. I pull out, and the condom is totally ripped.

"What?" she asks.

"The condom broke."

"Here, put this one on." She hands me another condom. I don't even think to clean myself before putting it on. Even more important, I don't even stop to consider how calm and collected she was when I told her the condom broke. I am thinking with nothing but my penis now, my bad little friend. I am on full throttle. I put on the new condom and enter her again. It's then that I notice blood stains on her bed and on me.

"Wait, wait, wait…" I pull out, take the condom off, and throw it away.

"What? Why did you stop?" she asks, panting.

"Anna, there is blood all over here. Are you on your period?"

"Yes, but I didn't think—"

"Wait, wait! You are on your period? That's not safe, Anna, not for either of us." I sit down on the bed and realize how stupid I have been. "Listen, you are clean, right? I mean, I was inside you, unprotected. No matter how brief it was, I was in you unprotected, and to make things worse, you have blood all over you and me. Are you clean?"

"Yes, I am clean, John," she responds very unconvincingly.

"I think we should both get tested before we move any further, Anna. We did something really stupid, and I would only feel comfortable if I knew your status and you knew mine before we moved any further."

"You're right. I am clean, but I will get tested this week and show you the results, if that will make you feel better." She gets up.

"Where are you going?" I ask.

"I want to go clean up." She heads to the shower, and I sit on the bed pondering the accident that just happened: the condom broke, I was inside this woman, unprotected, and to make things worse, she had blood on me. I think to myself, *Talk about sex going wrong.* I begin to wish I had taken Craig's offer and gone to that party. How many times will I put myself in these kinds of situations?

She emerges from the bathroom, and I go in to clean myself, remembering to take a piss for good luck and also possibly flush out any crap that may be lodged in my penis. Just a tip I picked up as a teenager from Al. She has already changed the bed sheets when I emerge. I lie down next to her but cannot sleep.

Instead, I stare at the ceiling, wishing I'd gone to Craig's party. Too late now.

***

It's Wednesday night. My accident with Anna seems a distant memory. Cesar invites me to this networking event going on at a hotel close to our office. I must admit that the real reason we are going is for free liquor and to see what girls we can pick up. You know how these professional women are: ladies in public and freaks in the bedroom.

So we decide to go hunting tonight. Shawn will meet us at the venue. We get to the place and are soon mingling with professionals and industry people. All this talk going on, but we are here for a specific reason. As I look around the room, I can't help but wonder if there are any other guys or girls like us here for the same reason. There are so many women here, it's unbelievable. Cesar and I decide to split up and scan the room for prospects. I see a group of girls chatting at one end of the room, so I move in, and introduce myself.

"Hello."

"Hi," they respond.

"I'm John." I tell them where I work, and they share their professional information with me as well. I do not notice that they are standing with a man who seems to be in his mid-thirties. He has a very calm demeanor, and his smile is refreshing. Within the group of girls there is one in particular who catches my attention; she has a beautiful face but more important for me, she has a sexy body. I can tell, even though she is wearing her work clothes.

Cesar joins me as we chat.

"So what do you do, again?" I ask the girl I am interested in, as I stare at her chest.

"I work for a nonprofit organization that helps raise money for homeless people right here in the city. I actually work with Ben over here."

"With who?" I ask.

"Ben, you know, you were just introduced to him," she says, pointing to the gentleman with the warm smile. I was staring at this woman's body parts for so long that I missed his name.

"Oh, hey, buddy, sorry I missed your name. So you guys work together?"

"Yes, we do," he replies. "And you work with sales, right?"

"Yes, I do."

"How do you find that?" the girl asks.

"What, my job? It's good; the money is great, you know."

"Is that why you do it, for the money?" the man asks.

"Well, yeah, of course I do it for the money. Money is power, you know, and this is the big city. You can't survive here without money."

"That's right," Cesar chimes in. "We make good money at what we do." As if to clarify his point, Cesar whips out a fifty-dollar bill and tips the waitress who brings him a drink. Some of the girls in our little group begin eyeing Cesar.

"Fifty-dollar tips. Hmm, don't you think that's a bit much just for a tip?" Ben asks. I have to admit I sort of agree with him.

"Hey, it's my money; I earned it so I can do whatever I want with it. I spend, on average, five hundred dollars whenever I go out to party. But you can do such things when you make the kind of money we make, right, John?"

I say nothing, even though I know in the past I have spent that sort of money with Cesar and Shawn.

"Hmm, yes, it is your money, and you can do whatever you want with it. I just find it excessive, especially as there are people at this moment who cannot afford anything to eat or drink, and you are here tipping waitresses fifty dollars. That money could do a lot for some people."

"Well, 'some people' have nothing to do with me. Homeless people need not be homeless; there are so many opportunities here that I feel no one should be without work. And when you work hard like we do, you get to spend money like we do," Cesar replies.

"Well, those homeless people, in most cases, are in that situation due to circumstances beyond their control, and you should not compare yourself to other people. Some people may not have had the opportunities you may have had, so you cannot think that your experiences apply to everyone. Yes, there are some who could work and are just lazy, but many did not have the same support systems you may have had. That money you gave away to the waitress or all the large sums of money you spend when you go out could go a long way toward helping some people who are less fortunate, and if you had a good conscience you would understand what I mean."

"Whatever, man, I worked hard to get to this point, and if I want to have some fun with my money I will do just that."

I stand with the girl I'd just met and watch Cesar and this gentleman go back and forth. There is some truth to what this man says.

But hey, it's Cesar's money, and he has the final say on how he spends it, and frankly, I don't mind spending five hundred or more dollars a night if I can afford it. Makes getting girls easier. It's an interesting conversation, but I came here tonight to have some fun and pick up some ladies, not save the world.

"Okay, guys, let's chat about something else," I cut in. "For starters, what are you guys doing this coming weekend?" I look directly at the girl I am interested in. We continue our conversation, and I make sure to get the girl's number before I leave the venue. Looks like I will have to add her to my collection.

I am with Darius tonight. We have just enjoyed another candlelit dinner at his place, and now we are both curled up by his fireplace.

"Hey, Michelle…"

"Yes?"

"I love you."

I cannot believe what I've just heard. I feel this thing go through my body; I think I am excited. But at the same time, I feel a little scared. How do I respond to this guy? Do I say I love him back? Do I feel the same way?

"I love you, too, Darius," I reply, not sure if I meant what I just said.

We kiss.

"I feel so much peace when I am around you, and you seem to understand everything about me. I hope we can make this thing long term," he says.

We kiss again. I want to say something, something along the lines of "Don't get too caught up in the moment," or something to that effect, but I stop myself because we are kissing so passionately, and I cannot control myself. He lays me down, takes off his shorts, and enters me. As we make love this image of Miss Pryce comes to my mind, but it quickly vanishes as Darius enters me again, and again, and again…

Chapter Ten

It is the Thursday after the networking event and I am at work. I have nearly forgotten about my accident with Anna this past Friday. I actually have been getting a lot of work done today. Finished three reports and am on my fourth. Closed three deals as well. I am doing pretty well, considering it is a Thursday. Business is usually slow on Thursdays. It is about 1:30, so I decide to grab a bite to eat.

It is at this moment that I receive the worst phone call in my entire life. I have just stepped outside my office building when my phone rings. Anna.

"Hey, Anna, how are you?" There is a brief silence. "Anna?"

"John, I took the test, and it came back positive for HIV."

I absorb this information, but I can't believe it. I refuse to believe it. So I laugh. "Anna, stop kidding around. Seriously, why did you call?"

She is still quiet. I suddenly feel something is very wrong. She must be kidding; maybe it's the city traffic outside that muddled up her words. Maybe I heard "negative" instead of "positive." I have to get to a quieter venue to hear what she said.

"Listen, Anna, I will call you right back." I walk hurriedly to a quiet location within my office building. My heart starts pounding. I feel something is wrong. No, this cannot be happening to me. No. No. I call her back.

"Okay, Anna, what did you say?"

"John." I hear sobbing in her voice now. "I am HIV-positive!"

***

Her words hit me like a freight train. I lose balance for a minute and stumble to the floor. My heart is pounding and my nerves are on edge. I get dizzy and feel like I want to throw up. I feel like I want to cry. I feel weak. I feel really confused. My throat swells up, and I feel choked. I shout, "No, no, no, no, no! Damn! Damn! Damn! Damn! *Damn!* You got to be kidding me! You got to be kidding me! Damn, damn, *Damn!*" I scream every obscene word in my vocabulary, words I hardly use on a regular basis. Not me, oh my God, oh my God, oh my God! I call God's name like the hypocrite I am.

"I am really sorry, John, I really am," Anna sobs on the other end of the phone. I try to pull myself together, but I can't. I feel as if I've just received a death sentence.

"Where are you?" I ask.

"Still at the testing center," she replies.

"Okay, I am heading there right now. I have get myself tested."

She gives me the address, and I set off. As I walk to the subway I can't seem to see anyone. My mind is a blank page, and my heart is pounding in excess. I have never been this worried in my life. I feel so scared, and I feel so helpless. My good friend Abel's words suddenly come back to me: "Keep on dodging bullets, John, and one day you're bound to get hit." Today might be that day for me. I am trembling; I feel my palms shaking in fear. I get off the subway and immediately throw up at the corner, right next to a bum, who I think is doing the same.

I meet Anna outside the testing center. She is in tears, and I give her a hug. I do my best to console her. It must feel horrible to receive news like that, but I cannot help but think about my own predicament. We walk into the testing center together, and it seems the staff there already knows about her plight and is expecting me. I discuss the situation with a doctor who is present, and then I fill out some paperwork and wait for my turn to be tested. I sit in the waiting room with Anna, who is sobbing. I feel really bad for her, but at this point, I am more worried for myself.

"I don't understand. I am always careful. I just don't understand," she sobs.

I listen, feeling blank; I am imagining all sorts of negative outcomes from this situation. Do I have HIV? Am I infected? What do I do? In the waiting room there is a video playing that shows the different STDs, their symptoms, and the effects. This makes the wait all the more unbearable. I am really trembling, and my heart is beating at an uncontrollable pace. It is beating so fast, and I feel this lump in my throat, and for some reason I am sighing every ten seconds. This is a living nightmare. I ask myself why this is happening. How did I get myself into this mess?

Anna has to go back to work. I don't know how anyone can work after hearing such news. I tell her I will call her and bid her good-bye. I hope she doesn't hurt herself.

"Mr. John Casey?" the nurse calls out. I am led to a separate room where my blood is drawn. A padded swab is then wiped on my gums. Apparently, this is to absorb my DNA to test for the HIV antibodies. I am then instructed to wait until my name is called for the results of the HIV test. I am so nervous. I am so scared. *Why me?* I ask myself. *Why now?* I feel so confused. I close my eyes, and call on God. "Master, I am sorry for what I have done. I am sorry I broke my promise to You. Please, please, I beg You. Do not let me be infected with this virus."

I say the same prayer for the next hour.

Then I hear my name again. Crunch time. My heart begins pounding again. I step into the counselor's office for my results.

"Hello, John."

"Hello, ma'am." I try to be polite, naïvely hoping that my politeness might change the outcome of the results in my favor. I sit down and brace myself for her next words.

"Negative."

Phew. I feel a breath of relief, and I immediately drop to my knees and thank God.

"But wait," she says. "These results only show your HIV status as of now. You will have to come back in a minimum of three months to see the results of your accident. All the results you received today tell you are that you were HIV-negative before your incident with your female friend." The words hit me, and they hit hard.

"Three months?" I echo. "Isn't there some other more rapid test I can take that can tell me my status now? I can't think about this for three whole months!"

"Well, unfortunately, that is the estimate for the minimum time it takes for the HIV antibodies to develop in your system. It is only after that period of time and beyond that our tests can determine whether you are HIV-positive."

I think about what she has just said, and the events from my one night with Anna come flooding back to me. I used a condom but it broke, and I was inside her for about twenty seconds, unprotected, before I pulled out. Not to mention I put on another condom right afterwards without cleaning up. And she was on her period; she got her blood on me. I suddenly feel all hope is lost. I relay my concerns to the counselor.

"Well, yes, it was a risky situation you were in, and it's all the more unfortunate because you did initially use protection. Studies have shown recently, though, that HIV is more difficult to transmit from women to men than it is from men to women. For you guys, the virus has to go through your urethra, which is hard to get into. For women, the opening is much larger. I personally think you will be fine, but you should come back and check again. And avoid sexual contact with anyone for the next few months until you are sure of your status."

I suddenly feel sick. I could have HIV! I feel dirty. I have heard so many unpleasant things about HIV, and I cannot imagine myself having it. But that fear might be a reality now. I fear I might join the ranks of people who actually have to deal with real setbacks in life. I feel reality knocking at my door.

"But counselor, there is a chance that the virus entered me. All it takes is one time."

"Yes, all it takes is one time, but the odds are in your favor that you did not contract the virus." Brief silence. She begins asking me standard procedural questions, such as, "Will you commit suicide? Will you let others know about your status if you do test positive in three months?" I feel so dirty and ashamed. Just one night of intended fun has turned into this? I just don't understand.

"John, here's my business card," she says. "Call me if you ever want to talk about anything, and remember, you have to think positive during this period. I personally think you will be fine, so just think positive."

I don't know if she is saying that to make me feel better, but I thank her anyway, and I leave.

On the way back to my office, I feel hopeless. I think about what I did wrong that night. Why didn't I go to Craig's party? Why is this happening to me? I feel so low, so lonely, so afraid. I feel like a reject, and most of all, I feel helpless. And I have to go through three months of being in this state? Of not knowing the future? Of dealing with so much uncertainty? Of having absolutely no control over anything? I want to cry, but the tears do not come out. I need a hug but have no one to hold. I need answers but have no one to ask. I feel lost and very insignificant.

This is one situation I have no control over.

***

I get back to my office. When I walk in, everyone is getting ready to leave. It is around 5:20, and the usual about-to-leave small talk is picking up. I slide quietly into my cubicle and turn my computer back on. I begin to type, but my mind feels like it wants to explode. I feel hurt and angry, but I'm not sure with whom. Not at Anna, because it takes two to tango, and I was as much into the act as she was. I'm not sure exactly with whom I am angry. I guess with myself, but I just do not want to admit it. I felt small, really small and vulnerable all of a sudden; most of all, I feel helpless. I feel helpless as I sit in my cubicle. I'm sure my face has a very ridiculous expression on it—not happy, not sad, just a ridiculous expression. I also feel very desperate. I want to ask someone to help me, but whom could I call? What could anyone possibly do to help me make things right? And I also feel so ashamed to pray to God. After all, I promised God that I would not chase women again after my first test, and I went ahead and did just that. Why am I so weak? Does my penis really have that much control over my will power? I guess this is a likely outcome when you let your penis do your thinking for you. Now I see what Jerry meant when he cautioned me earlier.

As I sit feeling sorry for myself, Cesar decides to pay me a visit. Of all the people in the world, why does he have to show up now?

"Yo, John, how are you man?"

"I'm cool, Cesar."

"You sure? You look a bit sick, dude."

I quickly force a smile. "I'm cool, man."

He looks at me for a few seconds, and then chooses to engage in random small talk. I really wish he would go away.

"Hey, have you heard from that girl, Anna?" Naturally, he would ask me about her.

"Nah, man," I lie. The fact is now I wish I had never met her to begin with. But they say everything happens for a reason.

He talks and I listen for about five minutes, after which he leaves. I do not feel like talking to anyone right now. I feel like ripping my penis off for putting me under all this stress. What a bad friend it has been to me. Whom can I talk to? Who will give me objective advice and not criticize me? Then I realize that a call to my mother is long overdue. I just hope she's ready for what I have to say.

***

I cannot sleep. I just stare at my ceiling. So many thoughts run through my head. I imagine myself with the virus and what I will do. I cannot imagine what I will do, so I just imagine myself with the virus. This leads to fear, restlessness, hopelessness, and despair. *There must be something I can do to fix this problem*, I think. *I made a mistake and I am sure I have the power to fix it. At least I hope I do.*

It is about 2:30 in the morning. I get out of bed and turn my computer on. Within seconds I am on the Internet, searching the Web for solutions for persons in my predicament. It's my life, and I am going to fix it. I see something, an HIV-support Web site. On it are the usual prevention strategies, with abstinence being the first choice. How I wish I could have read a copy of this before I went over to Anna's! But it's too late to wish now. What's done is done, and wishing makes me feel only more and more like a fool for putting myself in this predicament. I scan through the site, desperately looking for an answer. I soon see something that offers some hope: "PEP-Post Exposure Prophylaxis. PEP is usually prescribed for a period of four to six weeks immediately following a suspected exposure to HIV; however, they can be started as long as seventy-two hours after exposure. Although the results for the efficiency of this measure are mixed, statistics do show that the sooner they are started the better chance they have in reducing the risk of HIV infection."

This sounds like hope to me so I read on: "Thought has been given to prescribing PEP to people outside the healthcare field for HIV exposure from unprotected sex or injectable drug use. While no statistics are available as to the benefits, many have raised concerns that PEP will give people a false sense of security. For now, it appears PEP is still a viable option for occupational exposures to HIV."

I read the paragraph over and over again, examining every word, making sure I did not misunderstand any of this information. I feel my life is hanging, and I am running out of time. The article said seventy-two hours is the maximum time to hold off before starting the PEP treatment. It has been about a week now since my incident with Anna, but I'm sure it wouldn't hurt to ask or inquire if I can take this medication, especially if it has a chance of preventing me from being infected. I have to try. I decide to call in sick the next day. I'll go to a testing center and inquire. I lie back in bed and stare at my ceiling, my heart beating faster than usual. I have a feeling it will be a while before I can sleep well at night again.

***

I barely slept last night. I woke up today with my heart still pounding faster than usual. What a way to wake up. I want to shout, scream, cry, and curse all at the same time. But I can't. To do all those things would be a luxury that time will not permit me to do. Every minute I have now is dedicated to saving my life, I feel.

I call in sick and tell my boss that I have a fever. Afterwards, I take a shower and get dressed, then I rush to the STD clinic where I got tested the first time. When I get there, I recognize the counselor I spoke to the first time. She motions for me to step into her office. I avoid small talk and cordialities and jump right into my reason for being there.

"I was reading last night online that there is a procedure called PEP that, if done within seventy-two hours, can greatly reduce the chance of my acquiring HIV. It has been about a week or so since I learned that my partner was HIV-positive. Can I still obtain this PEP treatment, and can you tell me where to get it?"

She looks at me seriously. "The PEP treatment is theoretically only effective after seventy-two hours after you have been exposed. It is not likely that it would work in your case, but you can try. If you go to any emergency room, they should be able to provide you with the PEP treatment or an adequate assessment."

Emergency room. I remember seeing one when I passed a hospital on my way here. I must get there, and I must get there now.

"Thank you very much, ma'am," I say as I bolt out of her office. I am running at full speed down the street. I probably do not have to run, as it is only 11:30 a.m., and the emergency room does not close, but I am rushing because I feel my life is on the line. And I just cannot accept the fact that I might be HIV-positive. I just can't. I hop in a cab and tell the driver to get me to the hospital as fast as he can. As soon as I am dropped off I run up the front stairs to the main entrance. I'm sure with all this running I look like an escaped convict making a getaway.

When I get there, I sign my name on the sheet to see the nurse. Then I have to wait in line for about one hour. I pace back and forth in the room until my name is called.

"Mr. John Casey?"

I dart to my feet and rush into the nurse's office.

"Hello, sir, what is bothering you today?" She is a good-looking woman with a really nice body, but surprisingly, I do not find myself affected by her looks. My mind is in a different place.

"Umm, I had a little accident, ma'am. My girlfriend and I had unprotected sex, and I did not know she was on her period. I recommended that we both get tested, and she turned out to be HIV-positive, and I came out negative. But they told me I have to wait three months to be able to know for sure if I have been infected with the virus. I did some research, and I heard that there is a treatment called PEP that can be taken after a possible exposure, and I wanted to know if I could obtain it here."

She looks at me with concern and pity written on her face. "How sad. So are you going to leave her?" she asks.

I smile and shake my head, knowing I lied about Anna and me being in a relationship, so I do not look like the bad boy that I am to this stranger.

"You know, as a nurse, I got pricked by a needle once that was potentially HIV-infected. I used to work in an HIV ward. They put me on the PEP treatment as well, and let me tell you, it has some serious side effects; it can make you anemic, weak, and so on. I was vomiting and had diarrhea for a while before I stopped. And I'm fortunate that my insurance paid for the medication, because the PEP treatment can sometimes be as expensive as a thousand dollars a month. Luckily for me, we found out that the patient with whom the needle had been used was HIV-negative."

Her story does little to comfort me, but at least I feel she relates somewhat to my situation. She takes down my information, and then directs me to a patient room to be seen by the doctor. I sit down in the room and hope I can obtain this magical treatment called PEP. The doctor walks in, and I describe exactly what happened between Anna and me. He is a cold man without facial expression. He does not look angry; he just looks emotionless.

"Unfortunately, sir," he begins, "the PEP treatment can only be taken after a period of seventy-two hours. Even within that time frame, if taken, it is not totally guaranteed to hinder the development of the virus."

This is not good news to me.

"So, doctor, based on the scenario I described to you, do you think I acquired the virus?"

"I cannot say, sir; all it takes is a micro-abrasion on the penis for the virus to get in. It has to make contact with your bodily fluids to enter your bloodstream. Granted, the urethra is small and may prove harder for the virus to enter than the female vagina, for instance, but all it takes is a little of the virus to get in and make contact with your bodily fluids. In your case, you stopped and cleaned up, but you never know."

His answer makes me feel so hopeless. I cannot see this doctor being a counselor of any sort, but I respect his answer because it is raw and honest. I begin to plead my case with him, as if he has the power to remove any possible virus from me.

"You know, I thought I did everything right. I used a condom, I did not know she was on her period, the damn thing broke, and now I am here."

"I know, sir, and I am really sorry. For people like you, there are normally a series of tests you are required to take."

I am still pleading, praying for some salvation from this man whose profession it is to assist people who are medically unstable. I wonder if I am asking the wrong person for help. "I did everything right. I put the condom on. I thought I was safe and—"

"Sir, we have an HIV counselor on call right now. Let me get her in here and you can talk to her while I write up your chart."

He steps out of the room while I remain. I can't seem to make sense of anything right now. I start to ask myself why, but I am tired of asking that question. What I want to know now is how I can fix my problem. The door rattles and the counselor steps in. She has a warm smile, which I find welcoming at this point. We get down to the issue at hand, and I recount for the third time the exact details of that horrible night with Anna.

"You know, it was an unfortunate sequence of events, especially as you did attempt to have safe sex," she begins. "Yes, it was unsafe for you to be inside her, unprotected, but studies have shown that it is harder for a man to acquire HIV than it is for a woman. It is harder for the virus to go through the urethra and make contact with your bloodstream, and even harder and less likely because you were not inside her for that long."

"But I was inside her, and she was on her period. I had her blood on my penis."

"Yes, true, but the HIV concentration in blood is not that much higher than it is in semen or in vaginal fluids. Theoretically the chances of a man getting HIV from a woman are 1 in 1000, but in your case I would say it would be 1 in 100. Off the record I would assume it's like me taking a drive upstate without wearing a seatbelt. The chances of my getting hit by a car are there, but it is not likely. But if I do get hit by a car because I have no seatbelt on, the chances of my obtaining serious injuries are very high because I had no seatbelt on. It's sort of the same analogy."

"So, miss, say I was an outsider looking in on this situation, and I asked you objectively, not because I am sitting here or because it will make me feel better, but objectively: if you were to bet on my having acquired the virus or not, what would you bet?"

"I would bet that you are clean, but you should get tested just to be on the safe side. Get tested once in three months and then in six months, to be absolutely certain. That way you can free your conscience."

I think about what she just said. "Three months is a long time to think about this issue."

"I know, I know, but think of it this way: at least now you know, and more importantly the girl knows. Now she can be more responsible and the chance of her infecting others has been reduced, if not eliminated. So in a way, you did her, yourself, and humanity a service by requesting she get tested. Here, let me walk you out."

I grab my things, and we leave together. What a stark contrast her assessment is compared to the one the doctor gave. Whom should I believe? We walk down the hallway to the exit doors.

"Are you going to be okay?"

"Is that a trick question, miss? I do not know. I don't know if I will be okay. This is all very new to me."

"Here, take my business card, and call me if you ever need to talk," she says, handing me her card. "And here is some information on anonymous testing centers in the city you can go to when you are ready."

"Thanks, miss. I just don't know why this is happening to me. Now I have to wait three whole months before I know anything. I feel like I am on death row, waiting to know if I will get executed."

"You will be fine. You have to be positive," she replies. "You should consider taking yoga classes or doing some activity to take your mind off stress and worry."

"Well, sex was that activity, but I'm sure I will not be thinking of sex for a long time now."

She smiles. "I'm sure you won't. Don't worry; I have a gut feeling that you'll be fine. Use this period to re-evaluate your life and your priorities. This may be a good time to do so."

Wise words. I take her advice whole-heartedly. "Thank you, ma'am. I will be in touch."

I step out of the hospital and go over what I accomplished by coming here. I did not get the PEP medication; rather, I got two different opinions on my condition. I am leaving here more confused than I was when I arrived. But I felt the lady had more sincerity as she spoke to me. I will trust her opinion for my sanity's sake. One thing is for sure, though: I have to wait three months before I know where I stand. Three whole months within which I have to do everything I can to prevent this virus from consuming me. But no doctor can help me now. I feel that for the next three months, I will be dealing with the unknown, a realm most human beings are reluctant and afraid to deal with because of the risk and uncertainty involved. And now I find myself stuck in it.

On the way to work today on the train, I saw the girl I usually flirt with in the morning; she smiled at me, but I had no smile for her.

My mind was in a completely different place. I hope she forgives me. I got in the office today with worry written all over my face. I could not think in an adequate manner. I do not even know how I got my projects done. I just had so many thoughts happening at the same time. "What do I do?" seems to be the question I keep asking myself. Around me everything seems normal, and the usual small talk is going on. But I can't seem to hear anything. I begin to say a silent prayer to God, but then I take it back, feeling ashamed to even come to God after all I have done.

As the day wears on I begin to feel helpless, and I feel I have no one to talk to regarding my "problem." It's then I think of my mother. Now might be a good time to give her a call. But what will I say to her? I have never had a conversation about sex with her in detail. Now I have to tell her I had an accident with sex? Should I even bother mentioning it to her before I am certain of what my status is? What should I say? I play with the thought of not sharing this information with my mother, but then I realize that I am all alone, and if I do not share this burden with another who will understand, I will definitely go crazy. I decide I will call my mother. I wait until the office clears out after work, and then I walk into the lunchroom and call my mother.

"Hello, John, I was just thinking about you."

At the sound of her voice I suddenly feel ashamed. At the same time, I feel the maternal comfort only a mother can provide. "Ma, I think I just got into a little trouble."

"What's wrong?" I know she senses the desperation in my voice.

"I, um, I, um, I, err…"

"What is it, John?"

"I had an accident with this girl I was dating, Ma. We slept together and the condom broke."

Brief silence. "Well, you have to be more careful, John. I'm sure you are fine, as long as you didn't stay inside her for that long."

"But that's not all, Ma. She was on her period, and I didn't know. So there was blood involved. I suggested we both get tested before moving further—and her tests came back as HIV-positive."

My mother does not say a word.

"Ma, are you there?"

"Yes, I am." Her voice is remarkably calm, considering the information I just shared with her.

"I am really sorry, Ma. I know I disappointed you, and I am really sorry. Please, please, forgive me. I meant no harm. I did not mean any harm for anyone, and I thought I did everything right and—"

"It's okay, son. Tell me exactly what happened."

"Well, I was, I was, um, dating this girl, and I slept with her twice. The first time I used a condom and nothing happened. The second time I slept with her the condom broke, and I pulled out and put another condom on. She was on her period, so there was some of her blood on me."

"I see. Well, first of all, stop panicking. What's done has been done; accidents happen." I am amazed at how composed and calm my mother is. "Commit it all to the Lord and make sure you stay away from women until you test again. I have a feeling you will be fine."

"You think so, Ma?"

"Yes."

"I spoke to a counselor in a hospital, and she said the same thing."

"Oh, yes, in fact, studies have shown that it is harder for a man to contract the virus than it is for a woman. But you must still be careful. The poor girl; she must have been devastated when she heard her status. You must be nice to her, but please do not see her again."

"Absolutely, Ma, I will not even think about being around her again."

"But you can call her to check up on her once in a while. She probably needs all the support she can get right now. That's why I have always cautioned you to be careful when dealing with women, John, but you would never listen. You are in the city, and there are all sorts of women there who are not decent and loosely have sex with many random men. I know this because I am a woman myself; do not be fooled by the fact that I am your mother and have always presented myself in an innocent way to you. I know the ways of this world. You must be careful, my son; there are reasons why certain rules are in place. Most times, they are there for your own protection."

"I know, Ma, and I am really sorry."

"Don't apologize to me. If anything, apologize to God and to yourself. Maybe this was a blessing in disguise. If you had not suggested that you both get tested, she might have slept with more people and put more people at risk. And you might have seen her again if no accident had happened and that might have increased your own risk of contracting the virus. God works in mysterious ways. You should never forget that. I will pray to God to spare your life. You should do the same with total humility and sincerity."

"Thank you, Ma. I am amazed at how composed you are. By the way, I thought you would yell at me or get paranoid."

She laughs. "Yes, it was disappointing information to hear, but I am happy you told me. If I panic, it does little to comfort or calm your anxiety, and you are the one with the problem, not I. I am calm because I have faith in God, and I always commit my all to Him. You should use this period of time to get to know your God. Maybe this is God's way of speaking to you."

"Three months is a long time, Ma."

"Yes, and it could be the best or worst three months of your life, depending on how you use it. Don't worry; I am always here for you if you need anything. Next time, I suggest that you find a good God-fearing woman, and you both get tested. That would allow you to have a healthy relationship without fear of any infection. When you do meet her, I hope that you will decide to marry her as well—and give me some grandchildren."

We both laugh. It is amazing how, with relative ease, my mother relaxes me. She quickly changes the subject of our conversation.

"So, how is work?"

"Work is fine, Ma." We talk about family, friends, work, and most things average sons talk to their mothers about. Then we end our conversation, but not before agreeing to speak more often. I feel rejuvenated and full of life after speaking with her. I ponder everything she said. Maybe there is some significance in what happened and the way it did. Maybe this is God's way of speaking to me. Whatever the case may be, I have to use the next three months wisely. My future depends on it.

I have not heard from Anna in about two weeks. I called her cell a few times but she did not respond. I hope she is okay. It is very unusual for her not to call me and fill me in regarding what guy she is seeing. And she never told me how it went with the guy she met with her European friends. Well, I'm sure that when I do see her, she'll have some very spicy stories to tell.

I decided to give it a shot with Darius. He is a very nice guy and is turning out to be quite a keeper. He said he loved me again, and again I replied that I loved him as well. So I guess he is now officially my boyfriend. I call him about five times a day, and see him about six days a week. Alexia agrees with my train of thought. And he is such a good guy and so sweet; I feel so safe with him. I know I can trust him for sure.

Today is Friday, and I am excited because I have some plans with Alexia to go see a new movie that just came out—just the two of us, so that should be fun. We might stop at a café before the movie starts and grab some coffee. No boyfriend, no work, just my best friend and me spending time together.

As I get ready to leave the office, my phone rings. It's Jess.

"Hey, Jess."

"Hey, Michelle. Umm, something happened."

"What happened, Jess? Is everything all right?"

"I think so. Well, I don't know. Remember the guy I told you I was doing stuff with in school?"

"Yes, what about him?"

"Well, he was in my room with me the other night, and normally I don't let him sleep over, but we became kind of close, so I let him, and we were cuddling and stuff."

"Oh, boy, I see where this is going," I say, giggling. "Go on."

"Well, we started kissing and stuff, and I got really turned on, and umm…"

"And what, Jess?"

"He entered me."

My mouth drops to the floor. "Jess! You let him enter you? You guys had sex?"

"Well, it was a little awkward, and it hurt, but yes, we did, but now I feel as if I shouldn't have, and I feel very awkward."

"Why do you feel awkward?"

"Well, I don't know if this is the guy I was supposed to lose my virginity to."

"I understand. Wow, I am speechless. How did the sex itself go?"

"It hurt for a while, but it got better."

"How has the guy been since you slept with him? Has he called you?"

"Yeah, he called me this morning to check on me. He is a nice guy."

"Well, that's a good thing. Congratulations, Jess, you're officially a member of the non-virgin club now. Have you told Anna? What did she have to say?"

"No, I haven't told Anna. In fact, I have not spoken to Anna in quite some time now. I meant to ask you if you had spoken with her."

"No, I haven't, and it's been a few weeks now. I hope she is okay. I will stop by her place to check on her if she does not call any of us by the end of this weekend."

"Yeah, okay, let me know and I can go with you."

"Okay, Jess. Well, listen, I have to go meet up with Alexia, but let's all get together tomorrow and talk. We have to discuss your first sexual experience!"

"Oh, boy. Okay, Michelle, have fun with Alexia. I will talk to you later."

"Bye."

We hang up. I cannot believe what I've just heard. Jess is not a virgin anymore! This is crazy. What is this world coming to? I mean, I can understand Anna, Alexia, myself, but not Jess! This will definitely make for good conversation when I meet up with Alexia. I pack my things and head out to go meet my best friend.

***

We get to the movie theatre a bit early, so Alexia and I buy our tickets and head to a nearby café for some coffee before our movie. I am so excited about Jess's latest info, and I cannot wait to tell Alexia.

"I have some very, very, very, very interesting gossip for you, girlfriend."

"Really? Do tell!" Alexia replies.

"I don't know if you can handle it."

"Will you let it out and stop playing games? What do you know?"

"Nah, maybe I shouldn't tell you."

"Michelle!"

"Okay, okay. It's about Jessica."

"Yes, what about Jess?"

"Miss Jessica…how do I say this? Miss Jessica is not a virgin anymore!"

"What?"

"Yup. She called me right before I left my office to share the great news."

"Jessica had sex? I can't believe it!"

"I know; I was speechless when she told me as well."

"Is this a new guy, or is this the guy she told us she gives blow jobs to?"

"Blow-job guy."

"I kinda liked Jess as a little virgin. Now she is really going to start acting up, now that the beast is loose!"

"Don't talk like that, Alexia. We have to watch her so she doesn't end up like Anna."

"We're all like Anna. We are just a bit more discreet about the way we do things."

"I don't know. I might disagree with you. Anna is quite extreme."

"Speaking of Anna, where is she? I have not heard from her in a very long time. Did she travel or something?"

"Dunno. Last time I spoke with her she told me she had some friends in town from Europe. She was taking them out to meet some guys at a bar, and then I did not hear from her again. I tried calling her a few times, but she never picked up her phone. I left some messages. This was a few weeks ago."

"I see. It will be funny to see what she has to say about Jess losing her virginity."

"Yeah, I know. I can't wait."

We finish our coffee and head to our movie, and soon the thought of Jess and her new status becomes a distant memory.

Chapter Eleven

have been a really busy boy since I got Anna's somber news. I have been doing a lot of research on HIV and have learned a couple of very interesting things. HIV stands for the *human immunodeficiency virus.* Every human being has an immune system, which is how we fight off diseases and infections. The thing about HIV is that it attacks the immune system itself, the very thing that protects us from other viruses. It specifically attacks a special kind of immune system cell known as a *CD4 lymphocyte.* Sometimes these cells are called *T-cells.* HIV is a very tricky infection: it has a number of ways to evade the body's defenses, such as rapid mutation. This means that once the virus has taken hold, the body's immune system can never really get rid of it. Hence, a person can look and feel perfectly fine for years, until the body's immune system no longer has the ability to fight off other opportunistic infections the virus lets in.

AIDS is the latter part of the infection, when a person's damaged immune system lets in severe infections, such as certain cancers or when his immune system drops below a certain cell count. So in other words, the virus attacks the immune system and slowly destroys it until it gets to a stage where it can no longer fight off nor prevent most infections, diseases and cancers. HIV can enter the bloodstream through mucous membranes lining the vagina, rectum, and mouth. Also, the opening of the penis has mucous membranes that can transmit HIV through a man's urethra. As the counselor said, the transmission of HIV is more probable from an HIV-positive man to a negative woman than vice versa. I learned that the transmission of HIV is higher through anal sex than regular sex, because the lining of the rectum is thinner than that of the vagina, so during sexual intercourse, the rectum is more prone to tear. This torn opening is a good place for the virus to get into the body. So sex between men is a great risk for HIV infection, provided one of the participants is HIV-positive. Heterosexual anal sex under the same circumstances is also a high-risk endeavor.

I also learned that, in theory, the transmission of HIV through sex involves many different factors: the presence of any STDs in either person, the immune system, and the CD4 and/or viral load count in the HIV-positive person. The viral load count measures the level of HIV present in a person's body. So, the higher one's viral load count, the more likely one is to transmit the virus. But just because someone's viral load count is low when he was checked does not mean it was low at the time of sex; other infections, especially sexually transmitted infections, such as syphilis, gonorrhea, and Chlamydia, can temporarily raise someone's viral load.

After reading, I have less and less hope. The accident that happened while I was with Anna would be considered a high-risk endeavor. The condom broke. She was on her period. There was blood. Granted, I stopped early, but that doesn't mean anything. That really doesn't mean anything. I could be infected, and from what I read, there is no cure for the virus.

What will I do if I am infected? I will lose my friends, my lifestyle, my comfort. My health and my social life will go down the drain, and I will lose everything I am used to. One night of fun has turned into a nightmare for me. I begin to think about how fragile life is. There are so many healthy looking people walking around. How can you tell who is infected from who isn't? It would make life a lot easier if people had signs on their foreheads, indicating who had an infection and who didn't.

But it is really amazing. You see and meet so many people on a daily basis, and it is probable that some of them may even carry the virus and not even know it. I am beginning to see why HIV/AIDS is considered to be a number-one killer in the world. What I would give to be able to go back in time and correct my mistake! How I wish I had gone to Craig's party instead of to Anna's bed! How I wish Cesar had gotten together with her before me! How I wish I had not met Anna in that club! But then again, if I had not met Anna, it might have happened with someone else. Who is to say that the girls with whom I had accidents were not HIV-positive? Have I been lucky all this time? Have I been "dodging bullets," as my good friend Abel once said to me? I am not sure exactly what it is I should do. I don't know if I have the virus, and even though my research tells me that it is harder for a man to contract the virus than a woman, the possibility is still there. And there is no medication, no human effort, and no technique on this earth that can heal me if I am infected. Is there not anything I can do within this three-month period to save myself?

I suddenly think of my brother, Alfred. He would know what is best in a situation like this. I feel so embarrassed to share something of this nature with him, as I assume he thinks very highly of me, despite our different opinions on life. But my time is running out, and I need to make some moves. I have a little over two months left before my big day. I decide I will go visit him during an upcoming weekend and see what he has to say.

***

I couldn't sleep after absorbing all the information about HIV. I stayed in bed with my eyes wide open, staring at the ceiling. *I wonder what Anna's vi-*

ral load count was/is, I thought. I grabbed my phone and sent her a text at 2:30 a.m.: "Sorry to bother you at this time, but do you by any chance know what your viral load count was? I am sorry if I seem rude, but I really need to know."

I felt like such a jerk after sending that message. I couldn't even begin to imagine what she must be going through. Imagine just finding out that you have HIV. I really hope she's holding up well. Twenty minutes later I get a response: "The doctor said the viral load is in the 50s. I will check again when I go in next week." This must be so hard for her, and I feel bad. I can imagine her crying in her apartment all by herself. But hey, I'm also worried about myself as well. I'm sure that having this virus will finish me.

I couldn't get Jessica to come out with us to this lounge to catch up on current events because she had some tests to study for, but this past weekend, I finally get her to meet Alexia and me at a lounge downtown. I also managed to finally get a response from Anna! I sent her a text message, asking her if she could join us, and she replied saying she would.

We all meet at the lounge and soon are chatting like old times about many different things. For some reason Anna's spirits are not as high as they usually are. But I am sure she just needs some cheering up. Perhaps Jess's update will do the trick.

"So girls," I begin, "I think Jess has some information that she wants to share with us."

"Let's hear it, Jess. What's going on?" Alexia asks. Surprisingly, Anna says nothing. She usually would have said something.

"Well…how do I say this? I had sex for the first time a few weeks ago."

"Yay! So how was it?" Alexia asks.

"It was good. I actually have had sex a couple more times since then."

"Ah, Michelle, see? What did I tell you? I told you that once she starts, she won't stop."

"No, no, I won't be bad, but it feels good," Jess replies.

"So all the times you've had sex since then have been with the same guy?" I ask.

"Blow-job guy," Alexia comments. We all laugh.

"Yes, yes, the same guy, and his name is Terrence, Alexia."

Anna is quiet, and it begins to make me a bit nervous. She smiles here and there, but her mind seems to be in a different place.

"Anna, are you okay?" I ask.

"Yeah, I am fine, Michelle," she replies.

"You don't look fine. You look stressed out," Alexia remarks. "What's going on, and where have you been? We've all been asking about you."

"Oh, I am fine, and I am sorry that I didn't let you guys know what was happening with me. I had to go back to France for some time." Anna replies.

"Oh, but Anna, you usually let us know when you are about to travel. We just thought it was odd that you disappeared for some time, that's all," Jess says.

"And we were worried," I add. "And you don't look too happy."

"So, like Michelle asked, are you okay?" Alexia chimes in.

Anna eyes well up with tears, and I get really scared. Something is definitely wrong.

"I, umm…I, umm," she says as she looks this way and that, appearing very confused and looking as if she was trapped. My heart starts beating really fast.

"Anna, it's okay. You can talk to us. What's wrong?" Alexia says.

"I, umm…my, umm…my, umm…my …my…my brother passed away back home, so I had to go back for the burial," Anna says as she bursts into tears.

"Oh, Anna!" I say as I place my arm around her. We all move closer to her as she breaks down in tears.

"It's okay, guys" Anna sobs. "I am okay. It just affected me, but I am okay now, and I really don't want to talk about it."

We all surround Anna, comforting her as she cries.

"I should probably go," Anna says.

"It's okay, Anna, we understand" Alexia says.

"No, trust me, you don't," Anna says as she gets up, grabs her coat and walks out. We all look at each other and spend the rest of the night questioning Anna's behavior.

Chapter Twelve

It's Friday the thirteenth, and I've promised my old party buddies from college, Carl and Luke, that I will meet them for a drink after work. After college, they both got jobs in the city. Luke lives on the outskirts, and Carl moved into the city, like me. I don't know how I will talk to them in my present state of mind. But I have to maintain my composure and try to be myself in front of them. We agree to meet at the subway station nearest to my office and then go to a lounge Luke has recommended downtown. I honestly am not in the mood to meet with anyone, but for the sake of courtesy, I agree to make an exception for them.

As I head out to the station after work, I get a call from them, saying they will be about thirty minutes late. So I decide to sit down at a café nearby to escape the winter cold and collect my thoughts while I wait for them. *Why me?* I ask myself. *Why does this have to happen to me? Why do I have to be the unlucky one that has to sleep with a girl with HIV? Why?*

As I sit and contemplate the harshness of my reality, I again think of Alfred. This would be a good time to call him. I retrieve my cell phone and dial his number.

"What's up, John?" he says.

"Hey, what's up, man?"

"Your mother told me your situation. How are you doing?" he asks.

I am glad he saved me the trouble of getting to the point.

"I'm okay, Al. I have to wait two more months before I know what my status is."

"I see," he responds. "You know, some people suffer all the time, and some people don't. You probably now know which category it is you fit into."

"Well, yeah, this experience so far has definitely taught me a lot about life, humility, and patience. For once, I feel I am in a situation where I do not have any control. I have prayed to God, but God does not speak back to me."

"Maybe He does, and you just choose to ignore it," he replies.

"Maybe." I spot my friends approaching. "Listen, Al, I am meeting some friends for a quick drink. Let me call you later."

"Cool, man, I'll be waiting. Have fun with your friends."

I hang up and prepare myself to meet my friends.

"Hey! What's up, John!" my buddy Carl calls to me.

"Hey, guys."

We chat for a brief time, and then we decide to hop into Carl's car, parked up the street, to drive to the bar. While in the car, the conversation shifts from college days, to politics, to careers, and finally rests on the male species' favorite topic: women. Normally, I would have led this conversation, but this time I choose to remain quiet and play the role of listener. Of the two, Luke is more of a womanizer; a very athletic man in his mid-thirties, who I am sure has indulged in every sexual sin known to man.

He begins, "Man, it must feel good to finally live in the city, eh, John? There are so many women here, all shapes and sizes, all colors. I would be in heaven if I lived here. I would have sex for breakfast, for lunch, as a snack, and for dinner. Maybe it's a good thing I don't live here, knowing what I am capable of."

Carl chimes in, "Yeah, there are a lot of beautiful women here. But everything here is so fast-paced; it's hard to find a decent woman in this city."

"Man, forget about a decent woman," Luke fires back. "We're young and successful. This is the time to have glorious sex, not just for yourself, but for all the men out there. Think about it, there are so many women in this city and half the guys here are gay. Do the math, Carl. Right, John? I'm sure John over here has been doing his thing, eh?"

He pats me on the back as he says that, and I suddenly feel strange. I begin thinking of my predicament, and I force a smile as I look out the window.

"Besides, Carl," Luke continues, "the city has a lot of temptations. To do well, I can imagine you would have to learn how to balance your priorities. And my priority, if I lived here, would be to make money, and screw every girl in this city. Besides, do you know how hard it is to find a good woman these days? The women you see walking around are either damaged goods or stupid, with no education. If they are good-looking, at least by society's standards, they turn out to be either stuck-up or money-lovers, and a lot of these young girls have kids fathered by losers. It's very rare you find a humble girl who has her stuff together, man. You never see those walking around. So like I said, I'll screw till I die."

"Well, good luck with you and your lifestyle, Luke" says Carl. "And I agree with you about a lot of women these days being no good, but you know the same can be said about guys as well. And with the women who have kids at an early age, I see them all the time in my area. They're young, sometimes even in their teens, pushing babies along in their strollers. The fathers of their children are never on the scene, and if they are, in most cases, they are abusive."

"Yeah, I definitely agree with you on that, Luke," says Carl. "I don't know if these girls just choose not to have sex without condoms or just want to have kids, but I think that children should be brought up in a nurturing environment. Sad thing is, most of these kids having kids come from broken homes themselves, so they are not even capable of thinking outside the box."

"And, Luke, in most cases, single mothers who are young choose to settle with losers. It seems they realize this only after their child is born. But everyone is unique, bro. You can't say a woman is no good because she is single and has a child. I personally know some good people who are single mothers. If you are going to sleep around the way you implied, you gotta be careful. Just remember to use a condom every time. We don't want you getting burned. Remember, HIV is a real thing. In fact, I heard from one report that one in every three people has the virus. So, there are three of us here. Which of us is it?"

They both laugh, and I give a slight smile, but in reality my heart starts pounding at Carl's joke, which I find tasteless. That one person with the virus could be me! Normally, I would have found that funny, but now I feel anxious discussing HIV, women, and sex with these guys. I continue to smile at Carl's joke, but deep inside I do not find it funny at all. We chat for a little while before stepping into a bar, where Carl and Luke seem to comment on every girl's rear end and breasts. I feel sick to my stomach and out of place as I watch them, thinking how uncomfortable I would feel if I passed comments on every girl here, especially with what is already on my plate. It was that behavior that got me in trouble to begin with.

So I just play along and act interested, but in reality I cannot wait to leave.

***

Today is Wednesday, and it's been almost week since I hung out with Carl and Luke. I got a text message from Anna: "My T-cells are above 600. My viral load is undetectable." Is this good news to me? I guess so; the more T-cells a person has, the healthier the person is, so if her viral load is undetectable then I guess that works in my favor. I will have to do more research. "Thank you, Anna," I reply. "How are you feeling?" Even I realize how stupid my question sounds after I send it, even though I meant no offense. She does not reply, and I do not chase after her for a reply. Actions speak louder than words.

***

One and a half weeks have passed, and I decide to take some time off from work. I need time to myself, to evaluate my situation, and to be around people who love me for me. I have been feeling very depressed and lonely, and I do not want to be around friends. I feel very dirty, and I keep imagining "what if, what if…" What if I have this dirty, horrible disease?

I need some family support. So I decide to make a trip back home for an extra-long weekend. While on the train, I stare out the window and gaze at the calm scenery as the train gets farther and farther out of the city. I see some squirrels running up trees. I notice the ripples in a few ponds. I notice the way the wind moves the straw and weeds that grows in the marsh. I notice the calm feeling that is generated from nature itself, and briefly, I feel some peace. The scene I am witnessing is such a contrast to the smog-infested, overcrowded, dirty, and chaotic concrete jungle I have just left. And the farther away from the city I get, the calmer I seem to feel. Soon, I reach my destination: home. I am greeted with open arms and smiles. Al assists me with carrying my luggage inside, while my mother makes me feel welcome. I am informed that my father is away on another business trip. I can smell the lovely scent of what seems to be steak and fried rice coming from the kitchen. Good; I am hungry. Pretty soon, Al, my mother, and I are enjoying some good food as we talk. Surprisingly, the conversation does not begin with my issue but rather with a discussion on bad practices happening at the church that Al and my mother frequent. The preacher has been accused of using money from the church for his own personal profit. The conversation is mostly between the two of them. I play the observer, only because I know very little about that church. I think they really want to discuss my situation, but they don't want to jump right into such an intense conversation, especially over lunch. So we eat and laugh—well, they laugh, while I act as if I am laughing, and they discuss different points of views on the subject. After lunch, as is customary in our household, we sit on couches in the living room and sip chamomile tea to relax ourselves. It begins to rain, and my mother lights some scented candles around the room. I feel so relaxed after such a good meal, and this environment is perfect for a nap. But I know I can't do that right now. So we sip our tea, and my mother begins the conversation about me.

"So, John, do you feel any better?" she asks.

"Yes, well, somewhat. I still get a bit nervous when I think about the possible outcomes. I do not want to be told that I have HIV. I cannot even begin to think of what I would do."

"Yes, it would be devastating for me," she replies, "especially after all the praying I have done for you. I have always cautioned you boys to be careful with women, but you wouldn't listen. Now, see where you are? Sometimes I wish your father would have played a more involved role in your upbringing. It's a shame he's in Korea. When he gets back, it should be interesting to hear what he has to say. Well, from what I've heard, it's harder for men to catch the virus than it is for women, but that doesn't mean anything because the possibility is still there. One time, a thousand times, a million times—all it takes is one exposure and you get it. Let's just pray that the virus did not enter your body."

There is a brief silence, I break it by saying, "There must be something I can do to prevent any bad outcome from happening. There has to be. I will do anything, anything at all to prevent myself from having that virus."

"Well, you have exhausted all your options, at least materially," Al chips in. "You couldn't get the PEP treatment; that could have been your ticket. So, there is really nothing you can do to prevent anything from happening."

"Thanks, Al, that makes me feel much better," I reply sarcastically.

"I wasn't trying to be funny, John. Hear me out. The big question now is, what can we do? It is funny how God works; I see God's Hand in this. Who else can you turn to now, John? No doctor can save you, and if there is some medication you can take, we probably do not know about it. You previously debated with me on the existence of Jesus, of God, and now you might be forced to turn to what you disbelieved."

"I never said I do not believe in God; I just said I had a problem with understanding and believing in Jesus Christ," I reply.

"Okay, I am sorry I misquoted you, John, but the fact is that you are in a tight situation that only just believing in God hasn't solved."

"So what are you saying? That if I believe in Jesus then all my problems will be fixed? Jesus Christ is a character in a book written by people over time. Why should I take what another man says as the truth?"

My mother cuts in, "Because of testimony from those who believe and from our faith. Faith in what you may not necessarily see but can feel. The spiritual world is very much a part of our lives, despite what most of us are brought up to think."

"But Ma, that's exactly it. Why can't just believing in God be enough? I believe in God, and I pray to God, so what does my faith in this Jesus have to do with praying to God?"

"Well, you believed the PEP treatment would save you. You believed if you took the pills that you never even saw you would be healed, or at least that it would decrease your chances of being infected dramatically. In other words, John, you had faith in those pills, faith because you were desperate. You suddenly valued your life, and it became apparent that you might have this virus that could rob you of that life. So much faith that you rushed to the hospital and waited for hours before being told that it was too late to take the treatment. Well, my son, Christianity sort of works in the same way, only it's that we, as Christians, try to be desperate for life every single day, not just when something bad happens to us. A true Christian is desperate for life every single day, life under God's divine direction, sort of like how you were when you sought after that PEP treatment. For us, Jesus Christ is our treatment."

Interesting analogy; I like the way she broke it down for me.

Al cuts in: "Listen John, your options are extremely limited. Besides, what do you have to lose by committing your life to Jesus? Nothing else is working for you now, anyway. There is nothing in this world that can save you; it is either you have it or you don't. God is the only one who can help you and possibly save you, if it is in His plan for you. Why don't you call on Jesus? God knows your heart, so do not think you are lying."

He may be right. I really do not have any choices left. Only God can save me now. And I do not see what I have to lose by trusting Jesus. Just as I wanted to try the PEP treatment to save my life, God is also worth a try. We kneel down, and my mother says a sincere prayer for me and for our family.

Afterward, Al and I play a game of cards, while my mother retires to spend time reading in bed.

"So, what do I do now, Al?"

"Well, it is a journey when you make a decision to follow Jesus. And it is not always an easy one. It might be a good idea to try to give up a lot of your old habits, like random sex, drinking, and all the other things you do that are not fulfilling and useful to your growth."

"No sex?" I question.

"No *random* sex, John. Besides, God forbids it. And I am not trying to make you feel bad, but what if you do have HIV now? You cannot go around sleeping with women and infecting them. No, no sex, John, at least until you are certain of your status."

He's right. Soon, Al heads to his room to watch some television, but I choose to lie down on a couch in the living room and stare out the window at the falling rain. It is the most comfortable I have felt in a very long time; I feel relieved and relaxed, and feel that there is still hope for me. I close my eyes and thank God for my family. Then I let the chamomile tea put me to sleep. Tomorrow, I will have to pay a visit to my old friend Jerry by the railroad tracks.

***

I wake up the next day before anyone else, put on a track suit, and decide to go jogging. I pack a little sandwich in a paper bag to give to Jerry for breakfast. I head to Jerry's shack and spot him sitting outside his abode, smoking a pipe and humming his favorite tune.

"Hey, Jerry!" I greet him as I arrive at his place.

"John, my boy, good to hear your voice, yes sir. Did you bring some money for me from the city?"

"No money just yet, Jerry, but I brought you this." I hand him his sandwich.

He smells it and gives me a really bright smile. "You're too kind, John, too kind." He begins immediately to attack the sandwich, like a man who has not eaten in three days. I watch him as he eats, happy to see my friend enjoy his meal. I prepare what I am about to say to him.

"Jerry, I need some help, some advice, something," I begin. He pauses with his chewing and turns in my direction. "I got into some bad stuff, Jerry, some real, real, real bad stuff."

He puts his sandwich down with an expression of concern on his face. "What bad stuff, boy? Spit it out!"

I take a deep breath. "I, um, I, well, you see, I hooked up with this girl some weeks ago, and everything seemed fine. She seemed perfectly normal. Then I slept with her, Jerry, and the condom broke. Next thing I know, she's telling me that she is HIV-positive, and I feel like all of a sudden my life is finished. I got tested as well, and my initial test came out negative, but they say I have to wait three months before I will know for sure if I have been infected. Now, everyone I have spoken to so far seems to think that the odds are in my favor that I am not infected, but the truth is that it is a 50/50 matter. I could have this thing in my body right now as we speak, and it is freaking me out. I can't think right and I can't sleep. I get scared when I imagine the negative outcomes I may have to face when my three- month waiting period is over. I cannot imagine what I will do if I am told that I am HIV-positive. I just don't know what I will do. I get scared all the time Jerry. I do not want anything bad to happen. I was just having some casual sex—I mean, everyone has sex once in a while, but I was just unlucky that I had to have sex with someone who was HIV-positive. I was even unluckier when my condom broke. I am willing to do anything, anything at all that will prevent this virus from existing inside of me."

"So nothin' can be done about this, Johnny?" he asks.

"Well, the one possible option I had was this medication they call PEP that might have deterred the HIV from forming inside of me, but I passed my time limit for taking it. I just don't know what to do. I pray to God, but I feel God does not listen to me, and I feel so ashamed and dirty to even bring my problems to God. In a sense, I feel hopeless, Jerry."

Jerry has been listening attentively, and I see him take on a serious demeanor, one that I have never seen before.

"Johnny," he begins, "I told you…I *told* you to remember my words before you left for the city. I told you to control your little man and not let him control you. Now see what he has gotten you into? I told you, Johnny! But you wouldn't listen."

He's right; he did caution me, but I paid him no mind.

"I warned you, Johnny boy. Oh, this is not good. When we elders speak to you kids, you never listen; we speak, Johnny, because we have experience and have done and been through very similar experiences to what you're going through now. When we speak outta love, it's wise to at least listen, Johnny, but all you kids these days think you know so much, when you have seen so little. Even in my blind state, I see more than most of those with perfect vision. Well, I'm not sure what you want from me, Johnny boy. You say the doctors told you that basically it's either you got it or you don't, but the chances are that you don't. It's a 50/50 thing, is what your sayin'. Well, let's hope for the best, then. As far as a cure or something, I don't know. I don't think they have invented one yet for this disease they call the HIV, no, sir." He takes a puff from his pipe. "It's between you and God now, Johnny. If you didn't believe in God before, maybe this is the chance for you to do so now. Or look at it from a good perspective. Maybe this is God's way of revealing God's power to you! You ever think of that, Johnny?"

"I have, Jerry, but I can't just start worshipping God wholeheartedly without direction. I know there is a God, but how do I approach Him? My mother and all have told me that I can find salvation only through Jesus, and I respect them, but I have my reservations about Christianity and religion in general. I feel it is man's justification for his existence. His assumptions on how to live life. And I don't want to follow what any man says. I don't want to follow the crowd. I want to do what's right and ask God directly for help."

Jerry sits in silence, puffing away on his pipe. Then he speaks. "Johnny, my boy, you cannot define what God should or should not be, and how you want to hear from God. You are just a man; from the ground you came and to the ground you will go. If you asked God to show you the way, the way might not be shown in the way you want to see it. God may decide to teach you, Johnny boy, by taking away all that you have, to make you realize that you can't do nothin' without God, y'see? If you're waitin' for God Almighty to come down personally and direct you, that might never happen, Johnny. After all, who are you? You're just another soul and body among a million others, so what makes you so special that God will drop all that He's doin' and come make a personal visit to give you directions? God may decide, Johnny, to send agents, various people and experiences, y'see, to train you and guide your path. Problem with us here humans is that most of us are ignorant and blind toward such opportunities for growth, Johnny. We see each problem as what it is in its simplest form: a problem. And we fail to see the many answers it has to many of our questions."

I am amazed at Jerry's insight, but I have more questions. "Okay, Jerry, I understand that now, but I guess I should ask: how do you develop a relationship or communicate with God and find relief to all these problems?"

"You havin' a problem, Johnny, is due to your irresponsibility, and God's design for your life. I personally believe it was meant to be for you to sleep with this girl and find out the bad news. If you look at it as a problem, you're goin' to stress yourself out. Can you think of anythin' good that has come out of this?" He bends down to finish his sandwich while I ponder on what he just said.

Well, for one thing, I think, *Anna now knows her status and can be more careful with men, and she can also take better care of herself. For me, I am now more aware of my health, and I'm better geared toward living a healthy lifestyle. I doubt I will be sleeping around with random women after this ex-*

perience. And through my quest for life and a second chance, I am getting to know about God better.

So I guess those are good things. Jerry looks up at me as I speak. "Yeah, I can think of one or two good things, Jerry."

"Wonderful, Johnny, and as far as your second question about finding relief in God, I can't answer that directly, but I can share with you what God has done for me and how I find relief."

"No offense, Jerry, and please don't take this the wrong way, but you're still blind, and you walk with a bad limp. What relief could you have found in that regard?"

He suddenly puts on a big smile, and I can't believe how rude I was to ask such a question.

"I no longer see my failed eyesight as a problem, Johnny. I used to be a carefree boy, and when I had my eyesight I really had what I thought was a good time, being a wild guy. I had no parents; I was abroad in Paris, living alone and having the best time of my life, yes, sir. I snorted cocaine before; yes, John, and I even did crack one time. And I had lots of sex. Man, oh man. But I kept on feeling depressed. Then the doctor said I had diabetes—diabetic retinopathy—some sort of eye disease that comes from being diabetic. I paid no mind and kept on being a wild guy. Then one mornin' I wake up, but I can't see nothin.' All I see are blurs in front of me. Know what it feels like to wake up and your eyesight is gone, Johnny?" Jerry gets a bit emotional at this point, but he quickly resumes his story.

"I was a good guy, Johnny. Yeah, sure, I was partyin' and stuff, but inside, I was a good guy, and I ain't never hurt nobody. Those were dark times for me, Johnny boy. All my so-called friends deserted me 'cause ain't nobody likes bein' around a man with problems. I lost it all, Johnny: my money, my life with drugs, and women. I had to come back here, to nothin.' I was a bum on the streets. A blind one at that. Didn't take long for me to discover the drug scene through word of mouth. I was back on drugs again, and I was feelin' very sad and lonely and very sorry for myself. Then one day, I decided to kill myself, Johnny. I did not see the point in living. I couldn't see the beauty this world had to offer; people mocked me, I had no one and no family. I couldn't get a job, so what was the point in living? This is what I thought, you see, so I decided to kill myself. Couldn't hang myself. Damn, I couldn't have found the rope even if I'd tried. So I got a knife, and when I was alone, I planned on slicing up both wrists and just bleed to death. And just when I was about to, Johnny, just when I was about to hurt myself, I heard a baby crying in a trash can nearby, in the same alley where I was. Why would anyone dump a child in a trash can? But I guess in this life there are some things that are really beyond explanation. So I had to put my 'execution' on hold, Johnny. Here I go, wading through the trash, following the sound, and feeling around until my hands touched the most beautiful skin I had ever felt. I couldn't see, and I wanted to deliver this baby to the police. So I had to shout, 'Police, police!' for damn near two hours before finally a police officer came to my aid.

"Long story short, Johnny, with the help of the police I was able to rescue this baby and find her a new home and a new family. I felt happy to be part of something meaningful. The real reward came ten years later, when this same little girl, same baby I rescued, came up to my shack to tell me thank you. She was thanking me for rescuing her. Her new parents must have told her about me. Now she comes around here damn near every week. She's a big reason I get food to eat on a daily basis, and boy, oh boy, does she love taking care of me! I even have a tough time gettin' rid of her. Now, I can't explain it all as a formula, Johnny, but I felt satisfied and good that day. I felt peaceful. And I felt God was giving me an experience that no drug I had ever used could ever come close to providing. God gave me a feeling that even people who think they have it all—the money and the best jobs, and all that they are privileged to experience—cannot comprehend. A feeling that goes beyond sex, money, cars, and all them fancy things, Johnny. I think God revealed true beauty to me that day. Through that little girl, God revealed true beauty to me. And I couldn't even see, but as a blind man I found true beauty. On that day I realized what my true talent was, Johnny; my capacity to love another unconditionally.

"Suddenly, I didn't care about my blindness. All I wanted to do was live my life for God, to get that feeling again, that feeling that made me so happy, to help others, and to be the best I could be. I live for that feeling, Johnny, and since I believe God gave me that special feeling, I live for God. That's when I realized that life has no meaning without God, Johnny. Life has no meaning without that feeling. That's when I realized that there is a difference between existing and living. Existing is what most people do; living is what I am doing right now. Now I dunno much about Jesus, y'see, and I was never really religious, but I don't think God Almighty is one dimensional. If God can reveal godliness through a little girl, then I am sure God can come in other forms as well. So maybe this Jesus is another form God comes in to touch other people, just like He touched me. Isn't that what them Christians talk about: Father, Son, and Holy Spirit? Different forms but all one God.

"I mean, think about it Johnny, if God can speak to you through different people and experiences in your life, what is so hard to understand about Jesus? I think it makes sense what them Christians talk. I know in my life that God has spoken to me through different people and experiences. Now as far as if Jesus Christ is the only way to gain salvation, I don't know. Maybe you should ask the source—God—that question and not rely on any man or your mind, and whatever experiences come into your life that are from God you should follow. I am sure if this Jesus is the way for you, He will make himself known to you." He raises his blind eyes to me. "You should talk to someone who knows more about that subject than I do, Johnny. I'm going to shut up now. I hope my story proved to be useful."

"Absolutely, Jerry, it put a lot of things in perspective for me. Thanks."

"No problem, little Johnny. You'll be fine; I feel it. You have to talk to God and ask for forgiveness as well as for direction, and then submit yourself to God. If your family is suggesting that you let Jesus into your life, I personally would give it a shot. They are closest to you and know what's best for you. But trust me, Johnny; you will live a very average life if you do not find God. And I am not necessarily talking about Jesus, Johnny, but God first. You see, in my humble opinion, I believe we humans just love to categorize things when we cannot understand them. People do it with each other, and that results in racism and other problems. The media does it and that justifies labeling and stereotyping: who's fat from who's skinny, who's pretty from who's ugly. People may see a dirty, old, raggedy blind man like myself and label me a bum, not even worth touching. But when they get to know me and they see how priceless my attitude is, their thoughts come back to bite them.

"We humans love to categorize, and they even do it with God. No one understands God, so they use words like 'God is love' and 'God is powerful' and so on. How can we even try to describe God with words when we have only discovered just a fraction of our universe? I personally think God goes beyond human definition, and there is not one word or collection of words that can illustrate Who or What God is. So all I can say is, 'God is just God.' And logically speakin', I think God will take care of you if you do what is right, based on what you feel is right, provided it does not bother other people and does not disrupt the divine nature of things. I try to do my best with my life, Johnny, and I always ask God for direction. And I feel that He listens, and because of that, I may be blind and livin' in my little ol' shack, but I am also one of the richest men in the world!" he says as he laughs.

Hearing him laugh somehow makes me laugh, too. And I feel much better after laughing with him.

"Now remember, all I said today is just my opinion. Don't go running and telling your folks—I don't want anybody coming here to my little shack and harassing me."

"Thanks, Jerry, and trust me; our conversation stays between us." I get up to leave.

"One more thing, Johnny. Before you head back to the city, grab me some food from your kitchen," he says with a chuckle.

"Will do, Jerry, and thanks again for the advice." I grab my things and head out the door. I can hear Jerry's laughter behind me. I can't help laughing, too, as I run back home, pondering over the wisdom Jerry just shared with me.

I have been trying to call Anna for the past couple of weeks, but she does not answer her phone. I went to her apartment twice and banged on her door but no one answered. But twice within that period she left me messages, saying that she was fine and that she would call me. I can't understand her sudden change in behavior. We were all in the lounge together, and I thought she would have a good time, but she appeared to be so depressed, and then she just walked out on us. Something is definitely wrong. Maybe the death of her brother really took a toll on her. I spoke with the girls about it and no one could understand her behavior.

I am at Alexia's place now, helping her organize her taxes and bank statements. She steps away to grab a drink from her fridge. Miss Pryce is still in town, spending time with her daughter and Tara. I plan on heading over to Darius's place afterwards. I just sent Anna another text, asking her to call me.

Alexia walks in, and I say, "I am really concerned about Anna. You think she's okay?"

"I don't know, Michelle, that was pretty strange and not like her at all, the way she just got up and left the last time we hung out. Very strange, indeed."

"Yeah, well having someone close to you die is not the easiest thing to deal with."

"Funny, but I don't recall ever hearing Anna talk about a brother. And Anna loves to talk. Don't you find it strange that we are only just now hearing about him?"

"Yeah, you do have a point. But maybe she is just the type of person who does not like to get into her family business."

"Maybe, and maybe not. C'mon, Michelle, you've known Anna since college when she was your room-mate. Did she ever mention having a brother back in France, or did she ever show you any pictures of him?"

"Come to think of it, no, she didn't. I mean she spoke of her father, her mother, and her sister, but no, never a brother. But Alexia, that is just an assumption we are discussing. She could have had a brother that she never talked about, or maybe that she never got along with, or was not in touch with. Just because we were roommates does not mean that I knew every single thing about her."

"You're right. All I am saying is that the way she left us was strange. Normally, a person that has had someone close to her die would want to be comforted by friends and family, and she would have at least stuck around and let us try to make her happy."

"Well, like you said, whenever something like that happens, a person normally wants to be comforted by friends and family. Maybe this is something that friends cannot help much with, and she would rather be with family."

"We are Anna's family in this country, Michelle."

"True. You have a point."

Miss Pryce walks in the room. "So what are you girls talking about?" she asks.

"Oh, nothing much, Ma, just about a friend who has vanished mysteriously. We are coming up with different theories to explain her recent behavior."

"Oh, and what theories have you both come up with?" Miss Pryce asks.

"Well, it's Anna. I hope you still remember her. We hadn't seen her in a while, and when we finally did see her, she was acting really strange and then she told us that her brother died, and then she just left, walked out on us."

"That seems like normal behavior to me," Alexia's mother replies.

"No, Ma, but that is not all. We have no recollection of Anna's ever telling us that she had a brother, and Michelle was her roommate all through college. If she had a brother, we would have known about it."

"So what are the theories again?"

"Well, Michelle believes that she did have a brother who passed away, a brother she probably never brought up for whatever personal reason, and I am saying that we should not just go off the face value of what she said, that there is probably more than meets the eye."

"I am just saying that we should give her the benefit of the doubt and be there for her," I reply.

"Of course we will be there for her, Michelle, but I am not convinced about her dying-brother story."

"Well, Alexia, you do bring up some valid points, but so does Michelle, because she may not have revealed everything about herself to you guys. If she said that her brother died, then I think you all should respect that and do your best to be there for her. But Alexia does have a point in that people usually share these sorts of setbacks in life with a close friend or two, so yes, there might be something more to her story. But that's not something you guys, as friends, should concern yourselves with."

"Agreed, Ma, it was just strange, the way her behavior suddenly changed."

"Well, maybe she has something personal that she is dealing with, something that might be related to this brother who died. Who knows? To be effective friends you should give her some space and let her come to you. Maybe she just needs some time."

"You're right, Miss Pryce. I will stop trying to call her. I've left her enough messages as it is."

"Okay, and lets pray that she's all right. How are your taxes coming along?"

We spend the rest of our time sorting through Alexia's messy paperwork, and soon I leave to go spend some time with my boyfriend, Darius. Until this point, it had been just us four—Jess, Alexia, Anna and me—spending time together, and now it just did not feel right without Anna.

Chapter Thirteen

bout a month has passed since my incident with Anna, and I feel like I have a cold developing. I have flu-like symptoms, having been nauseated and feeling fatigued for the past three days. I have also not been sleeping well because of all I have on my mind. I immediately begin to get nervous, because I think these symptoms have something to do with my exposure to HIV. Are there any specific ways one can tell for sure if one is infected? Are there any symptoms that present themselves in such a situation?

Tonight, I decide to do more research on the Internet to give me more insight into my dilemma. I would go to a doctor, but I am too embarrassed and scared. Plus, I do not want to risk any such information leaking into my workplace.

I grab a beer and a burger and soon get down to business. "HIV symptoms, HIV sickness, early signs of HIV infection…"—I type the words into a search engine. A bunch of results pop up. One link finally catches my attention: "HIV seroconversion." Before I click on the link, my heart begins to pound faster. I am really scared. But there is no turning back now. I click on the link. "Seroconversion is the development of specific antibodies as a result of infection or immunization. Prior to seroconversion, the blood tests negative for the antibody, and after seroconversion, the blood will test positive."

Makes sense. From what I understand, HIV is a virus that attacks a person's antibodies/immune system. If specific antibodies are developed by a person's body to fight off the virus, then it means that person has been infected, as the virus is in the body. And once the virus gets in, there is no way to get it out.

I read on: "HIV seroconversion illness is the name given to a group of symptoms that occur when someone is newly infected with HIV. Upon new infection, the HIV virus reproduces and duplicates in a person's white blood cells." I guess they are referring to the CD4 cells I researched earlier. "When this happens, the body launches a response to the new HIV infection via the immune system. It is during this reaction by the immune system to the virus that symptoms can develop. The symptoms of HIV seroconversion are not always related to HIV. They vary from person to person, based on each individual's immune system and range from no symptoms at all, to very mild, to very severe. Most people report of a flu-like illness that occurs shortly after infection. It is important to remember that virus levels are very high before antibodies to HIV are measurable in the blood through HIV-antibody tests. *Someone newly infected with HIV is very infectious to others and may not know that they can spread HIV.*"

Oh, my God. I'm finished! I read on. "Some people who become infected with HIV develop symptoms that may last anywhere from two to four weeks. The symptoms may include fever, rashes, swollen lymph nodes, lack of energy, or joint/muscle pain."

I pause with my reading and sit back in my chair. I have had flu-like symptoms. I have been feeling fatigued, but then again, I hardly get any sleep. And this is winter—lots of people have the flu. But then again, what if it is the HIV working in my body? What if I am developing these symptoms as a result of the HIV crushing my immune system? All this uncertainty is driving me crazy. I wish I could go back. I really wish I could go back in time and change what happened. I would not have even taken one step into Anna's apartment. I would not have even spoken to her at the bar. As soon as I saw her, if I had known all this, I would have turned around and run away like crazy, like a madman out of hell. I feel bad for saying this, because she herself did not know that she was infected, but this is reality, and if I could change my past, that is definitely one experience I would erase. But then again, if not with Anna, it might have been someone else. What about all those other girls, those with whom I had numerous sexual accidents?

Any one of them could have had HIV.

I was blinded by a woman's curves, by a woman's hips, hypnotized by a woman's seductive stare. I was blinded by ignorance. And now I am paying the price. All this stress is really unnecessary. For the sake of a few hours of meaningless, selfish pleasure, I may have acquired a lifetime problem. Well, it is what it is. I have to think positive thoughts to keep my sanity and assume that all the symptoms I am experiencing now are a result of my stress, my lack of sleep, and this horrible winter weather. My nausea I will blame on all the genetically modified food I eat here in the big city.

***

It felt good seeing my folks last week. I have been feeling really depressed since learning of Anna's condition, and I feel very dirty inside. I am hesitant to contact others, and I realize I have been avoiding all my loved ones. I left work early today in order to come home and do some soul searching. And to do some more research on my predicament.

I buy some chips and soda and decide to spend the evening in front of my computer. I begin my research by first saying a prayer and asking God to direct all my research efforts. Soon, I begin scanning the Internet for HIV and all its related topics. I soon realize that I am not alone in my predicament.

There are numerous sites dedicated to topics such as "HIV transmission," "HIV prevention," and so on. From what I find, I see that men are more likely to contract the virus if they have an STD, which provides a pathway for infection. How many men know their own STD status? I don't even know mine! How many men and women go in for checkups regarding their sexual health?

My eyes begin to open to the world we live in. It's very scary to face reality and its harsh facts. There was so much I've taken for granted with my carefree lifestyle.

I read on. I discover two large studies done in California and Europe, which found a per contact risk (the risk of a man's becoming infected from each instance of penile-vaginal sex) of 0.0001 (1 in 10,000) and 0.0003 (1 in 3000). That is assuming it is with a partner of unknown status. With a partner who is seropositive, the odds of infection are anywhere from 1 in 10 to 1 in 1000. Makes sense. The risk would then be higher if the HIV status of the partner was known. The fact is, these are just statistics, just estimates. The virus can be transferred through one single act; all it takes is one time. The words of my good friend Abel come flooding back to me: "Let me say this to you, though, John: you're gambling with your life and dodging too many bullets. Keep on playing, and one day you're bound to get hit."

No matter what statistics I read, no matter what any counselor tells me, I put my chances at 50/50. It's either I have it, or I don't. No one can give me a definitive answer to that question. The question now is, what can I do in the meantime to minimize the possibility of my having acquired the virus? Is there nothing I can do to save myself? I realize now that my life is not in my hands, and for the first time I truly acknowledge the fact that I have no control over anything. I realize it is time for me to develop a relationship with God. I have no choice. So I kneel down to pray, even though I am not sure how. Is there a specific ritual I must do? What do Al and Ma do when they want to pray? I know what they do physically, but is there a specific mindset I should be in? I decide to kneel and speak my mind to God.

"My Lord," I begin aloud, "please help me." I think for a minute about what to say next. "I am trying really hard, and if I offended You by chasing women, I am sorry, but please, help me. I beg You." I suddenly begin to get emotional, and I feel as if I am pleading for my life. "I know I have never had the chance to develop a relationship with You, but please find favor with me and help me. I have nowhere else to turn, and there is no one else who can help me. You made me and You made the world, so I am sure You can help me. Please." I end my prayer and feel a bit better. Let's see what happens now.

My mind goes back to my research. "1 in 10 to 1 in 1000." An idea hits me, and I decide to try a little experiment. I grab a paper cup and a sheet of paper and tear ten evenly shaped rectangles from the sheet. I fold each piece four times, so they are exactly identical, and on the last piece I write the word "H" before I fold it. I place all the pieces in the paper cup, making sure not too stare for too long at any of them, for fear of recognizing the H-labeled piece of paper. I then place my hand over the cup and shake it vigorously, and then pour all the pieces of paper from the cup out onto my desk. I close my eyes and randomly select a piece. "One in 10 chance; here we go." My heart begins to beat out of fear, even though I am here alone. I hold up the piece I selected, take a deep breath, and open it. It is blank. Phew! Man, that was scary. I could have easily selected the piece with the H on it, the H symbolizing HIV and my having acquired it. I decide that from now on, I will play this game every couple of weeks, to help put things in perspective for me. I hope I never pick the piece of paper I labeled with the red H.

***

I need to find an outlet, something to do to take my mind off this situation. The yoga classes, the gym, chatting with friends over the phone about pointless issues and so forth all offer me temporary solutions to a long-term problem. And I find that I keep on going back to such comforts because I always yearn for peace. No, I need something to do that will completely occupy my mind and will help put things in perspective. I have been selfish thus far and have been indulging in nothing but myself for so long. Maybe I could try indulging other people for a change. Helping others. Being there for others, just as others have been there for me; namely, my family and people like Jerry. Jerry said he always found joy in helping other people; maybe there is something to what he said.

I decide to go online to look up ways I can offer myself for others in need. Do something different for a change. I soon come across various volunteer organizations and Web sites here in the big city. Maybe the city isn't completely tainted after all. I scroll through the different types. "Cancer Society, peer groups, mentoring programs, sports coaching programs, after-school programs, HIV-counseling and peer-support programs, Aware…" Wait. I look back. "HIV-counseling and peer-support programs." That title catches my attention. I click on the respective link. "HIV counseling and peer support, must be twenty-one or older…fluent in English…outgoing and friendly…good listener…HIV counseling and testing certification…"

I don't feel like taking a test, but maybe I can find a church or something that offers support for people living with HIV. It seems my exposure to this virus has left me curious to meet someone who is actually afflicted with it. I proceed to look up various church Web sites that offer HIV counseling. Most of them state that you need to have an HIV-counseling certification to be a counselor. I soon strike good fortune. I find a clinic that needs volunteers in their billing department. I could offer my services there and maybe get a chance to interact with an HIV patient. I need to know how someone deals with the virus—mentally, physically, spiritually, and socially—when that person knows that he or she is infected. I have to know, in case I find out that I have the virus myself. I decide I will call the clinic tomorrow and find out how and when I can become a volunteer.

***

Today, on the way to work, I saw the girl I usually flirt with on the train. She looks like such a good girl. Whenever I see her, she is always dressed up professionally, and she always gives me a really shy smile. "Oh, God," I say to myself, "why can't I just meet a normal girl like this one, with her modest smile and classy demeanor? Man, I would like to have the chance to get to know her. I know I have not spoken to her, but she just seems to have it together." I guess I said that to myself because I feel so depressed about the predicament I am in, and I would like someone to give me comfort while I am here in the city, away from my parents. So here I am asking for something I know nothing about. I guess we'll see.

It's been some time now, about a month plus, since Anna started acting really strange around us, and we still have not heard from her, other than the occasional text message saying that she is okay and that she will call, which she never does. We are getting used to it. I personally am not motivated to call her and check up on her as I used to, and I think the girls all feel the same way. If she calls me, I will not be mean to her or anything, but I'm not going to call her anymore. I can understand a week or two, but cutting off your friends for over a whole month is a different story.

Anyway, I am at work at the Ethiopian restaurant. Darius is out of town, which sucks, because I usually love going to his place after working here. He treats me to the best back massages! I miss him, but when he gets back, I am sure he will more than make it up to me. Tonight, I will be taking my onion-smelling butt back to my place for a nice, long, hot bath and some good sleep. I have been in Darius's bed for so long that it seems like a new experience whenever I fall asleep at my place.

I finish clearing up the last set of dishes and hand them to the dishwashers in the kitchen. I am about to start counting all my tips for the night when my cell phone rings. It's Jess.

"Hey, baby girl, what's going on?" I ask.

"I am fine, I think."

"Uh-oh, what's wrong, Jess?"

"I feel fine, and nothing bad happened—he wasn't inside…"

"Jess, calm down. What's wrong?"

"I'm scared, Michelle."

My heartbeat quickens. This is the same way I felt when Anna began acting up. Not Jess, too.

"It's okay, Jess. I am your sister, and I am here for you, but you have to talk to me. Calm down and take a deep breath."

"Okay."

"Now tell me what's bothering you."

"I think I am pregnant."

"What? Pregnant! Why would you think such a thing, Jess?"

"Well, I missed my period, Michelle, and I have been really tired lately."

"Maybe it's school. Maybe you are just stressed out from studying."

"We are on vacation, Michelle. I am not studying for anything now."

"When was your last period?"

"Well over a month ago. I am really scared. What do I tell my parents? And what about school?"

"We don't know for sure if you are pregnant, sweetie. Why don't you take the home pregnancy test?"

"I am pretty sure that I am, Michelle. I feel different."

"Well, take the test and we will know for sure. Have you been having sex with just that one guy you told us about?"

"Yes." She starts to cry over the phone.

"Whatever happened to condoms? Weren't you guys using condoms?"

"Once or twice, we did not," she replies. She resumes crying over the phone.

"Oh, Jess, stop crying," I say. "Being pregnant is not a bad thing! Besides, we don't even know for sure if you are pregnant yet."

"Yes, Michelle, but I am still in school. I am not ready to have a kid yet. Where will I get the money to support a kid? How will I study?"

"There are many women who get pregnant, have kids, and still do very well in school. Look at Alexia, for example. She got pregnant while she was in college and look how well she is doing now."

"Alexia dropped out of school, Michelle."

"Oh. yes, bad example, but you know what I am trying to say, Jess. There are many strong women who have kids and do exceptionally well in school. You will just have to change your lifestyle. So you have to think positive."

"I just didn't picture this guy as the guy I would lose my virginity to, much less the person I would have a kid with. It isn't supposed to be like this," she sobs.

"Aw-w, Jess, stop crying. Listen, think of it like this: we don't know if you are pregnant or not, but if you are, it will be the best thing that ever happened to you because you are going to have a beautiful baby whom you will love more than anything else."

"Thanks, Michelle."

"What are you doing now?"

"I am in my room, huddled in a corner, crying, and talking to you."

"Aw-w, sweetie, listen—stop feeling sorry for yourself. Get up, take a nice, long shower, and get some rest. Tomorrow, you will take the pregnancy test and we can take it from there."

"Okay."

"Oh, wait, and one more thing—have you told the guy yet?"

"No. You're the first person I told."

"Good. Wait till you know for sure. That will be priceless to see his facial expression if you are pregnant."

Jess does not respond.

"Sorry, bad joke. I am happy for you, Jess. Get tested and then we'll figure out how to tell your folks and the guy. What do you think he will say? What if he wants an abortion?"

"No, I will never do that. I don't believe in abortions. And he is a nice guy. But then again, guys are guys."

"Yeah, well, listen, I have to leave this place—we're closing—but let's talk some more, okay? Keep me posted. And remember that I am always here for you, okay?"

"Okay, thanks, Michelle."

We hang up. My blood is racing with excitement. I retrieve my cell phone and call Alexia.

"Hey."

"Hey, guess what?" I ask.

"What?"

"C'mon, guess—something really crazy."

"Umm…you lost all your hair?"

"No, silly, I'm serious. You'll never guess."

"I give up, Michelle, what? Share the glorious news."

"I think Jess might be pregnant."

"*What?* Why would you say that?"

"She just called me and told me that she's late with her period."

"Wow. Is this with the same guy, blow-job guy?"

"Yup."

"Damn, that is crazy news. Well, it seems little Tara will now have someone to play with at home."

"Funny, but what about her school situation? This might affect her."

"Yeah, well, it's hard balancing a baby, classes, and work at the same time. It's really hard."

"That's going to be one distraught young man if she is indeed pregnant. All guys run, first chance they get, when it comes to handling kids—well, young guys at least."

"I agree. I hope this guy is as nice as Jess makes him out to be."

"Hey, she was giving him free blow jobs; he has to be a nice guy."

"That's not nice—we have to be there for her if she is pregnant."

"Keep me updated. I have to give Tara a bath."

"Okay, talk to you later."

We hang up, and on the way home I play out all the possible scenarios that could occur for Jess.

Chapter Fourteen

It's going on two months since Anna shared the gloomy news with me regarding her health. I am sitting here in my office, and I am tired beyond belief, due to my staying up at night, most times because I worry for myself. I am not as worried as I used to be; could it be because I am getting used to my situation? Who knows?

The day is progressing well, considering what I have on my mind. I pray to God, but is that enough? Is there an extra step I must take? Every problem has a solution, but for this I cannot think of any. Nothing in this world can save me. If I did contract the virus and it is possible to make a cure, the probability of my seeing such a cure within my lifetime must be very slim. So does that mean the theory of "every problem has a solution" only applies in a physical/materialistic sense? Could all this be happening for a reason? Could God, whom I have gotten to know better within the past month, be using this experience to draw me closer to Him? Or should I think like the average man and base my fate on luck? No, I will plead with God for my life.

There has to be a God. How can it be explained how every living creature is unique within itself? Who can explain the blueprint for life, the reason we are here, how the world began? Scientists do not convince me with the Big Bang theory. If so, then what sparked the Big Bang in the first place? And what started whatever started that? Everything has a beginning; and even scientists hit a dead end when they try to explain the unexplainable. I have decided that scientists cannot help me now, and neither can luck. It's all depends on whether it is in my destiny, my life plan, my life's blueprint that God has designed for me. And the only one who can change the design for the best is the designer Himself. I use the term "Him" objectively to represent God, because no one word really can encompass who or what God is. I personally believe He is beyond human definition. God is who God is.

As I stay lost in my thoughts, I notice Cesar across the office, and he notices me. We nod at each other, and he keeps walking, but he has a distasteful look in his eye. It's almost as if he has a grudge against me because I have not spoken to him in about a month. Maybe his attitude has to do with the night we hung out with Anna and her friends. I remember he was also trying to hit on Anna. Who knows? I have more important things to worry about. It's time

I worked on my game plan. I will call upon God to help me. I will change my ways. I will pray more often. And I will always strive to do what is right, no matter the situation. I must do this. I have only about a month left.

So Jess is indeed pregnant. She called me four days after we spoke and told me her tests came back positive. She also told me that she spoke to the guy, and he was very nervous at first but seems to be doing a lot better now. I am just happy that she got pregnant with what seems to be a decent guy—there are so many losers out there, so many lazy jerks who just get girls pregnant and do not take responsibility for the kids that they help produce. Alexia's ex is one of them. I mean, I don't understand these guys—if you are going to have a kid, the least you can do is take a little responsibility! In a way, I feel sorry for Jess, because she is so innocent, and we could have taught her better, I think. I told Alexia not to tell her that we spoke about her, and moreover, Jess herself said that she would break the news to us both over dinner sometime this week. So Alexia will officially find out "for the first time" then.

I have been spending time with Darius since he got back from his trip because I missed him so much! I go to his place every day after work, and I take care of him. We cuddle every evening by his fireplace and talk about life, good food, and those things that lovers talk about.

Tonight is one of those nights, and now we are snuggled up together, enjoying each other's company. Of course, sex is at the back of both our minds.

"How is your friend, the one you told me just got pregnant?" he asks as he plays with my hair.

"She is fine. We are supposed to meet for dinner and talk about it."

"I hope she does okay. She is lucky to have a friend like you around."

"Thanks. I just feel a little sorry for her, because she is such a sweet, innocent person. You know it's funny because Alexia said it, that once she starts she won't be able to stop."

"Starts what?"

"Starts having sex."

"I see. How will she balance that with school and stuff?"

"I don't know, but we'll do what we can to help, Alexia and I. I see myself doing a lot of baby-sitting in the future."

"You know, it takes a strong man to stick around when he gets a girl pregnant. Most men run away or don't fulfill their responsibilities."

"Yeah, I know."

"It helps that the guy is in school with her. That shows that he has some kind of focus. I personally know a lot of guys with very lazy attitudes who go around getting young girls pregnant. And these girls are not being responsible, either. It's a shame, indeed."

"What if you got me pregnant, Darius? What would you do?"

He leans away from me and looks me dead in the eye. "What do you mean? Are you trying to tell me something?"

"No, baby, I was only asking a random question. Don't worry; I am not pregnant."

"Oh, you scared me for a sec."

"So what would you do?"

"Well, I don't plan on getting you pregnant, sweetheart, and I know this because whenever I sleep with you without a condom, I never cum inside you. But now that you bring it up, maybe you should start taking the Pill."

"Maybe I should. But you didn't answer my question."

"What would I do? I am a responsible man, and if we were both not ready for kids I would suggest you take the morning after pill to stop the pregnancy process from beginning in you."

"Easy for you to say since you're a man, you can only take that pill after some hours you know, and that's only after unprotected sex, in the event that we wanted to prevent unwanted pregnancy. Plus I heard it really hurts and gives cramps. And that pill is made to prevent pregnancies. I am talking about if I was already pregnant and brought it to your attention."

"Well I wouldn't want you to go through any pain whether with the pill or through having an abortion, so I probably would suggest that we get married, seeing as how we already live like husband and wife. Wouldn't you like that, sweetie?" He holds me close.

"M-m-m, I definitely would," I reply as I enjoy his grip. "So maybe I should trick you into making me pregnant so we can get married, eh?"

He gets really quiet now. "I was just answering your question, Michelle. You don't have to take what I said literally."

I sit up in bed. "So what are you saying? That you didn't mean what you just said?"

"No, no, of course I did, baby, but just because I mean it doesn't mean you have to make it a point to get pregnant by me."

I pinch him. "I was just joking, Darius. Of course I wouldn't do that. I am not ready to have a kid myself."

"Hmm, I don't know about you. You are beginning to scare me, little psycho chick," he says playfully as he begins to play-fight with me.

We roll around on the floor, laughing and giggling, and begin to have sex by his fireplace, again without a condom. But I feel safe because I know that he won't cum in me.

Chapter Fifteen

After work today I decide to head to the HIV clinic. I had gotten in touch with them earlier, and they said they had one volunteer slot open and that I could come fill in if I had time today. So I seize the opportunity because it may not be there tomorrow. There is a slight drizzle, and the weather is a bit warmer than usual. When I arrive at the clinic, I proceed to the receptionist. I am introduced to a heavy-set lady, Bertha, who shows me where I will sit as I work. Then she introduces me to a few other volunteers who are present. I listen intently as she goes through my job orientation, but I must admit that I constantly itch to ask her about the HIV patients. I pop the question at the right time.

"Just out of curiosity, do you have in-house HIV patients?"

"Most of our HIV patients are with us as outpatients, but we do have a few AIDS patients who reside here for proper care."

"Really?" I reply. "Wow, that must be something. Do you deal with them yourself?"

"Yes, I do," Bertha replies.

"I see. Don't you get scared that you might get infected?"

"There is always that possibility, yes, but the virus has to get into your bloodstream, and the situations I am in with the patients are not high risk. Besides, we are required to get screened pretty frequently, and in case there is an accident, there are certain measures we take to reduce the risk of HIV transmission." I am sure she is referring to the PEP treatment.

"Cool, do you think I could meet some of the patients sometime?"

She grins at my request. "Normally, we would have to get their consent, but I think we can arrange something. As I show you around, we will make a little detour to that section, and maybe you can say hello to some of them. They are really nice people."

I like this woman already. We finish our orientation and she takes me on a tour of the clinic. Just as she said we would, we make a brief visit to the AIDS ward. The corridors are sparkling clean, as are the walls.

"We have to keep everything clean, as AIDS patients have weakened immune systems and are susceptible to all sorts of infections. By the way, you have to wash you hands."

"Oh, yes, of course."

I head to a bathroom nearby and do as she asked. Then we walk through double doors into the AIDS section. A nurse sits in the reception area. I guess she is on call. I see rooms on both sides of the corridor, with individuals in each bed. Most of them have blank expressions on their faces; a few have laid-back smiles. Some are watching television. In a few rooms I see what appear to be family members sitting by bedsides, and in others, the patients appear fast asleep.

"This is it, John, as promised. We have a policy here of allowing our patients to have visitors all day long, except when treatment is being administered. We do this because people with full-blown AIDS need positive support, and it is not advisable to leave them alone, as they tend to feel isolated and depressed. The world, in general, does not accept them for who they are, but they are very normal persons in unfortunate circumstances, so we do what we can to help them maintain some sanity before the inevitable happens. We sometimes have volunteers come in for those patients whose families intentionally neglect them or who have no family at all. Such initiatives enhance the self-esteem of patients as well."

Bertha leads me into one of the rooms, where an elderly lady sits in an armchair, knitting. "Hey, Josephine, look who I have with me."

The lady looks up at me.

"Hi," I say.

"Hello, young man, and what might your name be?" she asks with a smile.

"I'm John. John Casey."

"Nice to meet you, John Casey," she replies. "Is Bertha showing you around?"

"Yes, she is."

"Well, that's nice of her; it's always nice to see a new face around here."

Bertha's cell phone rings, and while she answers it, I continue my conversation with Josephine.

"How long have you been here, ma'am?" I ask.

"Too long. I've been here for way too long. Sometimes I feel like I am being sentenced like a criminal, even though I did nothing wrong."

"If I may ask, how did you find out that you had AIDS/HIV? Were you born with it?" I realized only afterward that my question might appear to be rude to her. But I had asked it already, and so I waited for a response.

She smiles at me. "I am not sure you are supposed to be asking me that, but I like you, so I don't mind."

"I'm sorry, ma'am; sometimes I do not think before I speak."

"You're young, so it's to be expected. I was not born with HIV; I was actually married to someone for thirteen years, and I thought everything was going well…and then one night, he told me that he was gay."

"I am sorry to hear that, but what does being gay have to do with your being sick? Just because a person is gay does not mean he has HIV. That's just a stereotype, don't you think?"

She smiles again. "You're right. Well, he was the only person I was with sexually, and I didn't know who he was seeing while he stayed married to me. So I definitely picked up the infection from him. If I had known he was sleeping around, I would have used a condom or something, but this was my husband, and I felt really comfortable sleeping unprotected with him. And now I am in this clinic talking to you."

"I am really sorry to hear that. Did you guys have any kids?"

"Yeah, we had three: two boys and a girl. They come here to visit me a lot, but my youngest, one of the boys, gets really uncomfortable when he comes over here."

"I see. And are you in touch with your husband?"

"Nope, and we are not married anymore. I hope he is not with another woman, because I would hate for her to go through what I have. I just wish he had told me earlier, so all of this could have been avoided."

At that moment, Bertha gets off the phone. "What are you guys talking about?" Bertha asks.

"He was asking me how I ended up here, and I told him about Phil and the kids."

"I see." Bertha turns and faces me. "Yeah, a lot of men and women these days feel it is okay to get married and have extramarital affairs with the same sex. Josephine had it rough because she had kids with this man, and to make it worse, he was HIV-positive and she slept with him on a regular basis. Really irresponsible on his part."

I nod in agreement. "I am really sorry you had to go through that, ma'am," I say to Josephine.

"It's all right; just remember to be careful and honest with those you deal with, okay?"

"Yes, ma'am."

Bertha looks at her watch. "Okay, Josephine, I will stop by later, but I promised John I would show him around a bit."

"Fine. It was nice meeting you, John. Stop by again."

"It was nice meeting you as well, Josephine," I reply. We step out of the room and stand in the hallway for a minute.

"Josephine's case is rather unfortunate, as it could have been prevented if her husband had been up front with her. Now she's sick with AIDS," Bertha remarks.

"Yes, it's sad, but, you know, HIV/AIDS is not just transmitted through homosexual acts—heterosexual sex can lead to catching HIV as well," I reply.

"Of course, John, I know this. I do work in an HIV clinic, remember?"

We both smile.

"Yes, I remember, Bertha; forgive me."

"It's okay, and as you mentioned, HIV/AIDS can be transferred through any sexual act involving penetration and the exchange of bodily fluids. But I guess the main reason a lot of people associate HIV acquisition with homosexuals is because getting HIV is so much easier through anal sex than it is with vaginal sex. And homosexual men don't have vaginas." I knew what she was about to say but I let her finish, to see if my research made any sense. "If you do not know so already, John, HIV can be found in the blood, semen, pre-seminal fluid, or vaginal fluid of a person infected with the virus. In general, the person receiving the semen is at greater risk of getting HIV because the lining of the rectum is thin and may allow the virus to enter the body during anal sex.

"However, a person who inserts his penis into an infected person is also at risk, because the virus can enter through the opening at the tip of the penis, called the urethra, or through small cuts, abrasions, or open sores on the penis. But yes, the risk of getting HIV is high with any kind of unprotected sex, whether homosexual or heterosexual."

As soon as she finishes speaking, we hear a loud laugh come from a room adjacent to us. I feel good energy from hearing this laugh. It is full of life and brings some light to the gloomy atmosphere in this place.

"Who was that?" I ask.

She giggles. "That is Sebastian. He is maybe a little older than you are, and he's really a treat to be around. He likes his video games and his cartoons."

I look at his room door with curiosity. How can someone laugh so genuinely when it seems all hope is lost? I have to know his secret, in case I have to eventually deal with what all these patients are dealing with now.

"Do you think I could say hello?" I ask.

"Sure, I don't see why not." We stroll to his door. "Hey, Sebastian," Bertha says. He looks up. "This is our new volunteer, who will be helping us in the billing department. His name is John Casey."

He fixes his eyes on me. He has powerful eyes; they seemed to carry so much life experience in them, and they appeared very dreamy in nature. He also has a very big smile on his face, but I can sense some sadness behind the smile. He actually is a very handsome man, but the disease has taken its toll on his body. I noticed that he has lesions all over his arms, some closed and many open. He is in hospital garb, but I can tell the lesions are also present on his torso. He catches my eyes wandering.

"They are lesions, and yes, I know they spoil my ravishing good looks," he says with a surprisingly deep voice, which does not match his physique.

"Do they hurt?" I ask.

"Sometimes, but I am used to them; I've had them for a while now. It's a cancer I have, called Kaposi's sarcoma, which results in abnormal growth of blood vessels under my skin. And don't ask me what causes it, because I don't know."

"Don't worry; I wasn't going to ask," I reply.

"One minute, boys," Bertha cuts in. "I need to have a word with the nurse down the hall. I will be right back."

Bertha leaves, and I am left alone with Sebastian.

"So, John, where are you from?" Sebastian asks. I tell him the name of my town. "Oh, I've been there, before I found out I had AIDS. Nice little town. What are you doing here in the big city, then?"

"I got a job out here working in sales for an asset management company."

"Nice. Bet you're making all the big bucks. How are the girls, or should I say the guys, treating you?"

"I'm not gay, and I guess the girls are treating me okay.

"I hope you didn't take offense to my question. I meant no disrespect."

"None taken. And how about you? How are you doing?"

He looks at me. "Well, I am alive, I guess. I've got food to eat this morning, this afternoon, and this evening. I've got a roof over my head. I've lost a lot of things and a lot of friends, but who cares? Such friends were not meant to be around me anyway. Besides, God knows that I have a good heart, and He always sends good people my way to chat with me. Quality people."

"God sends people your way?" I ask.

"You're standing here, aren't you?" he replies.

He is right. But I decide to test him. "So you think God sent me here to you?"

"Hey, I prayed for someone to chat with, and voila, that someone is standing at my doorstep. God is real, you know."

He didn't need to tell me that.

"Hey, listen, once you get situated with your assignments and stuff, you should swing by and visit me from time to time, so we can have another little chat like this one."

"Absolutely," I reply. "I will definitely come back to talk to you."

"Sounds good, John. I'll see you around."

Just then Bertha returns to take me away. As we walk away, I feel bad for leaving Sebastian all alone. I tell myself that I will make sure to visit him as often as I can.

My younger brother, Carl, is coming into the city to visit me today. I was hoping to set him up with Jess, but seeing as how Jess presently is preoccupied with another person inside of her, I don't think that would be such a good idea. What a shame, because I feel that they would have made for a good match. My younger brother is a really cute guy, and I know that Jess is his type, physically. They definitely would have looked good together. Anyway, he is coming in later today, so to kill some time before I go pick him from the airport, I decide to spend some time at Alexia's place. I'm here with her now, in her living room, talking about Jess, of course. Miss Pryce is taking a nap in Tara's room.

"Do you think it will be a boy or a girl?" Alexia asks.

"I think it will be a boy. Jess looks like a boy producer."

"A boy producer? What the heck is that? You're crazy, Michelle."

"I was hoping that I could set Jess up with Carl, but I guess that's not going to happen."

"Your brother is a cocky guy—no offense. He definitely would not have made a good match for a girl like Jess."

"Alexia! How could you say such a thing! Carl is a nice guy…well, he can be."

"Your brother is a good-looking guy and that's about it. I don't think he has much else going for him."

"Carl is nice. He is nice with you whenever he comes around, isn't he?"

"He is okay, and that's because you and I are best friends. But I have seen him around other girls and in public. He needs to work on his personality."

"Well, I still think he would have made a nice match with Jess. It's a shame she's pregnant. Well, it's a shame because of the timing."

"Yeah, now that she's pregnant, I wonder what she'll do about her classes. She'll probably have to cut back."

"Who is pregnant?" Miss Pryce asks as she walks in on our conversation.

"Hi, Miss Pryce."

"Hi, Mom. One of our friends is pregnant, and we were just talking about it."

"Which friend? The Anna girl?"

"No, Ma. It's Jess."

"Jess is pregnant?"

"Yes, Mom."

Miss Pryce sits down with a look of wonder on her face. "Are you serious? And how do you know this?"

"She called Michelle and told her. Then Michelle called me and told me."

Miss Pryce gives me a stern look. "Michelle, shame on you. If your friend calls you and tells you something that confidential, it means she trusts you, and you shouldn't go telling other people until she does, not even Alexia."

"But I—"

"But nothing, Michelle. What's done is done, but don't make it a point to share anyone's confidential business, understand?"

"Yes, Miss Pryce." I feel really ashamed now.

"So, how is she doing?" Miss Pryce asks.

"She is fine, Ma. She just recently found out."

"So what will she do about school? She's not going to drop out, is she?" Miss Pryce asks.

"We won't let her," I reply. "Plus, the guy who made her pregnant is also in school, and I don't think he wants to quit school."

"So she was not using a condom?"

"Apparently not, Miss Pryce," I respond.

"These days you young people just don't listen. I hope you guys apply more caution when you engage in your sexual activities."

"Yes, we do, Ma," Alexia responds.

"I don't know about that, Alexia. I know that whenever I come around to visit you in this big city and even back home, I see more and more teenagers and young women getting pregnant. It's almost as if it is becoming a trend with you guys."

"Yeah, I personally always take precautions with my boyfriend, and I have even decided to start going on the Pill," I say.

"Do you have unprotected sex with him, Michelle?" Miss Pryce asks. Alexia giggles.

"Well, umm, yes, he is my boyfriend, so yes I do. But I trust him, and he is a responsible guy. And besides, he never goes all the way with me."

"Never goes all the way? What exactly does that mean?" Miss Pryce asks.

"Yeah, Michelle, tell us what 'never goes all the way' means," Alexia instigates with a smile.

"Be quiet, Alexia. I mean he never releases inside of me—you know, ejaculates. I was just a bit embarrassed to use regular terminology with you, Miss Pryce," I reply.

"You mean he never cums inside of you?" Alexia asks.

"Yes, if you want to be blunt. Yes, that is what I mean. So I take precautions so I don't get pregnant."

"Well, for your information, pre-semen can make you pregnant. And second, pregnancy should be the least of your concerns. What about diseases and stuff?" Miss Pryce asks.

"C'mon, Miss Pryce, no one talks about that. My boyfriend is fine, and I haven't noticed anything out of the ordinary with him. And if there was something wrong, I'm sure he would tell me."

"I am amazed at how naïve you guys are. I have this same conversation with Alexia all the time. You guys have to be careful, you know. Sometimes I get scared for you all."

"There is nothing to worry about, Ma. We take care of ourselves, and we don't deal with dirty men. We're fine," Alexia responds.

"Hmm, if you say so. Well, I am going to leave you guys alone and go back to my nap. I just heard you guys talking and wanted to say hello. Talk to you later."

"Good-bye, Miss Pryce."

"Bye, Ma."

Alexia's mom leaves, and we are alone again.

"Your mom is right, you know; we should be more careful."

"Well, of course she is. Guys are guys, you know, and you never know what you're getting."

"The same can be said for girls, Alexia."

"Yeah, but we don't date girls."

"Yeah, but guys do."

"Good point. Okay, let's make a new rule then; we will always use condoms from here on out when having sex."

"But I am so used to sex without a condom. Plus, it feels better."

"Michelle, were you not listening to anything my mom just said? We have to be more careful!"

"Okay, so no sex unless with condoms. Deal."

We shake hands on that.

"I should go get Carl from the airport. Let's talk later, okay?"

"Okay, Sis, see you later."

I leave Alexia's place, and soon my mind is on my younger brother and also on my boyfriend, Darius. It seems my conversation with Alexia and her mom has suddenly become another memory.

Chapter Sixteen

I am feeling really depressed today as I get off work and walk to the train station. *Why is this happening to me?* I keep asking myself. As I walk through the city's streets, I notice nothing. As I wait in line at my train stop, I think to myself, *I could really use some attention and comfort right now.*

I sit down by the window and stare out as the train pulls off. Then I feel someone sit down next to me. I turn around to glance at who it is. It is the pretty girl I flirt with during my commute to work.

She gives me a very warm smile.

"Hi," I say.

"Hi," she responds.

I never noticed how beautiful she really was, because she always sat a little distance from me. She has clear skin, long hair, beautiful eyes, full thick lips, and an elegant sexy figure. And she has an irresistible scent. Physically, she is flawless.

"It's nice to finally sit next to you. I was wondering when, or should I say if, we would ever get the chance to chat on the train," I say.

"The feeling is mutual. I have always liked the way you looked in your suit every morning," she replies.

Wow. This girl doesn't waste any time. She is already giving me compliments. "Thank you very much."

"You're welcome."

"My name is John. John Casey."

"And my name is Andromeda."

"Andromeda? You have a very exotic-sounding name."

She appears to be shy every time I look her in her eyes, and with my last comment, she looks away with a smile.

"So tell me, Andromeda, do you work in the city as well, and are you originally from these parts?"

"Well, I am actually not from this area. I came in from out of town, but I do work in the city."

"And what do you do here?"

"I work in the entertainment industry, in television, to be exact. I am a producer. And you? What do you do, John?"

"I work with sales. That's cool that you are a producer; it must be a thrill to work with so many interesting personalities."

"Thank you, but it's not all it's cracked up to be, believe me. It looks nice from the outside, but once you're in it, you get used to the way things work."

"I guess you're right. I would have to be in your shoes to understand what your experiences are." The train finally pulls into my stop. "Hey, listen," I say, "if it's okay with you, why don't we meet up for lunch or something sometime? Or maybe we could grab a drink after work? That'll give us a chance to finish our conversation."

"Sure, I don't see why not. You seem like a nice guy. Here, take my card and give me a call," she says, as she hands it to me. I take her card and bid her good-bye.

As I walk to my apartment, I think about what just happened. I had asked God to give me the chance to get to know this girl, and now here I was with her card in my hand! Interesting the way things turned out. I will be on my best behavior with this girl and not view her as a piece of meat for sex, as I have done in the past. For once, I will try to do something right. She seems like a good girl, so she might be worth it. I guess time will tell.

***

Work is going well today. I am not as stressed out as I used to be about my HIV situation. As a result, I have been sleeping better at night. Maybe that is because I am getting used to the situation. The mind is indeed powerful. About halfway through the day, Craig stops by my desk.

"Hey, John," he says.

"Hey, Craig, what's up, man?"

"Nada bro'. Haven't seen you in a while. How have you been?"

"I've been okay, I guess. Been running around doing this, doing that."

We chat for about ten minutes on trivial issues that befit an office setting. Then he gets ready to leave.

"Hey, John, I am having a little get-together/dinner at my place this weekend. Just having a few friends over, all good people. Why don't you stop by and join us? Don't think I've forgotten how you stood me up when I invited you to that party before!"

If he only knew! I would give anything to go back in time and go to his party, rather than sleep with Anna. If he only knew.

"Yeah, Craig, again, I apologize about before. Your thing this weekend sounds like a good idea. I should be able to make it."

"Good, that's what I like to hear, and you can bring a guest with you, if you like. You'll get a chance to meet some of my buddies and my girlfriend. But please, there will be enough guys there, and we would like a good ratio of guys to girls, so preferably bring a girl with you. That shouldn't be a problem for you, playboy."

I laugh at his playboy joke. "Okay, Craig, I'll see what I can do. Send me an e-mail with directions to your place, and I'll be there."

"Okay, John, will do. Got to get back to work now, buddy. I'll talk to you later."

"See you later, Craig."

I think I will go to Craig's get-together this weekend. And I will ask Andromeda if she would like to accompany me. She presents herself as such a lady, and she is very sexy, so I doubt Craig will have a problem with her. It will also give me a chance to get to know her a little better, in a nice environment. I have been avoiding friends for some time now; this will be a good way to let off some steam.

My brother Carl has been with me for some time now. He sleeps at my place, and during the day, while I am at work, he's out and about with some of his friends in the city. But that is the way it usually is when he comes to visit me. Typical little brother. But I am a little concerned about some of the guys he hangs around with while he's here. Two nights ago, I got home from work to find that he was at my place with a friend of his. I did not think anything of it; I just said hello and went to my room. I had made plans to spend the night at Darius's place, so I began packing a bag for my sleepover. I left Carl and his buddy in my living room. I went to go use the bathroom, and I mistakenly walked in on Carl's friend in the bathroom, and I was not too happy with what I saw. He had his sleeves rolled up, and I noticed a lot of scars on both his arms. The scars were very pronounced; in fact, they looked like someone had taken a knife and jabbed his arm many times.

I was not sure of what to make of them, but later, I described them to Darius, and he told me that usually if a person has such marks on his arm, that usually means that the person is an injection drug user and uses drugs like heroin. That news certainly alarmed me. I called Alexia to verify, and she confirmed Darius's suspicions.

Tonight, I am home extra early from work to confront Carl regarding the people he hangs out with. I wait for him in the living room. Soon, he walks in.

"Hey, sis." His breath smelled of alcohol.

"Hey yourself. We have to talk."

"Talk about what? What did I do this time?"

"I am a little concerned about you, Carl. Every time you come here to visit me, you always run off with these strange characters that I know nothing about."

"Michelle, you are not my mother, so stop addressing me as if I am your kid."

"I am not your mother, Carl, but I am your older sister, and you should listen when I show some concern for you."

"Listen, I came here on vacation. Why don't you let me have a good time before I go back to school? I haven't caused any trouble for you, have I?"

"This is not about your causing trouble, Carl. Last night I accidentally bumped into your friend in the bathroom, and I noticed scars on his arms that looked like he uses needles. And I asked my boyfriend about them and he agreed with what I thought."

"What the heck does your boyfriend have to do with my friends? Tell him to stay out of my business!"

"Stop trying to evade the question, Carl."

"No one is trying to evade anything. If you are asking me if I use drugs, I do not use drugs. I have smoked weed here and there, but I don't inject heroin into my system."

"But why are you hanging out with someone who does, Carl? How can I believe you when you spend all your time with such people?"

"Listen, Michelle, just because a person does different things than you do for fun does not mean that person is bad. You don't see me criticizing you when you get together with your friends and gossip about other people."

"I do not gossip!"

"Yes, you do. And for your information, I know many guys who do all kinds of things: smoke weed, heroin, even cook cocaine."

"Cook cocaine? You mean crack?"

"Yup."

"Great, my brother hangs out with crackheads. I am going to stop letting you stay here if you carry on with this behavior."

"I am not doing anything bad, Michelle. I told you—just because I know these guys doesn't mean that I go out and do stuff with them. And you know what? If you don't want me staying here anymore, that's cool. I have many friends in this city. I do not need to stay with you."

"Why don't you listen, Carl? You are going to destroy yourself. How could you hang out with crackheads and think that is normal? I saw your friend with injection marks on his arm, and you are telling me not to worry about you. These are your friends, Carl!"

"Michelle, you are overreacting. I am telling you that I do not do any crazy stuff. Now, I have to go. I made plans."

"Where are you going?"

"I don't have to tell you that."

"Yes, you do. You are staying with me."

"I'll be out with some friends."

"You have to give me a location, Carl. I have to know where you are going to be if you are hanging around crackheads all night."

"Michelle, I told you to let it go. I will be downtown somewhere, okay? Are you happy now?"

"Please don't hang out with those losers, Carl. I'm begging you; please don't."

"You know what? I've had enough of this. I'm leaving."

"Carl…"

He walks out and slams the door shut behind him. I proceed to cry for a bit, and after I compose myself, I call Alexia.

"Hey. I just spoke with my brother."

"Hey, Michelle. So is the guy a heroin addict?"

"I think so. He got really angry when I confronted him about it, and he just walked off."

"He just walked off? He didn't even talk to you for a bit?"

"Well, he did, but he was really defensive. He also said that he has a lot of friends who use drugs like crack."

"Crack? So what are you saying is that Carl is a crackhead now?"

"I don't know, Alexia, but I'm scared. I feel like I can't control him. I don't even know where he's going to be tonight."

"He's gotta be careful; hanging out with such people brings nothing but trouble, even if he is not doing anything with them."

"What should I do?"

"I have no clue. Try to talk to him in a less confrontational way when he gets back and see how that goes. He's your younger brother, so naturally he will be defensive when you confront him."

"I think I will do that. I will go see Darius now, so he can make me happy, because Carl got me in a really bad mood."

"That's a shame that you need a man to make you happy. I'm happy all the time."

"Yeah, right, Alexia. Plus, you don't have a brother who is a crackhead."

"That is true. Yeah, you have a lot on your plate. Maybe you should go see your boyfriend. Let me know how it goes when you talk to Carl again."

"Okay, I'll talk to you later."

"Bye, Sis."

We hang up, and I cry some more before I head out to Darius's apartment. I hope all this will turn out to be just a nightmare. But something tells me that the worst is yet to come.

Chapter Seventeen

Today is the day Craig is hosting his dinner gathering. I invited Andromeda to accompany me, and she accepted, so we are taking the train to Craig's place together. She is looking especially beautiful tonight; she has on a fancy dress and a fancy coat, and she is in heels. The gentle breeze plays with her long hair. That, combined with her charming, seductive smile, seems to make the whole package complete. I am amazed that I am even able to walk next to such a beautiful girl. Andromeda is the sort of woman you would see on television on the arm of some big-name actor or tycoon. And here she is, on my arm. I feel very special tonight. She has been very polite with me and has carried herself very well. I don't know her that well, but I am beginning to like her already. As we walk though the city this evening, we attract a lot of stares from many different people. Maybe they think I am a celebrity. A pretty woman can have that effect on an average mind.

We get to Craig's place in good time, and soon we are mingling with his friends and enjoying some good food and good wine. As expected, all the men (and even a few women, I'm sure) drool over Andromeda. But she seems to remain composed and in good character. I feel a tug on my shoulder, so I turn around.

"Hey, man, this is my girlfriend, Susanne," Craig says as he points to a petite lady next to him.

"Hi, Susanne, pleasure to meet you. I'm John."

"Nice to meet you, John. Craig speaks well of you."

"Really?" I reply. "I would never have thought that. Thanks for having my friend and me over here for dinner."

"You're very welcome, but you've not even introduced me to your friend," she says, as she points to Andromeda.

Craig's girlfriend is very elegant, and for some reason I feel at peace as she speaks. She speaks well and wears a genuine smile. She comes off as a simple person with a lot of class. Craig is a lucky guy. I call Andromeda over for introductions, and she slips under my arm. I feel good as she does that.

"Andromeda, these are my friends, Craig and Susanne; Craig, Susanne, this is Andromeda." As they say hello to each other, I take note of the difference in the respective auras that Andromeda and Susanne give off.

Andromeda is beautiful, stunning, a bit overwhelming, actually. She wears a lot of makeup, has on very trendy clothing, and looks very sexy. She has on jewelry and her dress is designed in such a way that flirtatiously reveals her cleavage and accentuates all her curves. I really do not mind looking at Andromeda.

Susanne, on the other hand, is dressed very casually, in plain jeans and a T-shirt. She is a pretty girl, and I am sure if she got dressed up, she would make heads turn as Andromeda does. Susanne is dressed down, but there is still something very sexy about her. I think it's in her speech, the way she talks with confidence, and her ability to make conversation. I look at Andromeda again. Andromeda purses her lips as she speaks and stands in a seductive manner, and it seems she is more concerned with how she looks than the actual conversation. Susanne, on the other hand, seems very interested in what is being said and makes interesting comments. And even though I do not know Susanne that well, I can see why any man would be attracted to her; she holds herself well and knows how to carry on a conversation. She kind of reminds me of my mother. She seems to have substance.

I snap back to reality and join in their conversation, and afterward, we have dinner over white wine. After dinner, we move to Craig's living room and begin to chat. I notice Andromeda continuously staring at me and smiling as the conversation continues in the background. I smile back. I think this is a good time for me to talk with her and explore her mind. I sit down next to her.

"Hey, you—having a good time?" I ask.

"Yes, I am. Your friends are really nice. You look really handsome tonight as well," she says as she delicately places her finger on my chin.

"Thank you, miss, for the compliment. You look beautiful yourself."

"Why, thank you, John. You're too kind."

She reaches for a glass of wine. This must be her fourth. We chat, all of us in that room together, and as we do so, I notice Andromeda's eyes begin to get glassy. I take that as a signal for us to leave.

"You ready?" I ask. She nods in response. I thank Craig and say good-bye to everyone there.

On the train, I talk to myself: *Okay, Johnny, you have this hot girl right next to you. Just take her home and then go back to your place. Do not let your penis think for you. Do not let your penis think for you. Do not let your penis think for you. Besides, she's had quite a bit of wine, and you have no business sleeping with a girl who's had too much to drink.*

I decide to talk to her some more and try to get my mind off sleeping with her. But just when I decide to do that, I feel her wet tongue on my neck. Uh-oh. I giggle because honestly, it does tickle, but also I'm considering what I am dealing with. This is the last position I want to be in. She is still licking my neck, and I must admit that it feels good. It feels so good that I am too weak to stop her, even though physically I am stronger than she is. My mind fails me. Luckily, we reach her stop promptly.

"Okay, Andromeda, this is your stop. You'd better get off now. If you want, I will walk you home." I literally have to force myself to say that.

She looks at me and gives a sly smile. "Nah, I want to go to your place." As she says this, she touches my thigh. Oh, boy. My heart tells me to tell her she cannot come to my place, but with her hand where it is, my body is too weak to say no. I set myself up for this. I say nothing, and I watch hopelessly as the train doors close and we proceed to my stop.

Okay, Johnny, I say to myself, *she'll come to your place. Maybe she is a little tipsy from the wine she drank. Just give her some coffee. You sleep on the couch and give her your bed, and everything should be just fine.* In reality, this probably will not happen.

We get to my place, and she immediately plops down on my couch. Good. Hopefully, she'll fall asleep, and I will be able to sleep without falling for this temptation. But I am wrong. As I am in the bathroom, preparing for bed, she comes up behind me and starts touching me in all my red zones. My resistance meter gets lower and lower.

"I want to give you a blow job, John," she whispers in my ear as she un-buckles my trousers. I want to stop her but it feels so good. The best I can do is talk.

"You don't have to do this," I whisper to her. "You don't have to do this, Andromeda." But when I look at her perfect face and perfectly proportioned body, it is hard for me to say no.

"C'mon, you'll like it." She begins, and it is the most pleasantly engulfing feeling I have experienced in a very long time. But my conscience kicks in. I muster all my strength, and stop her.

"Andromeda, please, I get really weak in these kinds of situations. You really don't have to do this," I say, knowing that I don't want her to stop.

"I want to do this, John," she whispers seductively in my ear. I can feel the wetness from her breath on my neck. "I have wanted you since the first day I laid eyes on you, and tonight you are going to screw me." She straddles me against the sink and raises her dress.

It's then that I realize she's not wearing any underwear. She grabs my manhood and tries to put me inside her, even though I have no condom on. I feel so weak at this point. There is a battle going on inside me; one side wants to satisfy a temporary pleasure and have sex with this girl, and the other, my conscience, tells me that this is not the right thing to do, especially after all I have been through. It's funny, but a couple of months ago, had I been in this same situation, I would have been the one being aggressive with her. But I slept with a girl who turned out to be HIV-positive. And I have to wait three months to know for sure what my status is. Therefore, if I sleep with this girl now, I am putting her in jeopardy, placing her in a risky situation that she knows nothing about. And if anything, that alone is morally wrong. I cannot be that guy.

Besides, the mere fact that this girl wants my manhood inside her without a condom on is a very bad sign. Who knows what she is carrying? If she is willing to sleep with me when she barely knows me, chances are she has done this before. And if she has done this before, and I stick my manhood in her, then indirectly that means I am sleeping with whoever else she has been with. On the other hand, I carried myself in the same manner only a couple of months ago. Sex is not just about the two people involved; it's also about whoever else they have been with, provided no protection was used. I mean, in all honesty this girl could have HIV herself. I cannot think with my penis. I have to be strong. I have to be strong. I have to be…"*Strong!*" I shout, as I shove her off me. I quickly go to my living room and stand by the window as I zip up my trousers, panting as if I'd run a five-mile race. I am not out of breath due to any physical strain, but my fight with my body's desires seems to have drained me.

I hear Andromeda behind me.

"Please, baby, I just want you to screw me. Please, baby, you know you want it." She touches my back and tries to touch my manhood. But this time I am ready.

"Stop!" I say firmly, as I take her hands off me and face her.

"You're weird," she says. "Do you know how many men would die to be in your position? I can have any man I want. You should be begging me to sleep with me."

I am appalled. Is this the same girl I met on the train, the same girl I thought was such a class act, the same girl who always carried herself well in public and who I never would have imagined would be so loose about sex?

"Andromeda, listen. I don't know what kinds of men you are used to dating, or what your preferences are when it comes to meeting people. But honey, you don't even know me. You've just hung out with me once and already you want me inside you, and to make things worse, you want me to sleep with you without a condom!"

She pauses and digests my comment. "No, I wasn't planning on sleeping with you without a condom; I was going to ask you to get one."

"Stop trying to defend yourself, Andromeda. You were literally fighting to have my penis inside you. If you are so willing to do this with me, how do I know who else you have done this with? How do I know how loose you really are?" My words seem to hit her, and hit her hard.

"I don't do this with just anyone. I have always had a boyfriend and practiced safe sex."

"Yeah, okay, Andromeda, and I was born yesterday. I expect you to defend yourself, although I don't know why. I am not attacking you; I am just stating the facts. After seeing you so many times on the train, I was hoping, one day, that I could get to know you and hopefully build something with you, but I can't do that if I feel that you open your legs to every man who catches your fancy."

"John," she replies, "I just wanted to sleep with you, and if something else happened, something else happened."

I look at her beautiful face. "Let me ask you a question, Andromeda. With all these boyfriends you say you've had in the past, were you always so open to sleeping without protection with them as well?"

"Well, they were my boyfriends and I knew them, so I hardly ever used condoms; maybe once in a while."

"So you think because someone is your boyfriend, that automatically makes him clean? How do you know who he sleeps with when you're not around? You should try to be a bit more careful, Andromeda."

She stares at me, and then she finally speaks. "You're crazy," she says. "I'll leave your place tomorrow morning, but I'll need a place to crash for tonight, as it's too late for me to go home."

"Sure, please use my bed; I'll be out here if you need me."

She says nothing and quietly walks into my room. I leave her there and lie on my couch, while staring at the ceiling. What a night. She said I was weird, but I feel good knowing that I did the harder right thing, instead of the easier wrong.

***

I wake up this morning to the sight of Andromeda's beautiful face staring directly into mine. I wish I could wake up every morning to such a beautiful sight.

"Hey," she says.

"Hey, you. Are you leaving now?"

"In a bit. I gave some thought to what you said to me last night, and I apologize if I made you feel uncomfortable."

"That's okay, Andromeda. Please let me at least make you some breakfast before you leave. It's the least I can do."

"Okay, sure. I'll stick around for a bit."

I freshen up in the bathroom, and then go into the kitchen to prepare some breakfast. Soon we're munching on pancakes, sausages, and eggs while sipping tea.

"John, I want you to know that I do not normally carry myself the way I did last night. I have not had sex in some time, and I have been really attracted to you for a while now."

"It's okay, Andromeda; what's done is done."

"You probably think I am a slut now."

"Do you really care what I think of you?"

She smiles at me. "No, not really."

"Okay, then, so let it go. No matter what happens, I hope we're still on good terms when you leave here."

"Sure," she says with a smile. "You're a really sweet guy. Anyway, I have to go. Thanks for the lovely breakfast." She kisses my cheek.

I say good-bye and then she is gone. I sit back down on my couch and grab a sausage while thinking about last night. A couple of months ago, I would have torn that girl apart. I am still amazed at myself that I was able to say no to having sex with a woman that good looking. But the fact is, I slept with a girl who turned out to have HIV. Even though the chances are that I am clean, I cannot go around sleeping with women until I know for sure. I should not put others at risk. And I have been praying to God to please spare my future from such a fate. Engaging in such activities does not help in my plea with God. Besides, this girl was so willing to let me insert my penis in her without protection. If she is willing to do that with me, who else is she willing to do that with? I would never have thought that a girl who carries herself the way she does would be so open to engaging in such risky behavior. She only knows me from the train. What if I'd decided to sleep with her and, God forbid, I actually had something? What if I had nothing, and she had something, and I decided to sleep with her? And the sad part is that there are a lot of people like Andromeda who are willing to sleep with partners they hardly know without protection.

That is one way that HIV is frequently spread.

Things have been not so good for the past couple of weeks. Carl has gone back to school, but for the last couple of days before he left, he and I were fighting more than usual. I kept telling him that I did not want him hanging around drug users, and he kept insisting that he was okay and not doing anything bad. But his behavior drastically changed, and he was behaving very rudely toward me, which was behavior I had never seen before. I can't explain it; I am just happy that he left, because it was beginning to get too much. All the drama. But I am still very concerned about him. Who knows what he is doing in school? Who knows if he is being up front with me when we speak? I guess all I can do is hope for the best.

Anyway, today I am at Alexia's place again. Miss Pryce will be leaving in about ten days, and she wants to see us all more often before she leaves. Today she's made dinner at Alexia's for us all, Jess included,

We are all chatting—and there is a lot to chat about. We are sitting around Alexia's small dining table. Miss Pryce serves each of us the pasta she made. Jess has no idea that Miss Pryce knows about her pregnancy. But Miss Pryce *does* know about my crackhead brother, I'm sure, thanks to Alexia. Alexia tells her everything.

"How is school, Jess?" Miss Pryce asks.

"School is fine, Miss Pryce. I am doing just fine. How are you?"

"Oh, I am very well, thank you. I don't feel like leaving because I am enjoying little Tara's company so much."

"Oh, Ma, you can take her with you. I could use a little break from being a mother," Alexia cuts in.

"Well, Alexia I took care of you without complaints, so you can do the same for your daughter, I am sure."

"I was just kidding, Ma."

"And how about you, Michelle? Alexia tells me that there are some issues you are trying to work out?"

"Yeah, my brother was hanging around with guys who I suspect use drugs, and that got me a little worried, so I have been trying to talk to him, but he does not listen. And that worries me."

"Why do you think his friends use drugs? Did you see them using drugs?"

"No, but she saw what looked like needle tracks on the arms of one of her brother's friends, and her brother himself told her that he hangs out with guys who do all sorts of crap," Alexia responds.

"Is this true, Michelle?"

"Yes."

"Then that is pretty serious. And you said that your brother argues with you when you bring it up?"

"Yes."

Miss Pryce begins to tell a story: "A few years ago I knew a young man, Quincy—a nice boy, who actually had a lot of promise. He used to hang around the rough kids in the neighborhood—you know, all brawn but no brains, those kind of guys. And he was trying to fit in, but he himself did not do anything bad, or so he claimed. One day he was driving around with one of these rough kids, and the police pulled his car over. And what did they discover? This kid that Quincy was hanging out with had bags and bags of drugs stashed in the car! So they both got arrested, and now, for the rest of his life, he has that tag on his name, that tag that says he was in a car with someone who was carrying cocaine. The law does not forget that, and neither do people."

"So what are you saying, Ma? That Michelle's brother should not drive around with these guys in case they are carrying drugs?" Alexia asks.

"No, what I am saying is that birds of a feather flock together, and if you hang out with a fool, the world will see you as a fool, and you will get a fool's treatment. And this doesn't just apply to hanging out with guys who do drugs but just anyone in general who doesn't do anything to help you advance in life. Just food for thought. Your brother should be really careful with these friends of his."

"Yeah, I have been trying to tell him, but he is very stubborn, and he doesn't listen."

"His mind is used to being in that state, perhaps, and young men like their friends. In many cases, they would do more for friends than they would for family," Miss Pryce replies.

"If I were you, I would be more radical about it. I would print out all the stats and things that could happen to a person on drugs and send them to your brother on a daily basis. That way, his mind will always have that voice of reason in it," Alexia adds.

"And that it's dangerous to be around a guy who uses needles. I think I read somewhere that you can catch HIV if you share a needle with someone who uses drugs in that manner," Miss Pryce said.

"Really? How?" I ask.

"Well, think about it, Michelle. Someone is sticking this needle directly into his bloodstream and then he takes it out and gives it to you, and you stick it directly in your bloodstream. You are coming into direct contact with his blood, in a sense. And if he has HIV or any other virus, guess what? You're placing it directly in yourself. So your brother should be really careful," Miss Pryce replies.

"She's right," Alexia adds. "You should really sit down and talk to your brother, and hope that he's not doing anything stupid."

"Yeah, I will. He can be a bit stubborn sometimes, but I will keep on trying."

"Good, you should. You young people seem to have a lot to deal with. I almost feel sorry for you. But a lot of it has to do with ignorance as well. Anyhow, good luck with your brother, Michelle. I hope everything works out."

"Thanks, Miss Pryce."

"You're welcome. So tell me, have you guys heard from your friend Anna?"

"Nope. I tried calling her a couple of times but she never called me back," Jess replies.

"Same here. It's almost as if she cut us off for no reason. I would be curious to see what she has to say if we see her again," I add.

"Take it easy on her," Miss Pryce advises. "Everyone is different, and I am sure she had her own unique way of dealing with the death in her family. You should respect that."

No one says a word. We spend the rest of the evening stuffing our faces with Miss Pryce's delicious cooking. For the moment, Carl and his crackhead friends are just a memory.

Chapter Eighteen

It's Monday, and my three-month time limit is coming to an end. I decide to see Sebastian at the clinic after I complete my volunteer assignment today. So, with the manager's approval, I head into the AIDS ward to pay him a visit. When I get to his room, I find him in bed, jotting down something on a pad.

"Hey, Sebastian," I say.

He looks up at me with a big smile. "Hey, John. How are you?"

"I'm good; can't complain. What are you writing there?"

"Just saving some memories; just saving some good memories. When you know your time is limited here, you begin to treasure thoughts, memories, and emotions At least I do. Whenever I remember a time in my life when I was happy, I save it right here in this notepad, and whenever I feel down, I open it and read any story and have a good laugh. Good strategy, don't you think?"

"Yes, good strategy. I like how positive you are. It's very refreshing."

"Thanks, John. And how are you doing?"

"Well, umm…I guess I am okay."

He looks me right in my eye. "That wasn't a very convincing okay, John. Is there something you want to talk about?"

I look at him and debate whether I should share my secret, my HIV crisis, with him. Then I realize that that is the whole reason I signed up for this volunteer opportunity in the first place. I decide to tell him.

"Well, I, um, how do I say this? A couple of months ago I slept with a girl without a condom; she turned out to be HIV-positive. I have been worried sick since I found out, and I've been trying to do everything humanly possible to ensure that the virus did not enter my body. But I am scared, Sebastian, and the main reason I started volunteering here was to meet someone who was dealing with such a virus, someone to help me figure out how best to cope, in case I find out that I am indeed HIV-positive."

His expression does not change as he looks at me. "I see. Wow, John, you should come around more often and share some more interesting stories with me."

"I am serious, Sebastian; this is not a joke."

"Okay, okay, sorry. I know that is a pretty serious situation. So let me get this straight: you want to know exactly how I deal with this situation?"

"Yes, Sebastian, if you don't mind."

The smile suddenly leaves his face, and he looks more serious than I have ever seen him before. "You know, John, I have known that I have been infected for a long time. I was in a relationship with someone for six years, and all the while she was HIV-positive, and I did not even know it. I felt I could trust her because we were partners. But I guessed wrong. I never bothered to ask her about her HIV status, or her STD status for that matter. This was ignorance on my part. The possibility is always there, no matter the situation."

"The possibility that your partner could have an infection, even though, emotionally, you guys trusted each other?" I ask.

He pauses for a second and ponders my question. "Yes, but also in a more general sense that anything can happen, at any time. This life is so unpredictable, John. For one thing, I would never have thought that I, of all people, would be sitting here at this time in my young life, in a hospital ward, covered with lesions all over my body, waiting to die. I always thought HIV was something that happened to other people. I always heard stories about it but never took them seriously. But now look at me, John, look at me." His eyes begin to fill with tears, and I suddenly feel so much grief for him. "I have one problem after the next, John. Today I might have a new lesion appear on my body; tomorrow I might develop a cold; the next day, I have severe aches all over; and the next day, it is something else. As soon as one problem goes away today, there is another waiting to pounce tomorrow. Another hurdle I have to overcome. But I guess life in itself is similar to my daily struggles; life is full of ups and downs."

"I am really sorry you have had to endure all this, Sebastian, I really am. And I apologize for asking you such a question and upsetting you. We can end this conversation, if you want."

"No, it's okay, it is important that we chat about such topics; it helps to put things in perspective for both you and me."

"I agree."

"Anyway, finding out you have HIV—or even worse, AIDS—is a very hard thing to endure. It's scary from a physical standpoint, yes, but it is even scarier from the social standpoint. It is inevitable that you will lose many friends and in many cases be treated as an outcast. With me, even my family has abandoned me. The only person who understood me, my mother, passed away when I was sixteen, and my father and brother refuse to have anything to do with me. But the fact is people like me have feelings, John, and we do not willingly decide to contract this virus. It either happens through ignorance on our part or through accidents. But I did not ask for any of this."

His story is heart-wrenching. "Again, I am sorry you have had to deal with all this, Sebastian."

"It's okay, John, there is no need for you to be sorry; you did nothing wrong. I know how I cope with it, and my method of coping may not be adequate for another person, as we are all different; you know what I'm saying?"

"Yeah, Sebastian, but you know, you seem so happy and content. There are people with fewer problems than yours who cannot smile and laugh the way you do."

"True, but don't be fooled, John; people have problems. They might not show it to you outwardly, but people have issues, man. Looks can be deceiving."

"Yeah, I guess you're right. We all have skeletons in our closets."

"We certainly do, John. Well, I try to see the value in everything I go through, with the time I have left. Personally, what makes me proud and keeps me going is knowing that I have taken so much pain, but I am still able to think positively. Not too many people can do that, and I pride myself on having the strength to be able to do so. My peace and my happiness are all I have left."

A sudden sadness creeps over Sebastian's face, and for the first time in a long time, I feel like crying for someone else. But I hold my tears back.

"John, I've lost a lot; my family has abandoned me, my so-called friends gossip about me, and I am a focal point in many negative conversations between people I know. My body is deteriorating, and I am slowly withering away. And what makes this situation at times unbearable is that I could have prevented all this from happening if I had just taken some time to discuss our sexual histories with my former partner before we got intimate.

"And every day I lie here and punish myself with the same phrase: 'if I had known...if only I had known.' But it's too late for that now, John. You get one chance, and when you blow it, you blow it. It does not matter if you're a good person or even if you're a saint. The real virus that killed me was not HIV but ignorance. Ignorance is something that causes so much unnecessary trouble in the world today, and I fell for it. So now I guess I am condemned to sit in this my bed and watch new lesions appear on my body. I wither away while jotting down past memories to bring me temporary pleasure but leaving long-term pain."

I feel so bad for Sebastian. Here sits a good man, stricken by life and by its uncertainty, feeling all hope is lost. I feel a certain responsibility to help him. I feel a responsibility to support my new friend.

"Hey, Sebastian, listen, man, like you said, life is full of ups and downs, and I cannot even begin to comprehend what it is that you're going through. I would have to be in your shoes, and ironically, it is for that reason that I am here. There is nothing anyone can say to make you feel better; I believe we can give you supportive words of encouragement, but it is up to you to take your life back."

"Take my life back?" he replies. "How can I take my life back, John? I lost everything because of one stupid virus and my ignorance. My life is finished, John. All I can do now is wait to die."

With those words, my mind quickly darts to Jerry. "Listen, Sebastian, let me share something with you. I have a friend back home who also had a life-changing experience regarding his health. He basically lost everything: his possessions, friends, and all. He also lost his eyesight, and his health is also deteriorating."

"Does he have AIDS as well?"

"No, he has severe diabetes, I think. But anyway, I see him on a frequent basis whenever I am home, and in a sense, he reminds me of you—or what you could be."

"What I could be?" Sebastian asks curiously.

"Yeah, Sebastian, what you could be. His name is Jerry, and I was having a very similar discussion with him some time ago. He was about to kill himself when he found a new life through helping people and loving God."

"God? What has God done for me but bring me so much suffering, John? I am beginning to question the relevance of God these days."

"Well, I do not have all the answers for you, Sebastian, but I will tell you this: life is much bigger than you, me, and anyone else. People suffer on a daily basis, some even worse than you are suffering now, believe it or not."

"I seriously doubt that, John," he fires back.

"You doubt that? Well, for starters, at least you have me to talk to. We are having a conversation, and we are, in a way, supporting each other. What about people out there who have absolutely no one to talk to? Or people out there who have no health insurance like you do—how can they afford medical care? Believe me, Sebastian, you are suffering, but things could be a lot worse."

He says nothing, but he stares at me attentively, so I go on. "God works in mysterious ways, Sebastian, and I may not know much, but I do know that it is when you feel all hope is lost, when you are put through the fire, that your true nature shows. This might be the best time of your life; you have the chance to really live and see what this life is truly all about, a privilege most people do not have, because most people, unlike you, would rather quit when under pressure than take the test." I pause, and think to myself, *Did I really just say all that? What is happening to me?*

Sebastian sits in his bed and stares at me with a blank expression. I notice that the look of sadness that was once there is now gone. I look at my watch. Time to go.

"Listen, Sebastian, I have to run. But I will see you again so we can talk some more, if you want. You clarified some things for me, and I am grateful."

128

He still has that blank expression on his face. I get up to leave. As soon as I reach the doorway, he calls after me. "Hey, John." I look back. "Thanks, man. Thank you very much. I'll be here, waiting for your next visit."

"Sure thing. See you around, Sebastian. And hey, listen, would you mind giving me some contact info for your folks? Maybe I can talk some sense into them for you."

He smiles at my offer. "Thanks, John, but it's really none of your concern—no offense. It's no use; nothing will happen, even if you tried. It's not your problem."

"No, seriously, Sebastian, I would really like to do this. It's the least I can do. Don't worry; I will not be rude or anything."

He sighs deeply. "Okay, what the hell—what's the worst that could happen?" He takes out a piece of paper and scribbles a number on it. "This is my father's number; you can call him Mr. Summers. You can try him, but I guarantee you that nothing will happen. You're wasting your time."

"You never know until you try, Sebastian."

"Trust me; 'trying' is something I have been doing a lot of. Before you go, John, let me ask you: what will you do if you find out that you're HIV-negative?"

I pause to think about his question. "I don't know. I will be very happy, I'll tell you that. I'll probably want to tell everyone I know, and I might even jump around and act crazy. And you, Sebastian, if you were in my shoes, what would you do?"

He smiles at me. "I would probably go for a long swim in a pool or maybe even the ocean."

"A swim? Why a swim?"

"Well, that was one of my favorite activities to do before I got sick. Of course, I can't swim now with all these sores on my body, but yes, I would go for a swim; being in the water puts me at peace."

"Hmm, interesting. I'll have to remember that. Swimming as a form of relaxation. Maybe I'll try it sometime. Well, I have to go, I'll see you around, buddy."

"I hope so," he replies.

I leave the clinic with a smile on my face, and on the way home, I suddenly feel so fulfilled and full of life.

"So you told your parents?"

"Yeah, they were a bit shocked at first, but they took it for what it was. I could tell that my father was a little disappointed, but my mother took the news better."

I've met Jess after work for some coffee at a café near my daytime job. She'd told me that she was going to speak with her parents regarding her pregnancy earlier today, and we agreed to meet here for all the details.

"Well, that's good then, if, in general, they were receptive to what you had to say."

"Yeah. Now my mom wants to meet Terrence."

"Who is Terrence?"

"The guy I have been sleeping with Michelle. Haven't you been paying attention?"

"Oh, yeah, sorry I forgot his name. Do you think he will be up for meeting your parents?"

"I think so. I have a feeling that my parents will like him. He has really been responsible about the whole thing. I am lucky that this happened with a guy like him, because I have heard so many horror stories about how men can be when it comes to unwanted pregnancies, so I am grateful that he has been so mature about everything."

"Well, that's good, then."

"I hope I have a boy. I like boys."

"No, you should get a girl."

"Michelle! What do you have against my having a boy?"

"I like girls better; plus, Alexia and I are curious to see what Tara will be like around babies."

"We'll see what happens. How is everything with your brother?"

"Okay. We've been talking on the phone, and he apologized for being rude to me the last time he was here. So we'll see. I tried talking to him about his friends, but he still was not giving me his full attention. I will keep on talking to him."

"Cool. I'm sure it will work out. And what about Darius? How is everything with him?"

"He is fine. We are doing great, and I am actually going to see him after I am done with you. We're going out for a walk through the city."

"Oh, that sounds so romantic. I'm jealous. You're so lucky to have such a great guy."

"I know I am, but thanks. I am just happy that I enjoy his company."

"Well, I hope that Terrence and I can do things like you and your boyfriend."

"I'm sure you already do."

We chat for a few more hours; then I leave to go see my boyfriend.

***

I meet Darius by a park situated downtown. He surprises me with flowers.

"Aw-w, baby! You're so sweet!" I exclaim as I kiss him and give him a hug.

"For you, I'll do anything. C'mon let's go for a walk."

We begin walking through the park, hand in hand. The cool air brushes against our faces and makes me get closer to Darius as we walk along.

"You know, we've been seeing each other for some time now, Michelle."

"We have."

"And I really like you—you know that, right?"

"I thought you loved me. Isn't that what you've said to me in the past? Or did you just say that to get in my pants?"

"C'mon, baby, you know I meant it."

"I know you did. Is there a point here? Where are you going with this?"

"Well, I just want to be sure what we have is real, you know. I know I've said that I love you, but I don't think you feel the same way about me, and I don't want to get hurt or anything like that, so that's what I wanted to talk to you about."

"But why do you think that I do not feel the same way about you? Did I say something to make you feel like that?"

"It's all in your actions, Michelle. Yeah, you say that you love me, but you only say that after I ask you. You have never proactively said that you love me without my prompting you."

"But Darius, look at how I treat you. I am with you all the time; we talk; I tell you personal things about me; we make love—what about all that hints at my not loving you? I don't get why you are talking like this."

"But I don't know, Michelle. I mean, I am a very nice guy, and I have been pretty honest with you about everything. I get caught up in emotions when I start seeing someone, and I hurt hard, so before I get caught up with you, I just want to make sure that we are on the same page. Is that fair enough?"

"That's fair enough, Darius."

"So are we on the same page? Do you love me?"

I think about his question and I feel slightly hesitant to answer. That can't be a good thing. "Are you seeing someone else?" I ask. "Are you just asking me all these questions to make me feel guilty for something I did not do?" Whoa. I can't believe that I just asked that.

"What?"

"Well, I don't understand, Darius. We have been having a great relationship. I have already told you that I love you, and then you come out of the blue and start asking me all these bizarre questions. How do I know you're not doing all this because you are cheating on me?"

"C'mon. Michelle, you know me better than that. You know I wouldn't cheat on you."

"And how do I know? You are a guy, aren't you?"

"I am a guy? What the heck are you talking about?"

I am so caught up in this façade I have built that I start to cry. I am a good actress. "You guys are all the same. When you start cheating, you also start with all your lies and try to make us women feel guilty. I am the one who should be asking if you love me, Darius, not the other way around."

"Michelle, I am sorry, I didn't mean to—"

"Just stop it, Darius. You hurt me."

"Michelle, I am really sorry. I didn't mean to make you cry. I am sorry. Please stop crying."

"You hurt me, Darius," I say as more tears spill from my eyes. I start to walk away, and he runs up behind me and holds me. It feels so good to have him hold me like that, my comforter.

"Michelle, I am sorry, baby. I honestly am not cheating on you. I was just asking these questions because I wanted to be sure about us. I've fallen for you, and I love you. I really do. Please forgive me."

His sweet words make me cry even more. I know I am acting, but his consoling makes me feel so good. "But Darius," I sob, "you shouldn't ask me if I love you if you know that I do. I don't know, Darius."

"I know, Michelle, and I am really sorry," he says as he kisses me again and again.

I feel so good in his arms, but I have to resist and put my foot down. "No," I say as I pull away. "I think we need a little break."

"A break? What do you mean a break?"

"I think we need some time apart, you know, to really think about ourselves and where we are headed. Maybe you're right in questioning me."

"No, no, no, Michelle. We are fine. I know you love me, and we are fine as we are. I don't want us to take a break. We are fine."

"I don't think we are, Darius, if, after all the time we have spent together, you can ask me such questions. I think we should take a little break."

"Michelle, please, I said that I was sorry. Please let's just forget what just happened and move on." He draws me close, and I almost melt in his arms. But I pull back. I can't be too soft around him.

"No, Darius. I love you, but I think we need a break. I want to do some thinking myself. I'll call you when I'm ready."

"Michelle…"

"Good-bye, Darius."

I start to walk away, and he walks after me. "Michelle, please…"

I hail a taxi and hop in, leaving him on the sidewalk.

"Michelle!" he says one last time, before the taxi drives off. I look back at him as he stands there all by himself, and I feel so guilty. I want to run up to him and hug him and not ever let go. At least now I am pretty certain that he is a good guy and that he loves me. But I think I will give him a little time to think about it.

Chapter Nineteen

I am heading home after work when I bump into a really old friend of mine from school, Cody. We used to work out in the same gym when we were in school. We decide to go for a quick drink so that we can catch up on old times. I have been trying to avoid friends, but I have not seen this guy in such a long time, so I obliged.

We go to a bar, get some beers, and begin reminiscing about old times. It feels good seeing my old friend. We chat for about an hour, and that's when I see the most beautiful thing I had ever seen in my life.

***

She could be of any nationality; she seems to be of a mixture of different backgrounds. She has long hair, all the way down her back. She has absolutely beautiful, tanned skin, full lips, and beautiful, deep-set eyes. I notice the way her eyelashes serve as beautiful doorways to her deep, calm eyes. She smiles as if she is aware of her body, but yet her mind is free to go wherever it pleases. In other words, as I look at her, it is as if her presence goes beyond this room, beyond this bar, with all its drinks and people talking about concepts that, in most cases, are irrelevant to the grand scheme we call life.

I notice her and her positive energy. Without saying a single word, she captures my attention, not by her good looks, because there are other good-looking women in the room, but by her presence alone. Her calm demeanor radiates and seems to fill the bar. She is a queen, and I know I am looking at a real woman. Cody is in the middle of a sentence when I notice her, and I do not catch the rest of what he says from that point on. This girl is gorgeous. But what I find most attractive about her was not her long hair, her perfect skin, her curves, or the nice clothes she had on. No, it is her deep-set eyes, her eyes that have "experience" written all over them. It is her calm demeanor as she walks about and smiles, while the guy she is with introduces her to various people. He seems to be an overprotective type, and he is very loud. He seems to want everyone to notice the beautiful girl he has on his arm. I enjoy watching her and think to myself, *Now, that's my kind of girl.*

Cody continues talking, but I watch her as she moves across the room. Soon, she sits down, looks up, and our eyes meet. We look at each other briefly, and it seems as if she is sizing me up. Surprisingly, I become shy and look away, while still smiling, then glance back at her. She smiles back at me. Wow. I have to talk to this girl. The only problem is that this guy friend of hers is in the way. What do I do? By sheer chance, the guy heads toward the bathroom at that moment. As soon as he leaves, I move toward her, feeling a bit nervous. I don't have much time; the guy will return any minute. Being out of time seems to be a norm for me these days.

"Hi," I say.

"Hi," she responds. I notice she is playing with a book of matches in her right hand.

"Was that your man?"

"Nah, just a date," she replies. "Is that *your* man?" She points to Cody, who is staring in our direction from his seat.

I laugh. This girl has a sense of humor. I like that. "No, that's not my man, nor is he my date. Good joke, though."

She laughs. "I hope I did not offend you, but that actually was a serious question."

"You did not offend me. I should know better. After all, this is the city." I love the way she speaks. She had a very mellow voice, and I catch a slight accent as well; it sounds like a mixture of British and Caribbean.

She also makes very calm hand gestures as she speaks. I think she is absolutely beautiful.

"Listen, I don't want to talk for too long, especially since your date will be back shortly. You think maybe I could call you sometime? Maybe we could do lunch or dinner?"

She looks at me, right in my eyes. I melt. "Well, I don't know you, and I don't really give out my number to people I don't know." She is testing me.

"Well, the whole point of my calling you, miss, would be to get to know you, but I would need your number to do that," I reply. I sense she wants to play hard to get with me a little while longer, but she also keeps glancing toward the men's room. She knows her date will be back any minute, so she gives in.

"Sure, I like your style. Considering the situation we're in, I don't see why we cannot chat later. But I will take your number."

Just as she is about to retrieve her cell phone, I notice her date heading back this way. Damn. I quickly walk back to my seat before he has a chance to see me, and he resumes his position right next to her.

She looks in my direction. I have to do something. I walk back to her table; her date is laughing profusely with another guy. I tap him on the shoulder. "Excuse me."

He turned. "Uh, what's up, man?"

"I was just wondering if you guys have some matches I could use to light up my cigarette."

The girl immediately hands me the pack in her hand. "Here, take these," she says.

I thank her as if I have never met her before and go back to Cody.

Cody has been watching the whole thing unravel, and when I get back to the table, he is smiling and shaking his head. "You haven't changed, have you, John?"

I smile at him without saying a word. As I open the book of matches, I notice her number written on the reverse side next to her name: Aurora. A smile comes over my face. Smart girl. As Cody and I leave the bar, she winks at me and smiles.

There is just something about this girl, Aurora, that is a little different. And it is not only a sexual attraction this time. I look forward to speaking with her again.

It's been two days since I walked away from Darius, and I miss him so much. He has been calling me at least every thirty minutes, but I don't pick up. Maybe taking some time off will make us think more about each other and make him want me all the more. You know, like they say, "Absence makes the heart grow fonder." But I won't spend too much time away from him, because he is a good guy, and I do want to keep him around. It's hard to find good guys like him these days; all men want to do it seems is have sex, so it's rare to meet a guy like Darius. I mean, he likes the sex as well, but he also likes spending time with me, and that's all I could ask for. My last boyfriend, Cody, was a really nice guy as well, but I couldn't sway him as easily as I can sway Darius. Cody. I miss him. But he's history, and Darius is my boyfriend now, so I cannot dwell on Cody. But now that he's come up in my mind, I can't help but ask myself who would make a better boyfriend? Okay, Darius has more money, and Darius is a better cook. Cody is more of the athletic type and is funnier. They both look good, and they both are good in bed. Darius is a sweeter guy, but Cody has a bit more edge to him. And I like both qualities. So I don't know; it would be a hard decision. Maybe I should ask Alexia and see what she thinks. I dial her number.

"Hey."

"Hey, Alexia, I have an update for you."

"You do? Do tell."

"I broke up with Darius."

"What? Why? I thought you were happy with him?"

"I was…I still am, but I decided to take a little break."

"Why?" she asks.

"Well, two days ago we were going for a walk, and he started asking me if I really loved him and saying stuff like I never tell him that I love him without his asking, and I don't act like I love him, and all this crazy stuff."

"Was he correct in saying that?"

"Yeah, he was actually. But I don't normally tell anyone that I love him!"

"But he's your boyfriend, Michelle."

"Yeah, I know, but then I started accusing him of probably cheating on me as the reason for his asking all those questions, and then I started crying, and I felt bad because I made him feel bad."

"So basically, you used reverse psychology on him. You made up stuff just to take the pressure off you."

"Yeah, something like that. I am a horrible person. Does this mean that I am a horrible person?"

"Yes, it does."

"I feel so bad, Alexia! You should have seen him as he was trying to console me! He looked so cute!"

"You're evil."

"No, I walked away, because I don't want him to feel that I am helpless around him. That'll make him want me even more, don't you think?" I ask.

"It could. From the way you describe him to me, it probably will. So what are you going to do now? Act as if you're single?"

"Yeah, I guess, but just for a little while. I don't want to lose him."

"If you do, that'll be two good guys you would have lost: Cody and him."

"Speaking of Cody, I was thinking about something before I called you just now. Who do you think would make a better boyfriend, Cody or Darius?"

"That's a good question. They are both cute. Darius seems more sophisticated and charming, but Cody has that street edge to him. I don't know; personally, I like guys with some edge, and I already told you that I liked Cody, so I would go with Cody."

"Really? But Darius is so cute! Are you sure Alexia?"

"Hey, you asked me for my preference, and I gave it to you. But you're with Darius now, and Cody's history. You should be happy that you're with a nice guy, unlike a lot of the jerks out there."

"Yeah, I know. What about you? Which guy is in your life now? You're a beautiful woman, Alexia, and I know for a fact that at least ten or more guys hit on you per day."

"Ha, I wish. More like three or four, Michelle. But none of them is worth it. All they do is shout after me and use these stupid lines. And then the presentable guys who do approach me nicely turn out to be jerks. So I give up."

"What about the last guy you were seeing that you told me about? Did you ever see him again?"

"Who? John?" she replies.

"Yeah, him. You stopped telling me about him."

"I stopped telling you about him because there was nothing to tell. I saw him a couple of times, and then he stopped answering his phone when I would call and would not call me back when he said he would. So I just left it at that."

"You think he lost interest?" I ask.

"I think he just wanted some easy sex. Plus, I told him that I had a child, as I do with every man that I plan on dating. I think that scared him off."

"I'm not surprised. What a jerk."

"Yeah…but guys like that always learn, he will probably have some out of this world experience that will make him start being nice to women" Alexia replies.

"There are some women who don't mind guys like that—take Anna, for example."

"Anna! Where is she? She just completely vanished off the face of the earth!"

"I haven't heard from her in a very, very long time, and I just hope that she is doing fine."

"You think she cut us off?"

"I have no clue Alexia. Possibly."

"But why would she do a thing like that? I mean, I know that she said that her family member died and stuff, but we are her friends. By now, everything should be back to normal. Remember that I told you I think there is more to her story? I still think there is."

"Who knows, Alexia? I guess when she's ready to hang out with us again, she'll make an appearance."

"I guess. You think she has a boyfriend? Girls usually get like that when they get a boyfriend."

"Trust me; Anna would have told us if she had a boyfriend. I don't think that's the reason we've not heard from her. Could be that she is out of the country. Could be that she is still depressed. Who knows?"

"Yeah, I guess, that's the thing about life and people, right? Who knows?"

We spend the rest of our time talking about Jess, Alexia's daughter, Darius, and my going back to school. And my cell phone keeps on ringing, but I don't pick up.

Chapter Twenty

I t's a little over two months since I had my incident. I got back from work not too long ago and said a few prayers to Jesus, asking for forgiveness and for direction. The phone rings. It is Al.

"How are you holding up?" he asks.

"I am okay, bro, just trying to stay positive."

"Good. Have you been praying?"

"Yes, I have."

"Excellent. I will be around your way sometime soon, and I'll stop by to check up on my little brother. You think you could make some time for me?"

"Absolutely, Al, just let me know when."

"Okay, I will give you a call then. I gotta go. Later, bro."

"Talk to you later, Al."

After our conversation, I go to my computer to do some more research:

"On average, each time a monogamous, heterosexual couple in which one partner is HIV-positive has sexual inter-course, the probability that the virus will be transmitted to the uninfected partner is 0.11%, according to an analysis of data from rural Rakai, Uganda. The probability rises significantly as the infected partner's viral load (the amount of virus in the blood) increases, and it is elevated if the HIV-positive partner has genital ulcers."

I didn't have ulcers on my privates, and I don't think Anna has any either. I read on: "In 2007 alone, about 33.2 million people were believed to be living with HIV worldwide and 2.5 million are newly infected." Thirty-three-point-two million! And two-point-five million newly infected! Those are big numbers. Huge numbers, in fact. And those are just reported numbers. This means that there are people walking around with HIV who probably do not even know it, and they might be infecting others on a daily basis. I may even know many personally. God forbid, but I might even be one of the newly infected 2.5 million! Knock on wood. This is horrible, and scary, too, once I begin to seriously think about it. Those with HIV may pass on this virus to others on a regular basis. And this puts others at risk. Anna did not know for sure. And I, John Casey, was exposed to it through her.

***

Today was a slow day at work. I have been in this office for some time now, and I speak to fewer and fewer people. That could also be because I can't stop thinking about this HIV situation. I rarely ever see Cesar these days, and that's good, because I do not feel like getting into discussions on the subject of females right now. As far as the work itself goes, I think I am getting bored of performing the same duties over and over again. Maybe I need a vacation.

Tonight, when I get home from work, I'm going to give Aurora, that girl I met at the bar, a ring.

***

I find the pack of matches with her number. I can still smell her perfume on the pack. Her phone rings twice, then she picks up.

"Hello?"

"Um, hi, good evening, may I please speak with Aurora?"

She puts on her sexy voice; she probably knows it is me calling—or whatever other guy she gave her number to since we met that night.

"This is she."

"Hi, this is John. I met you the other night." I describe our meeting at the bar and she remembers.

"Hi, John. I was actually thinking about how you ended up with my number. I thought it was cute the way it all played out."

"I thought it was hilarious that we pulled it off with your date right next to you."

"Yeah, well, he was no one important."

"So would you have given out your number if he had been your boyfriend?" I ask.

She giggles. "Probably not, especially since I wouldn't want my boyfriend, if I had one, doing that to me. But that guy was just a date, no one special."

"I see, good to know. By the way, you were looking absolutely gorgeous that night."

"Why, thank you!" she replies. We talk for a while and agree to meet for dinner on Saturday. I like this girl, at least so far. She is very pretty, has a lovely body, from what I could see, and seems to have her head on her shoulders. But looks can be deceiving. And this is the city, so anything is possible.

***

After I speak with Aurora I fall asleep for about fifteen minutes. I wake up around 10:30. I feel so restless, partly because I have so much on my mind. I go to my bathroom and splash some tap water on my face, then I stare at my reflection in the mirror over the sink. I smile, and my reflection smiles back at me. "If only I could be as happy as you are," I say. I walk back into my room and notice the piece of paper Sebastian gave me with his father's telephone number. Maybe that's why I couldn't sleep. I decide to give him a call, despite the fact that it is almost 11:00. I dial the number, and the phone rings three times.

Then an elderly male voice answers, sounding stern and angry. "Hello?"

"Yes, hello, my name is John Casey, and I was wondering if I could speak with a Mr. Summers?"

Brief silence.

"This is Mr. Summers. Who is this, and what are you calling me for?"

I ready myself to say what I have to say. "I am calling with regards to your son, Sebastian."

Another brief silence.

"Yes, what about him?"

"Well, sir, I have been visiting Sebastian in the clinic, and he seems to be a bit lonely. He also mentioned to me that he hardly speaks with his family, so I felt the need to contact you. Sebastian really needs people around who care about him at this time, sir." I hope I sound convincing.

"I see. Listen, Mr. Casey, with all due respect, I appreciate what you are trying to do, but Sebastian is not a part of our family anymore. He has AIDS, and he cannot put other people in our household at risk. We send him post-cards and the like, so that should keep him entertained. And second, what happens within our family is none of your business."

"Yes, sir, I know it is none of my business, but then again, someone I have come to know is suffering, not just physically but also emotionally, partly because his own family refuses to even visit him."

"I told you, Mr. Casey, that he is not part of our family anymore."

"Of course he is part of your family!" I fire back. "You gave birth to him, didn't you? Listen, Mr. Summers, all I am asking is that you visit him once in a while so he does not feel so alone, that's all."

Mr. Summers sighs deeply. "Listen, our family has been through a lot of rough times, and Sebastian's case has not made it easier for us. The chaos with Sebastian started soon after his mother passed away. Things have calmed down since we placed him in the clinic, and we would prefer for it to stay that way. Sebastian has AIDS, and I do not want anyone in our family to be exposed to it and go through what he is going through."

"But sir, from what I understand, you can only catch AIDS through the exchange of bodily fluids, in most cases, so I don't see how simply visiting your own son would place you at a risk of acquiring the virus! If—"

"Stop right there!" he fires back at me. "I just told you that this conversation is over, and I was trying to end it in a polite manner, but you are pushing me. Now, I do not even know who gave you the authority to call my home at such a late hour. This conversation is over. We provide for Sebastian in an adequate fashion, and your concerns, while appreciated, are not needed. Please do not call this number again. Thank you."

"But sir, I—" I hear the click as he hangs up on me. I let out a deep sigh, then go back into my bathroom and put splash more water on my face. I look at my reflection in the mirror, but this time it isn't smiling back at me. How could a father—or any parent, for that matter—reason in such a way about his child? It just made no sense; it made no sense at all.

I am standing by an available table at my night job at the Ethiopian restaurant. There are not that many customers here tonight; only two tables are taken, and the customers at one of them are getting ready to leave. Normally, I would go to Darius's place after work, but we are still on our break. I miss him, though.

Cody. I have to admit that since Alexia and I spoke about him, he has been on my mind, and I am curious to see him again. I wonder if he has a new girlfriend. And I am curious to see if he is over me yet. But I can't call him; it's been so long since we last spoke, and we didn't break up on the best of terms. This really sucks. I retrieve my cell phone and pull up his number. I get this funny feeling in my tummy as I look at it. Should I call him? What on earth could I say? "Hi, Cody, I know it's been, like, over a year, how are you doing?" I feel so stupid, but I do want to call him. I look over at the remaining table, and the customers there are talking and laughing, so I don't think that they need me to get anything just yet. I have time to make my phone call. I take a deep breath, then dial Cody's number. It rings once, then twice, then—

"Hello?"

I hang up. Hearing his voice made me really nervous. But he would know that it was me calling, so I have to call him back. I call him again.

"Hello? Michelle?"

"Hi, Cody."

"Why did you hang up the first time?"

"Oh, I dropped my phone," I lie.

"Oh."

"How are you?" I ask.

"I am fine, doing well, thanks. And yourself?"

"I am well, thanks."

"So to what do I owe the pleasure of your call?"

"I just wanted to see how you are doing, Cody."

"That sounds very strange, coming from you."

"C'mon, Cody, I hope we are still friends. I was just calling to see how you are doing."

"I am fine, I guess, still doing the same old. How are you?"

"I am okay. I'm at work right now. There are not too many people here today, so I have some time to kill."

"Oh, yeah, the restaurant. I have missed eating there."

"You should come around and eat sometime, on me."

"Michelle, what's going on?"

"What do you mean?"

"I mean, I have not heard from you in so long after we broke up, and you just call me out of the blue, asking me how I am doing. Wouldn't you find that a bit strange, if you were in my shoes?"

"I understand where you're coming from, and trust me, there is nothing sneaky going on. I just wanted to see how you are doing."

"After all this time, you're just now calling me to see how I am doing? Are you kidding me? What's this all about?"

I feel butterflies in my tummy. Maybe I am not over Cody yet. "Listen, Cody, I know we split on not so good terms, but we did have some good times together—even you can't deny that—and I don't want to lose touch with you, because I think you are a great person, that's all. There is no reason for you to get defensive."

"I am not being defensive, Michelle. You hurt me once so I am just being careful."

"How did I hurt you? You were cheating on me, Cody! The whole entire eight months we were seeing each other, I know you were seeing someone else. That's why you kept on bringing up my working long hours and stuff like that, to take the attention off you and your cheating."

"You and your drama. And who is this mysterious girl I was seeing? You have yet to tell me her name. Do you even know who she is? Who is this girl? I would like to meet her."

"It's okay. What is done is done, and I've moved on."

"You're crazy, Michelle, you really are. You call me out of nowhere to tell me all this nonsense? Are you nuts? I've told you before that I never cheated on you, and I still maintain that you put your work and personal preferences over simply spending time with me. And I can't deal with a woman like that."

I still feel those butterflies in my tummy. "Okay, okay, okay, maybe I overreacted a bit. Can we just move on, please?"

"Move on to what, Michelle? We have nothing. I am not sure what you plan on moving on to. If you're asking if we can get back together, that's not happening. Like I said, you're crazy."

"Are you seeing someone now?"

"That's none of your business."

Ouch. That stung. "Fair enough. Can we at least get together for a drink or maybe some dinner? I promise I will behave. We will just hang out as friends."

"Michelle, whatever you have up your sleeve is not going to work. Sure, we can meet for a drink and chat, but that's about it. I am just letting you know how it is going to be between us from now on."

"Okay, sounds fair enough. So what time works for you? And what do you want to do? How does dinner sound?"

"We can do that, as friends. I am not sure how this week or the next looks, but I will send you a text message and definitely let you know when we can meet. I will let you know in a few days when I know what my schedule looks like."

"Okay, Cody, I'll wait for your message then. It was good talking to you again."

"Likewise. I gotta go. You'll be hearing from me. Bye."

"Bye."

Our conversation ends. I have to admit that talking to him got me a little excited. I am curious to see how it will go between us when we meet. I know he still likes me; if he didn't, he wouldn't have answered the phone. I have to prepare for him. I'll have to ask Alexia what sort of things to say, how to dress, how to smile. I am really excited. The last customers are ready to leave and signal me for the check, and I head over to take care of them and end my day. I am smiling and still have that funny feeling in my tummy. I can't wait to see Cody.

Chapter Twenty-One

As soon as I wake up today, I decide to play my raffle game. I shake the cup with the pieces of paper in it and close my eyes as I pick a random piece. I open it. No red H. Phew. Lucky again.

It's Wednesday, and I decide I will go home immediately after work and be in some good company. A conversation with Al and my mother sounds really appealing. So, after work I catch a train back home. When I get there, it seems no one is home, so I let myself in with my spare key. I call for Ma and Al, but no one responds.

They must have gone to the store, I think. *I'll just sit tight and wait until they return.* I sit down on the sofa in our living room, and it is then that I notice a figure lying down on another couch adjacent to mine. Dad. Apparently, he is taking a nap. I wasn't aware that he was back from his trip to Korea. He rarely hangs out in the living room, so what is he doing here?

"Hi, Dad, how are you?" I say.

He sits up and looks at me dead in the eye. I shiver because I feel ashamed that he might have been informed about my predicament. "I am fine, son. Your mother told me what happened. How are you holding up?"

Suddenly, I feel embarrassed. "I have been very worried for the past month, maybe even two; I've lost track. I am a mess. I have not been able to work well, and I can't seem to fall asleep. I tend to be careful around my friends, and basically, I am a nervous wreck. I cannot bear the fact that I might have HIV. That is something you hear about but never expect to happen to you. I am mad at myself, but at the same time I feel it is not fair what I am dealing with. I just don't know, Dad."

He continues to stare at me, a look of concern in his eyes.

"Well, son," he begins, "life is full of trials and woes. It's full of tests, failures, and victories. It is unfortunate that the girl you slept with turned out to be HIV-positive, but you need to see that as a warning sign for you and not a condemnation."

"Dad, I have been through so much stress because of this issue, and I wish I had never even met that girl. I had the worst luck of my life that night."

"Well, son, personally, I do not believe in luck. If it happened, it was meant to happen. Everything happens for a reason; we are all part of God's grand plan. You may not know the reason until years from now."

"I have been praying to God about it, Dad," I reply. "I have asked God to please help me. Ma and Al suggest that I ask through Jesus Christ, but I have always been skeptical about religion and its rituals. No offense."

"I see," he replies. "Well, look at it this way—what do you have to lose? At this point, you want every positive energy available working in your favor. You spoke to the doctor and he can't help you. You spoke to friends and they can't help you. Even we, your family, can only provide you with some level of comfort, but ultimately, we cannot solve the problem for you. Now you are questioning Jesus, and you are wondering if praying through him is the right thing to do. And you will question and question, as do most people who find it hard to see the truth.

"If you question the entire time, son—and this is wisdom, so pay attention—if you question all the time, you will do just that: question all the time and never find answers for yourself. This applies to anything in life. You cannot understand a concept, an experience, or a fact if all you do is question it and make assumptions. Remember: from assumptions come stereotypes. You have to experience it for yourself, and then draw your own conclusions. Sometimes risks and leaps of faith are necessary steps we have to take in this life, in order to see the big picture."

It was refreshing to receive wisdom from my father.

He went on, "Has God given you a list, John, of the right and wrong ways to pray and approach Him? I mean, has God come to you personally?"

"No, Dad."

"So what do you have to lose by doing it in the name of Jesus? Your overall objective is to approach God, and as Christians we have accepted that only through Jesus can we approach God Almighty. It is good that at least you agree that God is in control, but from your questions about your experience, it does not seem as if you're getting answers to all your questions. And that hints to me that you do not have a relationship with God."

"I do have a relationship with God, Dad. I ask Him all the time to help me and to protect me."

"That is not a relationship, son. That is you asking all the time like a spoiled child. If you had a friend, would you like it if every time you spoke to him, all he did was ask you for money or favors? You eventually would not be so keen on hearing from him! A relationship works both ways. You ask, yes, but you also have to serve and obey God's rules."

"Dad, I am a good person. Okay, so maybe I have been with one or two women. The average man today is even worse than me! Well, maybe not. The fact is, I did what most guys and girls do, and I unfortunately was just unlucky. That does not warrant being punished by having HIV! If, besides my sexual exploits in the past, I have been a good person, what has God done for me in return? Put me through all this stress!"

My dad shook his head. "First of all, I told you before that I do not believe in either good or bad luck. I believe what happened to you happened for a good reason. Maybe it was to open your eyes to God, maybe to clean up your act, maybe to punish you—who knows? I cannot answer that question, as I am not God. And second, you asked what has God done for you. Well, for starters, you are alive, son. You are breathing. You had food this morning. You did not have a problem getting here today. And it is not certain if you have HIV. In fact, studies show that it is likely that from your situation you do not have HIV. You were just in a risky situation, a very risky situation. That is just like my putting a bullet in a revolver with ten or more slots and telling you, in a couple of months we are going to point the revolver at your head and squeeze the trigger. I am sure you've heard of the game called Russian roulette. The odds of your getting shot are slim, because there are ten or more slots and only one bullet, but no one wants to gamble with their life like that in the first place!

"So, yes, it is a nerve-wracking situation, I am sure, and I cannot even begin to understand how you feel. But you are not condemned yet, if at all, so you have to think positive. Things could be a lot worse, John. You have it pretty good with the life you have here. For example, you think life is this easy in other parts of the world? You think in some parts of the world that men have the luxury of sleeping around with women as you did? There are places where men your age wake up with a gun to their heads, and live in fear of death on a daily basis. In such places, they don't play the game of Russian roulette and gamble with probabilities; in such places they actually get shot. You don't have to worry about that. You were born in this free society, but you take everything for granted. So I think that alone is enough reason to thank God."

He is right, I realize. I have had a pretty good life thus far. Compared to others my age and even younger, I've had a really good life. I should learn to start putting things in perspective.

He gets up and strolls into the kitchen, then proceeds to prepare two cups of tea. I pull up a stool and settle near him.

"You see," Dad continues, "to have a mere understanding of God, you have to be able to put things in perspective and learn to see the big picture. You were born, and you have grown up to be the young man you are now. You have had unique experiences all through your life that have shaped you into who you are today. You have emotions; you feel things that go beyond mere physical explanation: intuition, love, fear, courage, purpose—traits that science and other fields try to explain through mere human understanding but cannot.

146

"This is why your situation is unique, son, because usually in life, when people are backed up against a wall and have no one to turn to and nowhere to hide, it is then that they have only two choices: turn to God or take matters into their own hands. They turn back to the source, which is God—either that, or they go crazy, go on drugs to ease the pain, or worse yet, kill themselves. There are many people who have been in your shoes and did not have the attitude you have about trying to be logical and fighting the problem. Instead, they have taken their own lives, or gone into severe depression, or some other negative thing.

"God is real, John. Look at the flowers, unique in themselves. Better yet, look at human beings, with all our unique features and differences. No one set of fingerprints is the same between two people. There are different thought processes for each individual, and we all make different and unique journeys through this life. What generated all this magnificence in creation?

"If I were you, son, if I were drawing up a battle plan to tackle your problem, the first thing I would do would be to go to the source and ask for help. God created all things and all processes. He is the beginning and the end. If God created this world and everything in it, I don't see why God cannot show you mercy—if you go about asking for it in the right way."

"And that's what I have a problem with, Dad. How can you be certain that going through Jesus Christ is the right way?"

He pauses and looks at me seriously. "Well, son, I know because I had some faith and asked God to show me the right way to go. And God revealed Jesus Christ to me through the many life experiences I have had, and I have been content ever since. My belief in Jesus and God is based on my personal life experiences, not what can be explained through mere human rationale. It is based on feeling and faith, not numbers and words. But that is my own unique experience. You have to experience God for yourself. I know Jesus is real. I experience His love every day, but there is no way I can convince you of that by just telling you. If you want to know Jesus the way I do, just have a little faith that He is real and ask for guidance and mercy, and most importantly, ask for Him to reveal himself to you. Besides, the way I see it, your options as to what other alternatives you have are very slim.

"Give it a shot, John. If you value my recommendation, give it a shot. It's a win/win situation, so you have nothing to lose by asking Jesus for help. Don't just sit there and feel sorry for yourself, accepting the unfortunate hand that life has dealt you. If it doesn't work out, then at least you will know you tried, and you didn't just sit around being miserable, questioning and blaming everyone while doing nothing. And keep in mind that God has a unique plan for you. You may ask for something that appeals to your human understanding and that may sound right for the moment, but God knows all things and ultimately knows what's best for you. Your answer may not come in the way you planned. You can try other things if you want. You can sit and cry in your little apartment; you can keep on talking to me and questioning me; you can even join a yoga class or take up a hobby to take your mind off your issue. You can do all these things, and they might bring you temporary relief, but they don't solve the problem. And remember that you have limited time before you test again, so be sure to make the right decisions in terms of what you decide to do. Trust God, and have faith in Jesus, and all will be well."

He holds out a cup to me. "Here, have some tea."

As I sip Dad's tea, I meditate on his words. It all makes sense. Well, sort of, given my limited understanding of life. But Dad's right; only God can help me now.

"Okay, Dad, I will give it a shot, but what am I supposed to do?"

"First of all, don't approach it with that attitude. You are in no position to 'give it a shot.' Your only option is to not only to save yourself but also to have your eyes open and truly understand the world in which you exist. God does not owe you anything, and He does not have to fix up your mistake. You made the mistake, not God. In fact, God gave you rules through the Bible to help you avoid making such mistakes."

"But, Dad, as a man—and I am sure you will understand what I am about to say—as a man, especially in today's world, it is so hard to look at a woman and not have carnal thoughts. This is not the same world you grew up in, Dad. Sex is thrown in our faces everywhere we go, from the media to the way women dress and carry themselves. With my situation, Dad, this girl had everything that appealed to me sexually, and I tried to do things the right way. It is not my fault that the condom broke. So, yes, I made a mistake by going to her place and doing what I did, but I couldn't help it."

"Son," he sighs, "there is so much you have to learn about yourself as a human being and about yourself as an entity. Most people are absolutely clueless as to what life is really about. But I will explain that to you another time. To answer your question, yes, I agree with you that the world has become a very sexually immoral place, among many other things. All men experience what you experience, including me. Yes, I, too, am tempted to look at women and think all sorts of things. But succumbing to my flesh, to my body and its desires, only leads me to a dead end. Look at how your body has deceived you! You thought you were going for a night of pleasure, but that has now turned into months of pain. That is the risk associated with succumbing to the flesh: short-term pleasure for long-term pain.

"Now, by God's grace, there is nothing wrong with you. But for the sake of this conversation, look back at your decision-making process when you decided to go see this girl. You were powerless against your bodily desires! It is a blessing that you actually asked the girl to get tested. Most men would not have gone that far, so you should see that as a good sign. Son, nothing worth having is easy; I am sure you've heard that before. Easy sex is not worth having, and you have had to learn that the painful way. But at least, now you know."

"Okay, Dad, you're right. Do you have any rules you observe in your faith with regard to this problem?"

"Son, as a Christian man and as a smart man, the only rules I have and need are in the Bible. The Bible is man's instruction manual, God's rules and regulations that He gave us to know what to do and what not to do. Every human dilemma you can imagine is discussed in the Bible. It has rules and regulations, and just like any set of rules, when you break them, chances are you will get caught and pay the consequences, just as you are doing now."

I think about what he just said. "Damn, Dad, but following the rules in the Bible is so hard, especially when you live in an environment like the city!"

"Well, son, remember what I told you: nothing gotten easily is worth having. The rules are there for a reason, and if you break them, be prepared to face the consequences. But for now, if I were you, I would slowly try to wean my eyes off the sexual attributes of certain women and instead, try to get to know them for who they are. It's not easy, I know, but you have to try, and you can only be successful by asking the Holy Spirit to help you. Remember, son, all this stuff is in the mind. You only think you need to have sex so much because that is the world you live in. Let's say a prayer and wrap this up. I have work to do."

"I can't believe you called him!"

It is Wednesday, and I am home from work, having my regular evening chat with Alexia. I just broke the news to her about my calling Cody.

"Was he nice to you?" Alexia asks.

"Yeah, he was, same old Cody, always defensive."

"What did you guys talk about?"

"Well, we argued for a bit, which was to be expected, and then we talked, but not for too long."

"You still didn't answer my question: what did you guys talk about?"

"Just stuff, Alexia, nothing important, just stuff. He was still trying to defend himself and still trying to say that he did not cheat on me."

"But Michelle, like I told you before, you don't have any proof that he did."

"C'mon, Alexia, c'mon. You know that whenever guys start questioning you and stuff and putting all kinds of blame on you, it usually means that they are cheating on you. You know this."

"Hey, you can't just jump to that conclusion, Michelle. You said Cody was concerned about not spending enough time with you. Maybe that is exactly what is was, that he was concerned about you guys not spending enough time together."

"Or maybe he is just a damn liar. You can't just take everything a guy says as the truth, you know."

"You're nuts, Michelle, but that's why I love you. So enough on the past. What are you going to do when you see him? What are you guys going to do?"

"Not sure yet; we talked about having dinner or maybe getting a drink, so we did not plan anything official."

"Why not?"

"He said he was busy and that he would send me a text message when we can meet."

"Are you going to try and sleep with him?"

"We are just meeting as friends, Alexia."

"I know you. You are going to try and sleep with him. You won't be able to resist."

"Be quiet. Okay, fine, maybe the urge will be there. So what? I mean, the guy used to be my boyfriend, right? I am already comfortable with him, and I have slept with him already, so I know what that feels like."

"But how do you know he is not sleeping with someone else? Did you ask him?"

"He said that it was none of my business."

"Ouch."

"Yeah, that hurt, but I took it well. I don't think he has a girlfriend right now. If he did, he wouldn't have agreed to see me for dinner."

"Hey, guys are guys. How do you know he may not be looking for some quick action?"

"Quick action?"

"Yeah, you know, sex."

"I doubt it. Like I said, I know he likes me."

"Well, I guess we'll find out. And what about Darius?"

Darius. I'd forgotten all about him. "Umm, Darius? What about him?"

"Well, he was your boyfriend until recently. Don't you feel any guilt for planning on sneaking around with Cody?"

"I will not be sneaking around with Cody, and nothing is going to happen. We will be meeting as friends, to just catch up."

"You're so full of crap. You and I both know that is not going to happen."

"You obviously don't know me that well. I will be fine."

"I know you too well, Michelle, but like I said, I guess we'll find out. Okay, enough on men. Have you spoken with your brother lately? How is he doing?"

"He's okay. The last time I spoke with him we got along, and he was listening to everything I said, so I will take that as a good sign."

"Okay. Listen, with Cody if he doesn't text or call you by tomorrow, I think you should drop the whole idea and get your mind off him, at least till he calls."

"Why?"

"Because you just broke up with another great guy for very stupid reasons, and you might want to work on salvaging what's left of that relationship, rather than chasing after your past."

"But Darius is too nice. I don't like guys who are too nice."

"No one is perfect, Michelle, not even you. You have to accept people for who they are."

"Aww, Alexia, why are you always giving me a tough time? Okay, okay, I get the point."

"Hey, I am just trying to be a good friend, and being a good friend does not mean I will always tell you what you want to hear."

"Thanks, Alexia. But for now, I am excited about Cody, and you have to help me with handling him."

"I'm always here for you, Michelle."

"Okay, I gotta go, but as soon as he sends me a message, I will call you."

"Okay. Bye, Sis."

"Bye."

We hang up, and I think about what Alexia said. Does she have a point? Should I change my behavior toward Darius and my aspirations for Cody? Are my actions making sense?

I don't feel bad about anything, if that is what she is asking.

Chapter Twenty-Two

It is Saturday evening, and exactly two months and two weeks since my incident with Anna. I have two more weeks before I go in to get tested. I'm sure these will be the longest two weeks of my life. I had been avoiding women and saying my prayers regularly—up until last week, after which I began losing my motivation to pray. I wonder why? I will have to ask Dad about that.

I wake up this morning and see that I have a rash developing on my left arm. Immediately, I start to think of all sorts of possible causes of the rash: Could it be there because I really do have HIV? Could my body's immune system be weakening, therefore allowing a rash like this to pop up? Could I have an STD? Or could it just be stress? I worry myself sick from all these questions. I worry myself from analyzing all these *possible possibilities*. I get dressed, and put a Band-Aid over my rash. I hope it's just a fungal infection or just stress.

Tonight, I have a date with Aurora, the girl I met in the bar. I have to try to comport myself, even though I might be tempted to talk about my problem and seek comfort. I have to remain objective with her. We're meeting for dinner at an Ethiopian restaurant she recommended on the eastside of the city.

I get there first, seat myself at the table we reserved, and wait. I don't know; there is something familiar about this particular restaurant. Twenty minutes later, she walks in, looking as beautiful and elegant as ever. I feel honored to be dining with such a pretty lady.

"Hi, John" she says.

"Hey, you," I reply, as I watch her sit down. She smiles at me. I notice she has the same smile that Craig's girlfriend, Susanne, had. And she carries the same aura as well.

"How are you?" I ask.

"I'm good. Sorry I'm late. I was doing girl stuff."

"That's okay. I knew you'd be late."

"You didn't know anything, smarty pants. By the way, you look good tonight, sir."

"Why, thank you, miss. You look elegant yourself. Anyway, let's order dinner, shall we?" We give our orders to our waitress, and then delve into conversation.

"So, where are you from, Aurora?"

"Well, my parents are Jamaican, Italian, and Hawaiian, but I was born and raised here. I live right here on the eastside of the city."

"So, that explains your good looks."

"Thank you, John. You're not so bad yourself."

Our waitress arrives with our food, and we begin to eat. As we chat over the tasty meal, two gentlemen walk in and seat themselves at a table adjacent to ours. One of them begins talking out loudly and waving his hands in a flamboyant manner. This catches our attention.

"He's being really rude, talking so loudly," I say.

"Yeah, and he needs to stop waving his hands around so much. He might hit his friend in the face," Aurora giggles.

"You have a problem with gay people?" I ask.

"Well, how do you know he's gay? Just because he's flapping his hands around does not mean he's gay."

"C'mon, Aurora, that man is gay. Look at him."

She glances at him. "Yeah, okay, maybe he's gay. I don't have a problem with gay people. Do you?"

"No, I have never really thought about the issue. I don't think I have a problem with gay people. If that's what you do, that's what you do. I guess everyone is entitled to do whatever they want in this society. I am not gay myself, nor will I ever be, but if you enjoy homosexuality, whether you are a man or a woman, I would just be sure not to put your partner at risk." My mind suddenly darts back to all the research I did on HIV.

"Put your partner at risk?" she repeats. "What do you mean?"

"I mean in terms of getting him or her sick with HIV or STDs."

"But you can get such things from heterosexual sex as well."

"Of course, but anal sex tends to be associated more with homosexual men. I read somewhere that HIV is on the decline among heterosexuals but on the rise among homosexuals, particularly gay men. Now, I am not condemning gay men; I am really not. I don't want you to get the impression that I am homophobic or something."

"Are you?" she asks.

"No, Aurora. I am not homophobic, and I didn't make this up either. A lot of women these days who get infected catch viruses, whether STDs or HIV itself, from bisexual men. I do not know why homosexual men tend to have more risk associated with sex than heterosexual men. It may have something to do with anal sex, but they need to exercise more restraint and caution in their sexual activities. That's all I am saying. The same goes for heterosexuals; the same goes for everyone."

"But you're saying it's more probable that gay men transmit HIV?" she asks.

"I am saying it is more probable to transmit HIV through anal sex than vaginal sex, and anal sex is the only kind of sex I know of that homosexual men have, besides oral sex," I reply. "Of course, this is based on reading I have done, so don't quote me. But from what I understand, for example, one of the only holes a man has on his body—the rear end, the rectum, or whatever you want to call it—is more susceptible to bleeding when foreign objects are thrust into it because it has a thin lining, and it can easily tear and bleed. An example of a foreign object would be another man's penis."

She starts to laugh.

"Wait, hear me out. I am not trying to degrade homosexuality; I am merely telling it how it is. Also, the rectum has so much bacteria that, I believe, can facilitate the transfer of other diseases and so provides a pathway for HIV." I am amazed at myself and how much I have learned. I guess all my hard work doing research has paid off somehow.

"You know, a lot of homosexual men might disagree with you."

"Well, everyone is entitled to their opinion, Aurora. I am just stating what I have read and also what is common sense. And remember, I am not trying to degrade anyone; the same theory holds true for anal sex between a man and a woman as well."

"You know, you shouldn't believe everything you read," she replies.

"Maybe so, but I do not have to read anything to know that the rectum, or if I may be blunt, the asshole, was not designed to take things in, but rather to let things out, and I believe things get complicated when we try to change the course of nature to suit our personal desires."

"So what are you saying?"

"What I am saying, Aurora, is that first, I am not against homosexuality, nor am I for it. It is what it is, and I have absolutely nothing to do with it. Second, for the sake of others, if a man knows he is going to engage in risky sexual behavior with another, whether it's a man or a woman, he should at least know his partner's health status. And the same goes for a woman. Third, he or she has to understand that anal sex is more susceptible to bleeding, even if the bleeding is in the form of micro-abrasions, which, in most cases, cannot be seen with the naked eye. That is all any virus needs to get into your bloodstream. So, if he is going to engage in such activities, he simply has to be more careful. The same rule applies to heterosexual partners; women bleed during their periods and can bleed as well during anal sex. Fourth, men who sleep with other men, especially if they do not know their health status, should not sleep with women because if, by any chance, they acquired the virus from another man's bleeding rectum, they can transfer the virus to the woman, and women are more likely to catch HIV, as well as other STDs—one reason is the large surface area of their vagina. The penis releases, and the vagina absorbs."

She laughs at my last sentence. "You seem to know a lot on this subject, John. You have any personal experience with this topic or something?"

My heartbeat quickens, and I suddenly feel uncomfortable. "Of course not," I lie. "I just like to do research on my own."

"I see. Smart man. I like that. So you think gay men bring a big negative to HIV prevention?"

"No, not at all. Gay men, as far as I am concerned, can do whatever they want. It is when such actions infringe upon the well-being of others, gay or not gay, that it becomes a problem. Anal sex, in general, in my opinion, is a very high-risk sexual encounter. Sex, in general, is a risky encounter if not handled properly. So before having sex, it is advisable to know your partner's sexual history, to know his or her health status, and also to let your partner know yours. And if neither of you knows, get tested before engaging in any such activity. That's all I am saying."

She smiles at me. "Well said. I appreciate a smart man, and you appear to be consciously sound, but I wonder if you practice what you preach."

"Thank you for your kind words. Well, I try and do what I can. Unfortunately, we live in a crazy world, with all sorts of diseases running around, waiting for their next target. Too many ignorant people take things for granted, and do not like to take responsibility for their actions. This is just my opinion." I am amazed at the way I speak now. A few months ago, after having sex with numerous women I would just see them as pieces of meat; now, here I am promoting awareness.

"Anyway," says Aurora, "let's change subject and talk about you."

"What about me do you want to know?"

We spend the rest of our evening exploring our respective pasts and sharing experiences, as well as forecasting our futures. For the first time in a couple of months, I feel at peace and genuinely have a good time. Aurora turns out to be just as smart and classy as I had thought. I will definitely want to see her again, for the right reasons.

I also finally remembered why the restaurant seemed familiar—I brought Anna here for dinner before I knew her status.

Today was a good day. I worked at both my jobs today, in the morning at the office and afterwards at the Ethiopian restaurant. This morning I got a text message from Cody, asking if we could meet next week for a movie and a drink afterwards, and I said okay. Afterwards, I couldn't stop thinking about

Cody all day. He would make such a great boyfriend. I wish we could have stayed together, because we would have made such a great couple. He is a strong man, and he is smart, and witty…just my kind of guy.

A cute couple come in for dinner at the restaurant. The guy is very handsome and the girl is equally as stunning. I serve them and enjoy watching them as they eat, laugh, and talk. I can tell that they are really into each other. The girl must be very happy to be with a guy like that. I can tell that he is a good guy and very respectful as well. I know this because he was very polite with me when I went to take their order and when I served them. I'm sure he is the kind of guy who always treats women really well.

Watching them eat makes me wish that I had someone that special in my life. I'm sure I could have that with Cody, but I just have to play my cards right this time around.

After the couple leaves, I head home. I had a long day and all I want to do is take a nice, long, hot bath, call Alexia, and go to bed. But waiting for me, on my doorstep, is Darius.

"What are you doing here, Darius?" I ask.

"I missed you."

"Okay, but you can't just show up here unannounced."

"I need to know what's going on with us, Michelle. It's been some time now, and I have not heard anything from you."

"Well, maybe I am not ready to talk to you, Darius," I reply as I let myself into my place. He follows.

"When will you be? I can't stay around much longer, Michelle, and if you want to break up, I understand, but I need some closure."

"I just said I need some time, Darius, okay? Just give me some time. Don't worry; I don't have anything bad planned for you."

"Okay, that's it. I give up," he says as he heads to the door. My heart misses a beat. "I can't keep doing this, Michelle, playing these games with you. I am leaving; there is no need for us to see each other again."

I can't let him go just like that. "No, wait, Darius, wait!" I hold onto his arm.

He stops in his tracks and looks at me with those beautiful eyes of his, and I melt. "I have to go, Michelle. I am not playing games with you anymore."

"Don't go, baby…wait…I am sorry about the way I reacted. I just have so much going on."

"We all have a lot going on, Michelle."

"Yeah, but you know, with my brother, my friend Anna, work and stuff…I just have so much going on, and I am sorry I let out my frustrations on you. I just thought some time off would allow us to appreciate each other better."

"But I do appreciate you, Michelle. I told you that I appreciated you every day that we dated. What more do you want?"

"I'm sorry, Darius. I just get scared sometimes, that's all. And I do think that you are a great guy; I really do. And I always want you around me."

"So what does this mean? That our break is over?"

I think about his question. I have just gotten back in touch with Cody, and I am interested in him. But at this moment, I am feeling really soft with Darius. And his eyes. I can't stop looking at them. I am honestly not sure what to do. Still, I say, "Yes, our break is over."

He smiles and holds me close, then looks into my eyes. And I melt again. We kiss, head to my bedroom, and make love like never before.

Chapter Twenty-Three

I have not seen Sebastian in a long time, so I decide to pay him a visit today. I also decide that I have time before work to try to convince Sebastian's father to come down to visit him. I dial Mr. Summers's number. A different male voice comes on the phone this time. "Hello?" I guess it is Sebastian's brother.

"Hi, my name is John Casey, and I was wondering if I could speak to any relative of Sebastian Summers."

Brief silence. "This is his brother, Jeff. Is there a problem?"

I sense some concern in his voice, but he does not sound as rigid as his father. I take that as a good sign. "All is well, relative to the situation, that is. I have been visiting Sebastian at the clinic for some time now, and I notice he never gets family visits. At a time like this, he could really use you guys there to provide support for him as he goes through his ordeal."

The voice sighs deeply. "I see. Do you work with the clinic?"

"Yes, well, sort of. I am doing some volunteer work with them, and I struck up a friendship with Sebastian."

"I see, and they gave you permission to call our home like this?"

"No, sir. I took the initiative. You don't always have to follow the rules to do what's right."

He sighs again. "You know, Sebastian has not been a part of our lives for a very long time. When he first learned of his infection, years ago, he cut us off from his life and made it seem as if he did not want anything to do with any of us. And we did not want to risk catching anything from him, so we parted ways."

I think about what he has just said. "Well, Jeff, first of all, it is not that easy to catch HIV from just a basic interaction with a person. There has to be a transfer of bodily fluids, so in other words, you and your brother would have to exchange blood or have sex—things like that. I don't think visiting your brother puts you at risk in any way, shape, or form. Also, when people go through tough times, it can be a natural response to shut other people out of their lives, and a lot of the time people do that not because they want to, but because maybe they feel that regular people cannot relate to their issues. But sometimes, simply being there says and does a lot."

"You may be right, but too much time has passed, and there are a lot of open issues that have not been addressed, particularly between Sebastian and my father, from the way they parted. You cannot expect us to just get up all of a sudden, after all these years, and go pay him a visit. We would have to be diplomatic about the whole thing, maybe start with some conversations first."

I sigh deeply this time. "Jeff, you seem to be a very smart, understanding man, so I am sure you will relate to what I am about to say. In life, we usually don't get too many chances to do the right thing, even though sometimes doing the right thing can seem like such an impossible feat to accomplish. Your brother is very sick; his condition is fatal. So, despite anything that has happened between you guys in the past, I personally think you should go be with your family. You might regret it later in life if you don't. Life is short, man, and opportunities don't come by often. Please, just go see your brother. If not to make him feel better, then do it for your own conscience, if you have one."

Sebastian's brother does not speak for some time, and while he is silent, I pray to God that I have said the right things to him.

Then he says, "You know, my father will never agree with what you just said."

"That's okay, Jeff. What's important is what your conscience says to you. You don't have to do everything your father says to you. You are a grown man and can make your own decisions."

He sighs again. "Okay, I will give it some thought and run it by my dad. Thanks for your concern. I really appreciate it."

"You're welcome, Jeff. Here, take my number—you know, in case you guys have any questions for me about anything. I would be more than happy to help." I give him my telephone number, and we end our conversation. As I rush off to work, I think that I have done a good job of leaving him with something to think about.

***

After work, I go to the clinic to put in my rounds. Bertha, my manager, seems especially happy to see me.

"Well, hello, John."

"Hi, Bertha. Sorry for my prolonged absence. I had a few things to take care of."

"That's all right. We all have responsibilities. Sebastian has been asking about you. You seem to have left quite an impression on him."

I smile at her comment. "Well, we had an interesting conversation the last time I was here. How is he doing?"

Her facial expression changes from happiness to one of concern. "Well, he is much worse than he was when you were last here. He is very weak now; it seems the virus is taking its toll on his body. But he is in high spirits. You should pay him a visit before you leave today."

"I certainly will. Thank you, Bertha." After my rounds I head to Sebastian's room. His room is dimly lit on this particular day. Sebastian, as Bertha mentioned, looks very weak, and he's lost a considerable amount of weight since I last saw him. But his eyes light up and he manages a smile when he sees me in his doorway.

I am happy to see him as well. "Hey, man!" I exclaim.

"Hey, John. I thought I scared you off."

"Never." I sit down in a chair next to him.

"You sure you want to get close to me, man? In case you haven't noticed, I have AIDS."

I smile. "Well, from what I understand, transmission is only possible from the exchange of bodily fluids, and I don't plan on kissing you or sleeping with you, Sebastian."

He laughs at my joke, and I enjoy seeing him happy.

"You won't sleep with me? C'mon, John!" He coughs. "I thought we had something here."

"You're not my type, Sebastian."

He laughs again, harder this time. "You're a good man, John. I don't think there's anything wrong with you, at least I hope there isn't, but as you and I know, that fate is in God's hands."

"Yes, I know. I'm hoping for the best. How are you coping?"

"Well, I feel much better, believe it or not."

"Really? You look like crap."

"Thanks, John. I feel so much better after hearing that."

We both grin. "I was joking. You look great."

"Thanks. When I said I felt better, I meant mentally. The conversation we had previously put a lot of things in perspective for me."

"Care to share?" I ask.

"Absolutely. For starters, I have accepted my situation for what it is. I can't change what's happening to me. So I decided that I am going to change my attitude for the better and adjust my outlook on life."

"I think that's excellent, Sebastian. Do you have a specific plan in place to help execute your new strategy?"

"Well, just like you volunteer, I've decided to become a volunteer as well."

"You, a volunteer? And how on earth do you plan on being of service?" I ask.

"Well, with Bertha's assistance, and also with the help of one of the computer tech guys here, I created a Web page where I post daily words of encouragement for HIV and AIDS sufferers. I write positive words and explain in detail how I plan on bettering myself with the time I have left. I also post a little poetry that I write once in a while."

"Wow, I think that is absolutely wonderful, Sebastian! I never would have thought you were the poetic type! Have you heard from anyone since you started?"

He gives me a big smile. "I have heard from numerous people, all praising me and sharing their stories with me as well. We are slowly forming some sort of online peer-support network, I think, and I feel good that it was my hard work that made it happen."

"That is absolutely wonderful! I'm proud of you, man. And how did you feel when you started getting the responses?"

A tear rolls down his cheek and disappears into his bright smile. "I felt full of life." I feel good hearing him say these things. Even in his darkest moments, he is taking the initiative and making the best of his time by being productive and trying to help others. He is being a real man about things. I respect that.

"Yo, you have to give me the name of your Web site, so I can check it out, man."

"Absolutely. Just don't steal any of my poetry and use it with your women."

I laugh at his comments as he scribbles his Web site address on a piece of paper for me.

"I promise I won't steal your poetry, Sebastian, and I think it's really cool what you have done. Speaking about women, I met this really cool chick at a bar some time ago, and I have been talking to her. I hope it turns out to be something serious, because I really like this girl." I realize then that this is the first time I have brought up my relationships with females to Sebastian.

He looks at me and smiles. "Really? That's cool; what's her name?" he asks.

"Aurora."

"Wow, sexy name. What is she like?"

"Well, she's cool, man. She seems really down-to-earth, and she's a really smart person, from what I can tell. I have not gotten into her pants yet, so I guess that's a good thing, and she seems to be very conservative about those kinds of things. But she is really cool, man. You would like her, I think; she's real laid back and open-minded."

"That's nice, John. Just remember, this is the city and there are all sorts of people here. Just because someone is nice within the first couple of weeks does not mean that he or she is, indeed, a nice person."

"This is true, Sebastian, which is why I am taking my time to get to know her. I think she is a nice girl, different from most girls I have seen."

"Then that's good, if you have a good vibe about her. Just remember, if you plan on getting intimate, get tested first and have her do the same. That way, you can have a relatively stress-free sexual relationship. Unless you aspire to become like me."

I do not find his last few words funny. "Stop talking like that, Sebastian. There is nothing wrong with you. Trust me; you're a lot more normal than a lot of people I know."

"Thanks, John," he says with a smile.

"Anytime. And I will get tested if I plan on getting intimate with her, and I will ask that she do the same."

"Good. And if she has any hot friends, bring them by here so I can hit on them and seduce them with my charm. Maybe I can read them a little of my poetry."

"Shut up, Sebastian!" He laughs. I look at my watch and realize it is time to go. "Hey, man, thanks for the advice and for sharing your Web site information with me. I'll check it out and let you know what I think when next I see you."

"Okay, man, sounds good. I guess I'll see you around, eh?"

"Yeah, Sebastian, you'll see me around. Oh, by the way, I spoke to your family—your brother Jeff and your dad."

His expression changes from a smile to a frown. "And what happened?"

I think for a long time on how to answer his question. "They are nice people."

"Really?" Sebastian looks confused.

"Yes, your brother, in particular." I notice a slight smile on Sebastian's face as I say that.

"Yeah, Jeff is a nice guy. What did they say?"

"Well, I think Jeff agreed with me that a visit was and has been long overdue, so he might be working on something. You never know."

Sebastian looks at me keenly. "Hmm, I don't know how to take what you just said, but it is what it is. Regardless, thanks for your help and concern, John."

"Anytime, Sebastian, anytime. I'm sure things will work out for the better. Anyhow, I have to go now; you take care, okay? And don't stress yourself out."

He looks sad to see me go. "Okay, John, I'll be right here. See you soon."

I leave work early to head to a restaurant on the west side of the city to meet Cody for dinner. He called me two days back, and we agreed to meet and have a chat. Darius actually wanted to see me as well so I had to make up an excuse—I told him that I was going to do Alexia's hair tonight. He bought that. I am so excited to be seeing Cody again. My heart is beating really fast. I spoke to Alexia briefly over the phone, and she thinks I'm crazy for sleeping with Darius again and then making plans to see Cody after I told Darius that our break was over. But she doesn't want to accept that I can meet my ex-boyfriend for dinner as friends. Her mind cannot understand that. I just plan on meeting him and catching up, because I honestly miss him. I've been debating what I will say, imagining that I might be shy in front of him, and all that lovely stuff. Now, this is a man I truly fancy! But I thought I fancied Darius as well—he is cute, and he has those eyes....

About a block away from the restaurant I realize that I need some gum, just in case. I spot a small convenience store on the corner and walk in to buy some. As I walk down an aisle, I catch my reflection in a glass door to my left. Damn! Even I have to admit that I look really good. This silk dress and with my heels make me look stunning. Cody will not be able to resist me tonight. As I look at my reflection, something else catches my attention. I see a person moving behind me, a person that looks familiar. I turn around to get a clearer view, but the individual moves to a different aisle. Now I am curious. I walk up to front and pay for my gum, and then I walk back to that area to get a better glimpse of who it is. The person makes a left turn around another aisle as soon as I get close, so I circle around. My heart begins to beat fast. After I make the next turn, I will come face-to-face with this person. I hold my breath and make the turn, and that's when I see…

It is Anna.

***

She looks really…well…different. She is dressed really plainly, a stark contrast to the Anna I once knew. Previously, I would never see Anna in sneakers; she always wore heels. And it was very rare to see Anna in khaki pants, much less a T-shirt. But here she is, in a plain white T-shirt, a baseball cap, and khaki pants. I feel strange looking at her—it is as if this Anna in front of me is the old Anna's sister. She hasn't noticed me yet, as she is looking at the nutrition facts on a carton of yogurt. I move in closer.

"Anna?" I say. She looks up at me, and her immediate reaction is one of discomfort, it seems. But she still manages a smile.

"Umm, Michelle, hi…what are you doing here?'

"I have a date in the restaurant next door."

"Oh, how nice…lucky you…how is everything?"

"I am well, Anna. Where have you been? We have all been asking about you!"

"Oh, yeah, umm, well, you know. You know how it is… I just, umm, got a little busy, you know, but I'm fine."

"But Anna, you could call us, you know. We have been your friends for so long. It's a bit strange to just cut us off like you have."

"I…I …umm…I didn't cut you off. I just had a lot of things to deal with, you know, with my brother passing away and stuff, you know…"

"Oh, yeah, again I am sorry for your loss."

"It is okay. I have really missed you, Michelle." Her eyes well up with tears. She looks so sad, and I cannot understand why. But I feel like crying as well.

"I have missed you, too, Anna. You know you can always talk to me. We have always been there for each other. You can always come to me." I give her a big hug. She begins to cry in my arms.

"Thank you so much, Michelle. You have no idea how much that means to me. Sometimes I feel like I have no one to talk to."

"But why would you say that, Anna? We have been friends for so, so, so long! You know you can talk to me about anything!"

"There are some things that are really hard to hear, Michelle, even between good friends like us."

"Why? What is wrong?"

"Listen, you're going to be late for your date. Why don't we grab some coffee sometime, so we catch up?"

"I would love to, but are you okay? Friends before guys, you know that." I'm not sure that I mean that; I'm not sure I would pass up meeting Cody tonight for any reason. I don't get dressed up for nothing.

"No, no, no, I am fine. You go on to your date, and don't let me hold you up. Let's meet sometime this week for some coffee, and we can talk then."

"Okay. Are you still at the same number? I've called you, but you never pick up."

"Yeah, I'm still at that number. Just call me, and I promise I will answer. Call me tomorrow so we can arrange a time."

"I will call you okay? Please pick up. We have to talk."

"Okay, Michelle. Have fun on your date."

"Okay, bye for now, Anna. Love you. Bye!"

"Bye…"

I leave the store a little stunned. I cannot believe what just happened. She looked so plain and ordinary. Something is definitely wrong, or at least different, and I am curious to find out. Now, however, a new curiosity is in front of me—a man by the name of Cody.

***

I step into the dimly lit restaurant, feeling really sexy. I know Cody is already here; he sent me a text message asking where I was as I left the convenience store. I look around and finally spot him sitting at a table in the back. I fix my boobs, then walk over to him. He looks so handsome in the sports coat and jeans he has on. He looks really sexy indeed.

"How are you?" I ask as I sit down.

"Hey," he exclaims in his deep voice. "You look really good."

"Why, thank you. You don't look so bad yourself."

"Thanks."

"Sorry I am late. I just had a little weird experience before I got here."

"A weird experience? Let's hear it."

"I don't know if you remember my friend Anna?"

"Yeah, how could I forget? Your crazy friend, right?"

"Yeah, well, she had a death in her family some time ago, and then she just vanished."

"What do you mean, she just vanished?"

"She just vanished; none of us had heard from her in a very long time. It was almost as if she just cut us off."

"But why would she do that? Did you guys get in a fight or something?"

"No, that's exactly why it was very weird! We would call her cell, go to her apartment, but all to no avail."

"Damn, that's crazy."

"Yeah, I know, but Anyway, right before I came here I bumped into her again, quite randomly, actually."

"What did she say?"

"Nothing much. We had a brief conversation, but I told her I had a date, so we agreed to meet sometime this week for coffee."

"So we are on a date? Is that what this is?"

"I don't know, Cody. Are we?"

He grins. And of course he avoids answering the question. "Well, you should meet her for coffee as you planned and see what explanation she gives. And don't get on her case for not keeping in touch. You know, people have different reasons for doing different things."

"Okay, enough about her. Did you order already?"

"No, I was waiting for you."

"Okay, let's order then."

We place our orders and then just look at each other.

"What are you looking at?" he asks, with a smile.

"You. I did not think you would be so nice to me tonight."

"You think I am being nice?"

"Compared to your usual self, yes."

"Well, I guess I am happy to see you."

"Are you, Cody? Do you mean that?"

"Here we go with all the questions. Why can't you just let my yes be a yes, and my no be a no? Do you have to question every statement I make?"

I smile and stick my chest out just a little bit so my boobs protrude a bit, just slightly. I catch his eyes looking. "I am sorry. I just want you to say it, that's all. I came here as a friend, Cody. I don't want to fight with you."

"Wow, Michelle is being nice. What a change. Maybe time off was definitely what we needed."

"I am nice, Cody. You just never gave me the chance to be nice to you. But you know that I can be a sweetheart."

"You *can* be—those are the key words. You also think you're smarter than everybody else, but you're not."

"Why would you say something like that, Cody? What have I done to you to make you talk to me like that?"

"You know yourself, Michelle. Stop trying to play naïve."

"Well, I don't think you're an idiot, Cody, if that's what you're getting at. I actually think you're a pretty bright guy."

"Thanks."

Our food arrives.

"Listen, you know that we had some genuinely good times together in the past. Granted, our relationship was a bit rocky, but I think that allowed us to really get to know each other."

"You have a point."

"Yeah, and now I just want to us to grow as friends. I don't want to ever lose you, Cody, and you are one person I would fight for." He keeps quiet, just listening, so I go on. "So let's just put the past behind us and move on. We don't have to be together, but I think that you're a good guy, and I want us to stay as friends." As I say that, I lean over and hold his hand—he doesn't seem to mind.

"Friends, huh? I can do that. Like I said, it is really nice to see you again." Again, I catch him looking at my cleavage.

We spend the rest of the evening talking about old friends, past experiences, and future aspirations. Soon, we finish and step outside, ready to leave.

"I had a really good time tonight, Michelle" he says.

"So did I, Cody. So did I. I hope we can see each other again sometime."

"Absolutely."

"By the way, you never told me if you have a new boyfriend. Are you seeing anyone?" he asks.

Darius is the last person on my mind right now. "No...no, I am not seeing anyone."

"I see."

"Yeah, so about our hanging out again...do you have any plans in mind?"

"Well, I was thinking we could hang out at my place, at my apartment, maybe catch a movie or something."

"I thought you said you wanted us to hang out as friends. Isn't that getting too intimate?"

"Intimate? We will just be hanging out, that's all."

"I see. Well I have to go. It's getting late. Good-bye, Cody."

He gazes into my eyes, and all of a sudden, I feel a bit shy. Then he leans over and kisses me on my lips. I cannot move.

"Good-bye Michelle. I will call you."

I am still stunned by what he did.

"Are you okay, Michelle?"

"You kissed me."

"I am sorry. I know, I know, just friends, I know."

"I never said that I did not like it," I reply as a taxi pulls up for me. "Call me."

"Okay. Bye."

"Bye."

The taxi pulls off, and I cannot believe that he kissed me! Why did he do that? Is he trying to mess with my head? I mean, I enjoyed the kiss, but I don't get it. Why would he kiss me? I ponder these questions all the way home and briefly forget that I met Anna a few hours earlier.

Chapter Twenty-Four

Today has turned out to be a beautiful, sunny day. I have not called Aurora since my date with her two days ago, but we have been exchanging text messages. I will probably set something up with her again, probably for the weekend or maybe even during the week.

Today, as I headed to work, there were all sorts of beautiful women who pass by me. And even as I was trying to pray and turn my life around, they all seemed to smile and flirt with me. I've caught myself looking at various women's bodies as I walk in the city, and I find myself again undressing them with my eyes. I cannot stop myself.

When I got home today, I was tempted to surf the Internet for pornography, just to relieve this stress I'm experiencing from not having had sex in such a long while. I have been having this same issue for the past couple of weeks, and it is also influencing the way I pray. I have been trying hard not to succumb to the feelings that got me in trouble in the first place, but it is so hard, especially considering the environment I live in. I have to call my dad and ask for his advice on how to deal with this issue.

But first, I decide to call Abel, my best friend, and get his perspective. I dial his phone number.

"Hello?"

"Hey," I respond.

"John, what's up, brother? Where have you been? Haven't heard from you in a while. Are you all right?"

My trauma over this HIV situation had resulted in my losing touch with many people, including Abel. "I'm good, man, and you?"

"I'm good, Getting ready to go see this girl tonight," Abel replies.

"Weren't you the same one telling me to stop dodging bullets?" I ask.

"Hey, John, I gave you advice. I never said I was a role model."

"True. Anyway, I want to ask you a question, or maybe I should say, I want your opinion, on an issue I have."

"Talk to me. What's on your mind?"

***

"Well," I begin, "okay, look, I have been trying really hard to be a good boy and draw closer to God. You know I live in the city, and you know the kinds of women you find here. I am finding it really hard not to even look at women the wrong way when the visuals and temptations are constantly being thrown in my face. Do you have any recommendations?"

Abel stays quiet for a while, and soon I begin to think that he has hung up the phone.

Then he speaks. "I have never heard you talk like this. Did something bad happen?"

This is why he is my best friend; he has such sharp instincts.

"No," I lie, "nothing bad happened. It's just a decision I made, that's all."

"I see. Well, bro, I personally think it is perfectly natural for a guy to check out a girl. It is in our genetic makeup! If you're asking me about sex, I think you should stick to one girl instead of floating around. But why are you even questioning checking girls out? You turned gay or something?" He begins to laugh.

"No, man, I'm serious," I reply. I am tempted to share with him what happened to me, but I refrain from doing so, realizing the negative stigma I could generate from Abel for my honesty.

"I don't understand, then," Abel responds. "Dude, you live in the city, land of the sexy women. You have at your disposal every ethnicity, every physical type, and every background to choose from. You could have sex a hundred times in a week, if not more, plus you have your own place there. So, dude, what the hell are you asking me about how not to check out women? Are you crazy?"

I have to think of a quick excuse to explain my request. "Nah, man. Been there, done that. I am trying to settle down now, man, and find a steady girlfriend, and I do not want to lose my ability to do so. So I am trying to minimize checking out every single woman and focus on being with just one, get it?"

"No, I don't get it, John, but if that is what you want, that is what you want. On a serious note, in today's world, it's a bit hard not to check out girls and find them sexually attractive. But it's not something that happens all at once, John. I would say, instead of sleeping around with a million different women, find one steady one and settle down. You get to build a relationship with another person, and from a sexual standpoint, you can have sex whenever you want if she is your girlfriend. It is also healthier. Lord knows what sort of diseases people carry these days." Again, my heart rate quickens as I hear Abel's words. "Sounds like you're growing up, John."

"You could say that. Where do you find good girls, though?"

"You don't find them, John; they find you, I guess. Or maybe I should say, God sends them to you," he replies. "You just pray to God for one, and she'll show up in good time, I'm sure."

"You're right. Well, I am sort of talking to this one girl now, man. She seems really cool, but we just started, so who knows what will happen, so we'll see. So, how are you coping with life in Brazil with all your women?"

"First of all, John, congrats with your girl situation. I hope that works out."

"And how is Brazil?"

"It's great; I couldn't ask for more. I'm having sex like a jackrabbit."

"You're crazy, Abel."

"Yeah, well, I never said I was a saint, but my conscience tells me I had better slow down."

"Maybe you should listen to your conscience, Abel. Your gut feeling is usually right."

"We'll see, John. Maybe when I leave Brazil I will consider slowing down; maybe I'll join you in your new initiative. But for now, I think I'll continue having sex like a jackrabbit."

Some people just don't change, and Abel is one of them.

"I guess it is what it is. Well, you take care of yourself, buddy, and be careful with those girls, man. If you're going to get crazy with the sex thing, always, always, always have good condoms handy, please. And be careful."

"I always am. You take care, John, and be careful as well. And stop calling me only when you need something! Bye for now, bro."

"Peace, Abel, talk to you later." I hang up the phone. It seems you only know the true severity and seriousness of a situation when you're in it yourself. Abel gave what he thought was good input, but he does not know all the facts. He does not know that I slept with an HIV-positive woman. He does not know the odds that I am up against. He does not know that I have been living in uncertainty and am doing all that I can to save myself from realizing that I have been infected with HIV. He does not know that I am fighting for my life and not accepting the facts that I am in a risky situation and am waiting for the results. He does not know these things. I hope he doesn't have to have an experience like mine to bring him in touch with reality.

***

That same night I could not sleep. The stress I have been feeling with regards to this HIV issue has affected my sleep patterns, my social life, my work, and my happiness—all this, for just one night of sexual pleasure. It's just not worth it. Not worth it at all. And the funny thing is that if I had not asked Anna to get tested, I probably would have gone to see her again, and again, and again, increasing my chances of catching this virus, if I do not have it already. So many people—men and women—take sex so casually. They sleep with one another without protection. Others think that just because they begin a relationship with someone and they call that person their boyfriend or girlfriend, it is okay to sleep without protection, but it is not. The act of sex brings so much temporary pleasure but can cost such a high price if it is not handled responsibly. Unfortunately, most people (and I include myself, at least in the past) are so blinded by the pleasure that sex brings that they neglect the serious risks, such as unwanted pregnancies, STDs, HIV infection, and worst of all, AIDS. Look at me, the mighty John Casey, who at one point proudly slept with women left and right but who now is huddled in a dark corner in my already dark room, ashamed, disgusted with myself, and humbled by forces beyond my control. I am now aware of how fragile I am, of how insignificant I am in the grand scheme of things. Life does not revolve around my selfish desires. Anything can happen to anyone at any time, and we humans have no control over that. Something far greater than ourselves orchestrates our lives.

I feel the urge to pray, so I get out of bed and kneel down.

"Lord my God," I begin, "I am sorry for my sins against you. Please forgive me. I am in a situation that is far beyond my control, and I need your help. Please find favor with me and spare me. I beg You! I beg You, please. I would like to have a normal family someday, with kids, and a normal life in the future. Please, please spare me and find favor with me, please!"

I get up off my knees and switch on my computer; I want to take a look at Sebastian's Web site, hoping that maybe that will make me feel better. I type in the Web address and proceed to his site. In the top left-hand corner of the home page is a picture of a healthy Sebastian, wearing a big smile. Under his picture are the words "HIV is not the end of the world; having AIDS does not mean condemnation."

Interesting. Sebastian has posted a message in the center of the page, which reads:

HIV/AIDS is a condition that has taken much from so many people in the world today. It has taken family members, broken up families, destroyed relationships, and most importantly, it has taken away happiness from so many people. It need not be so. Your happiness is yours and yours alone; no one should have the right to take that away from you, because without happiness you have nothing. This site is designed to make people happy and to let people dealing with HIV/AIDS know that it is not the end of the world. In most cases, it is only the beginning. I encourage you all to post your positive thoughts on this Web site, and know that no matter what you may go through, there are people here who are willing to offer support and comfort, even if it is through the Web. Place your kind words in my guest book, and post your thoughts in my discussion forum, which can be accessed through the link below. You can also access some poetry I have written through the poetry link, and post yours as well. My name is Sebastian, and I thank you for stopping by.

I enjoy his opening words, and now I am curious to see what his poetry is like, so I click on the poetry link. He has posted three poems so far; their titles are "Sometimes," "Haud Voluntas," and "Thank God, Thank All & Thank Life."

Interesting titles. I decide to start with "Sometimes" and read the rest later. I click on the link, and this is what I see:

SOMETIMES

Sometimes I wish I could really just be free.
Sometimes I wish I could really just be me.
Sometimes I wish in life there would be no more pain;
Sometimes I wish, but it seems my wishes are all in vain.
Sometimes I wish the sun, moon, and stars would always shine, but these days
the world is so dark and we all seem blind.
Sometimes I wish all good dreams would all come to be; sometimes I wish
there was no such thing as reality.
Sometimes I wish I had a girl I could call my own; sometimes I wish because
it sucks being all alone.
Sometimes I wish people listened and had 20/20 vision, so they could see the
state of the horrible world we live in.
Sometimes I wish God was not so much of a mystery; sometimes I wish but I
know He knows what's best for me.
Sometimes I wish I didn't think so much about this life I'm in; sometimes I
wish God would come get me to go be with Him.
Sometimes I wish friends stayed friends and not fade to memories; sometimes
I wish acts of love were really given genuinely.
I wish I could change the times; I truly wish I could free my mind…
Sometimes.
***

Wow. I feel an overwhelming rush of emotions after I read his poem. I pictured Sebastian himself, in the clinic, reading it to me. He sounded so sad. Now, I find myself relating to a lot of what he wrote, but I have to admit that his poem sounds depressing. I decide that I will suggest to him to write about happier concepts. But maybe that's the way he felt at the time, and I have no right to object to what he felt like writing. I enjoy his writing, and I tell myself that I will encourage him to write more, to give him—and me—something to do, rather than dwell on problems we have no control over. I creep back into bed and resume staring at my ceiling. Soon, I am fast asleep.

After work today I agree to stop by Cody's place to watch a movie he told me about over the phone. He said it was supposed to be good, so I oblige. I had to tell Darius that I would be with Alexia again, doing her hair. I also told Alexia that I was going to see Cody, and she advised me not to. But I want to see Cody! I still cannot get over that kiss he gave me. He completely caught me off guard! But I like that about him—how I can never tell what he is going to do or say. I wonder what this movie is about that he wants to watch with me.

Oh, yeah, I also told Alexia that I saw Anna, and she could not believe it! She was shocked when I told her how Anna's appearance has changed, and she is eager to hear what Anna has to tell me when we meet in a few days.

I get to Cody's place around 8:00 p.m. I have not been here in a long time, and I realize how much I miss walking through his front door, sitting on his leather sofa, watching the fish swim in his aquarium, and checking him out as he walks around his apartment. I really like his athletic body. I make myself comfortable on his sofa while he makes some drinks for us.

"It's been a while, huh?" he says.

"Been a while?"

"Since you've been here."

"Oh, yeah. I've missed the place, especially this sofa."

"Yeah, we had some fun on that thing," he says with a sly grin. I giggle.

"This is the movie." He hands the DVD case to me.

"It looks interesting."

"Action flick. I know you like those."

"I'm actually into drama, romance, that sort of thing, but I don't mind watching action movies. I thought you knew that."

"I know you like those kind of movies," he replies. "I think you will like this one."

"You think so? And what makes this one so special?"

"Trust me."

He puts in the DVD and then sits down next to me on the sofa. I am not sure what to do. I want to jump all over this man, but I already have a boyfriend. Is this right? Being so close to my ex? Should I be doing this? But I really want to be around him. The movie begins as I sip on piña colada that he served me. The movie turns out to be interesting—at least, it seems to be from the little that I see of it.

Cody slips his arm around me, and I find myself not moving away or resisting. Plus, he smells good. The movie plays for about thirty minutes, and then I feel his hand rubbing my arm.

"What's on your mind, Cody?" I ask.

"I am just remembering how we used to do it on this sofa, that's all."

"Cody!"

"Sorry, you asked me what I was thinking about."

"Did you miss me after we broke up?"

"No, I didn't. Just kidding. Of course I missed you. I thought about you all the time."

"I think you're lying."

"I don't lie. It's the truth."

"I'll take your word for it, then. So if you missed me, why didn't you call me?"

"Well, you were the one being unreasonable, so I saw no reason to call. I was hoping that you would come to your senses."

"Come to my senses? We have already had this conversation, and I am not going to argue with you again."

"I am not arguing with you; I'm just telling it how it is."

"Okay, okay…why is it that you argue so much?"

"I don't argue with you, Michelle. You like fighting with me. I just answer your questions. Maybe I should ask you the same question: why do you like arguing with me?" He playfully nudges me.

"I don't argue. I am a good girl." I cuddle with him. Darius is the last thing on my mind.

"I guess we are not watching this movie, huh?" he says.

"You knew we wouldn't watch it, silly."

He starts playing with my hair.

"Why didn't we work out, Darius?" I ask.

"Darius? Who's Darius?"

"Oh, umm, sorry, just one of my brother's friends. Why didn't we work out?"

"Because you don't listen, and you play too many games, Michelle. You think I don't know you, but I do."

He didn't react to my mistake with his name; I thought that was a good thing.

"What do you mean that I play too many games?"

"Not tonight, Michelle. We are really snug and comfortable. Let's not ruin the mood."

"You're crazy, Cody."

We are in each other's arms at this point.

"Hey, look at me," he says.

I raise my head and look into his eyes. "Yes?"

Then he kisses me. I cannot move, and I feel really turned on. We kiss some more, then he picks me up and carries me to his bedroom.

***

After we have sex, we both lie down in his bed. He is still good in bed—we had a good time.

"That was nice," I say. "If I didn't know any better I would have thought you were seeing someone to keep your skills up."

"I never said I wasn't seeing anyone."

I sit up in the bed. "What do you mean, you never said you weren't seeing anyone? What do you mean, Cody? You just made love to me."

"I did."

"So what do you mean by 'I never said I wasn't seeing anyone'?"

He sits up in bed. "I am seeing someone, Michelle."

"But…how could you make love to me if you are seeing someone? Do you ever think about me?"

"I didn't think you would take it personally. We have been together before. I thought it would just be like old times."

"I hate you! I hate you so much! After I told you that I was not seeing anyone, you just let me come here, seduce me, sleep with me, and now that you got what you wanted, you tell me that you're seeing someone? Are you crazy?"

"Stop playing the victim, Michelle. You haven't changed much from the last time we were together. And who is this Darius guy, huh? You think I'm stupid?"

"I told you that he's no one—one of my younger brother's friends."

"So you think about your younger brother's friends whenever you get intimate with someone? C'mon, Michelle, I'm not that dumb. Give me more credit than that."

"You know you're wrong, and that's why you're bringing my brother's friend into this. You know you're wrong, Darius."

"You see! There you go again."

"I meant *Cody*!"

"Whatever…okay, listen, we had sex, and we enjoyed each other as we did. Let's just move on from here and continue being friends, okay? I told you from the start that we would meet as friends and nothing more. I don't understand why you're making a big deal out of all this."

"You are a loser, you are a jerk, you are a moron, you are a liar, you are a bum, and *I hate you*!"

"Michelle, I think you're overreacting."

I begin to get dressed to leave. I cannot understand why I feel so angry. "You hurt me, like you did before. Now you see why we broke up. You're a horrible person. You are a really, really horrible person, Cody."

"Michelle, stop. Where are you going?" he asks.

"I'm going home, and I never want to see you again. This is the last time I will let you hurt me."

"Michelle, what are you talking about? Please, don't leave. Let's talk about it."

"Bye. Cody." I say as I gather the last of my things and head to his front door.

"Michelle…wait…" he calls out, but he never gets out of bed.

I step outside and slam his door shut behind me. I felt sick in my stomach. How could he do such a thing to me? After the way I felt about him…he knew all along, he knew all along what he was doing. What a jerk. I feel very angry with him as I head back to my place, and then I cry as soon as I get home.

Chapter Twenty-Five

oday is a beautiful Tuesday. This morning, as I brush my teeth, I play my raffle game again. I do not pick up the paper with the red H. Phew. That gives me some relief as I start my day. I come to work and plan on getting a lot done—I have been slacking due to my HIV situation. I have about a week before my time runs out and I have to face the heat. The rash on my arm has grown larger. I have also been having a lot of aches and pains all over my body. Can that be attributed to my having HIV? Or could I just have all these symptoms as a result of excessive stress? So much uncertainty; it is exactly this aspect that is mentally killing me.

When I looked at myself after my shower this morning, I noticed that I have bags under my eyes. Fatigue. I need more rest. And besides, from what I hear, good sleep helps boost the immune system as well. After all, what does worrying do for me? It only adds to the problem. As it is, I do not know if I have contracted this horrible virus, but for my sanity, I have to assume that I have not, as all the statistics point in my favor. Then again, those are just statistics, just educated assumptions made by researchers observing a small sample of people. Small samples of people that I do not believe are effective representations of the entire human race. So, it all comes back to a basic truth; that with regard to my accident, or for anyone who engages in unprotected sex with a partner whose status is unknown, there is a chance of catching a disease of any sort, HIV included, and that chance is greater if the person is indeed HIV- or STD-positive.

How can one tell if someone is infected with an STD or with HIV?

In most cases, these diseases do not wear faces; they are not easily recognizable. Very few STDs show physical symptoms, such as if someone has a herpes outbreak or a genital rash. But for most, the plain human eye cannot observe the infection. And I have not heard of anyone taking a microscope with them to inspect their partner's blood or semen right before sex. We live in such a harsh, unhealthy environment with so many viruses. How is it that most people, including me, are so blinded by ignorance regarding the true state of the world we live in? Why do simple rules that promote order and healthy living get overlooked and traded in for chaos and confusion?

It just makes no sense. And yet, my last statement seems to be the bane of human existence: doing things that make no sense.

Anyway, let me snap back into reality. I have a date with Aurora after work today; I am taking her to a restaurant a couple of blocks away. I hope our date goes well.

***

We arrive at the restaurant and have to wait about ten minutes for our table. It is a dimly lit Brazilian restaurant, and we are finally seated at a very comfortable table in the corner, away from most of the conversation in the room. The background music is some relaxing bossa nova. This should be a good evening.

"I like your choice of restaurant," Aurora says. She looks especially elegant in her lovely dress. The candlelight between us reveals her beautiful bronze skin and deep brown eyes. I certainly am a lucky man to be able to stare at something so beautiful.

"Thank you. I thought you would like it. I chose it based on your demeanor."

"My demeanor? What do you mean?" she asks.

"Well, from all the conversations I have had with you, you seem very laid back, and you make good conversation. I decided on this place because it has also has a laid-back quality, and it is good for conversation."

She smiles at me. "I bet you use that line on all your women, but thank you. I will take that as a compliment."

"You're welcome, but I am speaking fact, not fiction. I think this place complements you and the conversations we will have here."

"Well said, Mr. John Casey, well said."

"Why do I feel you are being sarcastic with me? Do you always try this hard to impress?" I ask calmly, with a smile.

"Only when I am interested in someone."

My smile broadens. "And out of curiosity, what do you do when you're not interested?"

"Well, if I were not interested, we would not be having dinner in this lovely restaurant that 'complements my demeanor.'" She giggles.

"Funny, funny; you're a funny girl."

Our waiter arrives. We order our meal and are soon enjoying our dinner with white wine and good conversation. After the meal, we continue to chat, and I get lost in her eyes.

"What are you looking at?" she asks in a very soothing voice.

"You. I am beginning to find your company addictive," I reply.

She smiles. "I like your company as well, sir. So far, you've not tried any moves on me that would make me think you're only after sex. And that's good. You've been a gentleman."

I think about her comment. Truth is, if I was not going through this HIV situation, I probably would have approached her with purely sexual motives in mind. But I find that because of my horrible situation, I approach people differently, and I value conversation more and more over lust. It seems I am beginning to put things in perspective. Maybe bad things do indeed happen for good reasons.

"Are you spiritual, Aurora?"

She looks puzzled. "Where did that question come from?"

"You just seem like someone who is in tune with her spirituality, so I had to ask."

"Yeah, I guess I am. I was raised as a Christian, but I have my reservations about Christianity—well, I have my reservations about religion in general. I read about many different religions, and I think they all have a lot to offer; there are many religions but only one God. I have a special interest right now in voodoo and other religions of the Diaspora, such as Santeria, Macumba and others. It fascinates me to see how the motherland beliefs survived slavery and colonial oppression over the centuries and the dominant role they still play in the Diaspora. I mean, in Brazil you can still hear incantations being sung in Yoruba, which originally was a Nigerian language from West Africa! Another interesting fact is how most voodoo practices also believe the Creator to be both male and female."

I sense an interesting conversation brewing. "So you think God is both male and female?"

"Remember, John, I never said I practiced voodoo. I just said I was interested in it. And no, I personally do not think about God being male or female. God is just God, but Christianity, especially denominations like Catholicism, tend to speak of God in a masculine manner, and I simply think that it is a different perspective to say that the Creator is both."

"So what are your opinions on Christianity, then?" I ask.

"I think every religion is man-made, which does not imply that the contents of their holy writings are not true or do not carry wisdom. Christianity is a man-made religion, just like Judaism, Hinduism, and the others, and religions are there to help us on our way to God. Like I said I believe there is only one God but many religions, just like there is only one human race but many skin colors. But on our individual journeys, we should never be blinded by the actors, institutions, and false prophets who want to lead us to God. I think that is a danger in every religion."

"Interesting, Aurora. I never would have thought you would give this issue that much thought. I'm impressed."

"Why are you impressed? You don't think I am capable of thinking about such things? You think I look stupid?" she teases.

"No, I do not think you look stupid. Then again, what does a stupid person look like? I just thought your opinion sounded objective and well thought out."

"Thank you, John. I do enjoy talking about such things."

I am impressed by how intelligent she is, although intelligence is useless if used with a wrong perception. At this point, I am debating what is truth from what is not. Because I need God, in all God's mystery and infinity, to help me with my HIV situation. I cannot get tested and find out I am sick. I need God to help me before I go, because God is the only one with the power to do so. No man can help me. And to get God's help, I need to know how to reach God, if I am not doing so already. Suddenly, I notice the restaurant is closing up. "Why don't we finish this conversation another time? I think they want us to leave." I pay the bill and walk her to catch a cab.

"I had a really good time tonight, John. Most men do not provide stimulating conversation. I hope we can do this again."

"I had a good time as well, Aurora. Why don't we meet sometime next week?" I say as I hail a cab for her.

"Sounds good," she says as her cab arrives. "Call me."

She blows me a kiss and hops into the cab. I am beginning to like this girl. I can actually have meaningful conversations with her. But what if I get tested and find out that I am positive? How will that affect my relationship with her? Will I be forced to stop courting her? So much rides on my next HIV test. Because of one night of self-indulgence, my future path is uncertain. I really hope that virus did not enter my body.

***

I wake up today and say a prayer to God, asking for mercy. I am not even sure about how to pray, exactly, but I am giving it the best I can. That way, at least, no one can say I didn't try. No one can say I sat here and just accepted my fate, whatever it may be. Today is also a big day, because Al is going to stop by to check on me. He said his church has started a counseling program for cancer and HIV patients right here in the city and that he has someone he has to see here. Somehow, I feel my ordeal has something to do with this new program at his church, but I have not asked him to confirm my suspicion. I am looking forward to seeing him.

After my prayer, I pick up the cup with the pieces of paper and play my raffle game. I shake the cup vigorously to make sure the papers get mixed up properly, and I dip my hand in the cup. I grab the first piece I touch and open it. Again, I open a blank piece of paper. Phew. Seeing that makes me feel a bit better. I have drawn a comparison between having unprotected sex and my raffle game. The chances of my picking the paper with the red H is also the probability I have of catching HIV, or an STD, for that matter. Of course, as my previous research showed, a lot also depends on the immune system of the individual, the amount of virus, the situation, and all the factors involved. But at least I have made a general correlation. I feel fortunate that, so far, I have not picked the paper with the red H.

What if I did? What if I picked up the virus after sleeping with Anna? Should sex be approached with so much caution? Now I begin to realize why certain rules are in place, such as the rules in the Bible, as well as in other good books. They are there for our protection. But too often, we succumb to the pleasures of this life and hurt ourselves as well as others, knowingly and unknowingly.

If I could go back, I would change all that I did, but I can't. I have been humbled beyond imagination. Forces beyond my comprehension are placing my life on a different path than I would ever have imagined. I do not want to be sick. I really do not want to be sick. I have had to live through a period of not knowing what the final verdict will be. Sadly, like so many other people, I gambled with my life for temporary pleasure, failing to acknowledge the consequences that one mistake could have on me. Now I am pleading with God to spare my life, because no one else can. At the end of my three-month trial, I will find out if all my pleading has been in vain. One thing I have realized, though: my life is not mine to control. Condoms break. And accidents happen. Anything can happen, at any time.

My doorbell rings—it's Al.

"So this is where you cause all your trouble," Al remarks as he walks in.

"Yeah, this is where it all happens. How are you doing, man?"

"I'm good, bro. Nice apartment you have; it will be even nicer when you decide to clean up your mess. Here, I brought you some cookies from Mom." He hands me the cookies. I thank him and make some space in my messy living room so we can sit and chat.

"You know, just because you are under a lot of stress does not mean you should not tidy your place," Al remarks.

"I know man, I know. I'll fix it up as soon as you leave."

"Cool. So how are you doing?"

"I'm okay, Al. I have been praying and doing lots of research and have just been trying to lay low, I guess. I don't really party as much; in fact, I am pretty much here in my apartment all the time."

"I see. Well, yes, you are having a hard time now, but that does not mean that you should change your daily routines. I would say still go out and see friends, and do what you used to do. Just do it responsibly, that's all. Don't be reckless with your habits."

"Yeah, you're right," I reply.

My phone rings. It is Shawn, the last person on earth I want to speak to. I tell Al to hold on.

"What's up, Shawn?"

"Yo, what's up, John? Where have you been hiding, man? There have been so many parties going on and you've been missing out. What's going on, playa?"

"Nothing, man, I've just been busy with some family stuff. What's going on with you?"

"I'm good, man. Got this nice Swedish girl the other night; you would have loved her, perfect tits and everything."

"I see. Listen, my brother is here visiting me, and I was in the middle of a conversation with him. Can I call you back?"

"Oh, that's cool, man. I just called to let you know there's a big party coming up in a couple of weeks. Should be a lot of girls in attendance, and I thought you might be interested. I am actually driving around your area, and I have a few admission tickets on me and I could drop them off at your place, if you like."

I am about to say no, and then I think of what Al just said to me, about having fun but having fun responsibly. I have been home for a long time, so I figure maybe going out might be a good thing for me. I decide that I will take Shawn up on his offer. "Okay, man, you can stop by."

I hang up then and return to my conversation with Al.

"Friend of yours?" Al asked.

"Yeah, he is just dropping off something for me."

"Cool. Anyway, thanks for offering your brother a drink when he comes to visit you."

"Sorry, bro; forgot my manners." I get Al a drink from my kitchen and then we settle down to talk.

"So, how do you feel, John?"

"I guess I am okay. Like I said, I have been doing a lot of research on this thing. They say it's not that easy for men to pick up the virus. So I have been placing my hopes on that statistic. But that is just a theory; in reality, I could be infected by it."

"I see. Well, God is a merciful God; at least, the God I know is. You should pray to Him in utmost honesty and ask for forgiveness and for His healing. God is merciful, and you will be surprised at the extent of His power."

"I know, Al, but I keep on having these doubts."

"Doubts?" he asks.

"Yeah, for example, good people suffer all around the world, people I am sure who are even as upstanding than yourself. You know, there are good people who suffer, get killed in wars, through murders and the like. There are good people who are born with this virus. I met this really cool guy at an AIDS clinic, and he is such a good person, yet he is dying from the progression of HIV to AIDS, and Al, if you meet this guy, you'll ask yourself why God would let such a person have such a disease."

"You went to an AIDS clinic? What for?" Al asks.

"Not sure. For myself, I guess. I wanted to meet someone who could tell me how to deal with it if I found out that I was indeed infected."

"I see."

"But man, I guess what I am trying to say is, if all these people who look good in my eyes are suffering or have suffered, and I am sitting here in uncertainty, not knowing if I will join their ranks, what is to show that I am not infected? If they suffer when they do no wrong, what does that mean for me, a certified playboy who has disregarded women and has nothing honorable to say about himself? That's what I am scared about, Al—that even though I have been praying and hoping for the best, it might be in my life's blueprint to have to deal with this virus."

Al looks at me seriously. His powerful frame is motionless as his eyes stay fixated on me, like a tiger stalking its prey. Somehow I feel a bit comforted and protected, knowing that my big brother is genuinely listening to me. And then he speaks.

"Well, bro, life is a mystery. I do not have all the answers for you about how life works, and I doubt anyone else does either. A lot of people talk and come up with all these theories as to what life is about: who we are, how we should act, blah-blah-blah. But the truth is, we human beings don't understand even one percent of the mysteries that comprise our existence. There is always something new we discover. All these discoveries scientists make on a daily basis are nothing new; they are truths that we are only now beginning to understand. And there is so much we do not know. We humans just recently ventured to the moon, and already our world is falling apart; and yet there is so much out there that we know nothing about. In addition to all of this, some people here on this tiny planet act as if they own everything, when they could drop dead the next day. I cannot answer your question as to why good people suffer, John. I am sure God has His reasons for everything, and we cannot expect to get human explanations for everything that happens to us, good or bad. But I will tell you that everything happens for a reason, and God has a very mysterious way of operating in people's lives.

"Yes, John, you could be infected with this virus as we speak. You could go in for your test when your three-month period is up and find out that you are indeed HIV-positive. And you have no one to blame but yourself. In the Bible there are numerous references about the dangers of casual sex; if you don't believe me, go look through the books of Proverbs and Ecclesiastes, as examples. Other religions have advice on this issue as well, not just Christianity. In society there are cautionary measures given to avoid problems related to sex, like what you are experiencing now. Abstain from sex, and if you have the urge and cannot resist, use a condom. Know your partners before you sleep with them. But you broke even those simple rules, so if you have to pay the price, you have no one to blame but yourself."

"Yes, I know, Al. You're right."

"I know I'm right. Casual sex has become a norm these days, but just because everyone is doing it doesn't mean you should join the crowd, like an idiot, even though it sounds and feels appealing. And if you cannot help the urge to sleep around with women, at least use a damn condom, and use it properly. In other words, check the expiration date, make sure it's new, make sure it's the right fit, and make sure you put it on properly. And it helps if you know the status of the person you're sleeping with as well, you know. You just don't know what people have these days. Usually, people live a carefree lifestyle until something drastic happens to them that puts things in perspective. For me, it was when I came back from school and found my parents tied together with plastic bags over their heads, dead. Going through that experience certainly changed my life, John, and I searched for years for a reason why my parents had to die in such a manner and why I had to witness such a thing. The result has made me who I am today.

"I now realize that God has His reasons for doing certain things, and nothing I can do will change that. I could sit here and be mad and upset about my parents' death and search for the killer my whole life. I could dedicate my whole life to hatred and never realize my true purpose for being here. That would be an easy path. But remember that nothing that is worth something is easy. A lot of people these days like to dwell on their bad past and preach negative messages to kids, who have no ability to decipher right from wrong. That's a coward's mode of expression, and anyone can do that. I chose to do the right thing and help others by trying my best to be a positive role model, and I pride myself in knowing that I have the guts to do the right thing, something that not too many people have the guts to do.

"I think in your situation, John, seeing that you do not know if you have this thing, your best bet is to bring it to God in prayer. I recommend going through Jesus Christ, based on my experience with life."

My doorbell rings. It's Shawn.

"Yo, Al, I've got to let my friend in for a sec, and then we'll get back to our conversation, okay?"

"Sure thing."

I go to the front door and let Shawn in.

"Yo, Johnny, my man, what's happening?" We shake hands.

"Hey, why don't you come in and meet my brother; then you'll have to leave because we are having some family talk."

"Cool, man."

I lead Shawn to my living room, where Al sits patiently.

"Al, this is my buddy, Shawn. Shawn, this is my brother, Al."

"What's up, Shawn?"

"What's happening, Al? You guys don't look alike. I would never have thought you were brothers."

"Yeah, we get that a lot," Al replies.

"Cool, well, it was nice meeting you. John, here are the tickets I promised you, buddy, and here is an extra one in case your brother wants to come as well."

"Thanks, man," I reply.

"Yeah, thanks," says Al.

"Cool. Say, John, think I could get a glass of water before I hit the road? I am a little thirsty."

"I don't have any bottled water, but I have some orange juice, or if you prefer, I could hook you up with some tap water."

"Tap water is cool, buddy."

I bring him a glass of tap water.

"So, what were you guys talking about? Oh, I'm sorry; I forgot you said you were discussing family business."

"Nah, that's cool," Al says before I have a chance to speak. "I was just discussing God and Christianity with John, that's all."

Here we go, I think.

"Oh, really?" remarks Shawn. "So what's the verdict? Do we all agree that Christianity makes no sense, and that religion, in general, is just man's interpretation of the way the world should work?"

"No, we don't agree with you," Al replies.

"C'mon, man, you can't possibly believe that Jesus Christ is the Savior and that Christianity is the way to go."

"I do," Al replies calmly.

"Okay, so how do you explain how Christians, who are supposed to be so holy, are responsible for so many mass murders throughout history? The Crusades are a perfect example. So many people go around killing innocents in the name of Christianity. And it's not just Christianity; so many people have died in the name of religion for no apparent reason. How do you explain that, huh?" Shawn chuckles.

Al suddenly wears a very relaxed grin. "Well, buddy, yes, a lot of people died during the Crusades. And a lot of people have died in the name of religion, many of them innocent. But for you to say that Christianity makes no sense, based on the actions of a few people, makes no sense to me. The choice those people made to cause so much chaos was a result of their own poor decisions, not a result of anything Christianity or any other religion made them do. And who are we to say that people who go around killing are really doing it in the name of religion? What are you following? The religion or the people in action?"

"C'mon, man," Shawn replies, "look at all the crap going on today—people killing each other in the name of religion. Christians are behind much of what is going on. Look at how relaxed Christians are; the same Christians who go to church are the same ones you see being immoral! I am not convinced about Christianity, dude. The way I see it, you have to live fast 'cause you don't know when you'll die. You have to have as much fun as you can, and you and you alone control your destiny, and that's that. I don't believe in following other people."

Al sighs deeply. "Well, you've made some interesting points, and I do not feel like debating with you, so I will end our chat on this note. We humans have traits unique only to us, such as having a conscience. And we all have the freedom of choice; that is what separates us from animals. That is what makes us human. Now, we have to remember that our decisions, no matter how small, affect others in ways we might not even know about. I am a Christian, and I try to live by the true Christian values, which are embodied by the teachings of Jesus Christ.

"He had two very simple rules, which go beyond Christianity, and which embody human existence itself: 'Love the Lord your God with all your heart, with all your soul, and with all your mind,' and 'Love your neighbor as yourself.' In other words, understand and respect the sheer infinity of God and have respect for your fellow man. Everything else he said is based on these two rules. Now, I cannot speak for the reasons individuals choose to distort his teachings to suit their personal desires. Like I said, we all have the freedom of choice. But I personally try to live my life by these rules. I know that there is a God, which I cannot even begin to fully understand, and I prefer to live in harmony with everyone else. These two rules pretty much embody all I strive to be."

"I see," Shawn replies. "Well, I guess to each his own."

"To each his own," replies Al.

Shawn turns to me. "All this religious talk has got me a little tired. John, I gave you the tickets, so you know what to do. I hope I see you there, dude."

"Yeah, we'll see" I reply.

He turns back to Al. "It was nice meeting you, Al. Maybe we can continue this conversation another time."

"Sounds good to me," says Al.

I walk Shawn to the door and then return to Al. "You have to excuse my friend; he can be opinionated at times."

"That's okay; I used to be like that."

"So tell me about this counseling program your church started. Did you say you guys are offering HIV counseling?"

"Yeah, we got in touch with a few of the clinics and outreach programs right here in the city. We take on some of their patients and provide support and counseling."

"That's a very noble thing to do, Al."

"Yeah, in fact I will be seeing this girl who just found out that she is HIV-positive the day after I leave your place. She's quite a pleasant girl."

"Hmm…hearing that scares me a bit."

"You shouldn't be scared if you've prayed to God. From this point on, whatever happens was meant to be."

"You're right, Al. I should have more faith that I will be fine."

"Yes, you should. Anyway, enough serious talk. Why don't we rent some movies, order some food, and spend the rest of the day having some fun."

"Sounds good to me."

And that's exactly what we do.

I have to see Alexia. My last encounter with Cody really upset me. That's the thing with guys—they just sleep with you and see you as a piece of meat to be discarded when they are done. I feel so used. And to think that he had that planned from the very beginning! What a jerk! I should find out who this girl is that he is seeing and tell her all about him and see how he likes that! Jerk! I ask Alexia to meet me at my place for some girl talk around noon today, and she obliges. Later on, I'm going to meet with Anna for some coffee.

Alexia watches as I pace around my apartment.

"I can't believe that jerk!" I exclaim.

"I can't believe *you*, Michelle."

"What do you mean, you can't believe me?"

"Well, I told you not to go over there, but you didn't listen."

"That's not the point, Alexia. The point is that I went over to his place, and he made it seem as if he wasn't seeing anyone, and then it was only after we had sex that he chose to tell me that he was."

"But why do you say that he made it seem as if he was not seeing anyone?"

"Well, he was flirting with me the whole time, and he kissed me the last time we had dinner!"

"So maybe he wanted you. Did you want more from him besides sex?"

"No…well, I mean, yeah…I don't know. He is my ex, you know, and I did have feelings for him before."

"So you wanted more from him."

"Yeah, okay, fine, I guess I did. But it was still wrong of him to lead me on like that. If he had a girlfriend he could have at least mentioned it."

"Did you tell him that you were seeing someone yourself?"

"No. Well, it almost slipped out, but I didn't tell."

"So you're saying that you're angry that he is seeing someone, yet you are doing the same. Michelle, you knew full well what you were getting into before you went to see him, and you're just as wrong as he is."

"Whatever, Alexia."

"Whatever? What about Darius? I thought you told me that you guys agreed to start seeing each other again?"

"Let's change the subject. I don't feel like talking about this anymore."

"No, no, we are not changing any subject, Michelle, and you can't keep on bouncing between boyfriends like that. I'm saying this to you as a friend. Yeah, we all know guys can be a bit flaky sometimes, but that doesn't mean you have to lower your standards as well."

"Okay, okay, Alexia, geez, fine. I was wrong for going to see Cody. I was just hoping that we could work things out, that's all."

"You already have a boyfriend. There is nothing to 'work out' with Cody, and you have to make yourself understand that."

"Okay. Can we please change the subject now?"

"Okay. What's up with Anna? When are you meeting up with her?"

"Later on today. She agreed to meet for some coffee."

"I wish I could go with you. I kinda miss Anna."

"No worries. I am sure we will be able to meet again, and next time you will be able to join us. I don't see Anna having a problem with that."

"She must have been going through a lot."

"Well, she looked really…umm …how do I say this? She looked very ordinary when I saw her. Very plain, no makeup, no fancy clothes…she looked very different. And tired."

"Hmm. Well, people and things change, I guess."

"Yeah. I am sure that she's okay, but we'll see what she has to say," I replied.

We spend the rest of our time together talking about men, and then we part ways; she goes back home to be with her daughter, and I head off to meet up with an old friend called Anna.

***

I get to the coffee shop around 7:00 p.m. for my rendezvous with Anna. It begins to rain, and I am happy that I got there before the rain got really heavy. I walk in the shop and spot Anna sitting in the back. She still looks very plain, and she also looks sad. She is smiling, but her face still looks sad. I walk over and take a seat.

"Hey, you," I greet her.

"Hey, girlfriend," she replies, "how are you?"

"I am okay. Just had a bit of a rough week, but I am okay."

"Is everything all right?"

"Yeah, just guy issues, the usual."

"Oh, did you end up dating the Darius guy you told me about?"

"Wow, you still remember that? Yeah, I dated him; we're still seeing each other, I guess."

"You guess?"

"Yeah, well, remember Cody?"

"Your ex? Of course I do."

"Well, he sort of came back into the picture."

"How? Did he contact you?"

"Actually, I contacted him."

"Oh, what made you do that? Did you miss him or something?"

"Yeah, I think I did."

"So what happened?"

"I slept with him."

"Wow! I thought you were dating the Darius guy?"

"I am."

"Well, does he know that you cheated on him?"

"No, and I don't think I will tell him."

"You should be careful with these guys. Being with one good guy is a better way to play the dating game."

I can tell that something is up. Anna would never talk like that—at least, not the Anna that I remember. She is usually the first one to talk about sex and being with every man on the planet.

"Wow, look at you talking, Anna, telling me to be with one good guy. That doesn't sound like you."

"Well, people and things change, I guess."

Those were the same words that Alexia used. "So what's changed about you, Anna? Other than your dress code and that you talk funny now. But enough about me; let's hear what's been going on with you."

She purses her lips and looks away. Her eyes begin to well up with tears.

"Aw, Anna, what's wrong?" I take her hand. "Talk to me, Anna. Is this about your brother who died? You can talk to me."

She looks at me and takes a deep breath. "No one died in my family, Michelle."

"What? But you told us that your brother died, and that's the reason that you became so distant. So you're telling me that never happened?"

"That never happened, Michelle." Tears begin to roll down her cheeks.

"I'm really confused, Anna. You have to help me out here. Something is definitely wrong."

"I…umm…I …umm…"

"Listen, you don't have to say it if you don't want to."

"It's okay, Michelle, I want to say it, so we're both on the same page. I have been holding this thing in for so long, and I have to talk to someone about it."

I continue to hold her hand. "Okay, I will listen, whenever you're ready."

"Thanks, Michelle. Okay…" She takes a deep breath and squeezes my hand as she looks me right in my eyes. I begin to get a bit nervous. "You have to promise me that what I am about to tell you stays between us."

"I promise."

"No, Michelle, I am dead serious. Promise me again."

"I promise."

"Now understand that what I am about to tell you most likely will change the nature of our friendship forever, but please, no matter what happens, please don't judge me."

I wonder what on earth she could be talking about. Change the nature of our friendship? Did she sleep with someone I know? Did she say something behind my back? "I won't judge you, Anna. I am your friend, and I won't judge you. Now tell me what you have to say."

"I'm scared."

"Why? I am your friend; there is nothing to be scared about."

"Okay…okay…Michelle, I'm…umm, I…err…"

"Just let it out, Anna."

"I am HIV-positive, Michelle."

I almost fall out of my seat. My heart begins to beat really fast, and I immediately pull my hand away from hers and place it in my lap. I do not know what to do; she has caught me off guard, and I do not know what to say.

"What? What are you talking about Anna?"

"I am HIV-positive, Michelle," she repeats, her demeanor much calmer now.

"But…but …that can't be. Why are you saying this?"

"Because I got tested, Michelle, and the results came back saying that I was HIV-positive."

"No…"

"Yes."

"No…" I begin to cry.

"I know it sucks, Michelle. It was hard for me to hear the news. I was so scared, so scared…I did not know what to do."

"But are you sure? Maybe the tests were wrong? Maybe they made a mistake with the testing, you know, like mix up your results or something?"

"I got tested twice, Michelle. I am HIV-positive."

"No…" I cry some more. "How did you find out?"

"I was sleeping around with some guy, and we had an accident, and he suggested that I go in and get tested, so I did. And that's when I found out."

"So this guy is the one who gave it to you?"

"I doubt it, because I only slept with him a few times over a short period, and if it was him I don't think my results would have shown as positive so quickly. I've probably had this thing for a very long time, before meeting him."

"Oh, my God…this is really messed up. Not you, Anna!"

"It's okay, Michelle. I am doing much better now. I have learned a lot from the whole experience. The doctors say that there are many people walking around who have this thing, so I am not alone. I just have all this medication to take now, and I just have to keep myself really healthy. So I can't party and do all the crazy things I used to do before."

"This is not right. You don't deserve this, Anna. You're too good a person."

"It is what it is, I guess."

"Is there anything I can do?"

"No, like I said, I am doing much better now. I was advised not to tell too many people that I have this thing, because people, in general, are very ignorant and will treat me really badly. I am only telling you because I felt bad about lying to you and also because we are good friends. But please, don't tell anyone."

"I won't. So what are you going to do?"

"Well, I joined a church for starters, and they have been really supportive of me. They listen and don't judge me, for the most part, so that has been helpful. There is also this counseling program that was started by some church located outside the city, and I spoke to one of its members over the phone a few days ago. I am actually meeting him tomorrow, and we are going to talk and pray about my situation. He seems like a very nice, genuine person, so I am looking forward to seeing him."

I am still crying.

"Stop crying, Michelle. Everything, I guess, happens for a reason, and you shouldn't cry. I am not doing that bad. I have HIV, but look on the bright side—I don't have AIDS, at least not yet. I am feeling healthy and I am taking steps to make things better. It's just the people aspect that can get hard sometimes."

"I am so sorry, Anna. I am so sorry that you have to go through this. It's just not fair."

"It's okay, Michelle, it's okay. I am just paying the price for my mistakes. I am not living day to day anymore. My mindset has changed, so I am just a lot more careful with who and what I deal with. There are a few things that scare me, like how to deal with people—guys, for instance. No guy wants to deal with a woman he knows is HIV-positive, but that's just something I will have to live with, I guess."

"And there is no cure for this thing, this HIV?"

"Nope. Well, there might be, but we common people don't know anything about it."

"This really sucks," I say as I dry my eyes. "I am so sorry, Anna."

"It is okay, Michelle." She reaches out to hold my hand. I move away from her touch, then realize what I have done, and I feel bad. Too late. She looks at me and gives me a gentle smile. "It's okay. I understand. You're scared because you do not understand. But just so you know, there is no way I can infect you by just touching you, Michelle. But it's okay. I understand how people think." She gets up and grabs her coat.

"Wait, Anna, wait! I did not mean to do that. Please, give me some time to get used to the situation. I am really sorry. Please…"

"It is okay. I have to go now. Like I told you before, this might change our friendship. Don't feel bad for anything. All I ask is that you keep this between us, okay? I don't want people walking around calling me the HIV girl and stuff, because people can be very mean. Okay?"

"I promise I will not tell anyone. Are you going to be okay?"

"Yes. I have to go to the gym to get some exercise. I will be changing my phone number soon, so maybe I will keep you posted."

"Okay. Please call me if you need anything. You can always call me."

She gives me another gentle smile. "Good-bye Michelle."

"Good-bye Anna. Please, call me later, okay?"

"Okay."

I watch her walk out of the coffee shop. I do not know what to think or what to do. My heart is beating at an alarming rate. I feel my body tighten. I feel like throwing up. How could Anna have HIV? The same Anna who I partied with for most of my young adult life, the same Anna who made me laugh and told me all of her boy troubles, the same Anna who was my roommate through all those years in college. How could this be? I get up to leave, but I stop to wash my hands in the bathroom before I go.

Chapter Twenty-Six

get to work the next day in a better mood than I have been in for a long time. I have not been with a woman since my incident with Anna, and I have been praying on a pretty regular basis. I have done everything my parents suggested. Will all be well with me, then? Is this like a deal sort of thing, where I pray with honesty and the problem goes away? I decide I will have to talk to my dad about that concept. He might have some answers for me.

As the day wears on I feel more at peace. Then I receive an unexpected call from one person I did not want to hear from again—Shawn.

I see his number flashing on my caller ID, and I hesitate to answer the phone, but I finally do.

"Yo, John! How have you been, man? I haven't heard from you in ages!"

I can already see where this is going. "Hey, Shawn, how are you?"

"Yo, John, your brother was cool, man, a really deep dude. Must be something being around him all the time."

"Yeah, that's my bro, man," I reply.

"Cool. So what's up with you and the ladies, huh, Mr. John? Don't think I didn't see you being smooth with that girl at the bar the last time we hung out. Yeah, I remember. So what happened with her? Did you hook up with her?"

Anna. He is referring to Anna. A sudden chill runs down my spine, and I become very uncomfortable about speaking with this guy. "Nah, man, I never hooked up with her. Saw her at the bar and that was it."

"Shame, man, she had a really nice body. I would have screwed her. So tell me, man, what else is going on? I'm sure you got a whole bunch of women lined up by your bedroom. C'mon, talk to me John." He laughs.

I really do not feel like talking to this guy. A conversation I once would have found entertaining is now disturbing to my ears. "Nah, man, I don't have any girls by my bedroom."

"You liar! Anyway, I was calling to find out for sure if you wanted to come with me to the industry party that I gave you the tickets for. I think Cesar wants to come as well. There will be a lot of women present, buddy—so many beautiful women, all just waiting to get laid. So you definitely have to come with us, man. You'll love it; trust me."

I think about his offer, and for the first time, I realize I do not want to be around anything or any situation that reminds me of that night when I first spoke to Anna. And that includes Shawn. "Nah, man, I'll pass."

"What's up, John? You flakin' on me, man? Did you not hear me? You need to be there, man. All these girls will be drooling for a guy like you. C'mon, don't bail out on me."

"Nah, I'm cool. I'm not really in the mood to go out this weekend, but I'll call you if I change my mind."

"Okay, dude, but don't say I didn't let you know about this."

"I appreciate it, man, and if I change my mind, I will let you know. Promise."

"Okay, then, give me a call and let me know."

"Sounds good, man. Bye for now."

"Bye, John."

The simple thought of Shawn and his inviting smile brings back the memory of that night, the next few days of sleeping with Anna, and the day I received the gloomy news. And I do not want to revisit that whole episode ever again. I decide that this weekend, rather than stick around this city, I will go to see my father and get—I hope—some answers to some of my questions.

That night when I get home from work, I decide to do some more research into the virus. I soon find a topic that catches my attention: "Circumcision and HIV." That sounds interesting. "Circumcision significantly reduces the risk of HIV infection" is the title of this article. Apparently, this is a study that was conducted with two separate groups of men, nearly 3000 in Kenya and almost 5000 in Uganda. These men were not initially infected with HIV. The men were given safe sex instructions, and then regularly checked for infection. In the study the Kenyan men were found to have a reduction of 53 percent in contracting new cases of HIV, and the men in Uganda showed a similar result with a reduction rate of 48 percent.

As I read on, I can't help but ask myself how ethical it is to run such an experiment.

But that is another issue.

Apparently, there have been other studies that yielded similar results, leading many researchers to the hypothesis that circumcision reduces the risk of HIV transmission. This is due to two possibilities. First, the "underside of the foreskin has a heavy concentration of Langerhan cells, a type of dendritic cell that are the first lines of defense of the immune system." Langerhan cells...I have never seen that name before, so I decided to do some research on that. I opened a new browser and ran a search on that name. "Langerhan cells are likely initial targets for HIV following sexual exposure to the virus and provide an efficient means for HIV to gain access to lymph node T-cells." So I guess that Langerhan cells serve as a sort of transport module for the virus to reach the immune system cells. I read on. "The probability of HIV infection is a function of both the number of infective HIV virons in the body fluid which contact the host and the number of cells available at the site of contact that have appropriate CD4 receptors." I figure the Langerhan cells are an example of appropriate CD4 receptors, and the viral load would be the number of HIV virons in the body of the HIV-positive individual.

It all begins to make sense. I hope that I did not have enough Langerhan cells that were exposed to Anna's HIV! But of course, I can't tell. I would need a microscope and most likely a blood test to be able to know for sure. I guess it was a good thing that I took a piss and washed up when I was done. But you just never know. Which means I took a bad risk, even though I thought all would go well.

I go back to the previous Web page and read up on the second possibility as to why circumcision reduces the risk of HIV transmission. The report says that while circumcision can provide a reduced risk, it does not completely reduce the risk of infection. It only lowers the risk of HIV transmission during heterosexual intercourse, as it increases the reduction rate of HIV transmission from women to men and vice versa. Interesting—that is good news for me, because I am circumcised. But again, these are all just studies done that yielded results relative to a specific group, a specific sample that does not represent the entire whole. The chance of HIV infection, from what I learned, varies among individuals, based on genetic makeup, the immune system, the presence of certain cells, and the amount of HIV in the infected person or carrier. And all it takes is to get a little of that virus into your system.

All it takes is a little.

I have to see Alexia. I have so many thoughts and so many questions running through my mind. How could Anna be HIV-positive? How could this be possible? Why her?

I tell Alexia about my meeting with Anna, and she is shocked. She just could not believe it. So I agree to meet her at her place tonight for some girl talk, because this is a hot issue.

I get to her place in the evening. She had just put Tara to bed and had made some hot chocolate for us. I plop on a seat in her kitchen.

"Oh, by the way," she whispers, "my mom is here. She's asleep right now."

"She is? Why didn't you tell me? How long is she here for?"

"She is just here for two days. She came for this class reunion some of her college classmates are having here in the city."

"Oh, okay."

"So…Anna. That is so sad, so sad. I can't believe that she is HIV-positive!"

"I know," I reply. "I couldn't believe it myself."

"Do you know how she found out?"

"She said that she was having sex with some guy, and they had an accident, whatever that means. Then the guy asked her to get tested and that's how she found out."

"Damn. She's probably had it for a while then. What a shame."

"Yeah, that's what she said."

"See what happens when you sleep around? Anna probably slept with the whole world. Now look at her. This is so sad."

"Yeah, I know."

"What do you know?" Miss Pryce asks from the doorway. I always hate it when she sneaks up on our conversations like that.

"Oh, nothing, Ma, we're just yapping," Alexia says.

"No, you weren't. What were you talking about?" Miss Pryce asked.

"It's okay, Alexia, you can tell her," I say.

"Okay, Ma. Well, remember Anna?"

"Yes, your friend? What about her?"

"She just revealed to Michelle that she is HIV-positive."

"And Michelle came to tell you what Anna revealed to her, did she?" Miss Pryce gives me a stern look. I bow my head. "Did Anna ask you to share this with anyone, Michelle?"

"No, Miss Pryce."

"Michelle, I told you before not to go around sharing confidential information with other people, even if they are your friends. We had this talk before, when you came here saying that your friend Jess was pregnant, remember?"

"Yes, Miss Pryce. But Anna is a friend to all of us, and I did not think that it would be that big of a deal."

"You really need to be quiet right now. Of course it is a big deal! Don't you realize how sensitive the subject of HIV is? You don't just go around discussing that with your friends over hot chocolate, as if it is men or some other random subject you are talking about. You have a big mouth, Michelle. In life, don't talk about other people to other people, and don't run your mouth unless it is absolutely necessary, because that is how trouble starts. Do you understand?"

"But Miss Pryce—"

"*Do you understand?*"

"Yes, Miss Pryce."

"Good. You are friends with my daughter, so I take you as one of my own, but I will stop Alexia from hanging out with you if I catch more of this behavior from you. Gossiping only starts unwarranted trouble, Michelle, no matter where you are or who you're doing it with."

"Okay, Miss Pryce. I am really sorry."

"Don't apologize to me. If you see Anna again, look into yourself and see if you have the guts to apologize to her, and do so."

"C'mon, Ma, you're being a little harsh, don't you think?" Alexia says.

"No, I am not, and I will not endorse gossiping in any way, shape, or form. The mouth is a very dangerous tool, and it can destroy you if you do not use it wisely. Trust me."

"Ma, you really think you can stop Michelle and me from hanging out?" Alexia asks playfully.

"My dear, I can only advise you both to do what I feel is best for you. Whether or not you listen is up to you. Like the saying goes, you can lead a horse to water, but you can't make it drink."

"Okay, I was just kidding, Ma."

I feel really ashamed.

Miss Pryce turns to me. "That is pretty sad about your friend. This is why I always tell you girls to be careful. Are you girls being careful?"

Alexia answers, "We've made our mistakes here and there, Ma, but for the most part we are—at least, I am."

"When was the last time you had sex, Alexia?" Miss Pryce asks.

"Geez, Ma! What a question!"

"I am serious. We are all grown women, and we should be able to talk about such things openly. I have experienced everything you have and probably more, so don't feel bashful around me."

"Okay, Ma…well, I last had sex a couple of months ago," Alexia says.

"Was this with a boyfriend? I wasn't aware that you had a boyfriend recently."

"No, Ma, this was with a guy I met in the neighborhood. I found him attractive, and he was funny, so we went out, and I slept with him."

"I never thought you would be so random, Alexia" Miss Pryce says.

"I was lonely, Ma!"

"Yes, I know, but having sex does not solve the issue of loneliness; having a companion does that. Did you use a condom when you slept with this man?" Miss Pryce asks.

"Of course I did, Ma. You know me better than that."

"Good. How about you, Michelle?"

"What about me, Miss Pryce?"

"When was the last time you had sex?"

196

"A few days ago!" Alexia chimes in.

"Thanks a lot. Alexia...big mouth. Yes. Miss Pryce, a few days ago."

"And did you use a condom?"

"Umm...no, I did not."

Alexia seems shocked. "Michelle! I thought we agreed that we would start using condoms when it comes to sex? What happened?"

"I don't know...I mean, the sex was with my ex-boyfriend, so I did not think that it was that big of a deal."

"Hmm," says Miss Pryce. "So how many partners have you guys had in the past year?"

Alexia speaks up right away. "Besides the random guy I just mentioned, I haven't slept with anyone besides Tara's dad."

"Okay, and you, Michelle?"

I suddenly feel like an idiot. "Well, I, umm, I have slept with about three guys in the past year."

"Three guys, huh?" says Miss Pryce. "And did you use protection with all three guys?"

"Well, we started out using protection, but stopped when we started seeing each other more. But it's okay. They were all boyfriends at different points in time, so I felt comfortable with them."

"No, it's not okay, Michelle," Miss Pryce argues. "You think that just because a man gets the status of being your boyfriend that he magically becomes clean, even if he had an STD or HIV? You're not that dumb, are you?"

"I am not dumb, Miss Pryce, and every guy I have dated has carried himself really well. You know, taken care of himself—well groomed, that sort of thing. None has been a player or a junkie. They all have been good, clean-cut guys."

"Sometimes I am amazed at how foolish your generation is," Miss Pryce says. "It's kind of like people get dumber and dumber as the years go by. Have you ever discussed your previous boyfriends' sexual histories openly with them? Or do you just go along because they are 'good' people, and you are in love?"

"Well, they seem like decent people, Miss Pryce. I talk, and we get to know each other, and if we have chemistry, then we date."

"And when you say that you get to know each other, do you ask them about their sexual histories? Do you ask them questions like 'Do you have any STDs?' or 'Are you HIV-positive?' Or you just start sleeping with them because you feel that they are good people?"

"C'mon, Miss Pryce, nobody asks such questions when they are dating. It's not the norm to talk like that," I insist.

She shakes her head. "You girls need to be really, really careful. This world is not as pretty as you think it is. You have to be very careful with whom you deal with and how you deal with them. And this applies to just about anything. Think about it like this: do you just let anyone into your apartment, Michelle?"

"No."

"Do you invite a person you just meet on the street, who seems like a nice guy, into your place for hot chocolate and spicy conversation, as you guys are doing now?"

"No."

"Why not?"

"Well, I would have to get to know him first. A lot of guys who seem like nice guys turn out to be psychos, you know."

"Use that same analogy with your body. The same way a seemingly nice guy can come into your place and steal your possessions, mess up your apartment, and even hurt you is the same way a man whose sexual history you know nothing about can enter you and cause a whole lot of mess. You shouldn't let just anyone into your 'house,' and the same applies for guys. A guy should not enter a room or a woman when he knows very little or nothing about it or her. And if you feel that it is absolutely necessary to let someone into your place, at least have some protection, Michelle, and don't base it on how you feel or how attractive a person looks. Looks can be very deceiving."

"You're right. I have been making some bad decisions, haven't I?" I say.

"You think?" Alexia responds. "Why do you think I said we should start making guys use condoms, Michelle? I wasn't just saying that to say it."

"I know, I know…I just got caught up in the moment. You guys are making me nervous."

"I am sure that you are fine," Miss Pryce says, "but just use more caution from now on. You can't just have unprotected sex with different men; that's very risky, Michelle. Do you know how many women the average man sleeps with? And do you know how many other men those women he sleeps with have been with, and so forth? You have to be more careful—both of you."

"But Ma, even though I agree with you, it can get so hard sometimes. You know, right around when my time of the month comes around, I get really heated, and I feel like I have to have sex. What do we do when times like those come around?"

"It's all in your mind, sweetheart. Your mind controls your body, and if your mind is in the gutter, your body will follow suit. Yes, we are human beings, and naturally our bodies have certain cravings, sex being one of them, but even cravings can be controlled and managed wisely. If you get heated, don't go off and seduce some man for sex. If you have to do what you have to do, then do it, but don't go around sleeping with random men. And if you feel that you have to have sex, use a damn condom! Make the man use a condom, even if he is your boyfriend. The only time you should even consider having unprotected sex is if the man is your husband, or if you know for sure that he is disease-free. Men should be asking women those sorts of questions as well, but most men don't have strong wills when it comes to sex."

"But Miss Pryce, how do you ask a man that you're seeing if he is disease-free? I mean, most guys will think that you're accusing them of something, and will get mad at you and stuff," I say.

"Who cares what they think, Michelle? What someone else thinks of you should be the last thing on your mind. It is your body, not theirs, so don't worry about what they think. You have to put your foot down and learn to respect yourself. Sex feels really good, but like most things that feel and look good, it can come with a very high price, if not handled responsibly."

"My mom is right, Michelle. We have to be more careful. People are people, and you never know what you're getting."

"I feel very scared now. What should I do?" I ask.

"Well, for starters," says Miss Pryce, "why don't you have a conversation with whomever you are seeing now, and try to get to know him a little better? Then take it from there and start making better decisions."

"Okay, Miss Pryce. Thank you."

"Thanks for the pep talk, Ma."

"You guys are welcome. Okay, well, I am an old woman, and I am very tired, so I am going to rest with Tara. Don't stay up too late, okay?"

"Okay, Ma. Sleep well."

"Bye, Miss Pryce."

"Bye, Michelle. And remember to talk with your current boyfriend or whomever you've been having sex with."

"Okay, I will."

"Good night girls."

"Good night."

Miss Pryce leaves us in the kitchen, and Alexia and I continue to sip on our hot chocolate. I have a million things running through my mind.

"So what did you think?" Alexia asks.

"Your mom made a lot of sense. It's stuff I never really thought about."

"So are you going to talk to Darius, or should I say, Cody?"

"Not funny, Alexia. I think I will have a little chat with Darius."

"What about Cody and Braxton? You slept with them unprotected as well."

"Yeah, but I can't call them. I am not dating them anymore. Besides, they may not want to talk to me."

"I understand. Well, start with Darius and see how that goes. Looks like Anna gave us all a wake-up call, huh?"

"She sure did."

We spend the rest of the evening sipping our chocolate and doing very little talking. And I feel a little nervous.

Chapter Twenty-Seven

Even though it's the weekend, I decide that I will pay Sebastian a surprise visit. It's Sunday, five days before I can finally hear my verdict; I have exactly five days before my three-month trial period comes to a close. Five days before I am "pardoned" or "sentenced." Merely thinking about such a concept sends a shiver down my spine. I would never have guessed in my wildest dreams that I would find myself in this situation. I have heard of friends of friends of friends of mine getting infected. I have heard of people I know catching diseases. I have heard all sorts of stories. But how could this be happening to me, John Casey? How is this possible? I mean, I took precautions like every guy does: I wore a condom, and I thought I put it on the right way. But the damn thing broke. Who knows why? Maybe due to its age or its quality.

The fact is that accidents do happen. Even though I have prayed to God the best way I can, I still have the urge to do more research on my situation and evaluate my possibilities for escaping the clutches of this deadly virus. This is why, this evening I have chosen to do more research online to find more information that might bring me comfort, before I go to the clinic to see Sebastian.

I scroll through the Web sites and see pages I have been through already through previous research, but soon a title catches my attention: "Catching AIDS: The HIV epidemic in the United States." The article is dated 1993, so it's a bit old, but it might still prove relevant, so I read on. "HIV is no longer rare in the U.S. population. According to current scientific 'guesstimates,' 1 million U.S. citizens are currently infected with HIV. If this figure is correct, then 1 out of approximately every 270 people in the United States is infected."

Wow, that is a high number. And I have to remember that the number only takes into consideration recorded cases. The number is probably a lot higher. I probably walk past HIV-infected people on a daily basis. Oh, how foolish I have been, sleeping with women left and right without regard for their health or mine. I feel as if I have been a little kid playing with a loaded gun with the safety on—the more often the child plays with a gun, the more likely the child is to turn the safety switch off, switching that gun into firing mode. I turned the safety off when I slept with Anna and the condom broke. Now I am just waiting to see if the one bullet in the chamber is going to go off when I have to pull the trigger, in one week. I have been fooling around with my life. I have been such a fool; I have been so irresponsible.

I read on. "In an infected person, HIV is found in any body fluid or substance which contains lymphocytes (T4-cells). Substances containing lymphocytes include: blood, semen, vaginal and cervical secretions, mother's milk, saliva, tears, urine, and feces." Blood...when I had my accident with Anna, she was on her period, so I decide to try to find something in this article that relates to that. I am in luck.

"Females probably do not have an increased risk for catching HIV during menstruation. Menstrual bleeding is actually the shedding of the tissues of the uterus (womb). Menstrual blood flows from the uterus, through the cervix, and into the vagina. There is no vaginal wound for entry by HIV. Again, it should be noted, that the current consensus is that wounds may not be necessary, since HIV may directly infect macrophages, which rove the mucous membrane surfaces. Also, HIV may be able to directly cross the mucous membrane and enter the blood vessels therein."

In other words, there does not have to be an open wound or sore. The virus can simply infect the cells in that area. I read on, and soon find something that directly applies to my situation:

"Males can catch HIV from infected females. The method of transmission is not clear. It may be possible for HIV infection to come from menstrual blood or from contact with a female's vaginal or cervical secretions. The concentration of HIV in these substances does not seem very high (compared with blood and semen); still the concentration is sufficient for HIV transmission to take place. Small amounts of blood may also be present in the vagina due to rough sexual intercourse or to other vaginal conditions. In males, the doorway for HIV into the body may be very small wounds on the head of the penis, the mucous membranes lining the urethra (the "eye" of the penis is the opening of the urethra), or the glands which intersect the urethra at the base of the penis."

Well, I don't think I had any wounds on my penis, and I was not inside Anna for that long. But to be sure, I scan my little friend who got me in all this trouble. Nope. Nothing. But my check just now means nothing, as the accident happened almost three months ago. So reading this information makes me feel a little better but does not erase the possibility of my being HIV-positive.

In fact, it gives me more insight into the real unspoken seriousness of HIV in the United States and in the world today, but it does little, if anything, about telling me if I am indeed infected. All this tells me is that if I had known all of this then, I would not have acted the way I did. But there is no room for excuses; I am a man, and I am responsible for all my actions, and playing the ignorant card only makes me look all the more foolish. Only the test will answer that question. My selfish, risky, sensual lifestyle that brought me so much temporary pleasure has left me with nothing for the long term but pain. I now realize that selfish desires, whether in the form of money, power, attention, or even sex, may satisfy temporary cravings, but they leave us like slaves, in constant need to satisfy that hunger, and as a result, they control our lives.

When I first came to the big city, my goals were to make money and sleep with as many women as possible. And so I slept with women, without taking into consideration if I was hurting them or hurting myself. I used sex in the wrong way; it is meant for procreation and as an expression of love between two individuals committed to a healthy relationship. Instead, I used it to satisfy my selfish desires. Look at me now. Look at me, the selfish John Casey. Look at me now. Turns out that I am the loser in my grand scheme.

***

I get to the clinic. Feels a bit awkward coming here on a Sunday evening, but…oh, well. I printed out Sebastian's second poem, "Haud Voluntas," to read on the train, and I decide to read it now as I arrive at the clinic. I plan to ask him what *Haud Voluntas* means; maybe it's another language he speaks or something. I open the printed copy, and this is what I see:

HAUD VOLUNTAS

I slip then I fall, then I get back up again
I smile then I cry, then its back to smiles again
I reach then I touch, then I lose my grip with friends
And its then that I realize that nothing makes any sense

I think for a moment about what I've just read, and then I suddenly feel very depressed, more for Sebastian than even for myself. Why does such a good person have to suffer? The irony and complexity of this life baffles me, and sometimes I wish I could change things for the better. Just like how Sebastian felt, I guess, when he wrote his "Sometimes" poem. He sounds really depressed in this poem, even though on his Web site he offers hope to others like him. I will have to cheer him up. I will have to step out of my selfish life and do something to help another, especially when that 'other' is my friend.

I get to the AIDS ward, and surprisingly, Bertha is sitting at the receptionist desk.

"Hey, Bertha."

She looks up. "Hey John, what are you doing here on a Sunday?"

"Oh, just thought I would stop by and pay Sebastian a visit. Break out of my regular Sunday routine. What are you doing here? Do you have to work today?"

She smiles. "The nurse could not be here today, so I decided to fill in. This is more than just a job for me, you know."

"Cool. Is Sebastian asleep?"

"Hey, John!" I hear Sebastian yell.

"I guess not. Bertha, I will see you in a bit."

"Okay, John, go see your friend."

I step into Sebastian's room. He is lying in bed, and he looks paler than usual and very weak. "Hey, you."

"Hey, John," he replies. "How are you, man?"

"I'm good, bro. How about you?"

"I feel ill, but I guess that's to be expected," Sebastian says. "How is your family?"

"Everyone is well, Sebastian."

"And how about that girl you told me about? The one you're dating now?"

"Oh, she's good, man. Things are going well between us. She appears to be a great person so far."

"Good stuff, John, so did you find out if she had any cute friends I could hook up with?"

We both smile. "No, Sebastian, I did not ask her about her friends. I promise I will next time."

He looks at me, still smiling. "There might not be a next time, John."

"Sebastian, you should stop talking like that. And that reminds me, I read some of your poetry."

His face lights up. "Really? So what did you think?"

"Well, I thought it was good writing, but very depressing at the same time. And if you're doing a Web site to help other people in pain, sharing your depressed thoughts is not the best way to start."

He smiles again. "Well, John, you have a point, but the point of the site was for me and others to express ourselves. And that is the way I felt when I wrote whatever you read. Which ones did you read, anyway?"

"I read 'Sometimes' and 'Haud Voluntas,' and I have yet to read 'Thank God, Thank All & Thank Life.'"

"Cool. Well, the 'Thank God, Thank All & Thank Life' poem is not done yet. I will let you know when it is so you can read it."

"Okay, Sebastian. What does 'Haud Voluntas' mean, anyway?" I ask.

"It's Latin. It means 'no sense,' I think. I figured if I made its title in Latin, it would make it sound cooler."

"No sense, huh?" I reply. "Is that how you feel, that nothing makes sense?"

"Sometimes, yes, that is how I feel."

"There has to be something you can say that makes sense to you about this life, Sebastian."

He sighs. "Well…my mother made sense, when she was alive. Yes, my mother was one of the few things in life that actually made sense to me." He sighs. "John, I don't know, with that poem in particular, I wrote it at a time when I was feeling really down and depressed. I have been in this state for a while, and nothing seems to last. Nothing at all, John. I have lost so many so-called friends who were there when everything was great and going well for me. I am happy one minute, for example, when I see you or anyone who has been kind to me, and then as soon as you leave, I get depressed and want to cry because I have no one who stays with me. One minute everything is going well, and the next minute I am so depressed and lonely."

"But that's life, Sebastian. Life is full of ups and downs; nothing is perfect," I reply.

"And that's why I wrote that poem, John, because if this thing we go through called life made sense, there would be order to the way things happen, not that one minute you're up and the next you're down. None of this makes any sense."

I think really hard of what I can say to cheer him up. "Well, my parents used to tell me that whenever we go through tests in this life, Sebastian, we go through them to get stronger, to see our true capabilities. It's kind of like going to gym; you never know how strong you really are until you push the weight, and you never know what your max is, how much you can take, unless you add more weight to whatever exercise you are doing."

"And how does that apply to me, John? I can see how that statement would apply to someone like you, but look at me, John! I am dying. How much stronger can I get, John?"

For a second, I feel as if I have nothing to say. And then I find myself asking God to speak through me. "Sebastian, things might not look so good, but you have to remember that life does not end here. If you focus on the here and now in your situation, then you will spend your time being a very unhappy person, in my opinion. When we die, where do you think all our feelings, emotions, fears, aspirations, and conscience go? Where do you think our spirit goes? You think it just vanishes into thin air? That would make no sense. We all feel certain things that are intangible, things that cannot be explained through mere human understanding. Call it what you want: God in us, our spirit, soul, whatever. The fact is that inner element is really who you are, not this shell called a body that you're in that is rotting away—sorry, I didn't mean to say that."

He smiles. "It's okay; go on."

"In my opinion, you are not dying, Sebastian; you are very much alive. The way I see it, being in your situation has put you in touch with who you really are, and that is a state of mind a lot of people, including myself, have not attained. And remember that the mind is a very powerful thing, and that part of you, in my opinion, is very much alive, more alive than most people who appear healthy. I know it hurts, man, and you must be lonely sometimes, and it is not right the way your friends and family have deserted you. But life is full of shady characters. I personally am very honored that in my short and unfruitful life, I have had the pleasure of becoming friends with a genuine person such as yourself. That is a pleasure not too many people get to experience; that is, meeting a real person." I can't believe I've just said all that.

Sebastian's eyes well up with tears. "Thanks, John. That really means a lot to me."

"You're welcome, bro, anytime. But you have to stop writing all this depressing poetry, okay? Start feeling good about yourself. I am sure you have touched so many people with your Web site; you have certainly touched me."

"Again, thanks, and I promise I will not write any more depressing stuff," he replies.

"Cool." I look at my watch and realize I should be heading to my apartment. "I have to go, Sebastian. I'll stop by tomorrow again after work and check you out, okay?"

But he doesn't respond. He's suddenly fallen asleep. I step out of his room quietly, bid Bertha good night, and make my way back to my apartment.

I am sitting here in deep thought at my daytime job. The last conversation I had with Miss Pryce got me thinking, as did Anna's situation. Have I really been so ignorant about all this sexual stuff? I always thought this thing was something that happened to other people, or people you see on television and stuff...but then, along comes Anna. And she is HIV-positive! And this is someone that I know on a personal level. I felt really dirty when I got home from Alexia's that night. Could I have infections in me from sex? Could I be a walking around with stuff? I looked at myself in the mirror when I got home and felt so dirty that I took a shower. After my shower I tried to sleep but I could not. I mean, Miss Pryce had a point when she said that you never know who these guys sleep with when you're not around. And the same goes for girls—look at me! I slept with Cody, then Braxton, then Darius, then Cody again—all unprotected. Granted, they were all boyfriends of mine at different points in time, but who's to say that they don't go sleeping around when I am not there, just like I did? After seeing Anna, there is no way I want what happened to her to happen to me. No way. I know Anna said that she is fine and all, but I can't even begin to imagine what she is going through as far as dealing with people socially, dealing with men and all that stuff. It's got to be really hard on her. And I know people generally look down on HIV-positive people. This really sucks; now I am nervous. My heart is beating really fast. I think I will have a talk with Darius as soon as I get off work. He wants to see me tonight at his place, and I think that will be the perfect opportunity to have a discussion with him.

***

I get to Darius's place after work. I let myself in with the spare keys he made for me, and I find him reading a magazine in his living room.

"Hey, baby" he greets me.

"Hey. How are you?"

"I am okay. I missed you," he says as he gets up and gives me a kiss.

"I missed you, too. What are you reading?"

"Oh, nothing much, just a basketball magazine I picked up today."

"Oh, okay."

"Are you hungry or thirsty? I got some juice today, and there is also water in the fridge."

"Thanks."

"How was your day?" he asks.

"It was good, I guess, pretty uneventful. Just did a lot of thinking."

"Oh, yeah? What were you thinking about?" he asks as he gets up. "I am getting some water. You want some?"

"No, thanks." I take a seat. "I was thinking about us."

"Us? Nothing bad is it?" he asks as he returns.

"No, well, I hope not."

"Are you pregnant?"

"No, no, no, Darius. I am not pregnant, silly."

"So what's on your mind, then?"

"I was having a little chat with some friends, and they got me thinking about a lot of issues."

"Such as?"

"Well, you know, issues with regards to sex."

"Sex?"

"Sex."

"What issues about sex are you concerned about? You don't like the way I make love to you?"

"No, it's not that. You are great in bed."

"What, then? What's the problem?"

"Well…we have had sex a couple of times, a whole bunch of times, actually."

"Yes…and?"

"I was thinking about the way we've had sex."

"The way we've had sex?"

"Yes."

"You don't like the way we've had sex?"

"No, it has nothing to do with that."

"Then what the heck are you talking about? Get to the point!"

"Okay, I'll just say it as it is: we have had sex a bunch of times unprotected, Darius, and you have not had a problem doing it with me, as I have with you."

"I see where this is going."

"Yes, my concern is that we did not know anything about our sexual histories before we slept with each other. We just got really comfortable and started doing it."

"So what are you asking me? If I have any STDs?"

"Well, that's part of the question."

"No, I do not have any STDs."

"And how do you know? Have you been tested recently? We've never had this conversation."

"I have no symptoms of any STDs, Michelle, and I got tested a couple of months ago."

"And how come I never saw these test results?"

"Wait, wait, wait! Where are all these questions coming from? How about you? I've never seen any test results from you, and you never told me your sexual history, so what's with all the questions?"

"I just think we should have known more about each other before we started with sex, that's all."

He has a look of concern on his face. "I am fine, Michelle. There is nothing wrong with me, but I agree with you; we should have known more about each other before we made love."

"How many girlfriends did you have before me, Darius?"

"About five, I guess, but we normally spoke about such things before we had sex. How about you? How many boyfriends have you had?"

I suddenly get uneasy. "Honestly? About three," I reply.

"Okay, I'll tell you what. Why don't we both go to a testing center and get tested together? That way, there will be no secrets between us, and we can move on with our lives."

I get a little nervous at the thought. Get tested together with Darius? What if he turns out to have something, or worse yet, what if I turn out to have something? No, I would rather go by myself, just in case, or maybe I can go with Alexia. I would like someone I trust next to me. Someone besides my boyfriend.

"I think that's an idea, but I would rather go alone. I think I would be a bit uneasy going in with you."

"Why? I have nothing to hide."

"Yeah, let's just do it separately, okay? But we have to be truthful when presenting the results to each other."

"And how will I know that you are truthful if I do not go with you?"

"Because I will bring the official results from the clinic, with my name, date, and everything, to you when I am done. And you have to do the same."

"Okay, that sounds like a deal. Let's do it then. When do you want to do this?"

"By the end of next week?"

"Sounds good. I will have some results for you by next week, Michelle."

"And I will do the same."

The mood between us suddenly changes.

"So...would you like to talk about something other than STDs and stuff?" he asks. "All this nasty talk upset my stomach."

"No, I think I will go home. I just came by to have this discussion with you."

"Don't you want to stay for even a little while?"

"Well, until we both get tested, I would say that we both don't really know each other that well. I don't think that I will feel comfortable with you until we get tested. I'm sorry, but that's just the way I feel."

"You're right. We don't really know anything about each other when it comes to certain topics, but I am prepared to do anything to fix that. Why don't we take a break from seeing each other, then, until we have our results. If that will make you feel better, then let's do it that way."

"You're a good guy, Darius. Thanks for co-operating with me."

"You're welcome, Michelle."

"I should leave now. I'll call you, okay?"

"Sure thing, babes."

I step out of his apartment, and for some strange reason, I feel a weight lift off my shoulders. I feel a little tense, though, because I have never had any tests done for STDs or HIV in my entire life. I hope everything turns out to be okay.

Chapter Twenty-Eight

I have four days before I go in to get tested and receive my verdict. Four days. Monday through Thursday. I decided to take off work for the next few days and get myself prepared for the inevitable. I have asked God for mercy and have learned so much about myself and how I react under pressure.

Today, as promised, I pay Sebastian a visit. I arrive at the clinic and do my rounds. I did not see Bertha today, so I left my volunteer chores a bit earlier than usual to spend some more time with Sebastian. I arrive at his door.

He is lying on his bed, barely awake. He looks really frail this time and very weak. I sit down next to him.

"Hey, Sebastian" I say with a look of concern.

He slowly turns in my direction and manages to crack a smile.

"Hey, John," he whispers back. "How are you, sir?"

"I am okay, Sebastian. I am doing okay."

"That's good to hear," he whispers. "As you can see, I am doing great myself."

I can't help but giggle at his comment. "Even at a time like this, you can still manage to laugh at yourself," I remark.

"Well, you are not making me laugh so someone's got to do it."

We laugh together, even though his laughter seems to bring him physical pain. It was a bittersweet experience.

"How are you today?" he asks.

"I'm doing okay, Sebastian; been doing okay. Been talking to my family a lot about my situation, and they've been giving me some good support. It certainly has been a life-changing situation for me."

"That's good, John. I have been doing okay as well. My Web site is doing really well, and more and more people have been writing, wishing me well and encouraging each other to be more positive. I took your advice about sounding more positive, and I am seeing results. After all, it's not the end of the world if you have HIV or AIDS. There are still so many ways we can make good use of our time."

"No, it's not the end of the world, Sebastian. And you've done a good job of illustrating that."

"Thank you, John. And how about you? How is everything else besides your worry over your possible HIV crisis?"

"Well, let me see…I have been talking to the girl I told you about. She is very sexy, and she has a good head on her shoulders, or so it seems. I can talk to her for ages on numerous topics man, and I get a good vibe from her."

"That's good, John. What's her name again? Aurora, right?"

"Yeah."

"Do you think she would like a guy like me?"

We both laugh at his question.

"I'm sure she would, Sebastian; I'm sure she would."

His breathing was labored. "In all seriousness, I am happy for you. Like I said before, I hope everything works out so you can maybe develop a good relationship with her, if she's right for you."

"Yeah, I hope so, too."

"Don't just go for good looks in a woman, John. The packaging of a product is not as important as the product itself."

Wise words. "I agree, Sebastian. I wonder why it took all this that's happening for me to realize that fact, but I guess God has His reasons for doing things."

"Yeah, well, stuff happens, John. You were meant to experience everything you have been going through; you were meant to go through this ordeal; you were meant to meet me, as well as everything else you have experienced so far. I also believe you were meant to have your outlook on life change. Lord knows that in the short time we have known each other, you have done so much for me."

I nodded my head. "And you have done much for me as well, brother. I feel more at peace whenever I come here than I do when I'm on my own in the city."

He smiles. "You see, as my time draws near, I have to admit that I am very scared about what to expect. I just hope God doesn't make me suffer the same way I have suffered here."

"Well, I cannot tell you what God will or will not do, but I don't think God has that sort of personality."

"Well, let's hope not, John, because for the most part, I have had one crappy life." We look at each other, and then we laugh again. "So, hopefully, when and if you find out that you're clean, what are you going to do with yourself?" he asks.

"Not sure. I will probably have to do some thinking and re-evaluate my life and the direction I am headed. Probably start making healthier decisions, and focus on making myself a happier person."

"That's good, John. That's wise. Just remember that every minute counts. Time is your most precious commodity, John, because you don't get it back."

With those words, I see a brief look of sadness come over him. I want to say something to cheer him up, but I choose to remain silent. Sometimes, simply listening to another person is more than enough. "I think it's time I knew God, John."

I look at him. "What do you mean?"

"Well, I will die soon, and I don't know where I am going. So, it only makes logical sense that I try to ensure I go to a good place. And the only thing with the power to make that happen is God, I would assume."

"Yes, you're right," I reply.

"So let's say a prayer and ask God to find favor with me when I pass."

"You want to say a prayer now, in here?"

"Yes, why not? Are you shy or something, John?"

"No, not at all."

We both close our eyes, and Sebastian speaks: "God, I don't know you that well, but you created me and I am sure you know where I am going from here. I have never really been the religious type, but I am a good man, and I have suffered for so long. Please find favor with me, and take me to a good place when it's my time to go. Thank you for hearing my prayer, God."

"Amen," I say as I open my eyes.

"See that, John? I asked God to watch over me, so I am sure I am in good hands now."

"Yeah, I'm sure you are," I reply. Sebastian seems to have a lot of faith in a God he hardly knows. I look at my watch and realize that I have to get going. "Sebastian, I have to go."

His face turns sad. "You really have to go?"

"Yes, Sebastian. I would love to stay longer, but it's getting late, and I have to get ready for work tomorrow."

"I understand. Well, I guess it is what it is, until we meet again."

"Yeah, it is. I will come by again before I get tested. Maybe we can say a prayer for me then, as well."

"Sounds good, John. I will wait until I see you in a couple of days." He winks at me.

"Sounds good," I reply. I step out of the clinic, feeling privileged to be friends with such a good person.

It's been about three days since my chat with Darius. I was happy that he was very cooperative and understanding about talking about such things as

STDs. I told Alexia how the conversation went between me and Darius, and she was pleased.

But now, the more I think about it, the more nervous I get. I cannot change the fact that I slept with Cody, Braxton, and Darius while unprotected. I remember Miss Pryce's statement and a chill goes down my spine—she said that sleeping unprotected with someone potentially exposes you to everyone that they have been with. And all the men I have been with have all been attractive men. Lord knows how many women they have had sex with in the past.

I take the day off from my day job. I am sitting on my bed, thinking about these things, when my phone rings. It is Alexia.

"Have you heard from Darius again?" she asks.

"No. We are meeting next week to go over our results together."

"That's good."

"That's good, but I am scared. Getting tested must be a nerve-wracking experience."

"I made an appointment with this HIV counselor at a clinic downtown to go over some stuff and get some clarity on this STD stuff," she says. "I thought you would want to join me. Are you interested?"

"When are you leaving?"

"In about fifteen minutes."

"Okay, I'll go with you."

We hang up, and I hurry off to meet up with Alexia.

***

The clinic is a bit empty when we arrive. There are a few patients sitting in the waiting area with blank expressions on their faces. Alexia and I speak to the receptionist and are instructed to sit down in the waiting area. Not long afterwards, our number is called, and we are led into a small office by the receptionist. In the office, an elderly lady sits behind a desk. She has a very warm smile on her face. Alexia and I sit down.

"Hello, my name is Sylvia Tanson. What can I do for you young ladies?"

"Hello, Miss Tanson. My name is Alexia, and this is my friend Michelle. We came here hoping to get some sort of overview regarding STDs and HIV, and how those topics relate to girls like us."

"I have an appointment with another patient in about thirty minutes, so why don't we save one of the two topics for a later appointment? I can inform you about HIV, and we can talk about STDs the next time you come by. Or you can always use the Internet and do some research on your own."

"Okay, Miss Tanson. We can learn a bit about HIV from you and worry about the STD stuff later," I reply.

Miss Tanson smiles as she begins. "HIV stands for the human immune deficiency virus. It is a virus that attacks your immune system"

"How is that possible?" I ask. "I thought the immune system is what the body uses to fight off diseases and stuff."

"Yes, you are correct, but HIV is a tricky virus, in that it can mutate and evade the body's defenses. That is why it is such a tragic virus to acquire, because there is no cure."

"Damn, that sucks," says Alexia.

"Yes, it is rather unfortunate. AIDS, as you may know, is the latter part of the HIV infection, when the immune system is so weakened that it begins to let in certain opportunistic infections, like certain cancers and so forth. Your body basically deteriorates over time, and in most cases, death is the end result."

"That is pretty scary. And this is something you can pick up from just having sex? How does that work?" Alexia asks.

"HIV can only be acquired from the transfer of bodily fluids, and with sex, fluids are exchanged between you and your partner."

"How are the fluids transferred? I thought a man had to ejaculate in a woman before she could catch HIV." I say.

"You can acquire it that way, but pre-seminal fluids, which are the fluids that are usually present before ejaculation, can serve as a means for the virus to be transferred. Remember, the virus exists in one's bloodstream, so if you do anything to facilitate the virus's entering your bloodstream, you put yourself at risk of acquiring the virus."

"And how does this transfer stuff relate to us as women?" Alexia asks.

Miss Tanson furrows her brow. "I don't understand your question."

"I mean, we are girls, and the makeup of our sexual organs is a little different than that of men. So how does that affect us?"

"Good question. In theory, it is harder for a man to acquire HIV from unprotected sexual intercourse than it is for a woman. And if you think about it, it makes sense, as the man's penis is covered in skin and the woman's vagina is not. Skin itself serves as a line of defense against bacteria and viruses that exist all around us. HIV cannot permeate through a man's skin on his penis unless he has genital ulcers or sores from STDs, which is why STDs and HIV go hand in hand. A woman, on the other hand, has no skin protecting her sexual organ, so it is much easier for the virus to make its way into a woman's bloodstream from unprotected sex. This is also enhanced if the woman has vaginal ulcers or sores that may exist inside her vagina, which even she herself may not be aware of."

I suddenly become really scared. It seems I have been making some very careless decisions regarding my sexual habits and men.

"So this stuff is real, huh?" I ask, my heart pounding.

"Yes, it is," Miss Tanson replies.

"We just found out that a friend of ours tested positive for HIV. Are you saying that she is going to catch all these opportunistic infections and stuff?" I ask.

"I am sorry about your friend. If she is HIV-positive, her immune system will definitely be impacted to some degree. But many people with HIV can continue to live long, healthy, semi-normal lives. With the right medication, which can be plenty, and the right amount of exercise, the body can hold off the HIV transition to AIDS for many, many years. The hardest part about dealing with HIV is the social stigma that comes along with it. We live in a very ignorant world, and there are many ignorant people with bad intentions out there who live for nothing more than to feed off the misery of others. HIV is seen as a very dirty virus, so a lot of people do not want to even be associated with a person who is infected. It is sad, but it is reality. So to avoid all that trouble, the best thing is to avoid having unprotected sex, and do not take unnecessary risks."

"How did HIV come about? Do you know?" Alexia asks.

"There are many theories. But we have to remember that many of these theories have political, economical, social, and personal goals and agendas behind them. Remember, HIV in this day and age is a condition for life, and until a cure is found or until an existing cure is revealed to the public, managing HIV will continue to be a lucrative business for many people in powerful economic positions. How the virus came about is not as important as knowing how to effectively prevent yourself from becoming another statistic."

"Could you tell us some of the theories on HIV?" I ask.

"I am not an expert in that regard," Miss Tanson says, "but I will do my best. Let's begin with some background information. HIV is a lentivirus. All lentiviruses attack the immune system in animals. Lentivirus means 'slow virus,' or in other words, you could say that it takes a long time to produce adverse effects on the human body. Lentiviruses are part of a larger group called retroviruses. Lentiviruses are found in many different animals, including cats, sheep, cattle, and horses. Now, there is another immune deficiency virus that exists in monkeys that is called the Simian Immune Deficiency virus, or SIV. Many scientists believe that HIV is a descendant of SIV, because certain strains between the two viruses bear a close resemblance."

"What are you saying? That the SIV strain in monkeys morphed into the HIV strain in humans?" Alexia asks.

"I do not know much about how those concepts worked out. I am just giving you some of the different theories that have been presented."

"But obviously there has to be some connection between how the SIV strain from a monkey would create HIV in a human?" Alexia says.

"Well, that's where the theories come in. Whenever a viral transfer between animals and humans takes place, it is called 'zoonosis.' So you're asking me how zoonosis occurred between the monkeys and men? Before I go on, let me remind you that it is believed that the HIV strain is related to the SIV strain, based on the similarities in their structures. Nothing is definite, at least not to my knowledge. One theory suggests that the SIV strains were common in monkeys from West Africa, and hunters there got infected by eating these monkeys or getting wounded and having the monkey blood enter their bloodstream."

"They ate raw monkeys? Wouldn't they have cooked them at least? And I thought the lining of the mouth was an effective barrier against viruses," Alexia says.

"Again, that is just one theory. Another theory is one regarding the use of contaminated needles in Africa. According to this theory, in the mid-1950s, the use of plastic syringes was very common because they were disposable. But for certain African health-care professionals, purchasing these syringes would have been expensive, so in many cases, one syringe would have been used on many people."

"And let me guess, if that hunter who ate the monkey or got wounded had his blood drawn, and that same needle was used on another, that would equal HIV transmission," Alexia says.

"Yes. Another theory deals with Africa during the colonial years. In certain regions, such as the Congo, when King Leopold of Belgium invaded, or in other places, like French Equatorial Africa, the conditions were very harsh, with brutality and disease being very commonplace. Many Africans in these regions were forced to exist in labor camps. The health conditions were poor, and food was scarce. So our monkey friends with SIV would have been a food source for many starving people."

"I don't know," Alexia says. "This whole monkey business seems a bit far-fetched to me. You said it is believed that the HIV strain is related to the SIV strain, based on resemblance, but no definite relationship has been established?"

"Yes, not that I know of."

"So that defeats the whole monkey theory, unless you have some hard facts. You can't make assumptions based on assumed information."

"Remember that viruses are capable of mutating, so it might not be so farfetched to have a connection between SIV and HIV."

"I didn't know that viruses could mutate," Alexia admits. "Are there any other theories?"

"Well, yes. Other theories suggest that HIV came about by *iatrogenic* means."

"What does iatrogenic mean?" I ask.

"It means that someone intentionally induced HIV to occur in humans, Michelle," Alexia replies.

"And how do you know this?" I ask.

"I went to school, silly, something you should finish. Remember what my mom said to you? Miss Tanson, please go on."

"Other theories suggest that HIV came about by iatrogenic means, as I said before, through medical interventions…there are other theories that HIV had its origin in the 1970s from a specific iatrogenic event."

"Are there any events that happened around that time to support these beliefs?" Alexia asks.

"In the 1970s there was much cancer research on animals going on; for example, the polio vaccine they say was cultivated in living tissue. It was grown in kidney cells taken from local chimpanzees."

"I see some connection here. Let me guess—these chimps had the SIV strains in them?" Alexia asks.

"Quite possibly. And some years afterward, the United States government sponsored hepatitis B vaccines in New York, Los Angeles, and other places—now the hepatitis B vaccine they say was developed in chimpanzees. See the connection?"

"So could SIV been transferred through these hepatitis vaccinations?" Alexia asks.

"Quite possibly. But remember, Alexia, just a minute ago you were saying that the SIV strain could not be taken as a definite relation to the HIV strain, because no definite relationship existed. You see how easy it is for people to believe anything so-called experts say? These are all just theories and hypotheses—no one really knows where HIV came from."

"What's a hypothesis?" I ask.

"An educated guess, Michelle. Be quiet" Alexia responds.

Miss Tanson laughs. "As I was saying, these are all just educated guesses, and there are many more theories out there. What's important for girls like yourselves is to not worry about where the virus originated or who caused it—those things cannot be changed. Instead, concentrate on how to prevent yourself from catching it and affecting yourselves and others."

"You're right, Miss Tanson," Alexia agrees. "Do you have any advice for us on how to lead safer lives?"

"At your age, I hope you know the basics regarding safe sex. Abstinence is the best policy, but if you're sexually active, don't have unprotected sex. Make sure the men you sleep with use condoms, and try to get to know the people you sleep with. If you are in a relationship, try to have conversations with your partners about their histories and health status."

"Sounds like what my mom said to us, doesn't it, Michelle?"

"It does," I agree.

Alexia has another question. "Have you seen crazy cases, working in a place like this?"

Miss Tanson grins. "Yes, I have. I've seen all sorts of cases, and majority of the negative ones need not even be. A lot of people take certain aspects of their health for granted, because they live in ignorance, until it's too late."

"Yeah, you're right, Miss Tanson," Alexia says. "Thanks for all the information."

"Thank you for stopping by. I have a meeting now, so you girls will have to excuse me. Why don't schedule another appointment for sometime next week, and we can cover STDs?"

"Thanks, Miss Tanson," Alexia says, "We'll do that."

"Thank you," I add.

We leave the clinic and head back to Alexia's place.

"What did you think?" Alexia asks.

"I thought it was informative." I reply.

"How do you feel?" Alexia asks.

"I feel numb. And I'm scared."

Chapter Twenty-Nine

have two days left before I go in for testing. Two days. I spent the past three days resting, meditating, and hoping for the best. I also went for walks. I visited museums. I went to a spa and received a massage. I did things I normally do not do. And it all felt good and relaxing. Last night I took Aurora on a date, which went really well. I really like this girl. She is very smart and makes excellent conversation. She speaks with experience, and I like that. She is a beautiful woman who is actually beautiful in many ways. She has the physical looks, she is smart, and she is witty. But what I like most about her, so far, is how calm and humble she is. I am really surprised that I found a girl like her in the big city. I keep asking myself what I will do if I find out that I do have HIV. What will happen to my relationship with her? If I get really close to her, how will I reveal such information to her? I just don't know. So much is riding on this test, and I seriously hope God shows me some kind of mercy. I just want to lead a normal life.

Mom gives me a call to offer emotional support, and I say a prayer with her over the phone. Tomorrow, I will stop by the clinic again to pray with Sebastian about my test, and then on Saturday, I will go in and do what I have to do.

***

I get to the clinic in a good mood and finish my rounds faster than usual. By sheer coincidence, Bertha approaches me as I'm walking to Sebastian's room.

"Hello, John."

I detect seriousness in her voice. Maybe even a slight tremble. "Is everything all right, Bertha?" I ask.

"Yes, yes, all is well," she replies, but her eyes are sad.

"Well, that's good, then. I was just on my way to visit Sebastian. I finished all my rounds, but if there is something else you want me to do, I wouldn't mind helping out before I go see Sebastian."

"John, there is something I have to tell you."

Oh, no. I sense that she has bad news for me. I saw it in her face when I greeted her. I hope it is not what I think it is.

But it is.

"What do you have to tell me, Bertha? What's wrong?" I feel my heart-beat quicken.

Her eyes get really teary. "Sebastian is no longer with us," Bertha says quietly. "He passed away earlier this morning due to some internal complications."

Her words are hard to stomach, even though I expected her to say what she said. I stare at the floor and suddenly felt overwhelmed by sadness and a really congested feeling. Strangely, I do not feel like crying, but I do feel as if I want to throw up.

"I'm sorry, John. I know you guys were becoming close." She turns away and wipes some tears from her eyes. "I am really sorry, John," she says again.

I take a deep breath. "It's okay, Bertha. Let's hope he is in a better place now."

Bertha wipes tears from her eyes. "Yes, let's hope so. He gave me this to give to you." She hands me a white envelope with a hand-drawn smiley face on the front. On the back of the envelope is a little note that reads: "Do not open until after you get tested." I smile, because I recognize Sebastian's handwriting. I give Bertha a hug to comfort her, and then I leave the clinic, knowing I will never go back there—now, I have no reason to. I can't believe Sebastian is gone. I just can't believe it. On the train ride back I think, *How is this possible? I just saw Sebastian a few days ago.* I place my head in my hands and let out a huge sigh. I feel sad that I won't have a chance to spend more time with such a good person. I feel sad that such a person had to leave in such a way. I really, sincerely, enjoyed his company. I want to cry, but I force my tears back. I hope he has gone to a better place, and I am happy for him.

I'd hoped to tell him more about Aurora and my family. I'd wanted to get to know more about him as well. I guess life had different plans for us.

I miss my friend. I close my eyes and say a short prayer for my friend who is gone. I spend the rest of my day in my apartment, sitting in my bathtub and staring at the wall, trying my best to comprehend the fact that Sebastian is gone and that after tomorrow, my life will never be the same.

I am sitting in my bathtub after working at the restaurant. I made a bubble bath, and I am thinking as I relax myself. Meeting with the counseling lady, Miss Tanson, proved to be very informative. I learned many new things. But it also made me very scared. Could I have something? That's the question that keeps running through my mind. I slept with Cody, I slept with Braxton, and I slept with Darius, unprotected. Granted, they were all my boyfriends, but that doesn't mean anything. I'm sure they would deny having any infection, but how can I know that they are telling the truth? This is all very scary and beyond me. I have to change the way I do things with people, especially men. Poor Anna. I really hope that she is okay. After hearing what Miss Tanson had to say, the seriousness of Anna's situation became very real to me.

My phone rings as I lay in the bathtub. It is Alexia.

"Hey, Michelle. How are you holding up?"

"I'm okay. I just can't get that visit to the clinic out of my mind!"

"I thought it was very informative, though, didn't you?"

"I thought so as well."

"As Miss Tanson spoke, I was thinking about every guy I've slept with. I just thank God that there were not too many."

"I wish I could say the same," I say.

"You've not slept with too many guys, Michelle."

"But I've had a few boyfriends, and remember what your mom said? Just because they are your boyfriends does not mean anything."

"I went in and got tested," Alexia informs me.

"You did? When?" I ask.

"The day after we went to the clinic. The conversation got me thinking, and I decided that I would take better care of myself in every regard, including sex."

"But Alexia, you're a single mom living on your own. You've never had time for men for as long as I've known you."

"But I do have sex, and randomly as well. Remember the guy I met in my area? The one I slept with?"

"Oh, yeah, the one you cooked for afterwards?"

"Yeah, the John guy. He could have had something and passed it to me! I mean, granted he used a condom but still. I mean, I could have caught an STD or something if he had something, and I kept on seeing him! And it's risks like that I cannot afford to take. I have a baby girl, and I cannot act irresponsibly and jeopardize her well-being."

"That makes sense, Alexia. How did your tests go, and what did they test for?"

"I tested for HIV, gonorrhea, syphilis, and Chlamydia. The HIV test was an oral test and that came back negative, thank goodness."

"You must have been relieved."

"I was. I will get the results back from the other tests in about a week."

"What was it like, waiting for your results?" I ask.

"It was very scary. Now I understand why a lot of people are hesitant to go in for testing. It takes a lot of guts to do it."

"Maybe I shouldn't go, then. Because I would be really scared."

"No, I think you should, Michelle. You owe it to yourself and to whomever you end up being intimate with."

"But my heart is going to be pounding, Alexia, and I don't know if I can sit through the whole ordeal by myself. Can you come with me?"

"When are you going?" she asks.

"Tomorrow. I'll just go tomorrow and get it over with."

"Sorry, Sis, tomorrow is a bad day for me. I have to run some errands for Tara."

"I'll wait until you get back then, so we can go together."

"You can go by yourself tomorrow, Michelle. You don't need me with you."

"But I will be scared."

"You will be fine, Sis. You don't need me there; trust me. I went alone, not knowing what the outcome would be, and I made it out. I think you should go tomorrow and get it over with."

"Yeah, you're right. Okay, I will just go in tomorrow and get tested. I know I will be fine. I feel fine, so I know I will be fine."

"Excellent. I have to go put Tara to bed, but call me if you need anything. I'm here for you."

"Thanks, Sis. I'll let you know how it goes."

We end our conversation, and I recline in the bathtub, wondering what sort of day tomorrow will be like. I take a deep breath, realizing that after tomorrow, my life might never be the same.

Chapter Thirty

Time's up. Today is the day. Judgment day. Last night I was thinking about how nervous I might be, waiting for my results, so I debate whether it is be a good idea to get really drunk before heading out. That way, even if I get bad news, I will not be as nervous. But something tells me that it would be a bad idea, so I let it go. I'll just be a man and face my demons. I hardly slept last night because I was pondering how this day would go, as well as grieving for Sebastian. For most of last night, I just stared at my ceiling, feeling empty.

My alarm goes off at the usual time, but I am already awake. I say a prayer this morning, and then I decide to play my raffle game one last time. I retrieve the cup with all the papers in it, including the one with the red H. I shake the cup vigorously. Then I grab the first piece of paper my fingers touch. I open the paper. I see a red H looking back at me. Damn. Of all the days, does today have to be the day that I finally pick that damned piece of paper? Such irony; what a way to start the day. I hope that doesn't equate to bad luck. I grab the raffle-game cup and throw it into the trash. It won't make a difference after today, because life itself is not a game, and I cannot base my outcome on a paper cup and a few pieces of scrap paper. I say another prayer and place Sebastian's letter in my pocket.

Then I head off to the testing center. Everything seems to be moving at a slower pace this morning, and I notice every small detail in everything around me. I get on the subway, and it seems like it is the same one I was on when I heard the somber news from Anna. As I sit in that subway car, I begin to think about my final test. What if I am HIV-positive? What will I do? Maybe I should just assume that I do not have HIV and go home. That way, I wouldn't have to deal with all the pressure of taking this test. No, I can't do that. For one thing, I have been through so much that to turn back now would be a waste. For another, I owe it to myself and those around me to know for sure. I have to be responsible and do the right thing.

So no, I am not turning back, even though I want to. Although now I do wish I had drunk that alcohol this morning, considering the nervous state I am in. My mind keeps racing; it's as if the devil is feeding me thoughts to break my spirit: *What about Sebastian? Remember how his whole body was covered with lesions and how sick he looked? Would you want to know that you will eventually look like that? Would you like to know that you could possibly have HIV and have your life changed forever? You did sleep with a girl who had HIV, so there is a chance that you might have it. Why don't you just play ignorant, hope for the best, and just go back home? All you have to do is be a little careful from now on.*

That thought does seem appealing. If I don't go, no one has to know what I did, and I could continue living my life and act as if nothing happened. But no, I cannot buy into such assumptions. I need to know my status before I get intimate with another person again. I need to clear my conscience and learn from my mistake. I need to get tested. I need to know. As my train gets closer and closer to my final destination, my heart begins to pound faster and faster as well. Oh, if I could go back in time, I would change everything I did! I would never have made friends with Shawn and Cesar, I would never have gone to that bar, and I would never have met Anna.

This virus does not wear a face, and condoms are not 100 percent effective all the time. This virus has taken so many people around the world, and here I am, face to face with it. I am scared. I care about my health, and if I come out negative, I do not want to relive this experience ever again. I have to be more responsible; it is so easy to pick up something when you have a carefree lifestyle. People might look nice on the surface, but underneath all the makeup, nice clothes, fancy cars, charming smiles, and lovely bodies may lie something not even worth looking at.

I reach my stop. I walk slowly up the stairs to the open street. My heart continues to pound in my chest, but now I am here, and I cannot turn back. I walk slowly up the block until I get to the front of the testing center. It certainly has been a long journey for me, these past three months. I have learned a lot. But I tend to do that when my neck is on the line. I find a quiet spot on the street and kneel down to say a short prayer:

"My God, I have reached the end of the road. I cannot tell what is going to happen to me, as that decision is in Your hands. I have realized that the situation is beyond my control. I admit to how fragile and vulnerable I am in the grand scheme of things, and for what it is worth, I am really sorry. Please have mercy on me and don't let me have this thing in me. Please, I beg You. I will be more responsible next time. Please." I finish my prayer and stand up in front of the entrance to the testing center.

Well, this is it. It's either I have it or I don't. I take a deep breath, look behind me one last time, and step inside the testing center.

I get to the testing center a bit early today. I could not sleep last night, and I was out of my apartment as soon as my alarm went off. My heart is beating really fast as I walk into the place. It is rather empty, and I can understand why. If everyone is as nervous as I am when it comes to testing, I don't see who would want to come in. I decided to wear my hair in pigtails today. I am not sure exactly why. Perhaps it has something to do with change, because I never wear my hair in pigtails. I speak to the receptionist, and she seats me in the waiting area. My heart is still beating fast, and I can't stop playing with my fingers. After about ten minutes, this guy walks in, and he speaks with the receptionist. He's not bad looking, but he seems to have a lot on his mind, kind of like me. He makes for a nice distraction from the monotony of my wait.

"Miss?" I look up. A nurse is standing in front of me. "What are you here for?"

"I want to get tested for HIV and STDs."

"Today we are only offering testing for HIV, syphilis, gonorrhea, and Chlamydia. Why don't you follow me so we can begin processing you."

"Okay."

The nurse leads me to a room and sits me in front of a mean-looking woman. I get the chills from just looking at her. "And what are you here for?" she asks.

"I came in to get tested for HIV and STDs."

She nods. "I will ask you some questions before we get started."

"Okay."

"Have you been with anyone you think is HIV-positive?"

"I don't think so."

"Do you have or have you had multiple sexual partners."

"Yes, but they were all boyfriends of mine."

"Miss, just answer the question."

"Sorry…yes."

"Have you ever practiced anal sex?"

"No."

She asks me a whole bunch of questions for about five minutes, and the whole time she's typing stuff on her computer. I wonder what she's typing.

"What made you come here today?"

"I have been having conversations with some friends of mine about safe sex," I explain, "and I wanted to get tested so I know where I stand."

"It takes a lot of guts to come in and get tested. Most people would rather not know."

"Well, I am a bit scared right now, if that is what you're asking."

"You have no reason to be scared. Have you done anything risky recently?"

"Well, I don't sleep around, but with every boyfriend I have had, we start out having sex with condoms, but soon we get really comfortable and then we stop using condoms. So that has me a little concerned."

"When was the last time you had sex?"

"Umm, about a week or two ago; quite recently."

"Well, that would constitute risky behavior. You shouldn't sleep with anyone unprotected, even if the person is your boyfriend. You do not know who he's been with in the past, and don't forget that a lot of people cheat when they are in relationships." I thought about myself when she said that. "You should not have unprotected sex unless you are certain of your partner's status, period."

"Yes, I know, that's a big part of the reason that I am here today."

"That's a good decision on your part. Follow me; I will take you to the testing room, and the doctor there will take care of you."

I follow her to the testing room she mentioned. An old man, who I assume is the doctor, is sitting across the room, inspecting different tubes filled with different colored liquids.

"This is Dr. Bernasko. He will take care of you. When you are done, go back to the lobby and wait, and I will come get you."

The lady leaves, and the doctor moves closer to me and begins to take a new syringe out of its wrapper.

"How are you, my dear?" he asks with a smile. His smile makes me smile, and I feel less intimidated by this whole process.

"I'm fine."

"Are you scared of needles?"

"Yes."

"This will only pinch a little, and if you don't like looking at blood, try to look away if you can.

"Okay."

He begins to take my blood, and as promised, it only stings a little.

"It is great that you decided to come in and get tested."

"Thank you."

"It's very important to know your health status. It keeps you and your loved ones safe."

I suddenly feel like expressing myself to this man. "I am just trying to do the right thing. I had some boyfriends in the past, and I never knew anything about their sexual histories, so I just want to make sure that I am fine."

"That makes perfect sense. You have to be careful these days. There are all sorts of viruses and things spreading around. Can't just go sleeping with people you know little about."

"I agree, and I am a little scared about what my results will be."

"Ah, don't worry. I have a feeling that you will be fine. Here—take this cotton swab, and run it all along the interior of your gums."

He hands me the swab, which looks like a Q-tip, and I run it along my gums and then hand it back to him.

"Sir?"

"Yes?"

"Why do you have a feeling that I am fine?" I ask.

"Well, my dear, I do not know anything for sure, but I know what my spirit tells me. And my spirit tells me to have faith for you. But you should have faith for yourself as well—that's where it all begins, with faith."

"What do you mean by faith? "

"Just believe. And you never know—something out there might just believe with you." He smiles at me.

I smile back. "Okay, I will try."

"Good. Well, we're done here. You can go back to the lobby. The counselor will get you when your results are ready. It was nice meeting you."

"You, too, sir."

Surprisingly, the testing center is empty. When I walk in, I only notice one girl, who had her hair in funny-looking pigtails, sitting in the waiting area. I expected to see a long line of people waiting to get tested. I expected to see a lot of sad faces like mine. But no, the center is empty. It is as if, behind the scenes, the whole place was reserved just for me. I walk to the front desk and speak to the receptionist.

"Can I help you?" she asks.

"Yes, I am here to get tested for HIV."

"Okay, this way, please." She directs me to the waiting area, and I take a seat, waiting to be called. I notice that the girl with the pigtails has disappeared. As in the other testing center, there is a television. Fortunately, it is off; I cannot imagine having to watch horrible, graphic images of the symptoms of STDs and AIDS as I wait, as I had to do before. Soon a nurse approaches me and directs me to an office, where a counselor is waiting to speak with me. She is a serious-looking woman, probably in her thirties, and not once does she glance at me. Her eyes are fixed on her computer screen as she speaks.

"Hello, sir. You're here for HIV testing?"

"Yes, ma'am."

She gives me a smile, but with her serious demeanor, I do not find it comforting. "Don't call me 'ma'am'; that makes me feel old."

"Sorry about that."

"There are a few questions I have to ask you before I take you in for testing. Is this your first time here?"

"Yes."

"Do you have or have you had multiple sexual partners?"

I think about the question. "Yes."

"Do you practice anal sex?"

"No."

"Do you sleep with men?"

"No."

"Do you have any STDs?"

"Not any that I am aware of."

"Do you do any drugs?"

"No."

"Have you ever used needles for recreational purposes?"

"No." For some minutes, we go back and forth with the questioning and answering, while she types away at her keyboard; I imagine that all this information I am giving her helps to feed their database, which in turn probably influences the statistics regarding STD/HIV data. Soon she is finished with her questions, but she says, "It is a good thing you're here to get tested; it shows maturity on your part."

"Thank you." I am beginning to get nervous as my testing time draws near, and I suddenly feel the need to speak. "So, I was just wondering…do you have a lot of guys like me come in here to get tested for HIV?"

She looks up at me. "Of course we do; this is a testing center."

"Yes, I know, sorry—silly question. It's just that I was in a pretty risky situation some months back, and I am a bit nervous as to what the outcome will be."

"What sort of risky situation were you in, exactly?"

I take a deep breath. "Well, I slept with a girl who I discovered was HIV-positive and am just now getting through the window period for testing, so I am here today to find out if I have HIV."

"Well, I cannot tell you if you have acquired HIV. Only the test will let us know for sure."

"Yes, I know, I know. I have been doing a lot of research on this thing. I am just a bit nervous, that's all. I feel like today is judgment day for me. I wasn't inside her for that long, and I did clean myself after I had sex with her. Previously, I had only slept with her once. But I am just a bit worried."

"And you should be, but from what you've said, I don't think you picked it up. The more times you sleep with someone who is HIV-positive, the more likely you are to pick up the virus, so from what you say, it is actually good that you stopped early. If your condom broke, it is probably because you used an expired condom or a condom that did not fit properly. You have to be careful with these things; always use the right-sized condom, and if you're unsure of the girl, use two, if necessary. Do not sleep with girls when they're menstruating, because menstrual blood is waste that the female body discards, and it is not healthy to have that on you, even if the girl is HIV-negative. If you had told me this had happened when you were having anal sex, I would have been much more worried for you, but from what you said, I think you'll be fine. Only the test will tell for sure."

She finishes typing and turns off her monitor. "Well, let's hope that you are fine and that you learn from your experience."

"Believe me, I have learned my lesson," I reply.

She gets up to direct me to the testing room.

"Here, follow me. Remember, the best way to avoid all these things is through abstinence. But if you insist on having sex, then at least do your best to make sure that your partner is disease-free. It does not take that long to get tested; the most it will take is an hour on your testing day, but that time can save you so much trouble in the future. But even with testing these days, you can never be totally sure. You never know what your partner does when you are not around, and people are people. You see, in our society, HIV is an unspoken evil; people know it's there but do not want to talk about it. And the media, I believe, does a good job of promoting ignorance on the subject, and it leads people to believe that HIV and AIDS are problems restricted to only third-world environments, like countries in Africa. But believe me, the HIV crisis is very real and present right here in this country and in this city. You wouldn't believe the number of cases we have coming through here. But as I said, people prefer to play ignorant and not acknowledge certain truths regarding life. My advice? Just wait until you're certain, find the right girl, get tested, and sleep with just that one person. The more you float around, the more chances you make for diseases to get the best of you. Now take a seat, and the doctor will be with you in a minute."

"Thanks for all the advice. I appreciate it."

"No problem." She leaves, and I find myself in a small room. I close my eyes and say another prayer:

"God, I know I never knew You before, but please, please, please don't let me have this thing in me. Please don't let this thing be in my body. I have been irresponsible, and I promise I will not be careless when it comes to sex again. Please."

Just as I finish my prayer and open my eyes, the doctor walks in. He is an elderly man with a very warm, gentle smile, the same sort of smile Jerry has whenever I visit him, and the same sort of smile Sebastian had on the last time I spoke with him.

"My name is Dr. Bernasko," he says. "How are you, young man?"

"I am fine, thank you, sir."

"Good. Please raise your sleeve and flex your arm."

I do so, and he takes a fresh needle and syringe to draw blood from me.

"I am a bit nervous," I say.

"Oh, don't worry. You look like a strong guy. This shouldn't hurt much."

"No, sir, I am not nervous about the needle. I am nervous about what my status will be."

He smiles "Well, if you are one of God's children, you should be fine."

"I don't know, sir; I've done some pretty bad things."

"We all have. But you must believe in God and have faith that He knows what is best for you."

"That's just it, you know. I've read and heard from people that sometimes God puts us through tests and trials to bring out the best in us, but I don't know if finding out that I have HIV will bring out the best in me."

"I see," he remarks. He inserts the needle into one of my veins and begins drawing blood. "Well, young man, God does not send punishment to His people. If you find out that you're sick, that is a result of your negligence to follow a few simple rules, and you can't blame God for that."

"But I did follow the rules, sir. I used a condom, but it broke while I was inside a girl who turned out to be HIV-positive."

"Well, if the condom broke, it is most likely because it was an outdated condom, you used the wrong size, or you did not put it on properly. If you had followed the rules, you wouldn't have been in that situation."

"You're right, sir, and if I could go back in time, I would change all that happened, but I can't."

"Ah, well, what is done is done." He takes the needle out of my arm and puts my blood sample in a funny-looking container. Then he retrieves a swab and hands it to me.

"Starting from your inner left cheek, move this swab across the outline of your gums; this is the oral test."

I take the swab and do as he says, and then hand it back to him. He places it in a container.

"Okay, now we have to wait for about thirty minutes or so before we'll know what your status is."

"I will go wait in the lobby till I am called." I open the door.

"Before you go, let me say something to you, young man." I turn in the doorway to face him and hear what he has to say. "I see so many young people like you walk in here every day to get tested. Most people are fine, but we do have quite a few cases with positive readings, and those people think that their lives are over. Having HIV is not the end of the world; if you maintain a healthy lifestyle, exercise regularly, eat healthy foods, and take your medication, you will live a healthy life like anyone else. But you will have to be a lot more responsible and careful in your interactions with others.

"Now, more important, if you are HIV-negative, what do you do from here? Do you go back to the same lifestyle you had before and take unnecessary risks? If you do, then all this was for nothing. All this stress you've gone through and coming here to test will be all for nothing. In life, we take tests to make us better people, whether it is a test in the classroom, tests at work, tests in the gym, tests in relationships, tests in life, or even HIV tests. If you take this test and you learn nothing from it, then, my young friend, you've wasted God's time, my time, the staff's time, and your time. And time, as you know, is too valuable a thing to waste, because you don't get it back. So, my young friend, as I say to every person who comes in here, young or old, learn from your experience because it is not what you do during a trial that is important but what you do afterward. Learn from your mistakes, and do not to make them again."

I look at him and marvel at his words. It seems God follows me in many different forms wherever I go. "Yes, sir, I will lead a healthier lifestyle from now on. Thank you so much for all the advice."

"You're welcome," he says with that smile that I'm beginning to learn signifies true experience. "Now you can go wait in the lobby; the counselor will come for you when the results are ready."

I take a seat in the waiting area while I wait for the counselor to come get me for my results. My heart is beating so fast. The doctor said that he feels I am okay, but he also said that I have to have faith. Faith? I slept with all my boyfriends without condoms, and anything could have happened. This is nerve-wracking. And it's scary, because I am here by myself. I wish I had someone to talk to.

The cute guy I saw earlier walks in the room about ten minutes after I sit down. He sits two seats away from me. He seems like a nice guy. I'm guessing he just finished getting tested and was sent here to wait like I was. Probably means that they will be calling me for my results pretty soon. I feel really scared now.

I step out of the room and take a seat in the lobby. I stretch on the chair and take a deep breath. I am not as nervous as I was when I walked in here. I begin to reflect on all that I have learned in these past months. I have changed drastically, and one thing I know is that I will not sleep around with women ever again—at least, I will try not to. It's just not safe, and it is just not worth it. I don't know where these women have been, who they have been with, or what they have done. People are people, and just because someone says one thing to you does not mean that is the way it really is.

I have learned a lot about God as well and what is truly important in life. I think I will start investing more time in creating more meaningful pursuits in my life, instead of spending my time fulfilling self-centered ambitions. Yes, it's time to put some purpose in my life; I came to the big city to make money and sleep with as many women as I could, but in my time of crisis, none of those things helped me or provided me with a center. Nope, the money didn't help me, so-called friends did not help me, and the girls did not help me, either. In fact, they were a part of the problem.

I am so deep in thought that I do not even notice that I am sitting only two seats away from the girl with the funny-looking pigtails. She looks very worried. Maybe she is fearful about her results, like I was. I think I will be nice and try to open some dialogue between us.

"Hello," I say to her.

She looks at me. "Hi."

"You looked a little disturbed, and I just want to make sure that you are okay."

"That's a bit of a weird comment to say in a testing center, don't you think?"

"You're right. Forgive me."

"Oh, no, I'm not angry or anything. I just thought it was funny to say I look disturbed in a testing center."

"Well, for what it's worth, I hope everything turns out okay."

"Thanks. You too."

There is a brief silence between us. But I don't like this silence; it just makes me more nervous.

"So are you from around here?" I ask.

"I don't particularly feel like talking about where I'm from as I wait for my test results. Sorry. Plus, I don't even know you."

"Sorry, I was just trying to make conversation. Waiting for these results can be nerve-wracking sometimes."

"Have you done this before?" she asks.

"Yeah, I always come in to check myself out. I prefer to keep myself healthy." That is such a lie.

"Well, that's good for you. This is my first time here."

Just then the counselor approaches the girl. "Miss, follow me, please" the counselor says.

The girl gets up and looks at me one last time. "Good luck" she says.

"Good luck to you, too. "

And then she's gone.

The counselor I saw earlier asks me to follow her into her office. Before she did, the cute guy I saw earlier sat next to me and started talking to me. I thought it was a little weird of him to start a random conversation with me while we waited, but this is the city, and there are all sorts of people here. Maybe he needed someone to talk to.

I can't worry about him, as I am about to get my results. I step into the counselor's office and sit down. She says nothing as she starts typing some stuff into her computer. Then she looks at me. "As I told you before, it is a good thing that you came in to get tested."

Oh, no. I don't like the way she starts the conversation. She probably has bad news for me. I probably have HIV and every STD that I tested for. I will have to be like Anna, and I will lose all my friends, and Alexia won't want to hang out with me, and I will lose my job, and I will have everyone tease me because of my status, and I will be looked down upon, and I will never get married, and—

"Miss?"

"Huh?"

"Miss, are you with me? I am talking to you."

"Sorry. What did you say? Do you have bad news for me? Am I going to die?"

"No, you're not going to die. Having HIV does not mean you are automatically going to die. You can have HIV and still live a long productive life, you just—"

"Oh, my God! Oh, no! I have HIV! How could this be? I don't deserve this! Oh, no!" I start to cry in front of her.

"Miss, you need to calm down."

"How can I calm down? You just gave me the news that I have HIV! What can I possibly do now? My life is finished! No, no, no!" I cry uncontrollably. My heart is beating at an uncontrollable rate. My vision gets a little blurry, and I feel like I want to throw up. I have to get out of here. I will just go and kill myself.

"*Miss*! Calm *down*! Your tests came back HIV-negative."

"What?"

"I said your tests came back HIV-negative."

"Oh. So why did you say that I had HIV?" I ask between sniffles. My heartbeat calms down, and I feel this extraordinary relief from hearing the news.

"I never said that you had HIV. I was letting you know that having HIV does not mean that your life is over. Nevertheless, it is not something that you want to have."

"Oh." I feel so happy now. "That certainly makes me feel good."

"It wasn't my intention to scare you, but you see how you just got really scared and started crying because you thought that you were HIV-positive? Imagine if you really were HIV-positive? You would have left here feeling like you just did but for a very, very long time."

She's right.

"Now, I do not know what risks you take with regard to your personal life, but I do not think that you want to feel like you just did, do you?"

"No."

"Good. So take this as a lesson, and understand that this thing is very real. Patients who are HIV-positive come through here all the time."

"Trust me; I have learned my lesson. I feel so much relief now."

"Well, don't get too happy just yet."

"Huh? Why? You said that I am HIV-negative. Isn't that enough of a reason to be happy?"

"When was the last time you had a possible exposure to HIV?"

"What do you mean?"

"Have you had unprotected sex recently? Or used needles? Or done anything that would have exposed you to HIV?"

Oh, boy. I did have unprotected sex with Cody not too long ago. And Darius as well.

"Well, I had unprotected sex with my ex-boyfriend not too long ago. And my current boyfriend recently."

"Was it within three months?"

"Yes. Why?"

"Your tests only show your status as of three months prior. If you've done anything risky within the past three months, you will have to come back in three months, and again in another three months, to know your status for certain. Technically, it is actually nine months from now, but most people just go for the six-month time frame."

"But we just had a test! Why do I have to wait that long?"

"Miss, HIV is a virus that attacks your immune system. When your immune system recognizes that the virus is in your system, it develops certain cells to fight off the virus. But because it cannot suppress the virus, it generates more of these types of cells as time goes. Three months is the minimum amount of time that is required for your body to develop enough cells that would be able to tell us if you are HIV-positive. But everyone is different, and each person's immune system reacts differently, which is why we suggest coming back six, then nine months from now, to know your status for sure."

My heart begins to beat fast again. "So I have to think about this for three whole months? Are you kidding me?"

"Do you know if the last person you slept with is HIV-positive?"

"No."

"Then you will have to wait. Either that, or find out for sure what the status is of the two individuals you had unprotected sex with. If they are HIV-negative, and they've not been exposed to HIV within the past three months, then you should be fine."

"But they seem okay. They take care of themselves."

"Don't assume anything. Make sure you know for sure."

"This really sucks."

"Welcome to real life. It's not pretty out here. But now you know, so you are responsible for taking better care of yourself."

"Okay. Thanks. Can I leave now?"

"Absolutely. Remember, come back in another three months to get tested again."

"Okay."

I step out of her office and head to the exit. I see her walk up to the guy who was trying to talk to me in the waiting area. Imagine if he has to hear the same thing she told me and has to wait three whole months to know his results.

This really, really sucks. Darius said he would tell me his results next week. What if, by some chance, he is HIV-positive? What if Cody is? Why didn't I make Cody use a condom? Why didn't I make Braxton use a condom? Why didn't I make Darius use a condom? Because it felt good? Well, I don't feel so good right now.

I step outside and head home. These are going to be the longest three months of my life.

The girl with the pigtails steps out of the counselor's office and leaves the clinic without saying a word. She didn't look too good as she left. I hope she didn't get some bad news. She didn't even say good-bye to me. I wonder if she just found out that she is HIV-positive. I hope that wasn't the case, but just imagine. I really hope she is fine.

Seeing her in that state makes my heart race again, and all the possible negative outcomes come flooding back. What if I am HIV-positive? What will I do? I shouldn't think like that; I should think positive, as that's what Al, my parents, and Jerry all advised me to do. I asked God to help me, as Al suggested, so everything should be all right. And I think I did the right thing by seeking God's help, even though I did not know God before. By God's grace I am learning valuable lessons from this experience, rather than pain and regret. Even if I am HIV-positive, at least now I will be in a better position to deal with it, due to my new relationship with God.

"Mr. John Casey?"

I am roused from my musings. Surprisingly, I am not nervous to hear my name. "Yes?"

"Your results are in. Please step into my office."

I follow the counselor into her office and sit down. She says nothing; she just enters information from my results slip into her computer. I wonder if she is building up some sort of suspense.

"So, am I negative?"

"You have to wait, sir. I cannot tell you your results until I enter everything into the computer."

Damn. Why me? I sit there and watch her type away at her keyboard for about five minutes. I have to admit that my heartbeat begins to quicken again. Why can't she just tell me? The result slip is right in front of her and yet she is not telling me. All I want is to accept my fate and move on, and it all lies on the little piece of paper on her desk. As I look at her, feeling like a madman about to go on a rampage, she gets up and gives me a smile.

"I have to double-check something with the doctor regarding your form, sir. I'll be right back."

"Wait, wait, wait! Can you at least tell me before you leave what my status is so I can avoid all this suspense?"

She smiles at me. "Sir, you are—wait, hold on a minute, sir. Just wait one minute," she says as she steps out of the room.

"Jeez! Tell me please!" I call after her.

She looks at me and then says these words to me: "You are HIV-negative."

Those have to be the best four words I have heard in a long time. I suddenly feel this weight lift off my shoulders, and my heart finally relaxes after three months of intense labor. I feel free, and I can breathe again. I kneel down right there in that office and say to God, "Thank You, thank You, thank You! Thank You so much."

The counselor comes back. "Okay, sir, you're free to go. You can come back in three months to check again, just to cover all bases, but you're fine."

"Thank you very much." I step out of the testing center and look upward to the sky, take a deep breath, then exhale. Phew. I close my eyes and speak to God: "Thank You, God, for being merciful. Thank You so, so, so much."

Just as I finish my prayers, my phone buzzes. I have a message in my voicemail. I call my inbox to listen to my messages. The new message is from Sebastian's family: "Hello, John. Mr. Summers here. I spoke with my son regarding your proposition, and we decided that we would like to come up and visit Sebastian. After all, it's the least we can do considering all that has—"

I hang up. There is no point in listening or even communicating with Sebastian's family, now that Sebastian has passed away. They should have taken the opportunity when they had it. My business with them is finished.

I smile as I walk down the street. I imagine that Sebastian, wherever he is, would be happy for me as well. As if to signify an agreement with my thoughts about Sebastian, a cool breeze brushes past me. It feels good against my face. The weather is clear and warm, considering this time of the year. I decide that now will be a good time to read Sebastian's letter. I take the letter from my pocket, and the first thing I see is the smiley face he drew. It's smiling up at me. I smile back. This is what he had to say:

Hey, John,

I do not feel as if I have much time left to live, and I fear that I may not have the chance to say good-bye to you, at least until we meet again. I wrote this letter after our last meeting in case, like I said, I do not have the time to officially say good-bye to you. By now you're probably either really happy or really sad, depending on the results of your test. But I feel that you are happy as you read this, because I feel that your test will go well. The important thing is that you learn from the experience. Relax with the women, dude, and be more careful when it comes to having sexual relations with anyone. Personally, I think you should get a good girl, because you are a good guy. I know you will be fine. I just wanted to thank you for everything you've done for me—for listening and for being a good friend; I've had so few of those in my life. We began developing a genuine friendship in such a short amount of time; most people cannot do so in a lifetime. Please accept my gratitude for your kindness. Thanks to meeting you, I will not die a sad man. I do not think there is anything wrong with you, and I am happy that this experience you've had has opened your eyes to so many ugly and beautiful realities about this world.

Please don't cry for me; I've suffered for too long, and now I hope that wherever I'm being sent provides me with a better life than what I have had here. Hopefully, where I am going I will be able to swim again. Now, wouldn't that be something? So do not cry; rather, celebrate that I am free. I'll see you around, buddy. I know you'll be fine, and you'll test negative. I feel it. Hopefully, we'll meet again. Please find life in life and value it, because as you have come to learn and experience, anything can happen, and we are so fragile. I hope I find life in whatever is next for me. I hope I am able to miss you wherever I go—that would be nice.

Your friend,

Sebastian.

P.S. I've attached that poem I did not finish to this letter. Maybe you can put it on the Web site for me later. Enjoy.

S.

I look to the sky and breathe deeply. Sebastian…I miss my friend. I peer into the envelope and find another sheet of paper, the one that contains Sebastian's poem. I find a bench on the street and sit down, and then I begin to read:

THANK GOD, THANK ALL & THANK LIFE

It's amazing the things I've done,
it's amazing in this short time the man I have become.
It's a shame most times I failed to appreciate the beauty,
the full spectrum of this life God had given me.
I have been blessed unlike most others, given the chance to see what this life
really has to offer…given the chance to be free,
even though being free sometimes costs pain and misery.
I have absorbed all I have done, experience making me what I have become;
given me a thirst for every experience that is new,
learned to see things from more than one point of view.
I appreciate the value of this one chance God has been so kind to give; I appreciate the value of this one life I have had to live.
I realize I am just one entity in this river of life that around me flows…and in
my world I am the lead character in what I
like to call "one very big talent show."
I thank all for being a part of this play that defined me;
for letting me try every line, every scene, till I found me.
And it is this experience, this kindness that "all" has been so kind to give,
which has made me aware of a secret about this one life I have had to live:
that we exist not to receive but rather exist to give.
So as the curtains draw to this my talent show,
I thank "all" for being a part of this one life I've come to know.
The experiences, good and bad, have all taught me a valuable lesson…that
everything, good or bad, happens for a good reason.
I thank all, I thank God, and I thank life
for being a part of this plot that was me…
And I pray that as this story ends,
it ends with me realizing my one true destiny.

I fold Sebastian's poem and place it in my pocket. I stand up and smile. I think he found himself before he passed. And I think I've found myself, at least a portion of myself, as well. I do not know Who or What God is yet, but I think I know what God is not. One thing I know for sure is that I cannot limit my understanding of God to my human comprehension, because there are some things we humans are just not capable of understanding. I have learned my lesson: HIV is real, and you never know what you're really getting into when you deal with people, no matter how presentable they make themselves.

I begin to walk down the street, with no set destination in mind. I am not smiling, but neither am I frowning; I am just aware. I have not gone swimming in a while. I think today will be a good day to go for a nice swim.

THE END

IGNORANCE

If I knew I could,
But that doesn't mean I would.
And if I fail to change I blame myself for pain.
And I can't hide and say that I did not know,
for the knowledge was given but I did not grow.

—Ben Hinson

References:

Chris Jennings, 1985,1986, 1988, 1993. "Understanding and Preventing AIDS: A Book for Everyone." Health Alert Communications. http://www.aproposinc.com/hap/catch.htm

STDResource. "HIV seroconversion illness." STDResource. http://www.stdresource.com/disease/index.php?page=edit&id=5&action= viewful (accessed June 19th, 2008).

Risk of HIV transmission is raised by a high viral load, presence of genital ulcers, Digest, Perspectives on Sexual and Reproductive Health, 2001, 33(5):240-241 http://www.guttmacher.org/pubs/journals/3324001b.html (accessed June 19th, 2008)

Ars technica. "Ars Nobel Intent: Circumcision significantly reduces HIV/AIDS risk." Ars technica. http://arstechnica.com/journals/science.ars/2006/12/14/6287 (accessed January 7, 2007).

FindArticles. "Female to Male HIV transmission." FindArticles. http://findarticles.com/p/articles/mi_m3225/is_n5_v41/ai_9101593 (accessed February 16th, 2007).

AVERT.org. "The Origin of HIV and the first cases of AIDS." AVERT. http://www.avert.org/origins.htm (accessed April 8th, 2008).

ORIGINOFAIDS. "The Origin of AIDS and HIV may not be what you have learned." http://www.originofaids.com/index.htm (accessed April 8th, 2008).

SERENDIPITY. "The Secret Origin of AIDS and HIV." http://www.serendipity.li/more/cantwell.htm (accessed April 9th, 2008).

UNAIDS. "UNAIDS 2007 AIDS epidemic update." UNAIDS. http://data.unaids.org/pub/EPISlides/2007/2007_epiupdate_en.pdf (accessed April 13th, 2008).

AIDSMAP.com.http//www.aidsmap.com/en/news/47AE661F-F92B-4073-B47E-45730410F81D.asp?type=preview (accessed April 13th, 2008).